NOPHEK GLOSS

Book One of The Graven

ESSA HANSEN

orbit

www.orbitbooks.net

ORBIT

First published in Great Britain in 2020 by Orbit

1 3 5 7 9 10 8 6 4 2

A CIP catalogue record for this book
is available from the British Library.

ISBN 978-0-356-51558-8

Printed and bound in Great Britain by Clays Ltd, Elcograf S.p.A.

Papers used by Orbit are from well-managed forests
and other responsible sources.

Orbit
An imprint of
Little, Brown Book Group
Carmelite House
50 Victoria Embankment
London EC4Y 0DZ

An Hachette UK Company
www.hachette.co.uk

www.orbitbooks.net

To family, born and found.
To my mother, for introducing me to worlds beyond.
To my father, who is already there.

CHAPTER 1

TENDED AND DRIVEN

The overseers had taken all the carcasses, at least. The lingering stench of thousands of dead bovines wafted on breezes, prowling the air. Caiden crawled from an aerator's cramped top access port and comforting scents of iron and chemical. Outside, he inhaled, and the death aroma hit him. He gagged and shielded his nose in an oily sleeve.

"Back in there, kid," his father shouted from the ground.

Caiden crept to the machine's rust-eaten rim, twelve meters above where his father's wiry figure stood bristling with tools.

"I need a break!" Caiden wiped his eyes, smearing them with black grease he noticed too late. Vertebrae crackled into place when he stretched, cramped for hours in ducts and chemical housing as he assessed why the aerators had stopped working so suddenly. From the aerator's top, pipes soared a hundred meters to the vast pasture compound's ceiling, piercing through to spew clouds of vapor. Now merely a wheeze freckling the air.

"Well, I'm ready to test the backup power unit. There are six more aerators to fix today."

"We haven't even fixed the one!"

His father swiveled to the compound's entrance, a kilometer and a half wide, where distant aerators spewed weakened plumes into the vapor-filled sky. Openings in the compound's ceiling steeped the empty fields in twilight while the grass rippled rich, vibrating green. The air was viciously silent—no more grunts, no thud of hooves, no rip and crunch of grazing. A lonely breeze combed over the emptiness and tickled Caiden's nose with another whiff of death.

Humans were immune to the disease that had killed every bovine across the world, but the contaminated soil would take years to purge before new animals were viable. Pasture lots stood vacant for as far as anyone could see, leaving an entire population doing nothing but waiting for the overseers' orders.

The carcasses had been disposed of the same way as the fat bovines at harvest: corralled at the Flat Docks, two-kilometer-square metal plates, which descended, and the livestock were moved—somewhere, down below—then the plate rose empty.

"What'll happen if it dissolves completely?" The vapor paled and shredded dangerously by the hour—now the same grayish blond as Caiden's hair—and still he couldn't see through it. His curiosity bobbed on the sea of fear poured into him during his years in the Stricture: the gray was all that protected them from harm.

"Trouble will happen. Don't you mind it." His father always deflected or gave Caiden an answer for a child. Fourteen now, Caiden had been chosen for a mechanic determination because his intelligence outclassed him for everything else. He was smart enough to handle real answers.

"But what's up there?" he argued. "Why else spend so much effort keeping up the barrier?"

There could be a ceiling, with massive lights that filtered through to grow the fields, or the ceiling might be the floor of another level, with more people raising strange animals. Perhaps those people grew light itself, and poured it to the pastures, sieved by the clouds.

Caiden scrubbed sweat off his forehead, forgetting his grimy hand again. "The overseers must live up there. Why else do we rarely see them?"

He'd encountered two during his Appraisal at ten years old, when they'd confirmed his worth and assignment, and given him his brand—the mark of merit. He'd had a lot fewer questions, then. They'd worn sharp, hard metal clothes over their figures and faces, molded weirdly or layered in plates, and Caiden couldn't tell if there were bodies beneath those shapes or just parts, like a machine. One overseer had a humanlike shape but was well over two meters tall, the other reshaped itself like jelly. And there had been a third they'd talked to, whom Caiden couldn't see at all.

His father's sigh came out a growl. "They don't come from the sky, and the answers aren't gonna change if you keep asking the same questions."

Caiden recalled the overseers' parting words at Appraisal: *As a mechanic determination, it will become your job to maintain this world, so finely tuned it functions perfectly without us.*

"But why—"

"A mechanic doesn't need curiosity to fix broken things." His father disappeared back into the machine.

Caiden exhaled forcibly, bottled up his frustrations, and crawled back into the maintenance port. The tube was more cramped at fourteen than it had been at ten, but his growth spurt was pending and he still fit in spaces his father could not. The port was lined with cables, chemical wires, and faceplates stenciled in at least eight different languages Caiden hadn't been taught in the Stricture. His father told him to ignore them. And to ignore the blue vials filled with a liquid that vanished when directly observed. And the porous metal of the deepest ducts that seemed to breathe inward and out. *A mechanic doesn't need curiosity.*

Caiden searched for the bolts he thought he'd left in a neat pile.

"The more I understand and answer, the more I can fix." Frustration amplified his words, bouncing them through the metal of the machine.

"Caiden," his father's voice boomed from a chamber below. Reverberations settled in a long pause. "Sometimes knowing doesn't fix things."

Another nonanswer, fit for a child. Caiden gripped a wrench and stared at old wall dents where his frustration had escaped him before. Over time, fatigue dulled that anger. Maybe that was what had robbed his father of questions and answers.

But his friend Leta often said the same thing: "You can't fix everything, Caiden."

I can try.

He found his missing bolts at the back of the port, scattered and rolled into corners. He gathered them up and slapped faceplates into position, wrenching them down tighter than needed.

The adults always said, "This is the way things have always been—nothing's broken."

But it stayed that way because no one tried anything different.

Leta had confided in a nervous whisper, *"Different* is why I'll fail Appraisal."* If she could fail and be rejected simply because her mind worked differently, the whole system was broken.

The aerator's oscillating unit was defaced with Caiden's labels and drawings where he'd transformed the bulbous foreign script into imagery or figures. Recent, neatly printed labels stood out beside his younger marks. He hesitated at a pasted-up photo he'd nicked from the Stricture: a foreign landscape with straight trees and intertwined branches. White rocks punctured bluish sand, with pools of water clearer than the ocean he'd once seen. It was beautiful—the place his parents would be retired to when he replaced them. Part of the way things had always been.

"Yes, stop everything." His mother was speaking to his father, and her voice echoed from below, muffled and rounded by the tube. She never visited during work. "Stop, they said. No more repairs."

His father responded, unintelligible through layers of metal.

"I don't know," she replied. "The overseers ordered everyone to gather at the Flat Docks. Caiden!"

He wriggled out of the port. His mother stood below with her arms crossed, swaying nervous as a willow. She was never nervous.

"Down here, hon." She squinted up at him. "And don't— *Caiden!*"

He slid halfway down the aerator's side and grabbed a seam to catch his fall. The edge under his fingers was shiny from years of the same maneuver. Dangling, smiling, he swung to perch on the front ledge, then frowned at his mother's flinty expression. Her eyes weren't on him anymore. Her lips moved in a whisper of quick, whipping words that meant trouble.

Caiden jumped the last couple meters to the ground.

"We have to go." She gripped a handful of his jacket and laid her other hand gently on his shoulder, marshaling him forward with these two conflicting holds. His father followed, wiping soot and worry from his brow.

"Are they sending help?" Caiden squirmed free. His mother tangled her fingers in his as they crossed a causeway between green pastures to a small door in the compound's side. "New animals?"

"Have to neutralize the disease first," his father said.

"A vaccine?" His mother squeezed his hand.

Outside the compound, field vehicles lay abandoned, others jammed around one of the Flat Docks a kilometer away. Crowds streamed to it from other compounds along the road grid, looking like fuel lines in an engine diagram. Movement at farther Docks suggested the order had reached everywhere.

"Stay close." His mother tugged him against her side as they amalgamated into a throng of thousands. Caiden had never seen so many people all together. They dressed in color and style according to their determinations, but otherwise the mob was a mix of shapes, sizes, and colors of people with only the brands on the back of their necks alike. It was clear from the murmurs that no one knew what was going on. This was not "the way things have always been." Worst fears and greatest hopes floated by in whispers like windy grass as Caiden squeezed to the edge of the Flat Docks' huge metal plate.

It lay empty, the guardrails up, the crowds bordered around. Only seven aerators in their sector still trickled. Others much farther away had stopped entirely. There should have been hundreds feeding the gray overhead, which now looked the palest ever.

Caiden said, "We'll be out of time to get the aerators running before the vapor's gone."

"I know..." His father's expression furrowed. The grime on his face couldn't hide suspicion, and his mother's smile couldn't hide her fear. She always had a solution, a stalwart mood, and an answer for Caiden even if it was "Carry on." Now: only wariness.

If everyone's here, then— "Leta."

"She'll be with her own parental unit," his father said.

"Yeah, but—" They weren't kind.

"Caiden!"

He dashed off, ducking the elbows and shoulders of the mob. The children were smothered among the taller bodies, impossible to distinguish. His quick mind sorted through the work rotations, the direction they came from—everyone would have walked straight from their dropped tasks, at predictable speed. He veered and slowed, gaze saccading across familiar faces in the community.

A flicker of bright bluish-purple.

Chicory flowers.

Caiden barked apologies as he shouldered toward the color, lost among tan clothes and oak-dark jerkins. Then he spotted Leta's fawn waves, and swung his arms out to make room in the crowd, as if parting tall grass around a flower. "Hey, there you are."

Leta peered up with dewy hazel eyes. "Cai." She breathed relief. Her knuckles were white around a cluster of chicory, her right arm spasming, a sign of her losing the battle against overstimulation.

Leta's parental unit wasn't in sight, neglectful as ever, and she was winded, rushed from some job or forgotten altogether. Oversized non-determination garments hung off one shoulder, covered her palms, tripped her heels. She crushed herself against Caiden's arm and hugged it fiercely. "It's what the older kids say. The ones who don't pass Appraisal're sent away, like the bovine yearlings."

"Don't be silly, they would have called just the children then, not everyone. And you haven't been appraised yet, anyway."

But she was ten, it was soon. The empathy, sensitivity, and logic that could qualify her as a sublime clinician also crippled her everyday life as the callous people around her set her up to fail. Caiden hugged her, careful of the bruises peeking over her shoulder and forearm, the sight of them igniting a well-worn urge to protect.

"I've got you," he said, and pulled out twigs and leaves stuck in her hair. Her whole right side convulsed softly. The crowds, noise, and light washed a blankness into her face, meaning something in her was shutting down. "You're safe."

Caiden took her hand—firmly, grounding—and backtracked through the crowd to the Flat Dock edge.

The anxious look on his mother's face was layered with disapproval, but his father smiled in relief. Leta clutched Caiden's right hand in both of hers. His mother took his left.

"The overseers just said gather and wait?" he asked his father.

"Someday you'll learn patience."

Shuffles and gasps rippled through the assembly.

Caiden followed their gazes up. Clouds thinned in a gigantic circle. The air everywhere brightened across the crowds more intensely than the compounds' lights had ever lit the bovines.

A hole burned open overhead and shot a column of blinding white onto the Flat Docks. Shouts and sobs erupted. Caiden stared through the blur of his eyelashes as the light column widened until the entire plate burned white. In distant sectors, the same beams emerged through the gray.

He smashed his mother's hand in a vise grip. She squeezed back.

A massive square descended, black as a ceiling, flickering out the light. The angular mass stretched fifty meters wide on all sides, made of the same irregular panels as the aerators. With a roar, it moved slowly, impossibly, nothing connecting it to the ground.

"I've never..." His mother's whisper died and her mouth hung open.

Someone said, "It's like the threshers, but..."

Massive. Caiden imagined thresher blades peeling out of the hull, descending to mow the crowds.

The thing landed on the Flat Docks' plate with a rumble that juddered up Caiden's soles through his bones.

A fresh bloom of brightness gnawed at the gray above, and beyond that widening hole hung the colors and shapes of unmoving fire. Caiden stood speechless, blinded by afterimage. Leta gaped at the black mass that had landed, and made her voice work enough to whisper, "What is it?"

Caiden forced his face to soften, to smile. "More livestock maybe? Isn't this exciting?" *Stupid thing to say.* He shut up before his voice quavered.

"This isn't adventure, Caiden," Leta muttered. "Not like sneaking to the ocean—this is *different*."

"Different how?"

"The adults. This isn't how it's done."

Caiden attempted to turn his shaking into a chuckle. "The bovine all dead is a new problem. Everything's new now."

The crowd's babble quieted to a hiss of fear, the tension strummed. A grinding roar pummeled the air as the front side of the angular mass slid upward from the base, and two tall figures emerged from the horizontal opening.

"Overseers!" someone shouted. The word repeated, carried with relief and joy through the crowd.

Caiden's eyes widened. Both overseers were human-shaped, one tall and bulky, the other short and slim, and as he remembered from his Appraisal, they were suited from head to toe with plates of metal and straps and a variety of things he couldn't make out: spikes and ribbons, tools, wires, and blocks of white writing like inside the aerators. They wore blue metal plates over their faces, with long slits for eyes and nostrils, holes peppering the place where their mouths would be. Besides their build, they resembled each other exactly, and could be anything beneath their clothes.

"See, it's fine." Caiden forced himself to exhale. "Right, Ma?"

His mother nodded slow, confused.

"People," the shorter overseer said in a muffled yet amplified voice.

The crowd hushed, rapt, with stressed breaths filling the quiet. Caiden's heart hammered, pulse noosing his neck.

"You will be transported to a clean place," the other overseer said in a husky voice amplified the same way. The crowd rippled his words to the back ranks.

"With new *livestock*," the first added with a funny lilt on the final word.

"Come aboard. Slow, orderly." The overseers each moved to a side of the open door, framing the void. "Leave your belongings. Everyone will be provided for."

Caiden glanced at Leta. "See? New animals."

She didn't seem to hear, shut down by the sights and sounds. He let her cling to him as his father herded them both forward.

Caiden asked, "Where could we go that doesn't have infected soil? Up, past the gray?"

"Stay close." His father's voice was tight. "Maybe they discovered clean land past the ocean."

They approached the hollow interior—metallic, dank, and lightless—with a quiet throng pouring in, shoulder to shoulder like the bovines had when squeezed from one pasture to another. Caiden observed the closest overseer. Scratches and holes scarred their mismatched metal clothes, decorated in strange scripts. Their hand rested on a long tool at their hip, resembling the livestock prods but double-railed.

Caiden's father guided him inside and against a wall, where his mother wrapped him and Leta in her strong arms and the mob crammed tight, drowning them in heat and odor.

"Try to keep still." The overseer's words resonated inside.

A roar thrummed to life, and the door descended, squeezing out the orange light. The two overseers remained outside.

Thunder cracked underfoot. Metal bellowed like a thousand animals crying at once. Human wails cut through and the floor shuddered in lurches, forcing Caiden to widen his stance to stay upright. His mother's arms clamped around him.

Children sobbed. Consoling parents hissed in the darkness. Leta remained deathly silent in Caiden's firm grasp, but tremors crashed in her body, nervous system rebelling. He drew her closer.

"Be still, hon." His mother's voice quavered.

She covered his ears with clammy hands and muffled the deafening roar to a thick howl. The rumble infiltrated his bones, deeper-toned than he'd thought any machine could sound.

Are we going up into that fire-sky, or into the ground, where the livestock went?

The inside of machines usually comforted him. There was safety in their hard shell, and no question to their functioning, but this one stank of tangy fear, had no direction, and his mother's shaking leached into his back as he curled around Leta's trembling in front. He buried his nose in a greasy sleeve and inhaled, tasting the fumes of the gray. His mother's hands over his ears thankfully deadened the sobs.

"Soon," she cooed. "I'm sure we'll be there soon."

CHAPTER 2

FEED THE BEASTS

The box roared for hours. The standing masses sat to rest shaken bones and cramped muscles. Bodies packed tight: sniffling kids, wailing infants, muttering women, swearing men. Arguments surged and faded. The sweltering hollow stank of sweat.

Caiden—numb from vibration, bruised from sheltering Leta—hugged his insensate legs and stayed alert. He could hardly see anyone in the dark.

But he could smell them. All of them.

Leta balled up next to him and clutched his arm like a buoy amidst the sensory chaos. Exhaustion towed her to sleep, while Caiden, twisted up, stayed still for her despite darting cramps.

His mother depleted weary tears, and her hands found him again, wiping the sweat off his forehead back through his hair. She kissed the top of his head. "Hopefully not long," she whispered, hot by his ear. "Soon. Imagine where we could be going. Green, do you think?"

Caiden recalled his picture in the aerator. Crystalline water. Knotted trees. Sand. "Maybe the place everyone gets retired to?" His hoarse voice broke, hardly cutting the roar.

"Maybe…"

His only way of marking time was stiffness and pain. He itched to get up and move, but his mother's arms belted him and Leta. "Soon," she whispered drowsily, until the word lost meaning.

There was no way to mark travel distance at all, and Caiden began to wonder if the box hadn't moved. "They wouldn't let us suffocate, would they?"

"No, sweetie, they need us. Who else will care for the animals?"

The animals are dead.

He shifted to rest his head on his other knee. Leta woke, wrung dry of tears. Caiden tilted his shoulder to make a better pillow for her, and winced as the cramp shot through fresh bruises.

Leta pulled away. "You're hurting yourself."

"I don't mind." His spirits lifted at having a job to do still. The crowded bodies, stench, and noise were unbearable for him, he couldn't imagine how they destroyed Leta's delicate senses. Her ribs quivered with each inhale, her body stiff. The best Caiden could do was squeeze her tightly, his pressure a comfort.

"Soon." His mother petted Leta's forehead. "Soon." She muttered until the words merged into a constant, sibilant stream escaping her lips, "Soon, soon, soon..."

A new stench emerged, worse than the carcasses. Defecation. Urine. The real smell of fear. One person started ranting, many joined, escalating to shouts. The overseers, some said, were taking them to new land, or were cleansing the old and they'd be released into fresh pastures, clean soil, sweet air. We're doomed, others declared, we're in here to die like the livestock, dropped under the Flat Docks.

Leta nuzzled deeper into the crook of Caiden's shoulder and he shifted, enduring torrents of pain. He said, "We'll get out."

"Soon." His mother completed his sentence with the hated word. "Soon, soon." She rocked back and forth, trapping them in monotony until Caiden's father pulled her away, hushing the fear that leaked out of her, the dead promise, *soon*.

The wails and sobbing lessened as voices grew hoarse, breaths labored and rationed. Puke ripened the muggy air more. Caiden fought back gags, suffocated in a soup of human reek.

Then the roar cut off abruptly.

The vibrations supporting his body vanished, leaving him empty, electric, a wisp. He hugged Leta, then rattled to his feet with everyone else.

A blade of light sliced the darkness, lancing his eyes and skull with fresh pain. The door howled upward and he squinted against radiance vibrating between his eyelashes, edged in every color.

The people closest to the door stood stunned, and the shoving began from the back, rolling into a stampede to the white slit of the exit. A new roar swelled: relief and cries and maddened feet. Twiggy silhouettes careened into the blinding light and disappeared. Caiden's parents struggled as the tide battered them toward the door.

His mother pressed him to the wall and shouted at him to stay out of the masses, then she and his father were lost in the chaos of flailing hands, screeching faces, twisting cloth. Children were trampled, yanked up, shoved. Big men waded forward. Slender women wedged through.

Caiden shielded Leta with his back as he inched along the wall to the farthest corner while the crowd drained into the light.

"You're safe." Caiden made her sit. His heart wrenched as he finally saw her face, wan and bruised, hair plastered to her cheeks with sweat and tears. In her wide eyes, something was shattering, something the travel hadn't already broken. "Everyone's just excited to be out, somewhere fresh, yeah? Stay here, really quiet. I'll come back for you."

His words were whittled frail by his own fear. Speech had left Leta, but she shook her head in protest.

"It'll be calmer here. Close your eyes? Cover your ears. It's all right to shut down." Caiden folded her gently into the corner. "Stay here until I come back?"

Leta nodded, managing a ghost of a smile, and a last tear trickled down one cheek as she closed her eyes tight.

"Brave of you." Something unhitched in Caiden's chest, soothed by the promise that formed a lifeline between them, keeping them connected even as he pivoted and rushed to the light.

"*Ma!*" The shout chafed his throat, lost in the din. He reentered the stampede and washed up through the blazing opening. Body-slammed by someone, he stumbled to the side of the pouring crowds and fell on sand. Cold sand. He gasped fresh air.

"Up, hon!" His mother shouted by his ear and yanked him to his feet.

Brilliance surged in his head, throbbing with blobs of afterimage. Sand stretched endlessly, studded in rock like scabbed skin. Caiden's head rolled back in shock. The sky was black. The ground and air glowed enough to see, but the sky was *black*. He'd never seen such a thing; the aerated gray of home had darkened in cycles but never like this. Grains of white speckled it, blurring into streaks as his mother pulled him from the stampede.

"Where are we?" Caiden yelled.

Bodies scattered from the dark transport cube like swarms of stirred insects. Shrieks severed the air and riveted Caiden in place, the raw pitches braiding into a chorus of terror.

Then he saw why. Russet creatures charged through the fleeing throngs. They were at least a meter high, four-legged, stocky and muscular. They leapt on runners and tore, crushed, gnawed. Blood sprayed. Caiden gagged, his stomach heaving with terror.

"Move!" his father bellowed, rushing over to shove them both.

His mother's face was flushed and fierce. She took fistfuls of Caiden, spinning him around.

Caiden's thoughts stuck as his heavy feet slogged into the horror. One of the beasts charged at his side, claws tearing up sand.

"Run!" His father's face shot past. Eyes bloodshot. Mouth wide, screaming.

Caiden's mother thrust him into a sprint. She shrieked his name, hands steering him. He gripped her arm and tried to run on sand slipping beneath his feet.

He swiveled his head back but his father wasn't behind them. Beasts mowed the crowd with giant paws and dagger nails. They snarled at one another and tumbled together on the sand, crushing already mangled bodies.

"The rock!" his mother said, hauling him with her. "Quick!"

Ache stitched Caiden's side. The knot in his stomach rolled up, and he retched, stumbling. He glimpsed a beast in pursuit, its eyes flashing white. Terror balled up but his mother's scream spurred him. He scrambled up and she drove him to a slanted rock just wide enough to squeeze under.

"Get in, in!" Face hard with focus, she jammed him under the ledge, strong arms shoving him as far as she could. Caiden groped handfuls of sand until he latched on to rock and pulled himself deep inside. He tugged his mother's hands but they skated from his, palms slick. *"Ma!"* he shrieked.

A beast crashed her against the rock. The thud echoed in Caiden's chest.

A wild scream gushed from him as she hit the ground in a spray of sand beneath muscles and jaws that filled the view from under the rock. Each bite was a yanking, crunching tear.

Caiden wheezed screams, his eyes stinging with tears and sand, but he couldn't close them. Teeth snatched her shoulder as a second beast arrived. The first bit a leg, and the two huge creatures wrestled over the body, flinging it from view as they fought. Guttural snarls resonated through their bodies, filling Caiden's hiding place with vibration.

He curled into spasms, a dreadful sound raking up his throat.

It had to be a nightmare. He'd fallen asleep, and none of this was real.

Two beasts fought over the remains. Over all that was left of her.

This isn't real. It's just a test, like the Appraisal. A nightmare to test that I can be strong. The anguish was a razor in his head like the beasts' copper-reeking blood, stinging his nostrils as he sobbed. He closed his eyes but the sound of one beast tearing up the other was no better than the sight, and images stamped across his mind. His mother's body. His father, lost in the crowd. Leta, hopefully hidden.

Hot blood splashed over him as one monster tore into the other by the overhang. The blood sizzled on the sand, seared across Caiden's tongue. He spat and balled up smaller.

The dying beast's moans dribbled out. The victor's huge head filled the opening between rock and sand. Jaws, countless teeth. Scaly, dark russet skin rippled with sleek fur. The details blurred behind Caiden's tears.

He clamped a palm over his mouth, stifling sobs and gagging on the tang of the beast's blood. Its muscular neck sloped from high withers to a boxy face with fluttering gash nostrils and eyes like reflective pits. Caiden saw himself flash in those pupils as they jerked to the crevice.

This isn't real. He clung to the words as if they were a rope that might pull him back to wakefulness and the green fields and his mother's arms. He imagined flowers and sweetgrass but his sinuses were colonized by the pungent, razor blood covering his skull.

The beast pawed at the red mud, sniffing, claws scraping and forearm clearly long enough to hook Caiden out from under the rock.

He pressed his hand harder against his mouth, but he couldn't stop the tremors or the *shush* his body made, drawing attention.

This isn't real. I can't die.

The beast's nostrils fluttered shut to slits then dilated scarlet. It grunted.

A knot of bile tried to rise. Caiden clenched his stomach, his jaw, his shoulders—everything. Warm wetness bloomed between his legs.

Just a nightmare.

The creature snorted at Caiden's face. His lungs were bursting, heart thundering.

A hot, ruffled inhale, tasting the air, smelling him drenched in blood. Then hard claws slid in and out of sand, paws thudding away. The beast left. Lost interest, not hungry enough?

It can't smell me through the blood? Caiden's exhale stuttered with relief. He opened his eyes.

Through the crevice slit lay the dead beast's body and other small, scattered fleshy masses. Caiden heaved, refusing to acknowledge what those pieces were. Whose.

None of it real. Just nightmare.

CHAPTER 3

AZURA

Half a kilometer away, the massive transport box looked minuscule and lonely. Black corpses scattered around it like seeds. Red like sprinkles of water. The sated creatures fought or prowled. There was enough food for all, and no other prey had escaped.

Reams of time passed and like his mother's promise, *soon*, Caiden repeated to himself that this wasn't real. Tears snaked down his cheeks and dripped, creating little holes in the sand. His eyes trained on the distant scene, hoping to see his father coming for him, somehow unscathed.

He caved at the thought of Leta—eaten, or still hiding in a dark corner of the horror. The promise he'd made shattered, and with it the lifeline between them. He curled in despair, the rock ceiling cutting into his side. Dredges of bravery urged him to rush back inside and look for her—but he knew... She had died and he couldn't bear to find her corpse. It would smash his will to survive and that was all he had now.

An idea sprang into focus, punching him with new energy. The beast blood scent stuffing his nose hadn't dulled a bit, and the monster had left, unable to smell him through it. There was a chance it could mask him. He shimmied out of the overhang and scurried to the big corpse. Claw marks rent it from cheek to tail. A smashed-open jaw revealed the inside of its enormous upturned skull, glistening pink and white. Blood pooled in the hollow.

He pretended it was just liquid, and not a carcass, and cupped handfuls of blood over himself, soaking the tangy heat into his clothes. He jerked back as his fingers grazed something that hummed. Nestled in the fleshy skull and violet liquid was a gem, translucent and scintillating every color he had names for, and many he didn't, mesmerizing amidst the savagery of this place.

Caiden plucked it out, expecting it to course through his fingers like a droplet of water, but it was solid, and hot, vibrating against his palm. He blinked back fresh tears and gripped the gem—the only thing that had any color besides blood and sand and the black sky above.

Sopping with stench that he prayed would protect him, Caiden ran through the desert until his legs throbbed and his side stabbed and he had no choice but to stop.

He couldn't run from the image of his mother. He cried until his face was too sore and puffy for more tears. He wept memories instead. His father, grimed with grease and soot; he'd worked himself and Caiden hard but laughed even harder. Caiden's parental unit had been assigned to him when he left the Stricture at four years old, and the two of them were strangers, their new child a temporary glue. But the three of them bonded fast and easy, and Caiden grew up knowing love. Leta had the opposite, isolated and scorned. It took Caiden ages to break through her protective shell, but every moment since was worth it. She'd been so shy of care and compliments, he'd given as much as he could. She would blush, and it would make his mother giggle. He felt her arms around him in the dark. The grainy slipperiness of her hand as it left his for the last time.

Keep moving. If this isn't real, it'll change. A nightmare—I'll wake up. He pulled on the lifeline of denial and trudged on, combing over all his memories until they seemed fake.

The desert sand emitted or reflected a glow that lit everything except the blackness overhead. The white speckles were sharp as nails piercing a far-off surface, but much too far to be a ceiling with tiny lights. Caiden wasn't sure what to make of it, except that he missed the gray vapor blanket of home.

Not home. It's all gone. Each step kicked sand in sprays.

"This is real." Caiden's voice cracked, raw and inappropriate here where there was no one to listen to his grief.

He plodded on, not worried about the beasts. They had eaten his whole world: they had to be full. The ones that passed by distantly sniffed the air, sensed his shield of blood, and loped on.

The crags sank while sand curved in dunes. There were no plants, trees, or tracks but Caiden's mind was too numb to wonder why. For kilometers in all directions lay an emptiness that scooped him out. When had he ever been alone? The Strictures had teemed with other children. He always worked with his father, or the duster pilots, or other mechanics. When he had free time alone, Leta came along. The bovines grazed with soft sounds and scents.

That world grew harder to imagine the farther he walked. Water pooled in the hollows of dunes, reflecting the sky's white nails. Half a kilometer away, a tall shape speared up, not a tree, but not as big as the transports.

"Shelter. People." Caiden picked up his shivering pace. The glossy black tower sliced up from a pool of water at an angle, mostly submerged, sides clustered with weird vanes and cylinders. It wasn't any kind of housing he was familiar with, but it was a machine, and Caiden knew machines.

He circled to where it overhung the shallows. Cracks and dents in its metal-glass surface warped reflections. A few panels were missing off the jutting end, and a hollow gaped open with enough room to climb in.

Caiden stripped off his bloody clothes. He scrubbed in the frigid water, chafing off the putrid smell and the memories burned in by it, bright as an afterimage. He washed his clothes, redressed, then rinsed the transparent gem he'd found—the only beautiful thing in that slaughter—and tucked it in a pocket.

He jumped to sling his wet shirt around a jutting piece of the machine's opening, and swung until he could hook a slippery leg over the edge and pull himself in.

Light spilled through the opening, and somewhere farther down in the darkness, a broad window let in a glow. The slanted surfaces were messes of metal seams, bars, and alcoves, far more complex than the aerators. Caiden sniffed familiar fragrances of iron and chemical. He lowered himself while tilting his head the way he imagined the machine was supposed to lie: longwise, not up and down.

Chill and grief killed his curiosity to rifle through compartments, and shriveled his desire to one simple thing: somewhere safe to curl up, not under a rock or covered in blood, not in the vastness of desert or sky. So what if he froze—he had a safe cocoon now in the machine. A grave familiar to him.

He lowered into the glowing bottom end, a smaller chamber like the cockpit of a duster. The slanted windows were submerged underwater, and through it the sky's white freckles swayed.

A ship?

Anchored to the tilted floor of the room was a single seat, covered in dust. Caiden peeled up a strangely cut coat hanging over the back. Adult-sized and leathery, it reached to his thighs, but he curled up in its cold weight and nestled in the slanted seat, staring up at the milky veil in the darkness. His body heat slowly soaked his damp clothes and the coat, and pillowed him in warmth.

Everything he'd been pushing aside welled up: the people he'd lost…a hot bath and his soft bed, and the comfort of the vapor gray.

"It *was* hiding something. Hiding worlds like this." His angry whisper hissed through a chattering jaw. The truth was smaller and more manageable in words than it was in his head. "Were the livestock dumped here too? All we ever did was raise food for those beasts. The livestock died out. What food is left? Us."

He rubbed the nape of his neck and the slippery lines of his brand. When he'd received it, the overseers had told him he was perfect, and confirmed he belonged, he was valuable, functional—not a piece of fodder that shouldn't have escaped the maw.

Pulse ratcheting tight, he curled into a smaller, hotter ball in the pilot's seat. *But I did survive. I need to make it matter.*

The overseers had arranged this. They knew everything.

A guttural snarl resonated through the machine bay. Caiden held his breath.

Could the beasts smell him now? He guessed the machine's opening was too high and narrow for them to squeeze into, but guesses and hopes hadn't gotten him very far in life.

He uncurled, snugged the warm coat around his body, and climbed up to the opening. Four beasts prowled along the pool's edge. Their lean bodies moved in serpentine jerks, struggling for footing in the sand on splayed, clawed paws. Their eyes were reflective circles in ridged black faces. One whined at him, two fought each other, and the last one rammed the side of the machine.

Caiden clung to the rim, ready to spring into action, while dread coiled up in his stomach. If these animals were valuable enough to feed with thousands of bovine from a world dedicated only to raising that fodder, then the overseers would come to tend them eventually.

He pulled out the spherical gem he'd pried from inside the beast's skull. It fit his palm. Through it, his skin looked watery pink, every wrinkle doubled along invisible inner facets. Light caught the surface and rippled iridescent colors like a butterfly's wing, definitely the strangest and most beautiful material he'd ever seen.

"Is this why the beasts are special?" he whispered. "A pretty rock? Is there nothing like this in my head?" He squeezed until it hurt, wanting to chuck it at the beasts, but thought better, shoved it back in his pocket.

He surveyed the empty world. His father hadn't knocked on the machine, yelling at him to come out. Leta wouldn't peer up from the ground, too afraid of heights to follow. And his mother was pieces. Ripped. Strewn.

Caiden surged away from those thoughts, crawling back into the machine. He sought a mechanism to get it working, or resources to stay alive, or some understanding to fill him up. His mother had always told him that focusing on the thankful things made more of them, and his father had insisted that hands at work were better at solving problems than hearts at rest.

He stuck his head inside a half-jammed door that opened straight down. The room smelled like an engine: cold iron and stale fluids, musty wiring, and floral chemicals that had dried up long ago. But it was *different*, too, like comparing butterflies and birds by the fact that both could fly.

Squeezing inside, he ran his fingers over a complex central engine bulk stretching the vertically tipped length of the room. He hadn't seen such materials ever, even in the deepest sections of the aerators: some white and fleshy, glassy and scaled, coppery rings that bristled when his fingertips drew near. It looked like a hundred different animals stitched together on one set of bones.

Caiden recognized signal flow. Cables connected modules, pipes ran from canisters to complex bulbs, and hair-thin wires threaded internal networks. Glassy nodes encrusted surfaces like barnacles he'd seen on the rare sea ships of his old world.

"Maybe you're alive. A huge creature wearing a hard shell."

Ridiculous. Machines weren't alive. But he smiled and swore that some of the materials he touched inside the machine were warm.

A shudder rippled through the hull, and he startled, almost slipping.

"*Are* you alive?"

A faint rattling.

Heart speeding, Caiden climbed back into the bay.

A howl passed by outside, but it wasn't any animal. Distant booms followed, building into pulsations that hummed in the metal under Caiden's grip. Light flashed across the upper opening and a high-pitched shriek tore the air.

Caiden climbed up enough to glimpse outside. A black shape ripped across the pool's reflection, followed by a brilliant tail that guttered out to orange.

"Crimes," he cursed. *More transports?*

A moan filled the air and something massive blotted the sky. Eruptions pummeled the dune pool. Colors frothed across the sky, and dark ships plowed through, much too high and fast, riding *air*—which was impossible. Electric light spidered through the darkness while waves of boiling air washed to the ground.

Nothing from his world had looked like this.

Caiden gaped and clung to the rim of the back opening. The whole machine juddered, rattling up memories of the transport, the stench, the beasts.

Another blast and the dune gave way, leveling out the ship. Caiden scurried backward to avoid falling out, and instead slid off a ledge into a lower hallway. Metal squealed, and something wet in the hull popped like broken bones and twisted ligaments. Whimpered swears poured from Caiden as he clutched an aching hip. He crawled up a ramp and crept back to the bay's opening.

It now nestled in the sand. Not high up, no longer safe.

The landscape beyond was rubble, mangled vehicles, body parts, charred globs of stone and glass. Veils of orange light waved through the sky, and broken metal fell, trailed by spirals of smoke.

A vessel screeched by overhead in a burst of pressure that thrust Caiden onto his backside. The sand peeled up in a wave and hissed inside. Following the ship, a second, translucent vessel sliced the air, made of glass or water or simply more *air*. It resembled a fiery bird, and inside its liquid skin, metallic gills rippled. Frozen on his back, Caiden marveled at the vessel as it hovered right overhead, suspended impossibly by nothing. Then its wings folded in and it sped away, thrusters pink and melodious.

The first vessel landed or crashed nearby beyond the dunes. Explosions popped, and razor-thin screams sliced the air. Animalistic sounds rioted: screeches, hisses, peals like snapping metal. Over a hundred meters away, two figures approached, human in silhouette, clad in chunky layers.

Overseers.

Sparks swelled in Caiden's insides. *If they find me, what am I to them? Meat?*

A third figure rushed them. One of the overseers raised a tool that fired a thread of white light. This pierced the rusher's chest, and their body expanded, ruffled, and dissolved entirely into a wisp of smoke. Only toppling legs remained.

"Nine crimes!" Caiden cursed. A *light* could obliterate someone?

He squirmed back inside the ship's twisted opening.

The overseers were heading right for him.

CHAPTER 4

SOUGHT AFTER

Caiden threw all his weight against the bent panel at the back opening, but it held firm. A sad creak escaped it. *Stupid. If I can bend it, so can they.*

He raced to the cockpit, but the console was dead material, no light, no language he could read. His heart sank.

"Blow it open." An overseer's voice outside.

Caiden ducked behind the pilot's seat.

"Can'na risk damagin' gloss," a second voice called. "Only hav'ta get th' one. Be happy yer not chasin' pups like the Graven boss."

Legs darkened the opening. A blue-masked figure crouched and peered in. "Oy, it's a stray thing, not a nophek." Metal banged metal. "Sand worm, wriggle out," they called inside.

Caiden felt desperately along the panels, switches, buttons, and strange surfaces lining the cockpit, pressing, punching, flicking—everything and anything, pleading with the ship to save him again. *Please.*

Metal rapped and echoed.

"Jus' blow it," the other said. They were too large to fit through, but there was plenty of room for their weapon.

Please, please, please. Caiden flailed against panels and controls.

"I see it. Human'ish, small."

"Freckles?"

"Can'na see."

Caiden pawed at a line of switches, smacked a glass panel, hammered a circle of button dots, exhausting every option in reach.

A high whine emitted behind him. That obliterating thread of light beamed out from the overseer's tool. It pierced the hull near the opening and chewed the inner panels' metal away with sheer brilliance, creating a hole big enough for the overseers to step through.

"A kid." One aimed the weapon at Caiden.

"Not worth the gloss 'less he's Graven. Fry 'im."

Their words mushed into the blood pounding in Caiden's ears. Ideas dribbled away and he stood there dumbly like livestock about to be slaughtered.

A thread of light sparked from the barrel of the overseer's weapon.

Caiden leapt onto the pilot's seat and stretched to reach the last strange thing in the cockpit worth trying: a crystalline swell in the ceiling. His palm slapped against it.

Explosive pressure blossomed through Caiden's hand. Vibration stripped him weightless, wrung of sensations. He felt turned to liquid, dumped on the ground, splashing into all of its hard angles.

But he was still actually solid, and watched an expanding sphere peel through the air, thickly rippling like the world folded inside-out along that traveling edge. Particles burbled outward, settling in a bright, peaceful wake. The expanding edge of the bubble shattered the overseer's beam of light inches from Caiden's face. He gushed relief as the ripple frothed onward, through the two figures, eating their screams and turning their writhing bodies into calm, dead heaps.

The metal walls sang with vibrations as the ripple passed through. Inside the bubble, everything appeared normal.

Caiden lay in a heap as well, his insides hot and seized up. His questions slithered through vertigo. The resonance of the singing walls stilled to a silken whisper lapping around him. The ship had saved him again.

The expanding energy bubble stopped and stabilized somewhere beyond the ship's shell, encapsulating it. Through the back opening, Caiden made out iridescent colors twisting like visible wind. Darkness and brilliance frothed in eddies. Beyond that heat haze veil, the desert was a suggestion of dunes and wreckage.

Caiden lay in this bubble of safety and simply breathed. Time slipped away.

The overseers' bodies never woke. A blue-black substance oozed out of the crumpled plates clothing them. How the weird bubble had killed them and spared Caiden, he didn't know, but he could tell that the world inside it was different and gentle. When he rose to his feet, he drifted farther with each step. The air tasted sweet. The musty scent of old chemicals and aged metal was replaced with a resinous fragrance that strung up memories of wildflowers and oak trees.

The ship had awakened. Panels lit with symbols, and lines in every surface gleamed with hidden life, as veins behind skin. The metal felt softer than before, and the hull's rattles quieted as if something solid had filled previous hollows, or muscle knitted between bones.

"Hello?" Caiden's cheeks tensed and tears finally spilled—but this time they were relief.

He marveled at all the things the darkness had hidden. One gel panel on the wall bore a ring of excited, circling light. Buoyant on his feet, Caiden walked over and pressed his palm on it. A whispery sound crawled around the back entrance of the ship. Jagged folds split open like a flower, letting in rays of light as the whole back of the bay unfolded and revealed more of the bubble that had expanded around the ship. It formed a stationary wall of billowing, iridescent air.

The open door plates formed a ramp straight through. Caiden reached out, one fingertip grazing the bubble's transparent surface. The hairs on his arm stood on end. Prickles of temperature played over his fingers; velvet, tingling.

A smile broke his face, and he strode through the warm sphere's surface.

Instantly, his guts twisted like snakes. Acid surged up as the surface passed through him, no better than before. He retched and crumpled on the sand outside the bubble. His eyes watered and lungs chafed, peppery and hoarse. *Stupid*.

Outside the bubble, the sky was still chaos. Wreckage spotted the desert, with unfamiliar bodies scattered as if they'd fallen from the sky or been vomited out with the debris. Streaks of radiance filled the air, darkness bubbled, ships flashed past in impossible motions. Many hit the desert in explosions of metal turned liquid turned flame.

Head craned up to the spectacle, Caiden didn't realize the beasts were back, until one squealed and sprinted at him.

He screamed a mangled swear. Paws churned sand. The monster leapt, and Caiden careened back inside the bubble on instinct.

Vertigo slammed his skull. His insides lathered again, bile sluiced up his throat. The convulsions tripped him as before, and he smacked the bay floor.

The beast rammed the bubble after him. A bellow shredded up its throat. Its muscles folded on themselves, bones fizzed, and gushing blood flickered apart into shining tendrils. A red-black foam was all that remained of the creature. Dust wafted in, settling gently on the floor.

Caiden's racing heart was primed to explode.

On the other side of the bubble's blur, the rest of the beasts scattered as several silhouettes drew closer, shooting buffets of light at the fleeing creatures.

A whimper leaked from Caiden. More overseers? He scrambled to his feet and hefted one of the dead overseers' weapons, holding it as they had, pressed along one arm through loops. It didn't light up. Caiden swore and ran his fingers over it, willing it to come to life as the ship had. He snatched a knife from one of the overseers too, and held it ready just in case. Knives didn't need power.

The five figures drew near, all human-shaped.

Caiden backed up to the cockpit. He bit the inside of his cheek, straining to focus. He'd defended himself and Leta against larger boys, and could maneuver around the bovines, but adult fighters were altogether different from bullies and animals. Especially if all that worked was the blade, and the bubble didn't kill all five.

The console behind him caught his eye: a blinking symbol with a series of eroding rings. *Power draining.*

"Oh no, no, don't fail now— *Shit!*" Adrenaline stabbed his exhausted body and soured his tongue. He swiveled to the door.

The bubble shrank, sizzling back up to the crystal in the cockpit ceiling. The edge's contact threw Caiden flat on his back. Dizziness melted the walls, but this time, his stomach didn't turn. He gasped what was now scratchy air and crawled to his feet, heavier than before.

The weapon he held lit up.

Five silhouettes approached the bay opening. They didn't look like over-seers. Instead, they wore strangely cut garments, draped portions over tight-fitted, and a mix of masks, veils, and hoods.

Caiden ducked behind the pilot's seat. The rail of his weapon shook in his grip and chattered against the knife blade. He itched his fingers around for some kind of trigger. When he grasped a handle near the front, the weapon's spine beamed with symbols.

The group halted in the middle of the bay. A tall man with a sharply muscular frame strode forward. He dropped his hood and unwound the scarf from his long, bearded face. He looked to be Caiden's father's age, but with features more wrinkled and scarred. He swiped back a shock of wavy hair marbled between gray and white. His expression grew rigid, brows drawn and eyes sharp.

He called out in a language Caiden didn't understand. Every syllable stopped in abrupt, hard-edged clicks.

A long pause stretched, while Caiden kept his heavy weapon raised. The knife wiggled in his sweaty grip.

The man tried a new language that rolled like water off his tongue, words buoyant and cadence soothing.

Caiden shook his head.

"How about this one, boy?" the man called.

Caiden straightened. "Are you an overseer?"

The man lowered his weapon. "So you speak slaver tongue."

"Slaver?"

Caiden had heard the word and the idea once before, in the Stricture. The livestock had been described like slaves. Were he and his people just animals to the overseers?

The man waved to his crew. They slung back or sheathed their imple-ments. Then he held out his hands, palms open. "I'm not one of the... over-seers." He glanced at the two crumpled bodies as he approached. "And you don't know how to use that. So, boy, let's not have an accident."

Caiden still held the knife, which he knew how to use. Overseers or not, he wasn't ready to trust, but he was smart enough to listen.

The cockpit lights illuminated the man's severe face. His right brow sloped over the corner of his eye and pinched toward a circular scar in his temple, matching an identical circle on the other side. Odd chevron staples ringed his dark-gray irises, more visible as he peered around the cockpit with an unblinking, too-sharp stare.

He asked, "Is this your ship?"

"It's mine." Caiden's voice cracked, throat still rough from acid.

"Well, let's get it working again." The man looked around, his gaze razor keen. "Then we can leave before this raid gets out of hand."

"*More* out of hand," one of the others corrected.

Caiden squeezed the knife and assessed the crew's casual stances. If these people knew what was going on, he could learn from them, understand this nightmare, maybe escape it. "Who are you?"

"My name is Laythan. I'm no slaver. Quite the opposite. What's your name, boy?"

Caiden laid down his weapon but gripped the knife tighter. Deep inside, he ached for someone to trust and let it all make sense, but if he was just an animal to them, too, he needed sharp fangs and claws.

"I'm..." No one who knew him was alive to speak his name. It seemed distant, left wherever he'd come from and bundled with all the lies. His gaze dropped to the floor, roaming to a painted square that read WI90NN-1238 among cheerful glyphs. "Winn," he finished.

Laythan laughed, and Caiden flinched. Could the man tell a lie? "And where are you from, Winn? A passager ship?"

Passager? Caiden's brows drew together.

Laythan frowned, surveying Caiden from head to toe. He turned to his crew. "Get the bodies out and scavenge a patch for the door iris." They surged into motion. The scars around the man's eyes whitened as he squinted at the round protrusion in Caiden's pocket. The gem. "Found something? Let's see."

Caiden wasn't about to let fear or fatigue sell his trust so fast. Laythan acted kind, but so had the overseers when they loaded everyone up to be slaughtered.

"I won't take it." Laythan shoved his hands in his pockets.

These people could have killed me and done what they wanted. Maybe they need a slave. Caiden thrust his tumbling thoughts aside. At the core of it he needed help, and these people could offer it. He pulled out the gem.

Laythan exhaled a slow whistle. His hands stayed in his pockets. "Nophek gloss. Boy, you're holding the most valuable substance in the multi-verse. No wonder everyone's heading this way."

Valuable enough to slaughter us all. Caiden squeezed the gorgeous, useless object, and fought the sting of tears. If he was worth nothing, he had only one option. "If you can get me to safety with what I need to survive, it's yours. Try to take it, and this blade'll find your neck."

Laythan's hearty laugh crashed through Caiden's defenses. "I admire your spirit. I can tell you've been through something you don't wish to remember. I've been through many." He tapped the white scar on his temple. "My crew and I, we're part of a people who call ourselves passagers, and we live by a fair code. Right now, you have a ship I need to get off this planet, and I have the crew you need to do the same. So, young pilot, have you ever flown your starship?"

Star? Caiden's grip slackened around the knife. "Flown?"

Laythan's forehead wrinkled. He softened his tone. "How did you end up here?"

"I was dumped." Caiden's throat itched. He swallowed. "Like years of livestock. We raised animals for the overseers...slavers. To feed the beasts. A disease wiped the bovine out, so we were all loaded up and dumped here. To be...To—" He couldn't finish. He scratched a fingernail frantically against the knife hilt, cutting off that thought with motion.

Laythan raked a hand through his stormy hair, then shook his head. Around the ship, a couple of the crew paused their work to exchange glances. "Winn, I have a lot to tell you, and you have a lot to hear. Put the knife away. Let's talk."

"How do I know you'll tell me the truth?" Caiden was too exhausted to be anything but straightforward. "Why wouldn't you just kill me, take the gloss and the ship?"

"Smart kid," a dark-haired woman muttered as she strolled by. "Can we keep him?"

Laythan grunted, but his lips crinkled in a smile. To Caiden he said, "Passagers do and believe whatever suits them, looking out only for themselves. I believe every being has a right to find their own place in the multiverse. I can't take that from you, no matter your origin. Many worlds means many riches. There's more than enough profit for all. As far as I'm concerned, you have claim to this ship and your own life. I'll take your deal: the gloss for your safety. My honor will hold me to that. If you believe me to be an honorable man, feel safe."

Laythan extended his hand. Tanned, wrinkled, and ripped by tiny scars. A hand with history. One that had worked, felt soil and metal, knew pain.

Caiden dithered, knife held awkwardly, as he fumbled with Laythan's foreign words. If he didn't trust someone, he would never escape this place, and he would drown in the sea of the things he didn't know.

He clasped Laythan's hand.

CHAPTER 5

PASSAGERS

Power filled the control pads and cockpit. A delicate hum spread inside the vessel's shell, pulsing like bloodstream. Two of the crew—one masked and the other wearing a tight-wrapped veil—fit a new panel to the damaged bay doors. Laythan talked to a heavily armed woman with slippery black hair of mixed lengths that she struggled to contain in a tie.

The adults' activity in the bay banished Caiden's loneliness, yet he felt ignorant and insignificant amidst their knowledgeable movements. He reminded himself that *he* was using these people, and he needed them to like him so they didn't change their mind about the deal. They could keep him safe and help him learn. Maybe Leta had stayed hidden and was found by kindly passagers too.

Maybe not everything was lost.

He paced a little corner, back and forth, and scratched at the leathery sleeve of his coat.

Suddenly, an explosion burrowed into the dune, tossing sand across the hull. Caiden ducked. The dark-haired woman dashed outside brandishing chunky weapons in each hand. "Two groups inbound!"

"Everyone else, gather up!" Laythan yelled. Another explosion rocked the ship. Darting whines peppered the air outside. "Various passager ships and that black armada are still roving the planet, snatching up gloss. The slavers must have gloss detectors. We need the iris fixed, engine refueled, and flight controls up. If this heap isn't going to fly, I want to know soon. Our ship's scrap, and no wrecks around are worth trying." He paused. "Winn."

It took Caiden a beat to register the name—*his* name. "Yes." He puffed his chest, ready for his task.

"Keep out of the way until we're off-planet."

Air punched out of Caiden's lungs. "I can—I can help, I'm a mechanic."

The affirmation came out meek and squeaky, his throat still sore from screams. He used to be familiar with every machine, useful and capable to his world. How swiftly he was reduced to worthless.

A gentle hand landed on Caiden's shoulder from behind. He swiveled, looking up into a man's brutish face, a trimmed beard framing his smile.

"A mechanic?" the man said with genuine surprise. His deep, soft voice didn't match his fighter's features. "That's no easy skill."

Caiden shrugged and pulled the too-big pilot's coat tighter around his shoulders.

The man wore a jacket similar in cut, but it was a deep, dark emerald like a blackbird's sheen, cinched to the throat with cross-shaped snaps. His hair was short and dark, his eyes the color of dull blued steel, and he wasn't young or old—somewhere in those middle years Caiden found hard to place. "Maybe you can help me with the console. My name's Taitn. I'm the pilot."

A pilot. Caiden absorbed Taitn's warming smile. He struggled to separate all their names, each spoken with an accent of original language, sticking out among the slaver speech. Even their names didn't belong in the world he knew. *Taitn... tighten...*

Laythan made an annoyed nasal sound. "Fine, short introductions. This is Ksiñe." He indicated the masked person, whose predatory posture didn't shift an inch. "Prefers 'he.' Ksiñe is Andalvian, and our scientist and medic."

Ksiñe's mask was metallic filigree over scarlet cloth or membrane, with tiny tubes threaded at the edges. The exposed skin at his neck was gel-like and matte, patterned with speckles and stripes, as if a layer of congealed water covered his pale skin with patterns. A furred sort of scarf looped his shoulders and collarbones, rippling indigo, black, and white as it... breathed.

Caiden simply nodded, crushing his curiosity at the word "Andalvian" in the pit where all his questions still lay. The name pronunciation slipped away at once.

"Panca is our mechanic. Like you. She's saisn." Laythan indicated the slender woman. Veils swathed her face and neck except the center of her forehead, baring a black, glistening circle the size of the gloss. The cloth was translucent enough that Caiden decided he wasn't ready to see what a saisn was. She touched two fingers to her forehead.

The blasts outside had ceased, and the final member of the group strode back in. Caiden blinked at their tall, muscular frame and squared face, different from the woman he'd seen march out earlier. Their tan skin was unusually smooth, with tiny black lines running along contours. They mussed the tie holding their black hair, which—Caiden was sure—had been even longer before.

"I can snipe, but we've got twenty arcminutes at most." They looked Caiden up and down, then up again. "I'm En, he for now. Dealer, negotiator."

"Gambler," Taitn added.

"Chiseler," Ksiñe hissed.

En grinned. "Guilty."

Caiden opened his mouth but hesitated to speak. The five of them— capable and seasoned—fit together like engine parts perfectly tuned.

Caiden was the misplaced part that didn't fit.

Laythan glanced among them. "Panca, Ksiñe, keep your masks on. And En, for now don't—"

"I won't." En winked at Caiden.

Everyone rushed to work while Laythan beckoned Caiden to follow him outside to the ramp. "We've got time before they get everything up and running. Let's talk. Come and sit."

En marched ahead of them, up to the highest bulge of the dune, where he lay and propped a long weapon lengthwise, then cuddled up to its scope. The tip of the rail flowered open, with translucent membrane stretching between the tines. A shrill blast pierced Caiden's ears and made him jump. Smoke and sparkles wheezed from En's weapon while a fat line of distorted air streaked across the desert at incredible speed.

"Over here." Laythan's eyes were sharp as ever, trained on the distance.

Caiden sat on the ramp edge and shoved at the sand with his boots.

"Until today," Laythan said, "there were only five known specimens of nophek in all the multiverse, but here…these slavers have cultivated hundreds, outside of regulations and observation. No one else knew about this world until recently, and now they're all after the gloss, prized for its energy potential."

Caiden pulled the gloss from his pocket and rolled it against his palm with a thumb, unwittingly recalling the nophek's sundered skull, pink brains, and iridescent fluid. He looked away and worried at it with his thumbnail.

"Small thing," he said, "to be worth thousands of lives." Worth more than all of him and everything he knew. His jaw stung with the threat of tears, but iron exhaustion held him together. He squeezed and scratched the gem, willing it to crack first.

En fired again, up on the dune. The blast kicked breath from Caiden's chest. *Shooting slavers. I want to shoot slavers.*

Laythan said, "We need to learn more about what happened with your people and this planet before we judge. Let the shock settle and shape you. You survived, and might find some good through it one day, with distance and understanding."

Laythan's words were a sour wind that rocked Caiden like a leaf on a twig.

Good . . . He kicked sand from his boots. Tan workers' boots, the same as every slave had worn. Laythan's boots were black and layered. Taitn's were leathery with steel toes and jangling laces. The attire of real people. "Nothing about any of this is good."

His left fist clutched the nophek gloss: the most valuable thing anywhere. With his right hand, he massaged the nape of his neck where the branding scar raised the skin, marking him as the least valuable thing anywhere. He had grown up believing the mark made him a valuable part of something large and important. But his parental unit, his friends, Leta—fodder. Ignorant, dispensable.

He scratched the brand's circle and six rays until his neck stung and bled. The stone of sorrow in his stomach heated into rage.

Another piercing blast cut the air.

"I should have died with everyone else." Tears brimmed, and Caiden shot to his feet to chuck the gloss into the desert.

Laythan caught his wrist mid-throw. "Easy! Its value might anger you, but that value is what will buy you a new life." His grip, too forceful, radiated up Caiden's arm. "Boy, everything you lose in this life is going to burr in until you let it go and move on. Even if it's your old self you have to let go. The sooner you do, the stronger you'll be to fight for the next thing someone tries to take from you. Settle down."

Caiden ripped his wrist away. "Leave me alone." He marched off the ramp onto the dune.

Behind him, Laythan groaned, pulled a flask from his coat, and took a swig.

En shot again, then deftly shouldered his weapon and slid down to the ramp. He tucked disheveled hair behind an ear. "I see you haven't improved at this stuff, Laythan. I mean, crimes, you can't leave him with that news."

The captain's gaze speared En. "You're the negotiator."

Taitn sidled up. "Let me talk to him?"

Laythan said, "Don't you have a console to get working?"

"Ksiñe's rebooting it first."

En snorted. "Well. Have at it, gallant."

Caiden ignored them and pushed his finger through the sand, drawing a word in the only language he knew. Slaver tongue.

His word was "home." He stood and kicked it.

Taitn joined him, approaching slow and indirect, the way Caiden had learned to approach skittish animals.

"I was like you once," the pilot said. "Plucked from what I knew and shown how *big* the multiverse really was...I felt smaller than ever." He pointed up to the sky. "Each of those spots are called stars. Some of them are worlds as big as this one."

Caiden craned his neck, taking in the twinkling white grains. "Impossible. They'd have to be really far away to still be as big as this one."

"Yeah." Taitn smiled, eyes sad. "They are. What do you say we get some space under these wings?"

"You mean fly?" Fast and powerful, destructive like those ships he'd seen before. A flutter of fresh energy coursed through him, and he gathered it up desperately. "Can you teach me to pilot it?"

When he'd stood before the overseers at his Appraisal, waiting for them to place a value on him and assign a designation, his heart had cried *Pilot*. But his cuts and calluses said *Mechanic*.

"Come on." Taitn gave him a gentle grin and turned him around. "A ship this beautiful shouldn't sit in the desert."

Finally free of sand and water, the ship perched like an insect, with gill-like arrays, translucent water-metal, gels that changed color at different angles, and countless plates with near-invisible seams. The ship was longer than it was wide, a thick nose and base tapering to blade tails, and two wings on either side, sharp and sickle-shaped like a falcon at high speed, preened back now tight against its body. The reflective black shell was chafed with white scars, fine cracks, dents, and a sand-wind burnish. A narrow strip of crystal was bared down the ship's spine from nose to tail. At its backside, silvery engine cylinders clustered, complicated and larger than any turbines Caiden had worked on. Even the dusters were like mites compared to this beetle. And he had never seen anything so beautiful.

The only thing he could trust for now was this machine. Real, solid, and contained.

Taitn said, "Sleeker but much smaller than Laythan's *Dava*, may she rest in the dust."

Caiden managed a brief smile, cheered by at least one ally among the crew.

They walked down the dune and back inside. The interior was a one-room bay, the cockpit an alcove at the end, and in the middle, a ramp led to a lower level with the long engine room and two other spaces. Smooth walls hid inner compartments, seats, and tools. The ship was a sanctuary compared to Caiden's old bed-pad bunk, or the insides of cramped aerators.

The memories ached. He thrust them aside and tested a new notion, "This ship is home."

"We should dump you here and leave," blurted Ksiñe, the medic and scientist, as he shoved Caiden aside and opened the cockpit console housing. His shoulders had a coiled angle, his short stature carried with grace and ferocity.

"Kis!" Taitn snapped. "Not the time for an ethical argument."

The masked Andalvian managed to glare by mere intensity. "Not time for strays."

"Layth made his call. This ship is the kid's; he can call it home. Have you got the interface working?"

Heart stinging, Caiden shuffled out of the way.

"Never seen half these parts," Ksiñe muttered, his accented voice purring. He fussed with the console's innards until the cockpit air fogged with light. The glow congealed into hovering diagrams.

Taitn wiggled into the flight seat, his leathery green jacket magnetizing to the metal of the chair. He raised his hands into the light, and it shifted into flowing patterns as he gestured through data. His fingers and dark-blue eyes moved at blinding speed, while the hard lines of his face softened with awe. "These...are the strangest wings I've ever seen. My bet's Graven tech."

"You say every time," Ksiñe accused.

Caiden watched mystified, bundling up a hundred questions. The diagrams flowed like a landscape: tiny rivers, layered ground, bits cut and replanted, branching. Even without knowing the language, Caiden understood signal flow.

"Winn." Taitn turned to Caiden. "You should give your ship a name."

Ksiñe sniped in, "She is 90-NN C-Center class."

"She *pretends* to be. Kis, this ship is like nothing I've encountered before, and I've piloted everything. Winn might've found a gem even more valuable than the gloss."

Caiden warmed at the praise.

"She *conceals*, not pretends." Ksiñe slunk from the cockpit. "Panca will find out what it is." The skin around his neck and collarbones clouded gray-blue, and what Caiden thought was a furred scarf wriggled off Ksiñe's shoulders and bound to his arm.

Caiden tucked his curiosity back beneath the soreness of rejection.

"Don't mind him," Taitn said. "You've displaced him as the newest, and he'd only just gotten his spots settled. It's a fine ship."

"Thanks, Taitn."

"Ready to pop engines!" the pilot called into the bay.

En strode jovially from the engine room, tied hair swaying. "Maybe we should all get out first? In case it just...blows."

Laythan closed the bay doors. "We can't waste time with tests. If this is the end... well, good run."

The captain's bravery didn't soothe the prickling in Caiden's gut. He was in capable company now, but a sense of urgency and dread was thick beneath their quips and Taitn's busy hands.

"Panca," Laythan called down to the engine room, "keep feeling the engines, make sure this heap's good for escape velocity."

"Quit with the 'heap,' Layth." Taitn's voice hushed with awe.

En cruised by and leaned over with a grin, whispering to Caiden, "I think he's in love."

Taitn swatted En away. "Winn. You're too short for the seat, so come here in front."

"Wait, you're really going to let me fly it? Now?" Caiden moved in front, facing the console and the sprawling desert.

Taitn's dark beard framed a kind smile. He gestured to two crystalline plates on the console. "Put your hands on these."

A surge of excitement turned Caiden's stomach prickles to butterflies. The plate surfaces were soft as skin, and yielded to engulf his fingers and cloud around them.

A rumble juddered deep in the ship's belly. Resonant metals moaned and a muted sound plumped up inside every surface.

Caiden shivered in anticipation.

Taitn laid his big hands over Caiden's. The surface sank farther. "Keep your fingers still but not rigid. This is called a twitch drive style. The bare minimum. Like riding without a saddle. Did you have riding creatures where you're from?"

Caiden opened his mouth to reply. He didn't feel Taitn's fingers move on top of his, but the acceleration hit. He stretched into a streak of a person, insides left his body, then snapped back against the jab of the console. His eyeballs bulged. Skull vibrated. Squeezed lungs reinflated.

Taitn's wild laugh resounded over the ship's song. "Graven tech never ages. She could've crashed yesterday."

Caiden's heart leapt as the ship roared. The sand outside rippled in fountains. A chorus of vibrations rose from a hard judder to a smooth purr as if the thrusters had narrowed into a sleek, powerful stream. The resonant materials relaxed, and the interior hushed except for the patch Panca had fitted over the bay door. The salvaged piece buzzed, secure but unhappy.

Caiden gawked. Through the windows, dunes slithered by at a sickening speed. The horizon brightened as they traveled, until a bright object finally surged into view, resolving into a faraway sphere of luminous, freckled blue.

"Relax." Taitn pressured Caiden's fingers up and down, singly then all together. The ship responded to each; built speed, banked, dipped its nose to a stop, glided over dunes, and spun around again. "It's like falling. If you're rigid and scared, it's going to hurt. If you're relaxed and drunk—well, you probably didn't even notice."

"Don't let him tell you drunk pilots are better!" En called from the bay.

Taitn rolled his eyes.

Caiden tried his own fingertip motions, to which the ship swayed side to side. Taitn's hands squeezed into a claw shape and the vessel slowed to a hover. Rolls of sand cascaded over the nose.

Caiden slid his hands free of the controls, then dragged in a deep breath.

"Right?" Taitn patted him on the back.

"I've never driven anything like this…" He massaged his knuckles as if they had changed, somehow.

Abruptly, the ship's metal shrieked. With no one at the controls, it nosed down hard, and Caiden slammed the console rim. Taitn's arms vised around him and hauled him back. Curses burst from the crew behind. A vessel ripped past the cockpit view, its velocity having thrown their ship forward.

The vessel in front of them was liquid glass. It shredded the air, the transparent layers of its hull clinging wildly to metallic bones within. It was the same weird ship Caiden had spotted before. An overseer ship. It had to be.

"All damned"—the swear leaked from him—"that's them, one of them."

The glass ship spun so it faced them nose-to-nose, re-forming its body more than it actually turned. Churning liquid wings solidified into sharp vanes.

"Crimes!" Taitn barked a curse, shoved Caiden back, and slapped his hands on the twitch drive plates. He plowed the ship forward to escape while En darted in and hooked Caiden's waist, pulling him back to the wall.

"Hold tight!" A thrill quavered Taitn's voice, as if the enemy weren't right on their tail.

Sand blasted around the ship, and the air shrieked as they tilted upward and gained speed. Caiden felt smeared into a streak of a person again at this velocity. Darkness filled the cockpit windows. The star spots turned to lines of pure speed.

The glass ship torched past their nose, forcing Taitn into a bank and Caiden's insides into knots. Taitn focused on evasive maneuvers while the crew somehow fended for themselves calmly, strapping into secure positions against the bay walls.

"You're a bit too short," En told him, fear well hidden in his voice but not his eyes. He lifted Caiden clear of the ground by his jacket collar, with one arm, up to the height of the wall's restraints.

Caiden wheezed, "How are you this strong?"

En laughed and pinned him against the wall, securing him with metal foot struts and cinched straps before letting go and strapping himself right beside. "Don't worry, we'll lose the pursuit. Taitn can fly out of anything. Welcome to the family, kid."

Family.

"Taitn!" Laythan bellowed. "Lose this Casthen cur! We don't have the fuel to play around."

"Casthen? Whose ship is chasing us?" Caiden yelled, but between the stress and the restraints, his voice was winnowed and no one heard him.

The transparent ship wheeled past the view, distorting the world through its morphing avian body. Taitn swerved and accelerated again, then stalled to fall behind and jet in a different direction.

Tones babbled through the fuselage as the vibration increased. The ship's shuddering returned Caiden to the huge cramped box, the roar, the stench. Horrific visions reared, and he sobbed while no one could hear him. He clamped his jaw shut and ran his palms up and down the straps, unable to move anything else. He closed his eyes so tight they watered through his eyelashes and tears jiggled sideways across his cheeks.

This box would crack like an egg and the beasts would rush in. The overseers would land in a splash of liquid glass and take him. His tears streamed, sorrow slipping out as his mind fissured.

The roar snapped off, motion halted, and like a light switch, Caiden lost consciousness.

CHAPTER 6

MULTIVERSE

Caiden regained consciousness, still in restraints. Beyond the windows lay an unmoving splash of milky dust and glittering "stars," and one small, dull ball hanging in the middle.

"Where's the sand?" he muttered groggily.

En said, "We're off-world. Taitn lost the Glasliq—the translucent vessel—in the fray."

Caiden blinked. "There's nothing holding the ship up... What if we fall?"

En sniggered and released the restraints, catching Caiden's stumble.

Stunned stiff, he stared at the expanse. He was shrinking in the vastness of all he didn't understand. He tried to imagine the faintly luminous sphere containing deserts and beasts and wreckage. Specks of light amassed around one side like flies at a carcass. "That's... But..."

"It's all very far away now. Those are passager ships wanting the gloss, fighting your 'overseers,' who are struggling to reclaim it. They can detect which mature nophek have complete gloss in their brains."

Caiden could have walked all the way around one of these "planets" and ended up where he started. His world had been a cage, keeping the population safe but stupid.

That horrific world shrank from view, and the things Caiden once believed were real and true shrank with it. But he knew one thing now: exposing the lies to save whoever else might have survived or be in danger was enough of a purpose to his life.

He drifted toward the view.

"Brave of you to get through this," En said. "You're safe now."

Brave of you.

Caiden had said it to Leta.

Said he'd come back for her. Ran. The end.

Cold sheeted through him. "We have to go back." His voice was half whimper, half choke. Panic surged him to the cockpit. Taitn twisted in the pilot's seat and caught Caiden's rush in the slam of one arm.

"Easy!" Taitn raised his other hand to stop En and Laythan from approaching. "You're all right."

"We have to—" *Go back for her.*

"How come?" Taitn's voice lightened.

Caiden glowered at that luminous corpse sphere amassed with flies in the dark, so very far away. Reminded himself how very small the hope was that she'd survived at all. Leta would have waited, like he—her hero—told her to...until the teeth came.

The reality snapped him. His shoulders twitched.

Worry pleated between Taitn's brows and he bent to look Caiden in the face, but Caiden's stare was locked on that distant wasteland and the reality, the failure, the hollow in his heart, because if he met the pilot's kind gaze, the cracks would spread. Instead, Caiden cinched up tight, clamped his quivering jaw, and let fury burn up the start of tears.

"We understand," Taitn said, soft as feathers. "You're safe with us. We won't push you to take your mind back there yet, or explain what you don't want us to. In your own time."

Laythan was sorting a bundle of salvaged weapons, and he boomed across the bay, "We're not going back, boy."

"I know..." Caiden belted his little knot of helplessness tighter. Despite being safe, he was within a well-greased machine of relationships still strange to him, even if En's nonchalant words from before—*Welcome to the family, kid*—still ricocheted in his heart. The moment he made a wrong move, these people could kick him away. Like Leta's family had rejected her, a bad fit.

"*Here* it is—" Taitn tapped a lit-up glyph on the console. The entire cockpit erupted in luminous, hovering lines. Translucent bubbles of all sizes stuck together, filled with tiny specks labeled with strange symbols. Unlike the paper map Caiden had once seen, with pasture blocks, road grids, and housing all squares and angles, this one was spheres, curves, and clouds.

"The multiverse," Taitn announced. "Each bubble is a complete universe with its own features. Some safe, others not. They can be any size. Think of them like rooms. We can pass from one to another through their walls, which are like membranes."

With a flick, Taitn zoomed the map out, revealing countless bubbles clustered into an intricate foam.

Laythan came over. "These are stars, and planets," he said, indicating specks with specific symbols.

Caiden squinted at the map, then out the window, wrestling with the immensity of the idea.

"These are stellar egresses—shortcuts." Laythan indicated tiny rings with lines curving across universes to other distant rings. "Unity." The largest and central sphere, without any smaller universes inside it. "Unity was the original universe. The rest bubbled off it. Unity expands continuously, as do the outer edges of the multiverse where new universes are born."

Caiden hoarded unknown words and concepts like treasures. He surveyed the breadth of the map: if Leta or his father had survived and escaped as he had, he would never find them in all these worlds. *We have to go back* sizzled desperately on his tongue again, but Taitn's soft words, and En's firm cheer, and Laythan's unwavering stance had all insisted, in their own way, *Move on.*

Taitn zoomed the display in to a little green chevron—the ship—hanging in the center of a red sphere that squished up against others.

"This universe is called CWN82, and the red means it was publicly declared a no-fly zone with unstable physics. But those dangers were all lies fabricated to conceal it. Nophek need both a special universe and a special atmosphere to survive in, and this universe was perfect. Passagers finally tailed the slavers here and learned it was safe all along."

The *scope* of it all hashed in Caiden's brain. He observed, "We're right next to a border...between universes?"

"That's right." Taitn whisked the map away and settled his hands in the twitch drive panels. He turned the ship all the way around and accelerated. The view filled with a gleaming surface of distortion cutting the darkness. It was the edge of a vast domed surface stretching out of sight, rippling with iridescent swirls.

Just like the little bubble that had expanded and collapsed around the ship—"but *huge*," Caiden blurted, eyes widening.

"That's a rind," Laythan said, "a border between universes. 'Crossover' is what we call travel through them. Universes can be *very* different from one another. Physics, probabilities, laws…A slight shift in parameters can either be unnoticeable or catastrophic."

"Slow down, Layth." Taitn twisted in the pilot's seat to give Caiden an earnest look. "Does this all make sense?"

Caiden recalled the dead overseers, and the nophek that had charged the ship's bubble only to be turned inside out into a red mist. His stomach flipped, but he nodded.

Laythan rushed on, "Material shifts phase, or gravity is inconstant, nonlocal memory or communication breaks down, other times electromagnetic variables render a ship unworkable. Passing through a rind requires a ship that can handle both the stress of the crossover and the conditions on the other side. Panca assures me this ship is so advanced, we'll have no problem. Generally, the more expensive a passager's ship, the more places they can go, and the more trade or exploration they can take on, which means more finances and ship upgrades to go even farther."

Still imagining the bloody mist, Caiden asked, "How are you sure *I'll* get through safely?"

"The newer, outer universes are the wild ones. Changes are usually minuscule this close to Unity. When we get to the Den, the Cartographers'll be able to sequence you and get a better profile of what universes are safe for you and which aren't."

Caiden curled his arms around his belly, recalling the sick punch he'd felt during crossover through his ship's rind—and that bubble had been tiny in comparison to the colossal surface they jetted toward at frightening speed. The approaching universe filled the view with oily hues in constant motion, snagging into a prickly, scintillating mess.

Air heaved against Caiden's ribs, pumped by stress. He backed up, right into En, who grabbed ahold of him. "It won't be so bad."

Brilliant, rumpled haze swallowed the cockpit. Taitn and Laythan's figures blurred and squished, unraveling into light. Then the rind engulfed the ship. Colors thrashed. Space boiled, and Caiden felt like his cells all squiggled in revolt, becoming a tingling fog, until the ship passed fully through into the new universe. The edge of the rind swept away behind them, and Caiden's sense of his body slammed back into place, solid again. The air in his lungs grew humid and his insides foamed, but the nausea was tolerable this time.

"Well done," En said, freeing Caiden from his arms. "Like I said, brave kid."

Brave. Caiden frowned and smoothed his hands over his body, ensuring he was all there. A flux of temperatures prickled his skin.

Taitn sighed contentedly. "Not a single complaint from the ship. Like silk."

Brave of you. Caiden snapped and unsnapped the magnetic seam of his pilot's coat. The *click* of his frustration. "The slavers," he said tightly, and the crew fell silent. "Who are they? You said that ship chasing us—that Glasliq—was *Casthen?*"

For a long moment, Laythan's piercing gaze assessed Caiden, judging what to say. "I know all this newness is frustrating, but we need more intelligence at a Cartographer Den before we jump to conclusions. That's where we're headed. You'll understand soon."

Soon. Caiden hated that word.

Laythan continued, "There, the Cartographers can find you a new home. A planet where you can get education and therapy."

Masked Ksiñe straightened sharply from his work in one corner of the bay. "You, rehoming?" He raised a gloved hand and made an exaggerated show of counting on his slender fingers; *one, two, three... four...* The number of crew members.

Laythan bristled, a hint of color flushing above his thick white beard. He rounded on Caiden again. "That's the deal. We all see your open wounds, boy. Each of us have lost things. We're not casting you out for having lost or for being different. We're taking you to the help we never had."

Caiden fidgeted with his coat seam. He didn't want a new home, he wanted the overseers to pay for all they had destroyed. How many others were in the same situation he'd been in, in a multiverse this vast where a large operation could be concealed for countless generations of slavery?

"At this...Den. Is there anyone who can track someone down in the multiverse?"

A last flicker of hope that Leta or his father had survived.

Laythan gave him another penetrative stare while warming up words or some other admonishment like that fact that they'd know more *soon*. In the end, the captain simply turned away, lighting the map back up. "We need to get there first. Crossover is safe but a stellar egress is another matter, and we're far from the nearest Den." He tapped lines on the display and drew purple hues from place to place. Taitn made a suggestion, which Laythan paved over, and they swiftly switched to a guttural language that escalated into an argument.

En whistled from the bay and motioned Caiden over.

"Best stay out of that, especially once Laythan's riled up." En twisted his black hair up into a weave. Metal specks trimmed each exposed ear. The venous black lines in his skin flushed into contrast for a moment before fading. He caught Caiden's curious gaze and chuckled, then yanked up one sleeve and flexed: the skin on his forearm turned translucent, revealing bundles of fat ribbons, wires, and porous metallic rods. Rapidly the whole construct deflated, muscles relaxed and shrank, and skin clouded back darker. By the time En pulled the sleeve back down, his arm and hand were slender.

Caiden looked up at En—but it was a feminine face, similar to but jarringly different from his features before. Finer bone structure, darker skin, smoky eye sockets, and wispy black bangs. The smile, tied hair, and slate iris color were the same.

"There's a lot you've never seen, isn't there, Winn?" En's voice was still husky but higher in pitch, smoother.

Caiden stammered sounds.

"Call me 'she,' or whatever you're comfortable with for now, I don't mind. You've had a huge dose of *new* lately, so don't overthink it, but get used to fluidity and choice. Those rule the multiverse, if anything does."

En laughed and laid an arm around Caiden's shoulders but withdrew when she noticed his trembling. "You're exhausted. This ordeal's a lot to absorb. And when was the last time you ate? Growing kids need to eat all the time. *Ksiñe!*"

In the corner of the bay, bent over his work, the Andalvian flinched. His masked face tilted her way, and the furry body around his neck stirred.

"Make us food?" En gave him a dazzling smile, then whirled and swept Caiden away.

Caiden's stomach did groan at the thought of food.

"Come on," En said, "Panca got the scour working. You need it. Did you have baths? Shed? Pristines? It's like that."

He thought of a bath, then the cold scrub he'd endured before Appraisal at ten years old—and he ejected that image fast. Dazed, he let En tug him down the bay ramp to the short lower hall, and whether it was the soft firmness of her touch, or the confidence of her lead, or her musical cadence, he wanted to lean closer, be led, assured, and comforted, because he *was* exhausted, and he flushed with gratitude at her care.

She pressed on the wall near one of the two sleeping chambers. A door slid back in a circular motion, revealing a cylindrical space. The glassy walls were dotted with bubbles and shiny textures. It smelled like peroxide and honeysuckle.

"Strip off your clothes, step in. Hold your breath."

Caiden blinked. His mind stuck on the very first thing.

"Look, kid, any part you could possibly have—human or xenid—I've seen it. Get in."

"Xenid?" He shrugged his pilot's jacket off and peeled away his grimy, sweat-damp standard-issue clothes.

"Good." En shoved Caiden's back so he stumbled inside, covering himself. "You'll enjoy it."

The door shut. The tube's radiant walls faded to lavender then black.

As cramped and void-dark as the transport cube had been.

The stale air, familiar.

Vibration filled his soles.

"*En!*" Caiden shrieked.

CHAPTER 7

FAMILY

The hiss of the "scour" tube devoured Caiden's alarmed shout. He held his breath, lungs burning, and squeezed his eyes closed. Light blazed red through his eyelids.

Like the transport cube when it had finally opened. Brilliance cracked the void.

Heat flushed from the center of Caiden's body outward. Chill shocked him in its wake, and he was instantly lightweight and emptied. A churning wave of density rolled down his body like a dump of feathers, a warmth that washed away the chill.

The breath he was holding burst from him, the chamber brightened, and he felt definitively *strange*.

The door rotated open to En, wearing a smirk.

Caiden fell to his knees.

En's mirth dissolved as she helped him up. "What's wrong? Too new? Scours work on all biology, it can't hurt you."

Caiden nodded vigorously. Words didn't come. How much of him was still back in that transport? How much still in the desert?

Irrational. Keep it together. He straightened and anchored himself in the present moment, where genuine amazement took over. The scrapes and bruises on his arms were gone. His skin was velvet-soft, his dark tan had vanished, and more freckles grew visible. He ran one hand through waves of pale hair and another over his belly. His bowels and bladder felt lighter. "It...How?"

"Takes care of dirt, elimination, parasites, and minor medical problems. Works for almost every species. We're all built of misshapen pieces shoved into a mismatched multiverse. On our homeworlds, our biology fit the environment, but now no passager's functions fit anywhere. With so much variety, species haven't homogenized, but technology has. Anyway. Stand back." En kept the pilot's coat and kicked the rest of Caiden's bloodstained clothes into the tube. After a scour, they came out stain-free, weave tightened, cream and green colors brighter. Caiden picked them up and dressed, relishing the warmth.

"Hold still." En sprayed something on the back of Caiden's neck and smeared it. "Can't have you showing a slave brand until you're old enough to fight."

Slave brand. It was almost funny . . . how far the brand was from the sign of merit he'd once thought it symbolized. "I can fight. I'm tougher than I look."

"Your heart's tough, I'll give you that." En examined the coat. "Can't scour this, needs polarizing." Ksiñe stalked by from the engine room, and En tossed the garment his way. "Hey, fix this morphcoat."

The scientist caught it, expression unreadable behind his mask but his posture all venom. "Needs jump start." He raised a tool with a snapping electric tip, and plunged it into the coat's material. Electric tendrils spidered across the leathery fabric and puckered it up, then slim feathers ruffled across the entire material as it transformed. The little plumes shrank to spiny points, then flattened into scales, finally melting back together into a shiny textured leather. A transforming material.

"Yeah, thanks." En snatched it back and handed it to a wide-eyed Caiden. "Good find. This morphcoat's whatever temperature, material, and resilience you need it to be."

Caiden put it on, better-fitting than before and steadily hugging him tighter. After the scour, he was warm and unburdened, soft and dressed in softness, but his fatigue welled up even stronger. "It's . . . incredible."

"Get ready for a lot of things to be, kid."

"Food!" Taitn shouted from the bay.

"Speaking of . . ." En led the way up the ramp.

The crew gathered on the floor around a spread of gourmet items. Caiden marveled at the meal's textures and colors, reminding him of the assortment of treasures Leta had collected on her shelves: colorful glass, shells, pressed flowers, feathers.

He pinched his fingernails in and out of his palm to drive the memory away. It didn't feel right to forget, but his *open wounds*—as Laythan said— carved deeper each time he recalled what he'd lost.

En tried unsuccessfully to sit and arrange her muscular legs beneath her. "There's nothing soft in this heap. First stop, we'll get you pillows."

"Enough already with the 'heap,'" Taitn grumbled.

Caiden sat comfortably on his heels, as he was used to doing when repairing the duster undersides. He was across the table from Ksiñe, whose hateful words from earlier still stung. The Andalvian's hands were ungloved for the first time, skin dark with speckles and striped rings.

"Where's Panca?" Caiden asked. The mechanic was the last crew member he needed to get to know. Did she want him gone as well?

"Pan rarely eats," Taitn said. "Saisn have a very efficient metabolism. She drinks fluids and feeds on vibration, mostly. The dark and quiet is nourishment and medicine for her."

"She is too thin," Ksiñe muttered. He stretched out a dense rubbery tube and flapped it in the air. Caiden watched transfixed as it puffed with steaming air pockets and expanded into a fluffy lattice. Ksiñe tore this into five pieces and laid them around a bowl of burgundy powder, the source of a heady, nutty aroma.

Taitn tore a chunk off. It attracted the powder when held close, and didn't seem to need chewing once consumed. Caiden's brow pinched as he watched. A plant or fungus, quickly grown? No *food* behaved this way.

The bare skin around Ksiñe's neck, beneath the straps and gills of his mask, paled and fluttered with peach-hued speckles. *Happy* speckles?

"You can..." Caiden wasn't sure how to ask. "Transform? Like En?"

"Not like En." Ksiñe ripped off his mask. His face had human features, in different proportions and shape, feline or piscine in a way. His skin was translucent and matte smooth over shifting patterns of spots that congealed into stripes across the bridge of his nose, peach above cream. His round eyes stretched to points at his temples. There the spots in his skin angled into black chevrons, the creamy hues reddening into a venomous glare. And his pupils and irises resembled an animal's eyes at night: disks of textured brightness in pools of black.

"Andalvians emote through their skin," En explained. "I'm augmented and can change skin, muscles, hair, and face, but I do so on command. Andalvians"—she lowered her voice and leaned close to Caiden—"are very blunt. They wear their feelings on the outside."

Ksiñe felt only vexation, if the oblique patterns and dark colors on his face were any indication. Slim chance of making a friend. At least there wasn't any ambiguity.

Caiden reminded himself of the patience it had taken to break through Leta's abuse-built shell. After a year of stumbling through unreciprocated small talk, he'd realized she needed depth, and that she understood a richness of unspoken things. Maybe Ksiñe's shell was just as tough.

The Andalvian plated a chunk of something so vibrant and purple it couldn't really be meat. The white marbling dissolved as he twisted it, and flakes of flesh-stuff crumbled onto a plate, furring up like velvet.

"Pakra," Laythan explained happily while snatching a chunk. "A delicacy. There's only one known universe with the right microgravity to support them. Try it."

Caiden popped a small piece into his mouth. Sweet, sooty, so buttery it melted on his tongue. He moaned in startled delight. En giggled.

"I've never... Wow."

Flavor. Who knew flavors could be as strong as scents?

As Ksiñe kept plating things, the happy pink sparkles around his jaw returned and the hate paled out of his face. He picked up one of the spongy fluffs and passed it over.

Caiden dipped it in the fragrant, electric powder, and paused with it halfway to his mouth—he scowled at En and Taitn's amused expressions as they watched him experience newness.

Caiden bit: flaky and chewy at the same time, coating his mouth in a hot, sweet spice. It warmed his stomach and expanded. He wolfed the rest down, filled with pure comfort and the realization that he'd never truly been *full* before in his life.

"So..." He fumbled the words over his tongue where the flavor lingered and a laugh bubbled. "So much better than the...the ration blocks." Those gray, tasteless things.

Darkness oozed over Ksiñe's collarbones across his strange skin, and he fretted his fingers together.

Caiden said, "Thank you, it's...all of it's really delicious. Ksiñe." He mangled the name somewhat but tried his best.

The Andalvian met his gaze with stiff shoulders, but a purple bloom around his neck slimmed into tight rings.

"*He says you're welcome,*" En whispered loudly.

Ksiñe's stripes darkened with bale as he flashed En a withering look, and muttered, "Would not wish ration slab on even enemy."

Caiden stifled a smile.

Ksiñe picked up a flake of pakra and held it up to the mass of fur draped over his shoulder. The pelt uncurled into an animal, nose rooting in the air. Nictitating membranes slid drowsily over huge round eyes, which dilated immensely as the creature spotted the meat. Barbed teeth in gummy jaws snatched the pakra in one bite.

"She is whipkin," Ksiñe said when he caught Caiden gaping.

The mammal was forearm-length, white body marbled in black with an indigo sheen. Spiral ears flicked on a leaf-shaped head as she crawled over Ksiñe's shoulders and arm, using webbed, long-fingered paws. Her body stretched long and sleek, then flattened out—with webbing rippling between her limbs—as she cuddled next to Ksiñe's plate of pakra to feast.

Caiden grinned. Ksiñe couldn't be all bad if he liked animals. "Leta would have adored her," Caiden said before catching himself.

He shut up as a tense silence hummed between the crew. En passed around a bottle with vapor in a bottom chamber and water on the top, which never emptied. Laythan and Taitn passed a chemical-smelling flask back and forth to each other.

The captain took a long swig, then said in the tone of trouble, "Earlier... you asked if a person could be tracked down in the multiverse."

Caiden ate another piece of buttery pakra. It tasted ashy this time.

There were no survivors to find. They were meat. All of them.

"Winn?" En prodded.

Ksiñe cut in impatiently. "He left someone."

More silence, abrasive.

"Family?" Taitn whispered, and the tight spaces in the word reminded Caiden that Laythan had said the crew all had wounds too. Taitn peered over, his bearded face kind, eyes crinkled with warmth. Caiden's poise frayed. "People you cared for?" the pilot asked. "I bet they knew how strong and brave you were to survive."

"I didn't feel brave," Caiden muttered. All the lovely tastes fled his tongue, the warmth grew hot, but under hunger and exhaustion and embarrassment, the crew grazed a part of him so thirsty for comfort, it seared.

Leta had asked him once, "Why do you help me?"

He'd answered instantly, "We're family."

"But we don't belong."

He stopped braiding grasses and looked over. Her gaze fixated on the distant herd.

"That's silly," he replied, "we trained in the Stricture to belong. The Appraisal will show you you're worthwhile, don't listen to your parental unit. You'll see in a couple years, you'll pass, don't worry." She was scared.

"We don't fit each other," Leta said, "can't you tell?"

"No?"

"The bovine. The little ones look like the parents, and they... all of them look alike. But we're all nothing alike."

He hadn't considered it. But Leta was always right, always observing patterns that no one else saw; even at eight years old she knew. He thought she just felt outcast, and had said, "So what if we're mismatched. You're still family to me."

All along, Leta had been right. They didn't belong.

En hummed, drawing Caiden back to the moment. "Whoever it is..." She read his face intently. "Ah, sibling?"

Heat flushed Caiden's cheeks. Quietly, he asked, "What's a sibling?"

The crew all paused again. Taitn blew out a long breath and accepted the flask for a swig.

En spoke. "Someone you grew up close to in your family. Did... did you have family?"

"Sort of," Caiden replied.

"Nine crimes," Taitn swore. "En, don't poke at him."

Taitn and En glared at each other across the table.

"Thank you," Caiden said, turning himself back to the meal. "But she's dead."

He ate and chewed, trying to find the flavor again.

Taitn nudged him with a shoulder and offered the blue-lacquered flask.

Caiden took it and sipped: bittersweet water, minty and crisp. It flashed down his throat and warmed in his breast. He took one more sip before handing it back, and nodded: he was all right.

He ate another puff of flavor, and held out a morsel for the whipkin, still as he could be while she sniffed around the table and considered him. Her rippled mass of black and blue fur stretched sleek as she rose on her hind legs and reached for the piece, her fingers splaying out huge and whiskers springing from her muzzle. Ksiñe *tsked* at her and she darted back to him, the morsel prize in hand.

Caiden smiled, which eased the sad mood that had fallen. The glorious tastes and textures returned as he ate. He relished the food as well as Ksiñe's generally softened demeanor, and the crew grew animated again, conversed and joked, slipping more and more into languages he didn't know. The whipkin discovered every scrap of food on the floor, and climbed each crew member to root for crumbs in their clothes before returning to Ksiñe and curling around his neck.

Caiden sat back in a pleasant daze as a toasty feeling spread through him. His morphcoat mimicked it as a downy fur the same blackbird green as Taitn's jacket.

He wanted the crew's happiness, their banter, camaraderie. The laughter and hugs and messiness. He felt left out—but that was to be expected. The crew was kind, but Caiden didn't belong.

So what if we're mismatched...

The meal wound down. Ksiñe packed things away with the little whipkin's help, then settled against one wall. Above one of his palms, four dimples of air formed a box filled with text that rewrote itself as he read. His pet cheeped sounds as she crawled around in his layered garments, looking for somewhere to snuggle.

Taitn nursed the lacquered flask and ambled to the pilot's seat to recline. In moments his breathing slowed to the husky rhythm of sleep. Caiden smiled. His mother had known that same trick, able to instantly sleep.

He worked a lump in his throat. Sawtooth nostalgia lurked in every moment. He didn't want to lose the lovelier memories, but they were twisted up with the bad.

"*That* look again," En said, "I used to wear it every time I looked in the mirror."

Caiden cocked his head.

En gestured him up and led him to the lower hallway. "Let time do its work. You're still raw. And focus on the balm, not the sting. Did you like the pakra or the efsä better? The Cartographers' Den will have so much to eat, I'm not sure where I'll take you first. No—new clothes first. And pillows."

She steered him to one of the two sleeping chambers, each on a different end of the hall. The door opened before they reached it and closed after they'd passed through. Caiden twisted to marvel at the door, then at the unlit room of steel-colored walls and geometric seams, functional and logical: the inside of a machine.

"Listen, Winn," En said, voice rougher. Caiden looked up to En's male face and physique: skin lighter, nose harder, brows deeper, and lips thin-pressed into a smirk. "There's gonna be a lot of weird in the Den, a lot of tech and a lot of xenids. What we've explained and what you've seen is nothing in comparison. You need rest if you're gonna handle a Cartographer Den." He sat Caiden on the bed and gently pushed him over. "I'm serious, kid. Rest."

Caiden crumpled gratefully on his side. The cushions heated beneath him. "Do you only have two faces?" he asked.

En's chuckle bounced off the walls. "As many faces, shapes, or colors as I want, of whatever kind, but I prefer these two and everything in between. Many options, in my professions, are a good thing."

"Why are you all helping me?" He meant to phrase it better but his mind mushed in spicy flavors and leaden fatigue, and Leta's voice still echoed, *Why do you help me?*

We're family.

"Because time goes on," En said softly. "And right now we're glimpsing a ghost of our pasts."

"Laythan said you all lost something."

"Laythan lost a prestigious position and the person he was sworn to protect...Taitn lost his 'family.' Panca lost her culture. Ksiñe lost so many things, I'm not sure what meant the most. Maybe his pet."

"The whipkin?"

"No...different creature."

An electrified silence settled in the dark and the warmth. It itched at Caiden until he voiced it: "And you?"

"Sharp thing, aren't you?" En clicked his tongue. "I started out human like you. I loved fights. Lost a lot of limbs and organs. I replaced them with machines, which I loved even more, so I bargained and gambled my way to completion. Now I'm whatever I want to be. Only my spinal cord and brain stem are the last history of who I was."

"You lost *yourself*."

The next silence stretched icy and void as En got up to leave.

Caiden curled into the blanket and ground his jaw as if the words could be chewed back and swallowed.

Mercifully, En's voice wafted from the doorway, "That's right, sharp thing. But I gained so much more. Now, get some rest."

Caiden balled up in the heavy morphcoat. Like the ship and the starry sky, its dark weight made him feel small and insignificant, but safe, and he relaxed into the knowledge that whatever new things awaited in the Cartographers' Den, they couldn't be worse than what he had already survived.

Nothing could.

CHAPTER 8

GRAVEN WINGS

When Caiden woke, warm and comfortable but alone, he stared up at a gray much darker than the sky of his old home.

Tears rolled down his temples. Free from the crew's momentum and scrutiny, he let the memories play. The rough limbs of the oak tree he and Leta would lie beneath and question the origin of the wind. The grass blades whispered. Laden seedpods chattered like insects. Their first glimpse of the ocean, dark and empty, which Leta had sketched so they'd remember. The rock ledge, like a mouth, which his mother had shoved him under to keep him safe from the sharper jaws of the beasts.

The visions grew bloody. He had to *move*. Caiden wiped his cheeks with a sleeve and made to shove off the bed. But beneath him was only air and the bed a full meter away. Caiden yelped and scrabbled for it, swimming midair, his limbs flailing and the blanket knotting around his legs as he levitated. His back hit the ceiling and he bobbed there, heart pounding. Everything seemed normal except this. He scrambled to grasp the door rim, glided carefully out, and almost ran into Panca, the mechanic, emerging from the engine room.

She snatched his arm and pulled him down as he spun. Her long, slender fingers were dense with weaves of muscle, surprisingly strong.

"What's happened?" he croaked. "Why are we weightless?"

Caiden's cheeks were damp, eyes puffy. Confused and panting, he scrubbed at his face again, and a teardrop flicked away, levitating impossibly in the air.

"Scalar gravity's off to conserve fuel," Panca said, her voice airy in a way Caiden suspected a bird might sound if it spoke.

"Scalar gravity" made no sense to him. Another new concept to struggle with.

Panca cocked her head to the side. The jeweled black circle in her forehead flushed with light and reflections, stark in the veiled blankness of her face. Hues of ocean and summer green swam through white.

"Is that...an eye?"

"To feel, not see. Your eyes're for solid things. Mine're for numinous things. Saisn exist in sense-sea. A textured world with broader sensory detail than yours."

Panca unwound her veil. At her forehead, her skull folded open around the embedded black core, sheeny and multifaceted like an insect eye. Her two *real* eyes beneath it were entirely black except for white limbal rings around each iris, which flicked as she examined wide-eyed Caiden. The fine muscles in her face scrunched like a fixed scowl under her velvet-soft, grayish-purple skin. Her flat nose had tiny teardrop nostrils, and her wide ears lay tight against her scalp. In place of hair, chevron ridges at the top of her forehead swept over her skull and down her neck like plaits. Eerie but beautiful in her own way, the saisn was not nearly as dangerous-looking as the veil had let his imagination assume.

She left him and launched off the ramp, gliding through the air to the bay ceiling. She spun right side up and grabbed a rung there.

Caiden tried to follow but his groggy instincts fired: he was falling. He flailed to catch onto a surface and stop himself, but swam in air until his hip finally bumped the bay floor and he could spider himself onto it.

"Panca?" Ksiñe said, worried, from across the bay. His skin was dark mauve with lightning patterns darting through. The whipkin clung to his upper arm, chittering grumpily.

Laythan and En were in other rooms, and Taitn lay fast asleep in the pilot's seat, snoring lightly.

Panca pulled herself along the ceiling of the ship, palpating the seams with her long fingers. Scaly material plated the surface, scored with gaps that glinted a crystalline material inside. She called to Ksiñe, "There's light-seep obsidian in this ship's spine, like I found in the engine."

"Impossible." Ksiñe floated up to the ceiling while raising his hand. His glove projected a field of dimples in the air, and a readout of symbols and numbers. The data shifted as he glided the scanning field across the ceiling to the swell of crystal over the pilot's head, the thing Caiden had touched that made the ship generate its universe bubble.

"Don't touch that," Caiden warned.

Ksiñe's gaze darted over. Crimson hues scowled across his cheeks. "What did you do?"

"I didn't, it—"

"Ksiñe," Panca said, "it's got a central seam." She probed the complex plating, then slid her arm beneath a panel. Something activated, moaning inside the walls. The ceiling panels and scales pleated open down the length of the ship, revealing a crystalline mass that had been hidden beneath it the whole time. It stretched from wall to wall and extended over the cockpit as part of that glassy swell Caiden had touched to emit the bubble universe around the ship.

A smoky lavender glow emanated, filling the bay. Not a digital light—something cellular, bioluminescent. Scintillations spread along branching pathways within. Inner facets shifted and flashed organically from different angles. Like so many of the new materials Caiden had seen, this spine existed between qualities and phases: glass, metal, jewel, and liquid.

Panca placed a hand on its surface and closed her eyes. The core in her forehead absorbed candescence. "Hybrid organic."

"*Laythan!*" Ksiñe shouted.

Taitn roused awake, anchored in the pilot's seat, blinking and scrubbing a hand through his short hair. "Kis, what's goin—" He cut off as he looked up.

Laythan glided up from a sleeping chamber, grumbling, and was also shocked still by the sight. He slapped a hand on the edge of the floor to steady his weightless momentum. "Taitn, get scalar gravity back."

"Right." The pilot's hands shot up, and the cockpit's bright displays sprang into the air.

Weight slammed Caiden. Every direction pulled his body, pummeled his guts, wrenched the air from him. Then everything snapped back to normal. His body stuck to the floor and he grew weighty again as he wobbled to his feet. The crew regained their footing like they'd done this many times before.

There was a loud thump in the engine room and a string of swears as En marched out, rubbing her hip. "All damned, warn a person before you—Oh." Her hand flew over her mouth, eyes wide.

All five seasoned veterans of this new world gawked up at the crystalline spine with as much dumb awe as Caiden.

"Explain," Laythan ordered.

Ksiñe's usually sharp posture drooped, and his skin's patterns curdled into uncertain swirls. His gloved palm still emitted a grid of air dimples, on which luminous data was strung. He read through it. "A holotropic resonator? Glossy technology, some lightseep, definitely Graven tech."

"Called it." Taitn grinned. "How much of this ship is shell? How much is crystal, lightseep obsidian, hybrid organics?"

"Cannot tell without full scanner."

En whistled as she ambled up the ramp into the bay, craning her neck back. "Winn, you found this ship in the sand *before* the raid started?"

"More importantly," Laythan butted in, "we approached this ship in the desert because we glimpsed a small universe from a distance. And we saw that universe shrink, which is impossible."

Caiden blinked. "You mean it really *did* create a universe?" He pointed to the cockpit ceiling where the spine's material swelled downward like a limpid eye embedded in the milkier quartz of the mass. "When I touched that, a bubble expanded around the ship. When the fuel ran out, it sucked back in."

Laythan squinted at it, his scars wrinkling more, then he shot Panca a quizzical, dread-filled look.

"Plausible." White rings in Panca's eyes flicked as she scrutinized it. "I've never seen such an engine, or material combination like this, or Graven tech in a ship. Possible this florescer can generate a small universe of its own."

"Florescer?" Caiden asked.

"Universe is bloomed like a flower, then closes like flower; fold, unfold. Implicate, explicate realities."

The ship was special, powerful. And it was Caiden's. He stood transfixed, bathed in light. Even if he had nothing else in the world, he had this—he could take on anyone.

"Amazing," Taitn exhaled.

"It's not amazing, Taitn," Laythan snapped. "It's terrifying. Have the damn sense to be wary of something so new, in a multiverse so vast."

Caiden frowned. Everything was new to him. How would he know what to be wary of, if even these people didn't? He would have to ration his questions. "What does Graven mean?"

"An ancient species," Taitn replied. "Some say they created the multiverse. Something wiped them out, but their technology remained. Like lightseep structures, stellar egresses, and devices hoarded by the Dynast, who govern Unity. Most of it we don't understand."

En nudged an elbow into Laythan's ribs, then motioned her head at Caiden. "Speaking of. Freckles."

Laythan's brow creased. "Not definite."

"But what do you think? You and Taitn should be able to tell."

Annoyed, Caiden scratched his freckled cheeks. "I'm standing right here. Is it a mark of poor quality? You're sizing up what to sell me for, in the Den?"

En winced. "Of course not."

Ksifie's eyeshine flashed red as he looked over. "Children fetch higher price as parts."

"Ksifie!" Laythan snapped. "No one's turning anyone to parts. The Cartographers can take him and answer all his questions. We need to avoid scrutiny. A vessel that can generate a new universe around itself could cross over into any world. That's a power that can be abused, and if the tech can be replicated for other ships, it would change how the multiverse is navigated. If anyone sees this tech, we'll have more than slavers on our tail."

Fear leached into Caiden as he tried to wrap his tired mind around it all. Maybe the ship wasn't such a good thing to own.

"Hurry up and make a plan," Taitn said, "we're here." He slid his hands into the twitch drive panels.

Light streaks marring the cockpit view slowed into a sudden vista.

The Den's blocky, light-studded mass filled space in front of them, growing larger as Taitn cruised the ship through an opening. The gigantic interior was crowded with walls and floors, up and down confused. Their ship glided through a narrow passage into one large "room" bigger than the combined area of all the pasture blocks of Caiden's old home. His mouth hung open and he leaned over the console to take it all in.

Vessels of various shapes flew past. Some were brightly colored, others reflected images around them or morphed shape and texture as they moved. Many were so fast they were mere streaks of afterimage. The slower ones were so huge they may as well have been vast walls.

Taitn chuckled at Caiden's expression, then aimed the ship through a membrane of light and nosed down into a tight canyon filled with haze. Cyan and orange luminescence frothed up. Walls blistered out in glass, with blurry activity swollen inside. Rows of ships docked at flowery airlock openings that stretched shimmering membranes across. The cockpit guides labeled it an "atmoseal" membrane.

Taitn spun to an open space in the row of parked vessels and backed up, hitting cushioning on the wall. A booming *clunk* riveted the ship in place and the engine hum faded to a whine. Taitn bent to detach his green jacket from the seat and crawled out, stretching noisily.

Laythan handed out salvaged weapons. "We head to the Cartographers' bar and assess the situation with the nophek planet raid and the slavers. Avoid trouble." He skipped giving Caiden a weapon and extended an open palm instead. "The gloss."

Caiden pulled it from his pocket. It sat warm and electric in his palm. The object was functionless to Caiden, but the dazzling ship, the morph-coat, and this gem were the only things that were honestly *his*.

The deal with the crew was nearing its end. Despite how little time they'd spent together, Caiden's heart ached a bit.

"Actually, the gloss is safer with me." En reached out. He'd grown taller, and muscles filled out his now too-small coat and trousers. "Don't worry, we'll get you to the Cartographers safely. That's part of the agreement. Right, Laythan?"

The captain grunted.

Caiden had gotten this far by trust—what was one more leap? Even if they abandoned him now, he was away from the jaws of the nophek and the cruelty of the slavers. He'd made it to this new world. Now he could learn the slavers' identity.

He dropped the gloss into En's hand.

"Good kid." En ruffled his hair.

"Hey! I'm not ten!" Caiden deflected En's wrist, but En's grin only widened.

Taitn hit the bay-door controls and glowered at the man's brawn. Taitn's face was built harder than En's, with strong cheekbones and brows, but somehow didn't look as violent. "En's more likely to start a fight than stop one, Winn. A little trouble in a Den can escalate quickly. The only place peace is enforced is the Cartographers' bar, where we're headed, so stay by me until then."

Caiden went rigid as the doors unfolded to reveal the Den.

CHAPTER 9

XENID DEN

The size struck him first. The Den interior was as vast and multi-leveled as the exterior. He blinked at colors and lights, surfaces flickering with imagery like windows to other worlds. Tiny ships and darts whizzed in the open air while beings of all sorts milled and streamed and... pulsed. Caiden couldn't tell what was beast and what was human or whether there was any clear distinction. Individuals and groups clashed. Language blurred the air: everything from guttural rumbles to birdlike trills. The space was stuffed from ceiling to floor with sensory stimulus.

"Follow me." Taitn guided him forward. "Just focus on your feet if you have to."

Caiden gagged at a waft of musk in the smoky air, fading to a floral taste and a pleasant spice. Babbling sounds whisked into airy syllables.

Two tall creatures sauntered by, svelte and congealed, like a gelatin coating on spongy bones. Their skin was smooth as a water drop, with an oily sheen that pooled at the extremities of too-numerous limbs. Atop it: a huge faceless droplet of tiny-veined mucus.

Bravery withering, Caiden shrank closer to Taitn, staggering as the space assaulted sense and sensibility.

A human shape drifted by, made of flowing cloud gauze draped over a transparent skeleton. She appeared more solid the longer he looked at her. A figure and face... a face he knew. *Leta? No.*

A familiar smile surfaced, vibrant and reassuring. Brown hair spilled from a messy bun around a strong jaw. Her stern eyes sparkled.

"Mother?" He lagged.

Taitn turned Caiden away. "Sorry, Winn, we see what we want to see in vishkant. They respond to exterior consciousness, conforming to others' thoughts and memories."

Vishkant.

Taitn steered Caiden from tripping over a small, scuttling thing covered in bristling scales. Its hiss razored Caiden's skull with a piercing tone. He winced and shut his eyes, but all the sounds without the sight was infinitely worse. He clutched the hem of Taitn's coat, like the ten-year-old he had told En he wasn't.

"It'll thin out soon. The concourse is always chaotic." Taitn dodged a waist-high creature with gaunt, translucent features and glowing eyes. "Should have borrowed one of Pan's sensory veils for you. Sorry."

A lanky bluish body lumbered past, and all Caiden registered was their horrific face: the nose an inverted pit of flowery bone, their phosphorescent eyes huge with diamond pupils and *things* swimming inside.

Taitn grinned. "Saavee. Friend of all. If you get separated from us, find a saavee."

Caiden gripped tighter, determined not to get separated. The pilot veered him into a wide corridor through a canyon of stacked rooms. The glass floor revealed sprawling vistas of activity below. Nauseous, he fixed his gaze firmly up and matched the purposeful gait of Laythan's crew. He'd entered the real world, and needed to be able to handle it to survive.

In front of a glowing wall, a stunning figure caught Caiden's eye. She was humanoid but ethereal and slender, with prosthetic scaffolding around tapered legs. Skin paper-thin and pearly. Her thick hair was so long it pooled onto the floor and clothed her body in dressy billows and braids. Wings spilled three to a side, formed of something plush: feathers, scales, petals, but soft, so soft-looking.

"Sweet young thing, how tired you are." Her words burrowed through the air into his head, caressing him in feather down. As he neared, her gentle hands wrapped his arm and the back of his neck to curl him closer. "You can rest with me."

En's brawny shadow fell on the creature. He peeled Caiden away. "Mauya company is overpriced every-damn-where."

Transfixion broken, Caiden back-stepped fast, bumped something hard, and looked up at a blue-black metallic face.

"Watch yer walk, vermin." The voice was muffled yet amplified. The same sort of voice that had said, *You'll all be taken care of.*

The chaos spiraled out of Caiden's vision until there was only that mask. *"Taken care of..."*

"Eh?" The overseer squared themselves and loomed. Glinting metals encrusted their wiry frame.

"People," they called us. But we were livestock to them. Caiden's clammy fear lit like a fuel and fired up wrath, powering him forward—but Taitn's arm hooked around him and a hand flew over his mouth, clamping in the shout that raced up his throat. He spun Caiden around as more overseers poured from a hazy side room. The overhead lighting glistened across mismatched metallic clothing, straps, weapons, and blue faceplates peppered with holes and slits. Their clatter settled to a jingle as they stopped. The conversation died to a murmur.

They loaded us up. Caiden fought Taitn pulling him onward. His gaze locked on the overseers and blurred with tears. Blood roared in his ears, drowning out the Den. All he wanted to do was hurt them.

"No..." Taitn hissed near Caiden's ear as he dragged. "No. *No.*"

Dumped us to be slaughtered. The event swelled around Caiden as if no time had passed and he was herded into the dark. He ripped free from Taitn's arm and swiveled around, only to slam into the leg of a beast half again as tall as Laythan and several times more muscled than En, chiseled solid as a rock from head to toe, naked, and covered in a rough purple-gray hide.

The monster threw a punch with a fist the size of Caiden's head.

En shot forward and caught the strike with both hands. His muscles bulged and his posture leaned full into it as he skidded back two meters.

En spoke in a language more like growling than words, yet he still managed to make his words sound cheeky. The beast grunted, withdrew, and lumbered off with steps that shook the ground.

Caiden twisted around. The overseers had left.

He wasn't in the dark or the desert, but there was sweat, and the roar, and he struggled to force himself to stop trembling.

En released a shaky sigh and shook out his arms. "Chketin," En explained. "Best to avoid them."

Laythan pushed En aside and swooped in, crouching to Caiden's level. "That was them, huh? Those armored passagers. Your slavers."

Armor...Caiden blinked, trying to take in Laythan's face and get back to his own body, the moment.

"I suspected as much," Laythan said. "They're Casthen, a publicly aboveboard organization. Most people don't consider them slavers, and a great deal of multiversal economy relies on them, so even if they were behind the nophek operation, they'll have strong allies who are invested in hiding it. There's nothing we can do yet. Deep breaths." He nodded and straightened.

Caiden gulped air. "What do you mean there's nothing we can do? A fist can do a lot."

En sniggered. "Seriously, Laythan, can we keep him?"

The captain responded with a glare. Like Caiden's father: allergic to questions.

The crew walked on and Caiden looked between his feet and followed one step at a time, telling himself he wasn't walking back into the desert, feeling the hot breath on his heels, hearing the bray of the beasts.

They entered a sector with self-luminous glassy white floors. Caiden focused on its blankness.

He and Leta used to lie tired in the field after tasks were done, and they'd stare up at a luminous gray sky like this. "Maybe nothing's up there, just gray forever," he had said, curiosity bobbing up as always. And Leta, younger but wiser, answered, "What if *everything* is up there?" And the idea had shut him up for a long while.

She'd been right.

Laythan brought the crew to a halt in a large chamber, the lights too bright, everything white all over. The space was colored by a variety of xenids passing through.

More of the Casthen slavers strolled by in the mix, and no one batted an eye.

Caiden crossed his arms and grabbed fistfuls of his morphcoat, which changed to scales in his grasp and bit the flesh of his palm. He couldn't restart life in a world where groups like the Casthen were allowed to do what they wanted and no one cared that an entire population had been part of a terrible machine and no better than meat in the end.

Taitn noticed Caiden's distress. He scratched his bearded cheek and lowered his voice. "There'll be an investigation into the universe you're from now that it's exposed. Passagers will uncover anything incriminating that's there. Meanwhile, you're the only survivor who saw everything firsthand. Let's find out what the Cartographers know, be patient, and let this untangle. We can get you settled in a new home."

"I don't want a new home." The hot itch of anger stampeded up Caiden's spine. "Can't we tell someone? I saw everything. Two of them, they...they loaded us up and then..."

En cruised over. "He's just a kid, you can't tell him the thing he needs to hit is behind locked doors. You have to let him hit it, or he'll end up hitting something else." En bent to match Caiden's eye level, hands on his hips. "This is the Cartographers' main district, so let's get you scanned, find out a little more about you, then we can think about what to do, all right?"

Caiden blurted, "I want to register as a passager. I need to be like you. To do what I want and go where I want."

Taitn made a strangled sound. En straightened, frowning.

Laythan walked over, saying, "You need education and counseling. That's not our job. The Cartographers will set you up somewhere safe."

"No." Caiden gazed over his hands where the scour had so easily erased years of calluses, stain, and scrapes, his entire life a waste. He'd been a tiny nut in a vast machine, fulfilling one purpose. Now he was a piece that didn't fit in any other mechanism, and would go unused, passed around. One of those homeless parts that always got discarded to a scrap heap in the end.

"I don't care about a safe life on some new planet. I'm registering." He rubbed the brand at the back of his neck; the concealing spray En had applied still smoothed over top, but the mark was permanent.

En huffed. "Did you see any other kids while we were walking here? You're too young to do anything about the Casthen. This isn't a world for children."

"I'm not a child."

Laythan said, "No kid chooses to become a passager. We're convicts, slavers, rebels, drifters. What you went through...no one should have to live with that experience, and it's going to take time for the past to feel like it's behind you. It took me decades to bury my own. We want you to learn the lessons we did sooner, without years of mistakes. Have more experiences before you decide if you're going to let hatred define your whole life."

"What if the hatred never goes away?" Even now, he hated the quaver in his voice, he hated the quiver in his body, and he hated Laythan's careful tone.

"You'll have to turn it into something else," the captain said. "Use it as fuel to do good."

A knot cinched in Caiden's chest like a drive belt too tight, overheating, ready to snap. He *was* trying to do good: becoming a passager to be free to destroy the slavers so no more people would suffer.

"Stay somewhere safe to learn and regrow," Laythan concluded. "There are plenty of quiet planets that won't feel foreign to you."

He wasn't going to regrow. The ordeal would *always* define him, like a chunk of rock reshaped by the chisel. He would always be misshapen, so there had to be something he was good for, something his new shape could unlock. Even if he never belonged anywhere with anyone, he could still serve a purpose. Justice.

In the corner of his vision, a figure approached behind a lengthy white counter. They had a formal posture and a uniform that matched others he'd seen on the walk over: angular and fitted, light gray and inviting purple.

They must be a Cartographer. Caiden snapped his spine straight and marched over, just tall enough to plant his elbows on the counter.

"I need to register as a passager."

CHAPTER 10

REGISTRATION

The Cartographer approached with a swaying gait. They were Andalvian, like Ksiñe: the tan spots dusting their pale skin pinched into wisps of sparkling blue. They wore a long, angular tunic pulled tight around their body, all light gray and purple. A black crown wrapped their head in layers of curving spikes—the jaw of an animal, upside-down. What creature was it from? Had they killed it?

"You look stunning as ever," En greeted, gliding in.

The Andalvian narrowed their eyes, which had black sclera and bright pupils like Ksiñe's, but their eyeshine was gentle blue. Wisps on their face thickened into dark streaks of scowl as En leaned against the counter. "And you look like you are trying too hard. I enjoy the *other* you better."

En changed. This time, Caiden watched him do it.

En's facial structure slimmed, feathery bangs stretched over her forehead, and her eyes creased in a smile as smoky paint oozed around them. Her skin tone darkened and cooled. She stretched her shoulders in an arc that carried down her whole body. Muscles relaxed and softened, frame shortened. In a heartbeat, female En was beaming at the Cartographer.

"Blue, right?" En's hair lengthened and brightened from black to waves of ocean blue spilling over her shoulders and back.

"Better." Stripes rippled down the Andalvian's neck into purplish sparkles, which rained into their shirt.

Taitn dashed his gaze away and pretended to examine a map on the ceiling. He wrinkled his nose and muttered, "Can't recall her name, but remembers she likes blue."

Caiden asked, "What *is* her name?" He warmed up his courage again.

"Sina," Taitn said.

Caiden turned back to the Cartographer, whose skin settled into a dusting of stationary spots as she focused on him. "Sina, I want to register as a passager."

"Winn," Taitn warned.

En raised her hand. "Let him decide. We're not his parents."

"Young, for passager," Sina said, her animal gaze flashing across Caiden.

"Please?" He flushed under her scrutiny. "I need to know more. I need to be free and—" *Better*. "You deal in knowledge, right?"

Sina cocked her head. "Correct. While the Dynast in Unity pays for technology, we Cartographers pay for knowledge. Technology grows old, but knowledge is always new to someone. With passagers buying and selling chartings, we map the expanding multiverse and make worlds navigable, together."

"Please. I have a ship. I need to be able to navigate worlds."

"Very well." Sina gave a formal bow. "It is a Cartographer's duty to see that all passagers are well and accounted for. Forehead here—" She indicated sections of the counter that lit up with starbursts. "Hands here. Eyes open."

Caiden bowed to the counter and was met with a blinding flash as his forehead touched. Heat pulsed to his soles and receded into chill.

"Sequenced." Sina's fingers flew in gestures across the counter display. "Name?"

"My name…"

En leaned next to him, blue hair coiling on the counter. "You can always change it. Make one up. I have thirty names."

"One for every lover," Taitn muttered, still glaring at the ceiling.

En shrugged proudly and leaned on tiptoes to peer at Sina's screens. "I *was* right about his makeup. There's a fair amount of Graven genes in there. Those freckles."

Caiden scratched his face, where light-colored freckles sprinkled across his nose, cheeks, and temples.

"A lot of unanalyzable stuff." En peered over at the data again, frowned, and glanced at Taitn. The pilot flinched, then mouthed, *What?*

"Sterile."

"What does that mean?" Caiden asked.

Taitn opened his mouth to speak, but hesitated. Caiden recognized the dullness in his eyes as he hid the truth. "It means . . . your genes have less risk of contamination."

They treat me like a child, but also say this isn't a world for children? "Tell me the truth."

Taitn winced. "You don't have the right knowledge to make sense of the truth yet. Be patient."

"I spent my whole life patient and stupid." Caiden swiveled straight. "Cartographer Sina, what does 'sterile' mean?"

Her blue-moon gaze flicked between the crew members, then back to him. "You are unable to procreate through biological means. It is a common result of selective breeding and mosaicism, which your genetic makeup suggests."

Selective . . . Caiden crushed his sleeves in his fists. Bovine breeding was the responsibility of those with husbandry determination—Caiden knew enough from questioning his mother—but no parental units on his planet made children. Four-year-olds graduating from the Stricture were assigned a unit based on their aptitudes.

He was a sterile hybrid, not born to a family or a tribe but created to be a slave, a cog in the Casthen's vast machine. The overseers' voices at Appraisal had been blunt: *As a mechanic determination, it will become your job to maintain this world.*

Caiden's only purpose had been to unwittingly perpetuate injustice.

"*Name,*" Sina urged.

"I'm . . ." *Caiden is dead, weak. Couldn't save anyone he loved.* "Winn."

She input more data into the display and showed him for confirmation. "Passager, tell me where your ship is docked and we will gather its specifics for the—"

"No scan," Laythan cut in. "A name is fine for registration now. Give it a name, Winn."

Only one name sprung to mind, inexplicably, the same syllables stacking together every time he thought of the ship, a name like the shape of her but in language: "*Azura*."

"Good. You are registered as a free passager, under the aegis of the Cartographers. You may provide more details at your leisure."

Caiden nodded, gaze stuck on the blank white counter, as he wished some new feeling would emerge. He was still nothing, from nowhere, and was one passager among millions.

En came up beside him, her blue curls tumbling over the counter. "Brave thing. We'll help you get on your feet. The *Azura* needs repairs and we need to buy a new ship for ourselves—might as well take yours to get to Emporia, where we can achieve both. Laythan can't argue against keeping you for at least that long."

Laythan grunted and stepped up to the counter. "What's the report from passagers returning from the previously restricted universe, CWN82?"

Sina's face sobered. Speckles bubbled at the edges of her cheeks. "That information is still being—"

"Please?" En leaned in, stretching on tiptoes. "I'll bet my heart that the gloss operation is driven by Dynast buyers. The Cartographers are letting passagers rough up CWN82 now to shake the blame loose, aren't they? What about the Casthen armada that flew in during the gloss raid?"

Sina sighed. "The Casthen's Prime, Çydanza, claims her ships stumbled on the planet at the same time as the passagers."

Çydanza. "She's lying," Caiden blurted. "They were there getting their gloss back, right? They started all this!"

The Cartographer cocked her head. "Where did you come from, Passager?"

Caiden gripped the counter's edge and unleashed the truth like a gale: "I'm from a planet in CWN82. The Casthen enslaved my people then dumped us as food for the nophek."

As brave as the admission felt, the reality of it all summed up sent a sour shock through his body.

Sina blinked her luminous eyes, and the spots on her cheeks slimmed to discerning pearly wrinkles.

Caiden wrestled with everything he'd learned. If the Dynast and Cartographers were rivals, and the Casthen slavers had been cultivating gloss for the Dynast, then the Cartographers should want to expose the Casthen as much as he did.

"You *buy* knowledge, right? I know everything. I saw them. I-is...is—" The rage sat brittle and dry in his throat, threatening to crack him again.

En patted his back, and he wasn't sure if he felt comforted or humiliated. Maybe both at once. In a tightly measured voice, En said, "Memories of Casthen involvement would incriminate Çydanza and her Casthen, and get every passager up in arms attacking their infrastructure, investigating every operation, station, and planet the Casthen have from here to Unity. Perhaps even exposing their Dynast buyers."

A slow green flush of recognition dawned across Sina's shoulders, while a dead pause followed from everyone else.

Panca shot to her feet off the bench. "Don't let him do it." Her aspirated voice was filed raw. Her white-ringed eyes flicked between Laythan and En.

Do what? Chills wormed down Caiden's spine.

Laythan said, "It's up to him."

"What's up to me?" Caiden asked, but was ignored. "Panca?"

She caved, her shoulders tense. "Laythan...side effects're unique to each brain. And he's a child. I was...It's not a decision he can make. The cost..." Her hoarse voice thinned and strained. Laythan drifted one step toward her, the very vision of a concerned but ill-equipped father.

Taitn straightened, just understanding. "You mean—"

"Don't talk like I'm not here!" Caiden said, and matched Laythan's intense gaze. "What do you all mean?"

The captain said, "You're the only survivor who's witnessed everything. There's a procedure, an uncommon one—"

"*Laythan!*" Panca shouted.

He raised his hand. "A tool that stimulates emotional memory. It monitors your—well, it lets us see and record your memories as they play out in your brain."

"It's not a nice tool," Panca hissed. "Trauma's not meant to repeat. It'll send you *back* there."

Back to the beasts. Leta whimpering his name. The heat of the monsters' breath and the stench of their blood-dripping manes. The crunching, tearing. His mother's clawing hands shoving him to safety with her final strength. And the last glimpse of his father's face. Eyes bloodshot. Mouth wide. *Run.*

Caiden's vision throbbed, pressure building. He crossed his arms and squeezed. *I ran like a coward. I survived and now I have to pay that back. One good thing, one purpose.*

Panca drifted over, took Caiden's upper arm, and forced him to sit next to her on a bench by the wall. Her velvety face hardened in an earnest expression. The luminosity of the white room seemed to pool in the jewel-like core in her forehead, setting it aglow. Her eyes were bright rings in black pools, a gaze that peeled back the layers of him.

"You're a small, wronged part of something large and twisted." Her airy voice pillowed around the edges of his misery. "Fear, resentment, hatred—those're your enemy. Not an organization. Untangle your feelings before you turn those feelings on others."

Taitn padded over and sat on the other side of him. He placed a gentle hand on the nape of Caiden's neck, over the slave brand. "Think about this. Don't rush all your decisions."

The velvet fog cleared to sharp edges. "If *I* don't do something, no one else will."

A jagged memory.

They hit me, Leta had told him once, *where the bruises don't show, so no one sees. People don't do anything if they don't know.*

Caiden met Panca's gaze.

Her face scrunched around sad eyes. "Be sure you're ready."

"It doesn't matter." Caiden inhaled, chest expanding. His trauma was all he had left, and it was worth something. "I want everyone to know."

CHAPTER 11

MEMORY JOG

We must contract payment first, for memory jog," Sina said as she curved around the Cartographers' counter.

"What sort of payment?" Caiden asked.

"Firsthand proof of the Casthen's guilt is worth a great deal. But you lack so much, most of what Cartographers could offer will have no immediate value to you." Purple spots clouded her nose as she hesitated. "Your ship won't help you if you cannot pilot it or navigate, and are too young for combat. You know nothing about stellar drives, machine spirits, neural interfaces, or xenobiology, and your body has not developed to survive in a fraction of worlds passagers frequent."

Caiden shrank as Sina pounded in his worthlessness.

She concluded, "For someone so young, we could offer acceleration."

Taitn inhaled sharply, then opened his mouth to speak, but En laid a hand on his tense shoulder. Taitn flinched violently, throwing her off. She said, "Let him hear it first."

Caiden raised an eyebrow.

Taitn exhaled the words. "Instantaneous accelerated aging takes years off your life span."

En *tsked* and added, "But spends those years growing your body, conditioning your mind with knowledge and skills that would've taken many more years to cultivate. Extremely expensive and rare."

"I would be older?" A delicate awe bubbled up.

Sina nodded. "We have the proper facilities in Emporia, in Unity. I can offer six years of accelerated age in exchange for the recorded jog of your memories."

"Six…" Caiden tried to imagine a twenty-year-old self. "I'll grow height and muscle?"

"The body is weakened initially," Taitn said, "stretched to a future state."

En sniped in, "But you can choose abilities and knowledge. It would be a chance to make up for being isolated so long, learning so little."

Caiden scratched the smooth bench with a fingernail as he imagined all the holes in him filled instantly, reversing what the Casthen slavers had made him. They had called him *perfect*, once, and branded him with belonging and value. Six years of acceleration was his chance to become everything those lies had promised. The memory jog would expose their brutality, and the acceleration could make him strong enough to hunt the slavers himself—starting with their leader, Çydanza—and not rely solely on his memories galvanizing others.

Taitn cleared his throat. "Memory jog first." His eyes crinkled, summoning the same brave smile that Caiden had used when telling Leta everything would be all right. "Who or what you want to become afterward can wait until you've put your past behind you."

"Passager Winn," Sina called. "If the payment is sufficient and you are ready, please have your medic inspect you. Cartographers will not be held responsible for calculable side effects of memory jog or your physical and psychological stability during procedures."

Caiden looked to Ksiñe, sitting on a farther bench. Dark, ragged bands swathed his upper face.

"Most xenids experience no repercussion to memory jog," Ksiñe said, shrugging. He pinned Caiden with a feral gaze as he rose from the bench and spread his gloved fingers, holding tensile bands of dimpled air between them. Caiden flinched back as Ksiñe began an unceremonious and handsy inspection, running the dimpled matrix across Caiden's body. His soft Andalvian skin and features were at odds with his stiff posture. His whip-kin pet scurried up and down him, stretching to sniff Caiden.

Satisfied, Ksiñe pulled away and said, "He is enough cur, will be fine."

"Cur?" Caiden twitched as Ksiñe stalked away.

"This way, Passager." Sina led Caiden through the Cartographers' zone to a small room buried among a warren of halls and pods.

The space was empty white, housing a chamber in the middle, one and a half meters square. The walls and ceiling of both the chamber and surrounding room were translucent glass so thick it became opaque pearl. Bubbles dotted the inside walls like watching eyes.

"Full-access biodata chamber," Sina explained. "It has many functions. Please, undress."

Caiden peeled off his slave clothes to his undergarments, shrank in embarrassment, and stood patiently while Sina stuck tiny cubes to his body. The objects flattened, spidery and milky under his skin. The backs were sheeny nodes the size of small rivets.

"Stand in the middle. Close your eyes, think about home and what happened. When you are ready."

"I'm ready." Saying it aloud made it feel more true. This was something only he could do: travel back into misery and lies, to make them real to others.

Caiden stepped onto the frigid, copper-colored gills of the chamber's floor. The entryway closed behind him in a series of square folding rods, completely seamless when sealed.

A silent pressure filled Caiden's head. His feet rose off the ground until he floated in place, and the air *filled*, like heat waves, buzzy against his skin.

The lights cut out. Caiden closed his eyes and focused.

Home. It's not home anymore. He pictured the false gray sky. The aerators spewing smoke lies and blotting out what must have been a view of sun and stars. He thought of his home unit, his simple bed pad and red coverlet, the steel kitchen, the bath after a day of work, the tools in the shop lined up on rotary cylinders. His parents, whose care hadn't been a lie even if everything else about his origin and upbringing was. He heard their laughter. He imagined the buildings and pasture blocks and roads arranged like parts of a machine. The air hot and muggy, the grass swaying green, and the gentle rips and grunts of grazing bovines reached his ears.

Beneath the oak tree, he and Leta lay down to gaze up at the sky.

She asked, *Where's the wind come from?*

He replied, *It just makes a big circuit.*

So it's the same wind every time?

Probably filtered, yeah.

Does the wind get tired, always being the same?

He didn't have an answer.

Leta said, *Maybe there's a wind that doesn't touch the same spot over again. A wind that just keeps going.*

The livestock died, and it wasn't a quick extinction. Pustules and abscesses developed on their lumbering bodies, sapping their strength until they dropped dead, infecting others.

Carcasses flattened the grass. Caiden jerked and covered his nose, still aware that his actual body floated in the biodata chamber. When he tried to open his eyes—they already were. His memories were all around him, inescapable. A nightmare from which he couldn't wake.

The sky parted like jaws. An orange throat. The black tongue of the transport box descended, surrounded by searing light. Shadow and fear blackened the crowd.

He tried to think of something else, to rewind to gentle grass and gray sky, and Leta's voice, but the scene wouldn't stop. One memory ricocheted to the next. The overseers emerged in their armor, their scratched blue faces and muffled, amplified voices. Caiden scrunched in the darkness of the transport, jabbed by elbows and knees, whipped by screams. He hugged his sibling while his mother whispered maniacally, "Soon, soon, soon…" Soon the rumbling would stop, the swelter would cool, and sweet air would waft away the feces and fear. They'd be greeted with a new world of vibrant green and a pure vapor sky.

Leta's pleading eyes looked up at him, clinging to the heroic promise that he'd come back for her. "Stay here, really quiet. It'll be calmer here."

Caiden stumbled onto sand. His heart pounded faster than the rhythm of the stampede. Madness propelled them, and terror stopped them short as the nophek beasts tore limb from body.

He spasmed, images jerking past, surrounding him: screaming faces, shredded bodies, red sand. Time rushed by in every direction as he ran. Vertigo tipped the landscape and he was lying on his side, squeezed beneath the overhang, staring at dripping jaws. Pungent metallic blood stung his head and seeped into his skin, never to be removed.

The rest came in a rush. Plodding across dunes. The ship, a pillar of safety. A battle in the sky. The overseers coming.

The lights in the chamber ceiling flashed on, and Caiden's vision burned white. He fell to the copper floor and stumbled to keep upright, hands slapping a wall, stomach threatening to heave. Sina clutched Caiden's arms and helped him up as the walls spun, all looking alike and everything too bright. Too white and pure and there should be blood everywhere.

"Sit." She lowered him onto a white bench.

Covered in sweat, Caiden leaned back and shut his eyes. His shivers and heartbeat raced out of sync, and he sat breathless, throttled, wrung out.

"Take your time." Sina pressed a cloth into his limp hands.

He squeezed it. Soft.

"Your crew is waiting for you when you are ready. It will take the Cartographers a short time to parse your recording into coherent playback, then broadcast in our districts for passagers to discuss."

Her footsteps drifted away.

The staccato *clink* of the folding outer door poked Caiden's ears. He opened his eyes and wrung the towel in his hands. The fuzzy yet slick greenish fabric left his skin energized where he slid it over his forearm, the sweat wicking away until his skin looked smooth and matte as it had after the scour. Cool. Astringent. Mint crushed in the fields. He grappled for that memory but it seemed squeezed from him, far off.

When the room stopped whirling, Caiden wobbled to his feet. New clothes were stacked beside him, softer and thicker than his old ones, without the rips and scorches from his old life. The dark trousers and long-sleeved shirt were loose when he pulled them on but shrank close to his body as he stretched.

Memories and slave clothes, shed like old skin.

The door opened for him, and En stood outside: light-gray eyes and smile the same, but black-skinned and long hair high in a tie. He held the morphcoat, which had changed to tiny scales, and whisked it around Caiden's shoulders. "I shooed Taitn away, he was a ball of anxiety. Not what anyone needs. You hold up?"

Caiden nodded but wasn't sure. His body tingled, dead-weight heavy, and something splintered at En's care, as if the reality of what he'd gone through was more apparent once recognized from the outside.

"Let's get food."

"Starving," Caiden croaked.

Narrow hallways returned them to a large common area in the Cartographers' zone. Circular counters formed islands among the crowd. Spherical maps of light hovered over these and morphed at the touch of well-dressed Cartographer attendants. Recognizing no languages, Caiden absorbed a wash of weird sounds across frequencies. All the people and creatures— what En had called xenids—moved stiffly around one another, navigating invisible borders, the way the bovines had moved around herders, reacting to every motion with a shift of their own. Eyes flicking, heads swiveling. The tension must have been because of the gloss from the raid: some people had it, everyone wanted it.

A backlit bar stretched against one wall, staffed by one of the muscular xenids called a chketin. Dim lighting hid most of their two-meter-tall, purple-gray body, their neck tapering up to a thick, round head. Muscular bundles defined all of the chketin's form, punctuated by crisp gold eyes and slit pupils that flicked toward Caiden instantly.

En steered Caiden onto a raised seat at the bar between Taitn and Laythan. The two men faced away from each other, with a generous gap between. Ksiñe sat outside Laythan, and En considered the arrangement a moment before choosing the seat next to the scientist.

Caiden was too fatigued to unravel family dynamics.

"You all right?" Taitn asked. "You did a good thing. Soon enough everyone will know what the 'overseers' are responsible for."

Caiden's head swam with daze, but he nodded, grateful.

Laythan slicked a hand through the wild waves of his marbled hair. Guilt or worry dug furrows in his brow as he preoccupied himself with a smoking golden drink. Ksiñe fussed with everyone's food, pushing ingredients to the side of plates or dabbing on seasonings and supplements from a little array of vials.

"Eat something." Taitn slid a dish in front of Caiden. The meal was a dense cylinder with a thin, velvety skin.

Caiden bit into it, savoring the rush of flavor as something juicy melted and another part crunched. His bite revealed at least a dozen different layers.

En laughed. "It's a ramia."

Crisp, salty flakes tore away, letting a layer of spicy orange sauce drip out. Long strips of vibrant meat lay inside and looked raw but melted on his tongue as no meat did. He wolfed it down and picked at the crumbs. "Can I have another one?"

"As many as you like," En said. "The ones Ksiñe makes are even better; I'll buy ingredients in Emporia so you can try his."

Ksiñe said nothing, but self-conscious red shivered up his neck.

"Emporia?" Caiden asked.

"A passager hub in Unity," En said, "right across the universe border. It's sort of like a Cartographer Den but much, much bigger, and all the factions are there. We'll sell the gloss, buy a new vessel, help you through your acceleration—"

Laythan interjected, "Then figure out what to do about the *Azura* after it's repaired."

Caiden bristled. "It's mine."

"You won't be able to pilot a sophisticated vessel until after your acceleration and some training. And if the Dynast finds out your ship contains unprecedented Graven technology, it and you will become targets." Laythan finally looked at him, expression softening. "You have an altruistic heart, and that'll get you nothing but trouble. I picked up four pieces of trouble, if you haven't noticed."

"Hey!" En exaggerated a scowl.

Laythan chuckled. "We need a new vessel in Emporia, and since your acceleration credits need to be redeemed there anyway we might as well—"

Ksiñe stiffened and cut in, "You said—"

"*We might as well go all together,*" Laythan finished with force.

"And I won't let Winn accelerate alone," Taitn muttered.

"And I," Ksiñe enunciated carefully, "told you we need to be done with the whelp." He continued in a different language, one that felt liquid and layered, the syllables crashing into rapids. Caiden's only hint at the emotion of the argument was Laythan's boisterous volume, Ksiñe's reddening skin, and the little whipkin's agitated pacing in his lap.

Caiden tried to ignore them, diving into another ramia on his plate.

The Andalvian finally shoved off his seat and stalked away. The whipkin's cries muffled as she burrowed into his clothes.

"Go after him?" Taitn suggested, swirling his drink. "He could cause more trouble than En. On top of everything, we don't need a whole Den murdered in a fit of pique."

"No," Laythan said. "He'll sulk back to the ship and Panca will take care of him."

They ate and drank in silence for a while. Caiden unraveled the tension and concluded the obvious: *he* was the wrench in this machine. He'd strummed all the latent tension built up between the crew. He didn't belong.

Caiden munched on the second ramia and got halfway through before Taitn's hand crept to the back of his neck and squeezed.

"What are—" Caiden cut off as a group of Casthen sauntered up to the bar beside him.

Half of them took a seat while the other half clumped nearby. They wore the dark metallic plates, mismatched weapons, and featureless blue masks that were lodged forever in Caiden's memory.

He quivered, jerking against Taitn's restraining hand.

"You've done enough," the pilot whispered. He punched a fist lightly into Caiden's chest. "Keep it in here. Breathe."

Caiden inhaled vigorously and held it.

En stared into his drink, eyes wide. He gripped the glass so hard it squeaked and his knuckles cracked.

Taitn glared at En and tapped the bar. "Keep it here."

A tall Casthen in the center of their circle was the leader, judging from the others' subservient and attentive body language. The man gestured to the chketin tending the bar, then he spun, leaned against the counter, and yanked his blue faceplate off. This Casthen had a human face, but his skin was too pale and fine, stretched over his sculpted bone structure. His eyes were bloodshot purple, and his irises were concealed in a blur of tiny, shifting hexagons.

Three others in the Casthen group removed their masks too. Their faces were as varied as their physiques, blending different features of the xenids Caiden had seen so far. Half this, half that.

"Keep it caged in the brig," Purple Eyes said to his crew. "Hopefully Çy's right about it. The second fleet bailed, got what they could."

Caged? Caiden envisioned a smaller version of the packed transport cube, with someone crammed inside. He twisted to face the slavers.

En reached over and pulled him straight, then tapped one ear with a finger. "*These* are your best weapons. Sit and listen. Your memory jog will do the most damage to them once it's released."

Caiden devoured the rest of his food and pushed the crumbs around. The Casthen group bobbed in his peripheral vision.

"Does it need eat?" said one who looked at least half saavee, the gnarled skin and diamond-shaped pupils giving them away.

"Sure whines like it." Purple Eyes surveyed the room. His gaze lingered over Caiden for a beat.

Caiden met the slaver's gaze and stared after it left.

One of the masked Casthen grunted, sliding a drink off the bar. "Is it worth anything, after? Maybe we keep it for ourselves, split it up." They ripped their faceplate off to reveal fine-furred wrinkles of skin. Their fleshy maw opened and consumed the whole drink in one pour.

"No fun and not worth nothin' young," the half saavee growled.

Caiden squirmed on his seat, imagining what they might be talking about.

I'm done running. I'll tell Sina they have someone caged. He shot from his seat. Within three steps, an armored hand yanked his wrist.

One of the other Casthen gripped him, but it was the leader's eyes he met.

Taitn leapt up, weapon drawn and pointed at the group. En swiveled and looked ready to lunge, hand on a knife at his hip and a smaller weapon raised. Laythan rose somberly, seat creaking. He stepped closer while the whole room noticed and shifted with him in a ripple, some brandishing weapons but unsure which direction to face.

"What's your business?" Laythan asked calmly.

Purple Eyes smiled eerily, keeping his gaze on Caiden. "Looks like he has something to add to our conversation. Also looks familiar, doesn't he, pack?"

The Casthen group shuffled with nods and grunts.

Caiden's captor twisted his arm, forcing him to bend forward. He bit back a pained curse and snarled, "Let me go!"

Purple Eyes cocked his head, surveying the back of Caiden's neck.

Where the slave brand was. The disguising material had wiped off.

The Casthen leader straightened and beamed. "Hi, Freckles."

CHAPTER 12

PROPERTY

The Casthen group's leader said, "Seems you're the property we've been looking for."

Caiden twisted free of his captor. "I'm not Casthen property."

"Step back," Laythan ordered.

Caiden couldn't move. His morphcoat bristled into tiny spines. He rocked on his heels, brimming with pressure.

En said, "He's a registered passager."

"That brand says otherwise." A wavy smile pasted across Purple Eyes's face. "Property can't be registered."

"He is," Laythan said, "so let's—"

"So he can handle this himself." Purple Eyes aimed the smile at Laythan before turning back to Caiden. "My name is Threi. And I think I know what you are, Freckles." He drew a silvery weapon of bundled rods from his thigh and offered it to Caiden. "You look like you want to hurt me."

"He's cur like us," the half saavee in the crew said.

"I'm not like you." Caiden snatched the weapon by its spongy grip. It resembled a smaller version of the weapons the slavers had dropped when they found Caiden in the ship. When they had called in, *"Not worth the gloss 'less he's Graven."*

Worthless. Property.

He pointed the weapon at Threi's face.

"Leave it be," Taitn whispered. "You've done enough."

En's grip creaked on his knife's hilt. "Violence fixes many things, but it can't change what's already happened."

The tiny hexagons covering Threi's corneas resolved into ice-blue irises. "Sometimes it's all about just feeling *better*. Go ahead, fire. Fast as you can."

Caiden's grip quaked. En had been right. He *did* need to hit something. Everything in him screamed to bash, to maim—to not be a coward this time. Everything he had gone through was fresh from the memory jog. The sky opening. The transport. The stench. Bodies opened with screams. And the voice: *Sand worm, wriggle out.*

Caiden squeezed. The weapon vibrated and fired a thin, blinding beam. It connected with Threi's face and burst into ripples of green-black smoke. An explosive pressure thrust Caiden back.

When the shivering iridescence of an energy shield settled, Threi's perfect face was still smiling.

"What." Caiden froze.

"*You!*" Thudding footsteps marked the huge chketin Cartographer lumbering around the bar. They grabbed Caiden's wrist with the weapon and hauled upward, lifting Caiden to his tiptoes. "Fights prohibited in this district. Take it to the ring."

Cartographer Sina called from across the room as she marched over, "A Casthen Enforcer should know better."

Threi waved his hands. "Guilty is the one who fired. Guess we'll have to have a talk about him."

Caiden had taken Threi's bait. The adrenaline washed out and left him cold. He wriggled in the chketin's grip, but five rough fingers each as thick as his wrist held him tight.

Sina took the situation in carefully, while patterns strobed across her skin. "Apprehend the Enforcer too."

The chketin obliged, grasping the man's upper arm, holding Caiden and Threi like caught rabbits. Threi shot Sina a perplexed look.

At that moment, a display in the bar's back wall switched footage to green pastures, bovine, gray skies: Caiden's memory jog footage. The imagery he'd experienced in the chamber had been reproduced in chronological snippets, both moving and static images. Some features blurry, others crisp.

Caiden's free hand curled around the back of his neck, body caving in. The chketin held him, he couldn't flee the sight, but some part of his mind detached anyway.

Murmurs carried through the crowded bar. More wall displays illuminated with his memory jog footage: the sky opening up orange, the transport descending on the Flat Docks. Then Casthen overseers ushering the population in.

Threi's smile withered as he stared, and his crew bristled as they watched their faction represented on the screens. The crowd reoriented at them, mutters rising as the gathered xenids realized that what they were watching had a Casthen source.

Fresh energy filled Caiden, and he blurted, "Now everyone will see what you did with your *property*."

Threi's head swiveled to look at him. Snarl lines gathered on the bridge of his nose.

"Passagers." Sina addressed the tense crowd. "We have acquired memory jog footage that will enlighten the situation in CWN82. The broadcast of it, as well as proof of authenticity, will be available here and through your personal databases." She turned to the chketin Cartographer who held Caiden and Threi in both meaty fists. "Take them."

"Sina," Laythan cut in, deploying his hard, fatherly tone. "The boy's with us."

"I am sorry, Captain. Even if we ignore a fired weapon on neutral ground, the fact of his Casthen brand must be addressed."

Terror skated through Caiden. He hadn't survived then doubled his trauma in the memory jog chamber just to be sent *right back to the Casthen*. His wrist bones creaked as he twisted in the chketin's grip.

En straightened, forming a strong line with Laythan and Taitn. "We'll come with him."

Sina frowned, spots flocking on her cheekbones. "If he is not property, then you are not his guardians, and he is a passager who can handle his own business. If he is one of the Casthen by—"

"*I'm not*," Caiden said, the pressure inside him corkscrewing the words into a squeak. "You saw..." He cut that thought right off. The memory jog's source was anonymous, unless he blurted it out. On the walls, the footage continued, showing the nophek and the slaughter, and if he had to watch it all again so soon he would shatter. He was already hot with sweat. "Let's get this over with."

"Winn," En warned.

Caiden shook his head. Dizzy darkness swarmed his skull in the motion. He had to get away from the screens. The memories playing on them threatened to spill out and engulf the room, become real again all around him.

Sina gestured, and the chketin hauled Caiden and Threi toward the Cartographers' main hall. They left the messy crowd, heading back through white warrens, into a naked room with only a circular white table in the middle. The chketin all but threw Threi and Caiden inside. "Sit, Passagers." Snarling inhales accented the chketin's speech. They had a face like a kicked bag of rocks, muscle bands bulging around eyes that were solid balls of black suspending orange pupils. The chketin was all brawn and rough skin, and Caiden shuddered at the size of their hand, big enough to engulf his skull and squeeze it like a fruit. He took an obedient seat. Threi slid into one chair and propped his feet on another.

The Cartographer grunted and took up station beside the door, crossing arms that were each two or three times as thick as Caiden's leg.

No escape.

Caiden glared sideways at Threi, his temper hot and scratchy. Sensing his mood, the morphcoat fused into padded scale armor.

Threi's own armor scraped and clinked as he propped an elbow on the table. He hard-blinked one eye and then the other, forcing out teardrops of the purple tech, which he plucked off and shoved in a pocket. "Let me guess, those captured memories were yours, Freckles? Figures you'd survive—skilled little Casthen pup."

Skilled. The affirmation that Caiden's heart quested for was rancid coming from Threi.

"I'm not one of you," he said.

"Again, your brand says otherwise."

Caiden's temper snapped, he shot to his feet, and the chketin boomed, "No fights! You wait for Sina."

Threi turned his ice-blue gaze to Caiden. His gloved fingers crawled through snarls of short, dark hair. "So, you're a heroic and temperamental passager now. I've always found it best to confront what you hate head-on, work out all those weak little bits of you. You know...if you joined the Casthen you'd have the best chance to do just that." Threi offered a gloved hand.

Caiden flinched as if a snake reared to strike him.

"I promise you'll get more opportunities to shoot me. Besides, don't you want to know where you're from?"

The poison words seeped to his marrow. Caiden paced the length of the room, escaping the pressure in his body. "I'm free, and I have nothing to do with slavers like you. Right now, every passager is watching what you Casthen did. They'll expose you. And I survived for vengeance, to free anyone else in Casthen claws."

He was a firebrand adrift from a burned-out blaze, and he would catch all of the Casthen aflame.

Threi laughed so heartily his forehead buckled into his supporting hand, fingers mashing through his wavy hair. "You *are* a darling pup. Çydanza would adore you."

Caiden stiffened.

Threi cocked his head up, chin resting in a palm that squished the edge of his smile. With his free hand he fished among his armor for something, then cast it across the tabletop toward Caiden.

He caught it: a marble-sized glass cube. When he picked it up, it unfurled in his palm and projected a small field of air dimples in a grid, like the devices Ksiñe used.

"That projects a holosplay for reading, and stores the Cartographers' public database. You can enter verbal queries. Have a learn later and see just how integral the Casthen are to this multiverse. One person, as young as you, can do nothing from the outside. And your memories are a pebble drop that *will* ripple, but it's rippling into a sea."

Caiden closed his palm and the holosplay field dissolved, the device re-condensed into a cube. He squeezed until its corners cut his skin. The multiverse already appeared built of a web of relationships he had no idea how to navigate yet.

"Your rage needs focus," Threi said, "and running amok as a passager flailing for justice won't focus you. If you want to face up to the Casthen, then come with me right into the belly of the beast and do it. Accept where you belong."

As guilty as Caiden felt about his temper, anger *was* the only way he could move forward and escape grief nipping at his heels. The brighter he burned, the less of sorrow he could see.

Caiden met Threi's gaze. "I'm never joining your kind."

The Casthen shrugged and lounged back in his seat.

The door folded open and Sina entered, her complexion all black and pink patterns. "The Cartographers have decided that if the young passager was free enough to register without opposition present, he does not qualify as property, any brands, marks, or genetics notwithstanding. We Cartographers cannot enforce his free status among others, but we can respect it within our own policies and domains."

The Andalvian's face speckled periwinkle, and Caiden gushed relief.

"That's a pity," Threi said, rising. "Because I know something about him you don't, Cartographer."

She cocked her head.

Caiden burst out, "He doesn't know anything about me."

Threi closed his eyes and took a deep breath, armor rasping as his chest expanded. When he opened his ice-pale eyes again, they brimmed with new intent and intensity. "I'd advise putting the Den on lockdown for a while."

Agitated billows strobed the skin of Sina's wrists and fingers. Her expression grew wistful. "Enforcer?"

Frustration creased Threi's flawless face. What was he expecting, she'd just say yes? He ambled over to the Andalvian until he stood less than half a meter away, peering down. "The passagers should be sent to their ships to avoid a riot against the Casthen until they can digest the memory jog footage and reach logical conclusions." The man's voice took on a melody. The same lazy enunciation, but wielded with purpose, like a carver's blade.

"Yes," the chketin boomed from across the room. They were already pulling up a holosplay.

Sina twisted to her companion, nonplussed.

"Cartographer," Threi said, pulling her gaze back to him. He seemed to almost curl over her slight frame as he spoke. "You can do that for me, can't you? And I should be returning to my ship as well. A little friendly fire isn't my fault."

Caiden was more confused than the two of them. "It *was* his fault! He should be punished!"

Pink glitters dusted around Sina's eyes as she blinked, tension melting from her face. "To avoid a riot, yes. A lockdown, then. Do as you will, Enforcer."

"Why does he get to go free!" Caiden shot from his seat. How was Sina falling for this shit?

Threi cast a dazzling smile Caiden's way, then rolled his head back to Sina. "I love fiery spirits like his, they are *ripe* for tempering. I think he really should be coming with me. The Cartographers are done with him anyway, yes?"

Sina hesitated, brows knit together under the edge of her crown.

A tendon jumped in Threi's jaw. He laid a hand on Sina's shoulder. "Do it for me?"

She actually *smiled*. "Yes, of course…"

"*Cartographer.*" Caiden swallowed a lump and tried to organize firmer words, trying to match the intent and intensity Threi had used to throw orders around. "You *just* said I'm not property. You said I'm a passager who can handle his own business. I'm leaving."

Caiden strode for the door but the chketin shuffled, and Sina raised a hand to stop them. Stripes crinkled across the middle of her face as she hesitated, mouth open to speak but silent.

Threi made a growl, and strode for the door, saying, "The boy should *at least* be locked up here for his own safety. His memories are out there flooding every passager's public feed—even if they don't know it's him, he's better off here during the lockdown. *Keep* him here. After all," Threi drawled, voice deep and honeyed as he glared at the chketin, "it's a Cartographer's duty to see that all passagers are well and accounted for."

"Yes," the chketin boomed again, staring down with…admiration?

Whatever was happening, Caiden caught the implication: Threi meant to store him in this room for later, like a predator would cache prey.

"Sina—" he started.

"He *is* safer here, for now," she said, as if Caiden weren't standing there shaking. Sina turned to the chketin. "Seal the room. I'll announce the lockdown and send passagers to their ships." She strode out.

The annoyance finally smoothed out of Threi's face. He retrieved his silvery weapon from the chketin and broke it open, poking at tiny rods inside. "You really are safer here," he said to Caiden.

"What did you...do to her?"

"You really should ask that database what exactly you're so bent on destroying. You might learn a little something about yourself in the meantime. Here." Threi smacked the weapon back together and slapped it on the table. "Keep the glave as a souvenir. I do admire your bravery—or maybe it's ignorance—for firing on a Casthen Enforcer."

Threi chuckled and strolled out, giving a vague salute to the chketin. Caiden stared daggers at the man's armored back as he melted into the shadow outside.

The chketin Cartographer exited and the door closed completely behind. Caiden raced for it but hit smooth wall, without any seam, panel, or button.

Crimes, what just happened? It would have made more sense had Threi intimidated them or convinced them with stronger logic. No one was charming enough to just change others' minds on a whim.

Caiden shoved the weapon—a glave, Threi had called it—into his belts, sat, and fished the database cube from a pocket. In his palm it unfolded and projected the holosplay above. He needed to know more. Six years of accelerated age would be enough to sharpen his body and mind into someone independent enough to take down such a large force, but until then he couldn't fight any of this head-on. Letting his anger burst out was getting him nowhere but trouble. He apparently couldn't even interpret conversational nuance correctly in this convoluted multiverse.

"What are the Casthen?"

Opaque words of light particles congealed, strung like handwriting on the holosplay's dimpled air grid: *A free-course faction composed primarily of hybrids and genetic mosaics from the Paraborn interbreeding project for private military operations. The Casthen deal in registered inter-rind trade of rare materials and xenids under free-course license. The xenids utilized in the Paraborn initiative were sourced by the Casthen. The faction's Prime is Çydanza.*

The words needled him. "What do you mean 'xenids utilized'?"

The answer resolved: *Paragon specimens were acquired or purchased for breeding.*

Caiden stared at the word "purchased."

He was a "cur" like them, one of Threi's crew had said...

"What's a cur?"

A slang term for a xenid crossed of different breeds or types. Resistant to a variety of foreign conditions and universal parameters.

Had the Casthen tried to create the perfect workers? Endless batches of them grown like the bovine were? Caiden got up and continued pacing, expelling motion as his thoughts spiraled downward.

"What is my...makeup?"

He had never thought about his origin—he just *was*. His parents had been assigned to him when he was four years old, and they bonded so swiftly he never considered they shared no relation. Caiden would smash his finger in a hatch and his father would joke until the tears turned to laughter, and for Caiden that was enough to mean family. He would smile as he balanced atop the fences to help his mother count the herd, and he didn't question that they belonged together.

Leta was cursed to see the truth but Caiden never stopped to listen, just asked all the wrong questions. "You're always working," she had said. "But I see and listen. Things are strange...like we don't belong here."

Words formed on the holosplay: *USER PASSAGER WINN 8-116-244.* A multi-pointed diagram appeared, strung with percentage weightings, webs of symbols, and red glyphs in a language he didn't recognize. Classified? Unknown? En had mentioned most of him was unanalyzable.

"What does the Casthen Prime, Çydanza, look like?"

Undefined.

"Where is the Casthen headquarters?"

The location of the Casthen Harvest is unknown.

Harvest...a fitting name.

"Who is Threi?"

Query too vague.

"Why did Sina believe his stupid suggestions?"

Invalid query.

Caiden huffed and paced the room.

"What is the Dynast?"

Governing faction of Unity, the original universe prior to multiversal furcation, ruled by the Dynast endarchy. The Dynast are seekers of knowledge who claim direct descent from the Graven. Their centralized government is led by an assembly under control of an appointed Prime who can claim a nine-two rank pure thread of Graven descent. The faction's current Prime is Abriss Cetre.

Being flooded by new terms wasn't helping him. He lacked the right *questions*, and could spend ages looping through all the things he didn't know. Meanwhile Threi was up to nothing good while the whole Den went under lockdown.

An acid fear trickled through him. He had to get back to the *Azura*.

He stopped where the door had been, but couldn't even discern an outline. There were no ventilation ducts anywhere, just holes drilled through the vitreous walls. No subfloor. Nothing.

Caiden groaned and leaned his forehead against the wall. He cleared his mind. Listened to silence.

Break stuff.

When he'd been twelve and Leta eight, he laughed when she said, "They really...They want me to fail Appraisal. That's why they leave and I'm alone."

She scowled, cross that he'd laughed at her anguish, but he said with a smirk, "Break stuff."

"Huh?"

"Whenever you're running into trouble, break the machinery. I'm closest to this sector and always get sent out for the small fixes, I'll come help you. And sometimes smashing feels good, you know."

Leta smiled and shyly picked more flowers. She had never been the smashing type.

Caiden rose to his feet in the featureless Cartographer room and examined its seamless white surfaces. In the center of the table lay a strange pit of gel. Caiden poked at the thick, grainy substance. White and red particles fizzed inside. He plowed his finger in circles. Sparkles skittered away like frightened fish.

He raised his arm and gave the thing a solid punch. The surface material shattered, and his fist was engulfed in frigid liquid deeper in. He yelped and pulled back, flapping his wrist.

An alarm whined outside the room.

Caiden scurried to the wall and flattened himself.

Booming footsteps approached.

The door's rods folded open. Alarms blared as the chketin Cartographer lumbered through.

Caiden was quick on his feet from working around large animals and vehicles. As the chketin's brawny leg whooshed past, Caiden slipped out the door in a corkscrew motion and darted as quickly as stealth and darkness would allow. The chketin roared expletives behind him.

Empty hallways, causeways, and rooms split off the main course. Strips of light on the floor were the only illumination, leading around obstacles and marking doorways.

He scanned for features that indicated he was backtracking in the right direction. After several wrong turns into disturbing confines and vast, impossibly textured spaces, a causeway opened to the multi-leveled docking concourse. The backs of ships lined the base level and many tiers above. They looked like giant faces; sharp, gnarled, or stout. Spotlights oozed around each one.

Caiden spotted the *Azura*'s spiked, slanted tail three ships down—and froze.

A group of silhouettes studded in contours of tiny lights ambled down the row of ships.

Caiden dashed behind a series of holosplay panels in the center of the concourse, and snuck through them until he crouched opposite the *Azura*. He slid his fingers around his weapon—Threi's glave—and pulled it from his pocket.

"'Nother one over 'ere," one of the group said to another.

There was no mistaking that stifled voice. Casthen.

CHAPTER 13

GLASLIQ

Caiden counted three sets of light-studded suits in the murk of the berthing concourse. One was the height and shape of a man. Another had a small head and sloped shoulders, and the last svelte shape stood two heads shorter.

Between them was a creature on all fours, less than half a meter tall. It whimpered and ambled in sluggish jerks. One of the Casthen kicked it, sending it rolling to the end of a leash before it was yanked to its feet.

Caiden almost lurched out of cover. Electric adrenaline whipped his muscles, twisted his insides, propelled him to take action. The image of Leta on the end of a leash rampaged through his mind. The Casthen said they had something caged: this was it.

The creature weaved ahead, and the group veered to follow it.

Caiden dug his thumbnail into his skin to curb the boil of rage. His heartbeat ratcheted. They hadn't reached the *Azura*, but were headed straight that way.

The group passed a swath of illumination, and their Casthen armor gleamed. The creature avoided the light, but it had paws, not feet or hands. Caiden's relief that it wasn't a child withered as he glimpsed its side riddled with needles and tubes. Its joints buckled every other step, pitching it into an ugly gait.

Eyes flashing, the creature jerked in the direction of Caiden and the *Azura*. He stiffened, afraid to shrink the last couple inches behind cover.

"Got something," said the Casthen who held the leash.

The creature rooted through the air then lurched against its tether. It let out a piercing yip and stumbled on its side as it tried to pick up speed.

"Should hurry," the stout one said. "Looks like it's gonna die."

"If you keep kicking it." The leash holder walked through a spill of light. *Threi.* His mask was pushed over the top of his head, shoving back the short hair to frame his bored expression.

Caiden's face twisted in a snarl but he stayed frozen, gaze locked on Threi's face before he even noticed the creature.

Though small and sickly, it was unmistakable: a nophek. Even young, it had the same boxy face, flesh-tearing teeth, and wavy mane.

Caiden choked back a cry.

Nophek had killed everyone he knew. Killed and *ate*.

It hobbled on seizing legs and bit blindly to gulp in air. Sick—about to die, they'd said. Caiden's horror sizzled against pity.

The group drew closer, following the sniffing pup. They were five ships away from the *Azura*. Threi appeared weaponless, while the other two held long glaves at the ready. Caiden had only the one glave and the element of surprise, which was about to be blown. He tightened his grip on the weapon, but his feet stuck in place, his arm shook, a sob clogged his throat. *Coward. Shoot them...But what if the crew isn't even in the ship?*

The nophek's luminous eyes danced through the dark. It whined and pulled in Caiden's direction again. Threi jogged with it.

Caiden stifled his panting with his free hand, stuffing terror down. The nophek veered and pawed at the foot of a ship two spots from the *Azura*.

"In here." Threi yanked the pup back. It bucked against the taut leash and whined.

Caiden choked on relief.

Threi's companions flanked the ship. The shortest one attached small objects to the vessel's tall, serrated tail, and stepped back. An electrical popping sound spread through the metal and ruptured seams, collapsing the ship's back doors outward. A lanky figure darted out, hooked instantly by the saavee, who prodded a weapon's muzzle into the figure's jaw. "Give it over, tal."

The xenid—maybe "tal" was its species, if not a slur—was made of a material that constantly moved. They squirmed in the saavee's grip. Limbs folded and unfolded from their body, but their flowery head remained pinned by the long glave.

The nophek yowled, eyes bulging, tongue lolled. It flailed against the leash.

"Give it some lact so it shuts up," Threi said.

The shortest Casthen chucked a vial on the ground. Pearly liquid splattered and the nophek scrambled to it, desperately lapping up the fluid despite glass shards lacerating its tongue.

Caiden struggled to bottle up his tremors and hear through the pulse pounding in his skull. Every nerve crackled. Sweat slicked his grip on the glave.

Threi sauntered to the tal and held out a hand. "It's mine, anyway, you understand. Give it here."

Confident and intent, as before.

But the tal hissed while their body fanned and rippled. The material of their morphing flesh looked like starchy cloth and was all the gray colors of dense smoke.

Threi snarled in frustration and leaned in until his face was inches from the tal's. He spoke in a language that fizzed with sibilance. The tal went slack and passive at once. Their lanky arm peeled from the trunk of their body and deposited an orb of gloss into Threi's palm. He cooed in the same language, pointed into the ship, and backed away smiling.

The tal plodded obediently back inside, their whole body quivering, more submissive than afraid. Like Sina.

The scheme clicked in Caiden's mind: Threi had suggested the Den lockdown so that all the passengers carrying gloss would be sequestered back in their ships. He was using the baby nophek as a detector to sniff out which ships had gloss inside, so he could cruise by and take it back, every piece of it. And the *Azura* was next. Caiden choked back a swear.

The short Casthen opened up a glowing satchel, and Threi dropped the gloss in. It *clinked* against more pieces. They'd been busy.

The little nophek quivered at full alertness and mewed until the satchel was closed. The saavee kicked the creature's belly. It yelped, staggering up to resume its hopeless search.

The glave in Caiden's grip rattled, slick with sweat.

The nophek's bright eyes saccaded. It sniffed.

He didn't have a plan. His heart rampaged, weight tilted to the balls of his feet, ready for something.

The nophek whined and tugged Threi toward the *Azura*. "Another in here."

"Good." The saavee hefted his glave. "Legs tire."

The shorter Casthen started setting charges on the *Azura*'s bay doors, about to break it open.

This is my moment. Caiden rocked on his toes. The held breath throbbed in his chest.

Threi's back turned to him. The nophek levered against the leash.

Caiden sprang from cover and closed the distance, bringing his glave against the back of Threi's head. "Don't move." His brave words mangled. The muzzle twitched in curls of Threi's hair. *Just shoot. Do it. Squeeze.*

An icy realization zagged through him.

The man had an energy shield before. What would shooting him do?

"I think that's mine." Threi turned slowly. The glave's tip slid through his hair, across his temple, and nestled into his forehead. He smiled.

Caiden squeezed the firing mechanism.

Nothing happened.

He squeezed frantically until Threi wrenched the glave from his grasp. "Thanks. It's nice to return something you've borrowed. I was going to let you keep it, though."

Threi twisted open the glave and slotted a thin rod into an inner chamber before snapping it back together. With the eerie smile still fixed on his face, he pointed the weapon at Caiden's head.

Threi shot. A blinding thread-thin beam screamed past Caiden's ear. He jerked aside and the beam connected with something behind. Waves of hot light scorched the area, throwing Caiden to the floor.

The *Azura*'s bay doors unfolded, blades cutting the spotlight.

Sensing the gloss inside, the nophek howled at a terrible pitch.

Panic ravaged Caiden's brain. He scrambled up and ran to the ship, half on all fours. Threi dropped the nophek's leash with a *smack* and the creature bolted after Caiden. Jaws bloody, eyes wild and flashing, claws scraping—and Caiden was back in the desert, running for his life. He hurtled inside, straight to the cockpit, leapt onto the pilot's seat, and slammed his hand against the florescer in the ceiling to signal a new universe to save him.

Light erupted as the universe bubbled outward, throwing him flat on his back. Air squished from his lungs. His insides became snakes. The iridescent sphere expanded to encapsulate the *Azura* in a fresh world. The rind shredded the pursuing nophek into red mist as it roiled past the bay doors.

Caiden's vision blurred with tears and dizziness, sickness tearing his gut, but he was safe. This wasn't the desert...just the emotion of it, ricocheting inside his weary frame.

Muffled sounds screwed into Caiden's awareness.

"You *damn fool*!" Laythan's voice crashed through.

Caiden was dragged up by the scruff of his coat and flung into En's arms. Senses tumbled in his head. En tucked him under one elbow to grab a glave with her free hand.

Ksiñe caught Panca, who collapsed to the ground.

"*Kis, shut the doors!*" Taitn screamed as he launched into the pilot's seat.

The blind, animalistic fear in Caiden still surged, raking up into a throttled sound as he twisted in En's grip to face the door. Threi's figure wavered darkly past the universe rind.

Threi was seeing it. Seeing what the ship could do.

Laythan plowed over to smack the door panel. The plates sealed closed while Taitn reached up to the florescer and collapsed the universe bubble. The rind surged backward, ripping through Caiden's body again. Without its universe active, the *Azura*'s engine sounded agitated as if once-tight materials loosened and clean fuel laced with filth. Discordant vibrations filed against Caiden's skull. He sagged in En's arms.

Taitn jetted the ship away from the concourse. Laythan rushed to the cockpit, bracing behind the pilot's chair and brushing frantically through the map holosplay. "Taitn, get us out of system, *fast*. That Casthen cur will be on our tail in a heartbeat."

The engines roared as Taitn pitched the ship upright and swung into traffic. Walls hemmed them in. Taitn dodged with gentle swerves, fitting into the crowd.

"*Panca*," Ksiñe whispered, cradling the unconscious saisn over one knee. His medical gloves cast a field of dimpled air over his palms as he palpated and glided his fingers across her body.

Laythan charged over and knelt by their side. "What happened?"

Ice knifed through Caiden.

"Stable, she is stable." Ksiñe's posture tensed, quivering with violence. "Told you. I told you he was not worth it." He glared up, red eyeshine leveled balefully on Caiden. His skin was a storm, coal black boiling over his eyes and bleeding down his cheeks.

Caiden choked, "Panca...Oh, crimes, is she—"

"Not a word from you!" Ksiñe flung open a case of medical supplies and fit vials into devices. His whipkin pet burrowed in the case and started to pull out and line up medicaments. Laythan held Panca steady across his lap, a big hand cradling her skull. She was breathing, her chest fluttering in and out. Thank the stars she was breathing.

Caiden wilted to his knees. "What happened," he whispered.

"The rind," En said, holding Caiden steady as the ship weaved through the Den interior. "Seems it's not very compatible with saisn biology."

Laythan shouted, "Don't make light of this, En. We haven't tested the ship's universe, it could have killed Ksiñe or Panca, or damaged your own parts irreparably."

Those black words soaked around Caiden's shame.

"The nophek," he blurted, not an excuse—he had no excuse for recklessness, senselessness, terror—but his mind tried to pick up the jagged shards of it all. The little beast had been trying to find its parents, yearning for its own kind. "Threi was stealing back gloss from the passagers in their ships. He ordered the lockdown, he—"

"I've had enough of your fixation on the Casthen." Laythan swore, "Nine crimes, you haven't listened to a damn thing we've been telling you."

Caving back in on himself, Caiden murmured, "Threi convinced Sina so fast. He just..." *Asked and got everything he wanted.*

Ksiñe muttered a stream of sounds in a foreign language. The whipkin fetched medical items for him as he gave injections, applied spidery nodes to Panca's skin, and stretched webbing over her mouth and nose.

Guilt chewed Caiden as he watched. And that nophek pup—

"*Shit!*" Taitn yelled. The ship braked hard; En and Caiden tumbled across the floor toward the cockpit.

In front of them, a mass of streaking liquid whipped to a stop. A transparent, avian ship. The glass of its wings rippled as it hovered.

"Th-that's the Casthen ship that chased us," Caiden stammered. "On the nophek planet. The Glasliq ship. It's Threi. It has to be." His voice whittled to a squeak.

The Glasliq's nose pilled out in concentric spikes that sharpened and amassed to spear the *Azura*.

"Brace!" Taitn shouted. Laythan and Ksiñe curled around Panca's body. En hooked an arm around Caiden's waist.

The Glasliq speared forward and Taitn yawed at the last minute, spinning through the Glasliq's wing and nearly colliding with fleeing passager ships. Curses poured from the pilot as he nosed the ship down and spun. Slender vessels and blinding streaks slashed the view. The cockpit's displays were alive with angry warnings and a blood-bright mark tracking the Glasliq's pursuit.

Caiden clutched En and a bar in the floor, and squeezed his eyes shut as Taitn raced the *Azura* away. Light seeped through the cockpit windows, the ship swerved around obstacles, filled with echoes, and sang with outlandish power. Caiden's organs bunched against his ribs.

Taitn piloted like a madman but the Glasliq was unreal. It flew straight into obstacles, its liquid wings slicing through harmlessly. At the same time, it gleamed like a blade, the ribby inner skeleton reshaping the ship as needed for speed, agility, or power.

Something slammed the *Azura*'s shields so hard it whiplashed Caiden's body. En caught his neck in a quick hand. He retched, dribbling sick down his front.

"I'm with ya, kid." En's fingers slid over his forehead. His skull juddered against the metal floor.

"You about done yet, Taitn?" Laythan bellowed, planting his boots and clinging to a wall strut while he cradled Panca. "We don't have fuel for this, and there's no time for games!"

"Not doing this for fun, Layth," Taitn growled. Sweat coated his forehead. His arm muscles and tendons corded, fingers clawed in the twitch drive panels. "If I can't lose him inside the Den, we're torched in open space."

The Glasliq veered beside them and matched Taitn's mad speed. Its shoulder reshaped into a bristle of cones ready to skewer. A beat before impact, Taitn winged the *Azura* over top of the Glasliq, upside down. Together they barreled toward the wall of a gigantic freighter.

At the last second, Taitn split downward and Threi up, cutting each other's path.

Taitn flew toward a void, out of the Den's labyrinthine interior.

They were free of the traffic fray: Threi's Glasliq had curbed the *Azura* into empty space with no escape or cover. In the holosplays wrapping Taitn, the Glasliq pursued as a smear of red fury in the map, and Caiden saw no helpful symbols—no rind or egress. Just one lone star in the distance.

Taitn shouted, "I have an idea and none of you are going to like it!"

"When do I ever like your plans?" Laythan snapped.

"Kis…" Taitn's voice broke. "C-can Pan take one more hit? We need the *Azura*'s universe for this…"

The ship pitched hard to one side as the Glasliq skimmed their belly, battering the shielding.

Ksiñe hissed angry words. His gloved hand rested on Panca's forehead over the core there. "Only if absolutely necessary. Harm is neutralized for now."

Curls of brilliant light soaked the cockpit from the approaching star. En's eyes bulged in alarm. "Wait. No. No, no, no, don't do it!"

"It's the only place he can't follow!" Taitn leaned into the twitch drive, fingers curling, powering forward as the Glasliq intercepted. He cut the tip of its wing, glass cracking into sticky liquid that splashed their cockpit windows. A screech of skeleton knifed the side of the *Azura* as Taitn powered ahead.

En cried, "*Taitn, you can't fly into a star!*"

CHAPTER 14

STARHEART

The star drew closer. The very *idea* of flying into it didn't fit in Caiden's mind.

Laythan roared curses and tipped Panca into Ksifie's lap. "I'll do what I can to optimize fuel. Without Panca and proper tests, this might be a death run." He bolted to the engine room, stumbling as Threi's Glasliq rammed the ship again.

Caiden's guilt shoveled deeper. He was a mechanic. He should have been able to help but knew nothing about his own ship.

The star engulfed their entire view. Scarlet eruptions of sticky flame ravaged its surface. The ship was headed straight into that massive, radiant, fiery sea of raw energy. Blooms of heat peeled across the *Azura*'s outer armor fields.

Taitn's hands shook violently in the pads to keep steady at immense speed. Unable to move, he screamed, "Hit the rind! *Someone hit it now!*"

Caiden lurched to the cockpit, vaulting up the back of the seat to slap the florescer.

A fresh universe engulfed them. The radiant bubble expanded until it passed through the ship walls.

The *Azura* sang. Happy in her own world, her metals grew soft and lost their shiver, resonant hollows filled with a silken rumble of speed, and the scalar gravity took on an aqueous thickness that lightened Caiden's body. He melted to the floor, his palms squeaking down the back of the pilot's seat.

He looked over at Panca. She was limp, pinned with blinking sensors and dermal devices, and Ksiñe curled over her, with waves of blue worry coursing across his skin. The whipkin mewled as she snuggled up to Panca's neck and chest.

The star grew closer. Eruptions of liquid fire raked across its surface. Light licked the rind of the *Azura*'s universe, sending shivers of iridescence across the view. Taitn really was going to fly straight into it and hope the universe kept them all from being melted. Caiden was too stunned to grapple with the reality of how a bubble of light could keep them safe from... so much fire.

Laythan stumbled back into the bay from the engine room. "There's only enough fuel to sustain the universe for a few arcminutes before it collapses again."

The Glasliq surged ahead of them. Its shielding burned in angry textures, and the glass turned rosy molten. Threi was forced to peel away. The Glasliq's watery wings foamed against its body and re-formed in a new position for a velocity thrust toward a safer proximity.

Taitn continued sailing the *Azura* straight into the roiling surface of the star's skin. Burning fusion bit against the resplendent rind but didn't pass through and inside. The ship sang serenely, muting the violent view. The windows sparkled with glitches as they shielded the intensity bleeding through.

They really were safe. While the fuel held out.

Like a bubble through water, they cruised into the plasma of the stellar core, a realm of whiteness without boundary, glinting colors Caiden never knew existed. The substance around them was a fiery, aqueous, crystalline *stuff* in constant motion. Tiny swirls of light built up into one great force questing outward.

By far, the most beautiful thing he'd ever seen.

Taitn looked as bewildered and adrenaline-ravaged as Caiden felt. The pilot peeled his hands from the pads and wiped rivulets of sweat back into his damp-curled hair. He put a weak hand on Caiden's shoulder as they both gazed out in awe.

The sight speared his soul in place. Between the resplendence and the *Azura*'s happy world, his worries melted away.

Even Ksiñe and Laythan looked entranced.

En stood up and braced a hand on a wall. "Are we dead already or do we have a moment? Wow."

"Fuel's dying," Taitn whispered, staring.

"We'll be obliterated the moment this universe fails," Laythan said, rousing himself to march to the cockpit maps and string together a course. "We jet out this way to the nearest stellar egress. With the twitch drive, we can fly undetected if we cut power, and escape the Casthen's watch, in a direction he won't expect. Go now," Laythan barked. "Now!"

Taitn leaned in and flew from the calm, white oblivion of the stellar core into its violent outer flux. Gold and red fusion twisted across the view. Caiden finally realized the incredible value of the ship's power. It really was able to traverse where no one could ever go otherwise.

And it was Caiden's fault that Threi knew it existed. His fault that Panca had been hurt.

The *Azura* sped out of the star, shedding veils of plasma. Taitn cut the power, the universe bubble shrank back into the florescer, and a dire silence sucked away all sense of motion. He kept one set of fingers in the twitch drive panels as the ship sailed stealthily into the void. He pulled out his other hand, and ran it shakily through his hair again, slicking back sweat. "The *Azura*'s universe . . . it was *made* for these engines. Or the engines were made for it." Taitn exhaled and twisted around to see behind him in the bay. "How is Pan?"

Caiden moved toward her, but Ksiñe stormed up, fist balled and face aflame. Caiden flinched and stood his ground, ready to take the strike.

En intercepted, catching the Andalvian with both arms. "Easy. Words first, fists second."

"*You* saying that?" Ksiñe shoved En away and stood breathless, on the edge of brutality. "Could have killed her. Winn spared not one thought for us."

"I get it," Caiden said quietly. "You can't make me feel worse than I already do."

"Winn," Laythan said, "you weren't thinking of the crew's safety because you weren't *thinking*. If fear and anger rule your reasoning, you'll hurt everyone around you when you lash out."

How do I heal fear and solve rage? Caiden backed to the wall and sank down it. He felt permanently misshapen. Could the acceleration fix him?

Ksiñe said, "We discard him when we reach Emporia."

"Hey!" Taitn said. "You aren't without your own mistakes, Kis. I've lost count of the universes we've had to flee because of you and En." Ksiñe's face blanched at that, then marred with jagged scarlet. Taitn flinched. "Sorry. But I would think you of anyone would applaud him, after all, you and the Casthen—"

"I do not applaud stupidity," Ksiñe snipped in.

En positioned herself in the middle of everyone and crossed her arms. "You're all overreacting. Panca is fine and I've gotten us in and out of worse disasters than this."

"I haven't forgotten those," Taitn said.

En glared. "Yet you all seem to forget how little time has passed since Winn escaped a brutal genocide."

Caiden warmed at his champion, but something else shut down, his body clammy, his mind churning on the events in the Den, the riptide between the crew…

"Laythan." En squared her shoulders at the captain. Long black hair slithered over her muscular shoulders, and the smoky stain around her eyes made their gray all the fiercer, rivaling even Laythan's flinty stare. "Did you stop taking in strays because they point out the fact you're too scared to deal with your own shit? At least Winn isn't running from his past. You two want to ditch him in Emporia? Has ditching inconveniences these past years really gotten you ahead?"

Laythan said nothing. Ksiñe hissed, "Yes," whirled on his heels, and went to pick up Panca. He struggled, and Laythan treaded over to help—avoiding En's argument, which seemed to prove her point. Laythan, much taller, easily hoisted the saisn in his arms.

Ksiñe led the way to the engine room and muttered, "Resonance will heal."

Laythan didn't spare En or Caiden a look as he strode past, and when he returned alone he dived right into organizing the weapons. He pulled out the small flask he and Taitn drank from and took a heavy swig.

If Caiden couldn't appear more stable, the crew would kick him out. And every stitch of care they showed him proved *how much* he needed something like family now.

"In the Den…" Caiden started to say, but hesitated. This wasn't the right time with the grim mood burgeoning between the crew, but the thought jammed in his mind. "Threi spoke to Sina…somehow…and just changed her mind. She said yes to his requests so fast. He ordered me locked up, and if I hadn't—"

Laythan cut him off. "If you hadn't tried to stop that Casthen Enforcer, we would have dealt with it and they wouldn't know there's a ship more valuable than even a Glasliq. We haven't uncovered half of the *Azura*'s secrets, and you're ready to throw it and your future away to vent a foul temper. Stopping one pack of Casthen won't stop the whole. You need to come to terms with not being able to win every fight or save every thing."

Leta.

Caiden had once struggled to protect her and himself against a pack of duster pilots who were pissed he'd taken a repaired vehicle for a spin. They beat him dizzy and added to ten-year-old Leta's legion of bruises. Caiden wobbled to his feet to march after them and pay them back in pain. Leta caught his inferno of a temper and said, "Let them go. If they stay away, who cares."

"I care," he'd said. "You're hurt."

"So, why hurt them back? They'll just hurt you more, nothing will change."

Smart girl.

Caiden released a held breath and headed to the *Azura*'s lower level.

"Hey, kid," En called, trotting over to join.

"Endirion," Laythan shouted, stopping her in her tracks. "A word."

En halted, expression bitter. She forced a smile for Caiden and swirled back.

Caiden entered one of the sleeping chambers and collapsed on the bed, stress-raw and sullen. He fished the glassy cube of the database from his morphcoat pocket. It unfolded in his palm and the holosplay emerged: light filled up a dimpled grid of air, ready for queries.

He asked about planets, xenids, universes. The database showed him magnificent worlds—and ugliness with it. The multiverse contained so much variety, everything had a value to someone, somewhere. For every story of safety and glory there was one of slavery and massacre. A twisted rhythm of being.

The Cartographers' laudable goal of exploration was corrupted by shady passagers into a search for profit. Only the Dynast, in Unity, ensured holistic safety and equality for all, adhering to a belief that the Graven civilization had a noble purpose that had been forgotten.

He queried, "What is the extent of the Casthen's business?"

An inexhaustible list scrolled. They were suppliers and buyers, controlled many universes outright, and were involved in every industry to some degree, from food to medicine to shipbuilding.

"What would happen if the Casthen were destroyed?"

After a moment of processing, its words re-formed: *One million species expired.*

He blinked at the letters. "How?"

Countless aspects unfolded, showing how the Casthen's influence or ownership would deteriorate industries. "Machine spirit" cloning operations would cease without the Casthen's proprietary germination techniques. The lack of new spirits would result in existing ones being forcefully desenescized—aged backward—to prolong their life span: beings wrung out and re-sopped like rags.

Five thousand other species would lose the ecological factors that sustained them. The cessation of predator harvest in five universes would threaten another twenty thousand species, each of which provided critical exports. Ecological links all over cascaded into catastrophe the moment a few key species were lost. Then a 3 percent drop in fuel-prism production would limit access to worlds in need of aid.

The Casthen appeared too large to destroy. The database reported that previous assassination attempts had all failed, and the Casthen Prime, Çydanza, had been in charge since anyone could remember, over multiple lifetimes. The location of the Casthen Harvest, their headquarters, was carefully hidden—not even the Cartographers knew.

He stopped reading and let the information flicker down the list. Noble things flourished off ignoble gains. The Casthen were the manure out of which beautiful things grew. They needed to be stopped, but as the crew was trying to tell him, the roots were too deep. He'd need a trowel, something sharp to dig under the roots and lift the whole structure up.

Would the six years of accelerated aging make him sharp enough?

Caiden squeezed his palm closed and the device furled back into a glassy cube.

He twisted onto his back on the bed and let everything he'd learned sink in. The darkness was warm but he couldn't sleep. He pored over Sina's strange obeisance, the sick nophek pup, Threi's bag of gloss, and the ship's beautiful universe protecting them all from a *star*. He tangled that all up until he couldn't make sense of it, and still couldn't sleep. In the end, all he could think about was the young nophek beast, destroyed by the rind.

CHAPTER 15

NOTHINGNESS

Caiden wielded a glave in his dream, and faced the stampede of nophek. Their gait was strange, as if they were tangles of scorched bodies tied up in the shape of beasts, given teeth and smeared with blood. He fired the glave over and over, blasting white tunnels through pink flesh.

His mother stood with him, the last vision of her he remembered: rod-straight spine, shoulders wide, bronze skin gleaming, and hair whipped free from its pile. She stood protecting her child from the teeth of the world.

Caiden fired over and over—because he knew what happened to her next.

One nophek leapt and bit his wrist, tearing forearm from elbow. The glave went with it. He was helpless when another nophek smashed his mother into the rock. Claws tore her sideways. Jaws opened, sharp enough to rend a soul.

Another slammed into Caiden and carried him to the ground.

He screamed, fell off the bed, and curled up shaking against cold metal.

Didn't the memory jog wring all these visions out of me? He whimpered into the floor and squeezed his eyes shut.

The door slid open and Panca swept to his side. He blinked at her. A waking vision? She crouched and placed a velvety hand on his cheek. "Your scream. You went back there?"

Caiden nodded and she wrapped him in a hug. He bowed his forehead against her and forced himself to breathe through jerking sobs. "It's punishment," he murmured. "I hurt you."

"Not punishment. I've recovered." Her arms tightened around him, her petting hands soft as wafts of vapor. He felt her heartbeats: two discordant, then three, four, a fluttering of pulses like a snared bird. "It's a burden you don't deserve after everything you've been through. You'll…" Panca trailed into a whisper and stopped petting him.

"I'll…?"

She pushed back to look at him, and tension swelled in her face. "I also underwent memory jog, which doesn't work for all species, and some've minds that repeat it after… Saisn do. I relive my past every night, and will for's long as I'm alive. Sometimes pieces, sometimes all. Whatever you are… you might too."

"Relive it? The rest of my life with—" Caiden's throat hitched and the dreaded words stuck there.

Panca curled him up tightly. "You're moving forward very, very fast for someone who went through's much as you did. Appreciate your own needs, make sure you don't break yourself still running—in your heart—from your trauma." She took his head in her hands, soft fingers caged around his skull. "Close your eyes."

He did. The darkness deepened.

"Breathe. Feel your ribs expand. Breathe in from your stomach to the crown of your head."

Panca's fingertips lifted from his skull. Without the pressure, his thoughts floated up like a flock of birds, tingles filled his body with each breath of air and he almost toppled over. Panca splayed a hand on the center of his chest.

"Focus on nothingness, just be here, breathing and present. Let your thoughts slide off and away."

She propped his shoulders square, straightening his spine. Her hands stayed there.

"Imagine you're wind. Nothing can snag it. It streams over and keeps going, because it's empty."

Caiden's fire guttered out. His breath was a circuit, washing sparks up and down his limbs. Clotted emotions whisked away. His body grew heavy, only Panca's hands keeping him upright.

After a while, he opened his eyes.

The bright limbal rings of Panca's own eyes flicked as she looked over his face and tucked stray hairs behind his ear. Feather-soft, she asked, "Better?"

"Y-yes." He still tingled, feeling as if he'd just been scoured. "How did you learn this... this nothingness thing."

"My formative years were nothing, as no one. I was born a clone, replacement body for a saisn high official, one day. Since my mind'd be rewritten, I was raised without stimulus or interaction."

"You were made as a replacement part," Caiden whispered. Expendable, like him. The sandy beach his parental unit would have been "retired" to— that was surely a lie. They had been meat, and he their replacement part.

She said, "My memory jog's another story... but after it, I was unnecessary, sold as a mechanic slave, confined to an engine room meant to be my prison. I made it my teacher. I grew up inside it, knowing only its vibrational language, energy, function."

Like the little birds that would perch on the livestock, picking at bugs. Symbiotic.

"The ship was attacked, lay dead for years. I'd nothing but nightmares and nothingness. I used one to solve the other. Then Laythan found me, and I found a new life, and filled my nothingness with good. We can all've second chances. Come." She took his hand, tugging him to the glittering, starry world of the engine room.

The hum of processes and whirr of small motors welcomed them. Caiden inhaled metallic and chemical fragrances: briny, powdery, floral. No grease scents, no soot or fumes.

Halfway down the dark mess of modules and conduits, Panca eased Caiden to his knees in front of a waist-high column of glassy material. Silent purple fire throbbed through ink within.

"When I relive my memories, or when I hurt," she said, "this helps too. Your ship's a healer."

She pushed his forehead against the crystal. Colors burst through his eyes. Sugar sweated across his tongue. The ship's singing vibration engulfed his skull, stilled his shivers, filled the ravine his nightmare had carved. Caiden went slack as pulsations rolled over him. Jagged bits of despair spilled free, cutting him on the way out. Warmth and gratitude infested him, and the ship's weave of tonal textures felt indescribably *right*, like a language he hadn't realized was his mother tongue.

If I have to endure horror every time I dream, for the rest of my life, at least I have you. I can survive it if I have you.

His breath reflected off the *Azura*'s surfaces and warmed his cheeks, as if he and the ship breathed together.

"Thank you, Panca. I'm so sorry my stupidity hurt you."

"Don't apologize for your wounds." Pink reflections glistened through her forehead core, sparkling on the vertices as she regarded the engine with a loving look. She ran her hand across morphing metals. "This ship . . . she's confused. Whatever drove her to crash, she remembers, keeps making the same injuries. Like you. Hate'll make you keep wounding yourself, and neither engine nor nothingness'll be enough. Either need someone to keep fixing you, or . . . learn to let it scar."

Caiden placed his hand near Panca's. Soothing tones slithered into his skin and pooled beneath his palm. The metal puckered into a field of tiny opalescent spots.

"She likes you." Panca's throat fluttered airily: a laugh.

"I like her." Caiden smiled. Warmth welled up around his fingertips.

"Machines're simple, talkative, honest." A tightness in Panca's fine musculature relaxed, ridges gone from her face. A smile in return? "They're the sum of parts. Transcend parts. Humans're the sum of experiences . . . and struggle to transcend."

"Machines are definitely less complicated than people." And Caiden was reminded of the arguments he'd fled from, the bad blood stirred up among the crew. "I'm so glad you're all right, Panca."

The core in her forehead glittered as she nodded, laughed, and rose to return to her work.

Caiden had tougher judges to face. He left the engine room, and in the little hallway outside, a fresh argument reached his ears. The crew was above and behind him, beyond the gouge that the hallway's ramp made in the bay. Caiden stalled.

"Sell," Ksiñe said.

"Keep." Taitn's voice was hoarse. He paced in jingling boots.

"There isn't room," En's feminine voice said.

Taitn argued, "With the gloss funds we could afford a pan-hauler, keep both. Think about it. A *universe*. Do you have any idea what we could cash in on if we can go literally *anywhere*?"

"No," Laythan said. "We don't know enough about this ship yet, and a damned Casthen Enforcer got eyes on it already."

The crew was discussing something that wasn't theirs. Had they already decided on discarding him? Caiden's morphcoat prickled into black scales, sensing his darkening mood.

Ksiñe said, "Dynast will pay fortune for unheard-of Graven tech."

"No," Laythan snapped again. "First we confirm whether the Dynast funded the nophek farming through Casthen ties, and we sell our gloss so we're not targeted. We get a new ship sorted, then leave Unity as soon as possible, as far from the *Azura* as we can get."

"Layth, let's…" Taitn growled in frustration. "Slow down. Let's see what Pan finds during repairs, once she's recovered."

Caiden lifted his chin and scrambled together confidence as he strode up to the bay and around, steeling himself to walk straight through their argument.

"Thanks for all your ideas," he said, "but the ship is mine. You have your gloss. What I do after the acceleration is up to me."

That sounded good. Puffed with pride, he marched to the cockpit, where a slew of doubts deflated him. He glanced over his shoulder, pleased by the silence that stretched in his wake, however awkward. Taitn looked stung, and slouched in the open collar of his dark-green jacket. Laythan stared as ever, pale gaze sharp as a spike, but his forehead furrowed. En *tsked* and looked ready to smack both men. She strode to the cockpit but Caiden angled his back to her. He didn't need pity, didn't want their opinions. He'd said his piece.

"Layth, can I speak with you below?" Taitn asked, and sipped from the little flask. Laythan grunted, and their footsteps retreated.

At the sight of Caiden, Ksiñe uncoiled and stalked forward. Purple ire strobed across his skin, and his eyes flashed like bloody moons. Something glinted in his fingers.

"Stop." Panca treaded up into the bay, straight for the startled Andalvian, and pulled him by the wrist to face her. She placed a palm on his collarbones, and looked at him intently.

Ksiñe's skin flushed cream and pink under her touch, and the colors slowly overcame him, down his arms and to his fingers, as his breathing settled too.

Some wordless communication passed between them, before the medic glanced around, self-conscious, and poured himself into work inspecting the monitor nodes and threading and other esoteric medical tech he'd installed on Panca's skin. The whipkin fetched or returned tools and medicaments from an open med case, her body a fast wiggle of black and white and indigo fur.

En said to Caiden, "Scary habit of Panca's. Seeing everything you want to hide." She eased herself into the pilot's seat at a crooked angle and propped her roomy boots on the console. Her oversized clothes fit loose with strategic belts and magnetic snaps to cinch them around her muscular curves. Long hair spilled over the arm of the seat like a black waterfall, too voluminous and slippery to contain. This face of En's was androgynous, and bore a pensive expression Caiden hadn't seen before.

He kept to one side of the cockpit, untalkative.

"Are you hungry?" En asked.

"A little."

"Good." En smiled at the vista, her dark eyes dancing with colors. "Cooking will settle Ksiñe. I didn't have time to get ingredients for ramia, but you'll like everything he makes."

"Thanks, En." Caiden wasn't cheered, but appreciated her attempt.

The ship cruised on auto-course into a landscape of cloud stretched over fields of stars. Clusters of scarlet light filled deep pockets of sea blue. Curtains of dust concealed bouts of wrinkled lavender fire, and beyond both stretched the iridescent surface of a new universe: Unity's rind, extending in every direction, too vast to even see its curve. Unfathomable colors birthed and died in the rind's hypnotic flux, so violently active yet feeling entirely serene. Some of the more distant universes were so small they were complete spheres, like hollow planets filled with sloshing colors and glistering stars.

Caiden glanced at medic and mechanic in the bay; Panca sat motionless as Ksiñe fussed.

En caught his eye line. "Panca was a big part of Ksiñe's rehabilitation. Taitn still isn't keen on us breaking up the trio family he got used to, but Ksiñe's tamed a great deal since he first joined. I, on the other hand, haven't tamed at all." She hummed. "Don't worry. Laythan never stays in one place very long, but I won't let him ditch you at the next stop. A family system like ours benefits from a little upset once in a while. We've been stuck in our ways lately, and you remind us how we can still grow too. Growing comes with pains."

Caiden worked that thought in silence, picking at the feathery sleeve of his morphcoat. Eventually he asked, "Ksiñe's newest in the crew?"

"Besides you. Panca was first. Taitn was next. Then me. I'm why Taitn—"

She cut off as the pilot returned from below, nursing the blue flask. He kicked the pilot's seat, still occupied by En. She smiled up at him, feet still on the console. A pink flush crept above Taitn's bearded scowl. He took a drink. En, with eye contact and impish slowness, folded herself out of his seat.

Caiden was too distracted by the approaching rind to sort out their dysfunction, and why En's feminine forms needled Taitn so much more. He gripped the back of the seat as Taitn settled in.

"Worried?" The pilot tilted his face back and smiled warmly. "This crossover won't be bad. Unity is the original universe, its rind the oldest and gentlest. Newer universes on the fringes of charted space are more dangerous."

Caiden squeezed his eyes shut as the rind passed through the ship. Radiant filaments swept over him, soaking his body with electric prickles. The rind swept by, and in the new universe on the other side, Caiden's breathing came easier, and the ship's scalar gravity field felt weaker.

Light threshed off the cockpit windows, revealing a new expanse of stars.

And Emporia: a structure a hundred times larger than the Cartographers' Den had been, and many times more unfathomable.

The entire thing was lightseep obsidian.

CHAPTER 16

EMPORIA

Caiden couldn't decide if having a name for the substance that composed Emporia made it more or less baffling to observe. The structure hanging in space was almost entirely lightseep obsidian, that bizarre multidimensional matter that composed parts of the *Azura*'s spine. The transparent walls and angles were there one moment and gone the next, slipping in and out of phase with one another like a great faceted jewel turned in the light.

Taitn said, "The multiverse is full of ancient Graven structures like this. Once discovered, they're gutted by the Dynast, scraped of any relics, leaving us the shells of things that once had purpose: a planet or a palace, a city, a creature—we don't know."

Caiden gawked. "*Creature?*"

"Well, anything is possible. Some think lightseep was chiseled, others say it's bones, or like an insect that's molted and left a perfect shell."

Emporia's fat middle tapered at top and bottom. As Taitn circled the *Azura* to one starlit side, the ridges were revealed to be the ends of long flat slices lined up close together to create the illusion of a single mass.

The lightseep glinted and slithered in and out of space: a bright wall where none was before, or transparency suddenly dense and dark. Each slice was built of small hexagonal hollows pieced together. Normal materials filled the inside of these transparent bones, colonizing the lightseep skeleton like a hive built around the limbs of a tree.

"Lightseep is the physical condensation of other-dimensional energy structures. Whatever event wiped out the Graven civilization also slowed down and crystallized the vibrations of lightseep over time. That's why it's solid."

Atmoseal membranes capped the hexagonal spaces, and the whole exterior was studded with lights and slathered with languages in luminous moving pastes. Activity swelled inside the rooms, while ships streamed in and out of the layers like bees.

"We're going to the mechanics zone," Taitn continued, "where Panca can fix up the *Azura*, and Laythan can buy us a new vessel. Probably cargo class." A bit of husky regret laced his voice. "The Cartographers' medical district has the acceleration chamber you'll use. It's rare enough tech we won't find it anywhere else, otherwise"—he hushed—"Laythan wouldn't come here."

Emporia's many layers immersed their view. Taitn navigated between two slices. The shift of viewing angle made the lightseep vanish for a moment, and the hive's cells appeared cushioned by an expanse of only stars.

Taitn flew against one long layer slice, through, up another wall, across, and Caiden lost all sense of orientation. They stopped in an area less vibrant and decorated, at an atmoseal-capped cell with a nondescript iris door. To one side, a strip of stars was bordered by obsidian. On the other, zipping lines of starship traffic dazzled among studded lights.

Taitn pulled his fingers from the milky twitch drive panels and raised them in the air. The holosplays congealed in the cockpit's foggy light, blinking and fading at his touch as he navigated the ship interface.

"Communications linked," the pilot said. "Request sent."

A throaty voice blared through a speaker in the cockpit. "*Laythan Paraïa! For too long I have not seen! What is this heap? Where is* Dava?"

Taitn rolled his eyes.

"Let us in, Pent, we have business," Laythan said.

"*Yes, yes, yes. Let me see it, let me eyeball.*"

The door iris before them dilated open. The *Azura* drifted inside through the luminous atmoseal.

The interior of the depository stretched half a kilometer, stuffed full of dead starships. Some were disassembled, or parts of one cannibalized onto another, while others were only shells or bones. Caiden didn't have names for most of the materials or shapes, and he gaped, leaning in the cockpit to see on all sides.

Taitn chuckled. "You have a mechanic's gleam in your eye. This place is pretty cool, huh?" The thrusters whispered as he flew carefully between the massive wrecks, finally stopping in a large open area. Landing gear slithered from the ship's belly. "Pent is an old friend. He can get any replacement parts we need, and we'll reassemble Laythan a new ship from the trove. This district is quiet and clandestine."

"Hey," En said, gliding over to drop something in Caiden's hand: a pair of small golden kernels. "Translators. Put these in your ears, they'll help shape your synapses. There are quite a few languages that your acceleration won't be able to give you."

Caiden fitted a kernel in each ear canal. They fuzzed up inside until he couldn't feel them, but when En said, "How about this?" the words lay heavy in his brain for a moment. He smiled, confirming they worked.

Floating spotlights, like bright insects, clustered in the nodes of the depository's scalar gravity. As Taitn set the *Azura* down, the lights swarmed all around, inspecting.

Pent's voice crashed through the speakers. "*Never have I seen! The wings! Oh! Open. Taitn Maray Artensi, please, please, yes, open, expose.*"

Taitn shook his head. "Excitable as ever."

Ksifie hit the doors open as everyone gathered in the bay. The back of the ship unfolded and the floating spotlights poured in, beaming rays across every surface. Caiden swatted a few away and backed into a corner.

"Friends!" Pent shouted as he approached the back of the ship, arms open wide. His voice was scratchy wet, vibrating in triplet through his big skull and the floral folds of his inverted nose.

Pent was a saavee. His large eyes sat high on his face, crisp fluorescent green dimpled by diamond pupils. He was Laythan's height but much thicker, brawny and callused, his body a mix of bumpy textures in slate and lavender hues.

Laythan greeted Pent on the ramp. They clasped wrists and thumped a fist into each other's chest. "We need repairs. She's been derelict for some time."

"Always for you! Always. Whatever need."

The floating scanner lights homed in on the ceiling, where the ship's crystal and lightseep spine was covered in scaly panels.

"What is?" Pent's diamond pupils flicked. He took a step back on the ramp.

Panca switched the ceiling plates open, filling the bay with blue light. The spine scintillated magnificent plays of luminescence and shadow.

"Graven!" Pent shrieked. His short ears curled back in alarm. The weave of his green irises came apart and wriggled as if he wanted to unsee what was before him. "No, no, no, don't you know—Dynast has detectors now! They would kill, kill for it!"

"They have *what*?" Laythan rounded on the saavee.

Pent swiveled his head anxiously. "Dynast set sensors up to detect vibrations of active Graven technology in all, all, all Emporia. They want to catch Graven things sold in secret. Quick! I have shielded hollow, can hide her! It is lightseep hole, pocket of weird physics, can hide things."

Laythan's face screwed. "Taitn, park there quick. Everyone else, out!"

"This way, in the back," Pent hissed. He shuffled outside, kneading his forearms anxiously.

"Wha—" Caiden was pushed out and left aside like baggage as the crew became a flurry of efficiency.

Taitn closed the bay doors and ignited the ship. The *Azura*'s huge thrusters were a pink whisper while a deeper vibration emanated from the base to push it off the ground. The ship crossed the huge depository to a far wall, where a gaping blister in the lightseep resembled a knot in a tree, a cavern of velvety light just big enough to house the ship. Taitn parked the *Azura* inside, and a creamy membrane slicked across the hollow's opening. The ship's sharp wings folded over each other, her outline svelte and so black it hid all the contours, seams, and sheen. The *Azura* looked like those dead insects that would collect in the pasture block light panels, impossible to remove.

Caiden walked over alone, watching the crew at work. En squeezed information from the saavee. Panca strode off into the shadowy depths of the depository.

The sound of Caiden's footfalls bounced lonely off the wrecks. The crew didn't need him at all, but he still very much needed them. The acceleration would make him twenty years old, stuffed with skills and able to fight, fix, fly, and speak real languages. Would he become good enough to contribute? Good enough to make them understand *why* he needed an impossible thing like vengeance?

Taitn emerged through the shielding hollow's membrane. His brow wrinkled when he saw Caiden. "You all right? Your cheeks are red. Don't worry about the *Azura*, she'll be undetected in there. Ksifie is modifying the traces we made as we were coming in. The Dynast's detectors rove, so we missed most of them."

"Yeah...thanks. Can we go to my acceleration now?"

Taitn blanched. "After we discuss. Soon."

Soon. That would forever be Caiden's most hated word. He would understand soon. He would accelerate soon. He would fly the *Azura* soon.

"A child!" Pent spotted him and gave a wide-jawed grin. His teeth were vertical strips of white barbs in dark gums. "A child. Do not tell me...Laythan! No, no, no. Surely, Endirion Day. You have misfired at last!" A hoarse cackle erupted from the saavee.

En scowled and folded his arms. "Not me. Sharpshooter."

"His name is Winn," Laythan said. "The ship is his, both of them from CWN82."

"Ah." Squiggles swam in Pent's eyes as he inspected Caiden. "Winn of Casthen."

"I'm not Casthen!"

"Then you would not have ship! Not be you." Pent grinned horribly again. "Bad things can make good people. Good people can make things bad."

Caiden's mind tripped hard over that. Was the opposite true too?

Panca approached, pushing a levitating cart of supplies and tools.

"Pan Carai! Oh!" Pent thundered to one knee and raised his arms in worship. "Pan, supreme, exquisite, tell me: have you heard *Azura* speak? What does she need? I have sulphur specs, you must see! And new coils, all the kinds—malta, halispar, all! Glossalith threads, I buy for you! Come, come. Come." Arms still spread, he backed sideways. His nose flared with great breaths like the petals of a gray flower.

Caiden shuddered. Panca followed with little reaction.

Laythan snapped his fingers and addressed the crew. "The sooner we wrap up the *Azura*'s bioprocessing repairs, the faster we can assemble and outfit a new ship and get out of Unity. I don't want to be anywhere near the Dynast while this Casthen dust settles. En, sell the gloss as discreetly as you can manage. Try not to bloody anyone."

"No promises." En saluted and jogged away.

Caiden tugged the morphcoat tighter around his shoulders. Laythan was still vexed, but Caiden had a goal and he didn't need to wait for the captain's approval. "Tell me how to get to the Cartographers' district."

Surprisingly, Laythan didn't fight. "Let's get it over with, then." He strode off to a nearby door on the depository wall and punched a keypad. Singsong motors brought down a lift.

Taitn charged after them both, face still pale and glistening with sweat. "Hang on, we have to discuss acceleration increments. He'll need—"

"He can do it all at once. It's only six years. Then he can make adult decisions and we can get out of Unity."

"*Only six*...You'd put him in danger just beca—"

The lift boomed to a stop, and the door to it opened by dissolving into particles. The three of them treaded inside, and the door re-congealed. The space was cramped, and there was no room for Caiden's anxiety as he sensed an old argument resurging between pilot and captain. The air was electric, and both of them towered, casting heavy shadows. Caiden shoved his hands in his morphcoat pockets and crunched the fabric between his fingers.

Laythan delivered measured, biting words. "We're leaving as soon as we have a new ship, which should only be a few days. If you want to take his acceleration slow, you can split off and stay here with him."

Taitn fidgeted. "You're trying to run from a threat that doesn't exist." He dropped his tone, quiet and deep. "En was right. Just because you spent decades stuck doesn't mean it's right to speed everything up for Winn."

Laythan's voice rose to take up the volume Taitn had lost. "Just because you went too fast doesn't mean others have your lust for patience."

"I'm not an adolescent, Layth."

"Stop arguing like one. It's not your choice, anyway, it's for the boy to decide what he does with his body. Winn—will you accelerate all six years at once and come with us when we leave, or space your time out safely and remain in Emporia?"

Alone dangled unsaid on the end of that.

Caiden stood, pinned by Laythan's unyielding gray gaze and Taitn's pleading blues. As much as he had fantasized about being older and capable, he had no sense of what he would become after that many years were slammed into him in an instant. And he couldn't imagine being alone in the multiverse without the help of the crew.

He desperately needed *both* the acceleration and their support.

"All six years at once." His voice quavered at the end, and he couldn't meet his hero's eyes.

Taitn looked away, face grim. He tousled fingers through his dark hair and slicked it aggressively to one side. Then, seeming unsure what to do with his hands and the silence, he fished out the flask from his jacket and nursed it.

Caiden pinched his arms against his stomach. His breathing felt loud in the cramped space. The lift stopped with a hiss and its door dissolved into a cascade of particles.

He blinked at the massive space beyond. Inside Emporia, the Graven ruin's hexagonal rooms that he'd seen from the exterior extended like long tubes. Xenids and wares populated the inner chambers.

Inside, the lightseep obsidian wasn't just a scaffolding into which solid, opaque materials were stuffed. It was a *canvas* onto which holograms projected. Light soaked surfaces, giving the illusion of moving landscapes much vaster than the actual walls of Emporia. To his left, waterfalls sixty meters high inhabited lightseep columns. They threw up whorls of mist that fractured rainbows. On his right, a forest of red-barked trees projected across one long, flat sheet of the lightseep stuff. Caiden touched the wall, expecting to graze the tree's rough bark, but his palm flattened on solid crystal, senses deceived.

Taitn ambled on, familiar with this place. Laythan strode stiffly, piercing gaze darting this way and that, parsing out the crowd. Caiden trailed behind, so captivated by the deceptive vistas, he barely noticed the new variety of xenids strolling past. Wonder started to unstitch his anxiety.

The inner facets of the lightseep obsidian shifted when seen from different angles, and the holo-environments projected inside transformed too. A tunnel passage they walked through was painted with fields of blue glaciers. In the next atrium, rainfall dangled like silver threads from an orange sky. But as he entered, the crystal facets shifted and there were clouds where the floor had been, and an underwater world in the ceiling.

The myriad views were all the more disconcerting and dreamlike because none had sound. And all of them were wildly different from Caiden's home of industrial buildings and green fields.

"Cartographers are purple," Taitn said, pulling Caiden's attention back. He flicked at a sinuous thread of colored light hovering in the middle of the corridor. Other colors bundled with it and shot off in different directions. In such a labyrinthine place it made sense there was some system of guidance.

"Dynast copper. Medics green. En will tell you red is 'fun,' I'd call it trouble."

Laythan snorted at that, his first sign of softening up.

The red navigation thread angled into a wide hall where tones swelled through glass walls and changed its hues. Lettering dripped in the air, painted in stylistic light, while laughter and sweet or rowdy voices pealed from moving shadows behind.

They followed the purple thread to a multileveled concourse over a kilometer wide and tall, crisscrossed with causeways and corridors. The lightseep wasn't holopainted; instead, it was like being inside a chiseled jewel with light sources casting all around.

As Caiden marveled, a lance of guilt cut him down. *Focus, idiot.*

He wasn't here to explore or enjoy—none of these worlds could be his—he was here to shore up his failings so he could put his worthless life to use. He would get one crucial step closer to the vengeance his whole dead world deserved.

Twenty years old. Caiden watched Taitn's back, the confident and unhurried sway of his shoulders, the straps crossing them with polished buckles that caught every light they passed. Taitn's boots had a jingling rhythm that Caiden tried to match, tried to measure himself and feel steady in his pace.

The acceleration would catch him up. Taller, stronger, knowledgeable. Caiden huffed, reenergized.

Taitn looked down and slowed. "Too fast?"

"Just right."

"Are you scared?" Taitn managed to summon a reassuring smile.

"What will it feel like? To be older, to know things, and be able to do things without any memories of how I learned?"

"It—it won't hurt," Taitn said, "but our bodies aren't designed to speed up or slow down. It'll take a while for the rest of you to catch up. I'll—we'll make sure you safely recover."

Caiden glanced at Laythan striding ahead.

Taitn took a sip from his lacquered flask.

Laythan reached a hand back for it. Taitn paused a good long moment before he shared.

In thickened silence, they treaded across storm clouds. Shops lined the long passageway on either side, while scarlet lightning danced in the ceiling and floor. Caiden flinched at every flash beneath his feet.

The purple thread streaked cheerfully into another atrium that had more passages shooting off from it. At the entryway, Taitn riveted to a stop. Caiden ran into his back. A crowd of humans and xenids clogged up the space.

Laythan's eyes widened in shock before he halted too. His whole posture cringed.

Caiden frowned up at them. There were displays pasted upon the walls of the space. Some showed footage streamed from passagers investigating the remains of his agrarian planet and RM28, the desert of death. Others showed footage from his memory jog. The imagery came in snatches and zips of detail, mosaicked from neural firing and painted by algorithms. A tightness screwed into him at how *wrong* it was to see his memories outside of himself, where they shouldn't be.

But Laythan and Taitn weren't looking at the footage. The whole crowd had their backs turned on the displays to look at a real person standing in the center of the room.

Taitn's cross expression melted into adoration. And Laythan's look of terror grew more complex, laced with yearning.

Caiden frowned and arched on tiptoes to see over the murmuring crowd.

Then a beaming female voice cast to him like a ray of light, and instantly, he understood.

CHAPTER 17

PRIMES

The voice was so compassionate and compelling, Caiden had to close his eyes to contain what he was hearing.

"—assure you, wholly unaware of the vulgar origin of the gloss and the violence that enabled its production. We are likewise dismayed to hear the response of the Casthen Prime, Çydanza. My stars have told me that patience and distance is the safest course until investigations are complete. Thus, all Casthen detachments in Unity are henceforth expelled by Dynast order, with ten ephemeris days to vacate before enforcement."

The reverberation of her voice stilled in the quiet atrium. Caiden exhaled and opened his eyes. Dynast officials formed a circle in the middle of the atrium's crowd, clearing a space. Their faces were masks of rapt admiration, the look of devotees. When Caiden finally spotted the figure in the center of them, he felt his expression melt into the same. Contentment blossomed in his chest; the warmth of an embrace, the delicate flutter of connection, excitement, willingness, the same complicated emotion that had overcome him when they'd flown in the heart of that magnificent star.

"Who is she?" he whispered.

Long brunette hair collected in a braid on one side of her head, pulled away from features that were at once mesmerizing and ordinary, imperfect but beautiful. Legions of freckles both light and dark stardusted across her tawny skin. She didn't smile, and wielded no charisma, but Caiden was fixated as if he knew her but couldn't place from where, and she might as well have been wreathed in an aura of warm light, a beacon of complete serenity. A star heart in the flesh.

"That's..." Taitn struggled, so fixated that Caiden had to tug the man's sleeve to remind him of words. "That's the Dynast's Prime, Abriss Cetre." His voice hushed, his eyes still wide and riveted, every cell of his body caught in her gravity.

"Why is...why." Caiden struggled too, trying to question everything about her in one statement.

"Of anyone," Taitn said, "she is the most Graven of all, claiming the purest, highest rank of descent. It is in the genes of all creatures to love that which is Graven."

Caiden looked back over the crowd, recognizing love in their expressions. In Laythan's, love battled with fear.

The people clogging the atrium orbited Abriss, inexplicably arranging into rings of species, some xenids only partially physical, some airborne, all organized by the same strange feeling that arrested Caiden too: a primal reverence that kept him at bay, and a burning attraction that called him in.

Is this what my freckles mean? How much of this do I have, and how would I tell?

The Prime wore a sheer black overdress embroidered with copper constellations. Beneath, she was clad in a dark, fitted flight suit, hemmed in bronze and lined with blue, woven of an expensive exotic gossamer he'd read about, called starspun silk armor.

"What's she saying?" Caiden asked. "The Dynast disagree with what the Casthen did?"

"The Dynast," Laythan began, his rigid jaw mashing up the words, "is pretending they weren't buying gloss from the Casthen. It's used to make starship fuel, valuable to all passager economy, but it's even more integral to the Dynast's research into Graven technology, which requires phenomenal energy loads." Laythan squeezed his eyes closed, face snarled with wrinkles as he struggled to focus. He raked fingers through his white beard. "The Dynast looks pristine on the outside, but they don't care how they procure things, as long as they get them in the end. The Dynast acknowledge that the Graven created the stellar egresses but not that the multiversal furcation was a Graven design in the first place. They believe it was a mistake, a catastrophe, but they profit from it like everyone else, since the Graven remnants they lust after are all over the damn multiverse."

Laythan flinched as Abriss spoke again: "To remedy the repercussions of this transgression, the Dynast will openly purchase gloss from any passager without inquiry or discrimination. My stars have told me this is the path of least conflict." The Prime spoke slowly, monotone, and enunciated with delicate precision. Her voice grooved shivers through Caiden, familiar...

His spine snapped rigid as he realized. This Graven effect was what Threi had used on Sina: her perplexed expression, clashing between obeisance and confusion. It wasn't intimidation Threi had used, it was love.

The Dynast Prime was only conveying information now, but if she had spoken an order, Caiden's heart would move worlds to obey. Threi had struggled to convey his orders, but even if the man was immensely less effective than Abriss, it was a terrifying thought. How many more Graven monsters did the Casthen possess, able to twist and fracture wills at their whim?

"Let's go," Laythan said. "We have to leave, now." He hooked Taitn's and Caiden's elbows, but Taitn was leaned against the Prime's gravity, his blue gaze still transfixed and mouth agape.

Serenely composed, Abriss showed no emotion, but every detail was a well of hidden secrets, every freckle a galaxy. Caiden leaned in, too, as she spoke more softly to the Dynast sentinels encircling her. They were all human and dressed in fitted black, midnight blue, and copper garments that looked like they would take ages to peel out of.

A broadcast crackled, coming online. The wall displays blunted to black. Caiden snapped from his lull. A symbol dominated the displays: a circle with six rays below. Caiden's hand drifted, shaking, to the back of his neck, his coat collar hiding the same mark.

Sound narrowed down in his ears. His mind fogged, turning the crowd into the masses at the Flat Docks, their brands all alike, herding in.

The voice piping through could not have been more different from Abriss's: female, but sandy and strained, a voice atrophied by disuse. *"The Casthen adherents are actively rescuing resources and refugees from CWN82."*

"Çydanza," Laythan spat, broken from the spell. He hauled Taitn and

Caiden sideways. "Let's go, we don't need to hear whatever lie she's weaved up in response."

Where the Dynast Prime had bewitched Caiden's attention with love, Çydanza's voice snared him with spite and pain. His feet stuck in place.

This being was the orchestrator of his trauma. This was who he had to reach.

"*I assure our dissidents that my adherents had nothing to do with the gloss operations discovered on RM28, and the footage released by the Cartographers— a supposed memory jog of a survivor—is entirely falsified, and we will prove it so.*"

"That's bullshit," Caiden whispered. Hatred threaded his ribs and throbbed like a kicked-up hive. He slipped from Laythan's grasp, but Taitn clamped onto his sleeve.

"It's just words," Taitn said. "Your memory jog paired with what the passagers recorded afterward incriminate the Casthen clearly."

"Çydanza said 'refugees.' Did others survive? Or they found more planets of people? And everyone's just letting the Casthen take them again!"

Laythan bent his face close, words hot beside Caiden's ear. "The Casthen are under everyone's scrutiny now, thanks to you. Not everyone cares, and many who *do* care never take action, but a good number of passagers will be outraged enough to detangle the Casthen's permissible actions from their illicit ones. You have to accept that justice will come over time, through your memories that you've already provided…at immense cost. Let's get your reward so we can leave Unity for good."

Laythan dragged Caiden through the dense crowd. Çydanza's voice continued to grate his ears. "*It's unfortunate that neither the Dynast nor Cartographers see eye to eye with me or agree to conjoin our reclamation efforts, a decision that will make all suffer a slower resolution, and who is to say that the Dynast isn't behind the gloss operations themselves, being now so eager to reclaim it from free passagers, so eager they've been putting a little worm of encouragement in the ears of Cartographers outside of precious Unity, so why don't you all think about that before you choose sides.*"

Caiden's fury flexed, but Abriss's clear voice cleaved his tension instantly. "Any gloss acquisitions freely sold to us will be used exclusively for glossy research and existing Graven programs of intent. These, as all denizens of Unity know, are for the benefit of all, and the comprehension of our reality manifesting from luminiferity."

There wasn't a single note of combativeness in her. Just serenity, which sounded a great deal like truth. Having said her piece, Abriss turned her back on Çydanza's broadcast display with the red Casthen brand, and drifted from the atrium with all the Dynast sentinels in her wake.

The spell broke when she left, and a warm veil peeled off Caiden. When that inexplicable love left, his temper lay raw and vile beneath.

Taitn helped push him through the crowd. "Words and promises are cheap. Let's get you moving forward, not looking back."

I'd promised Leta I'd come back for her. Cheapest of promises.

Around them the crowd came to its senses, half beginning to disperse. Çydanza kept talking, her raspy voice a file re-carving the shape of Caiden's hate. He dug his heels in and said, "I need to hear this first."

Laythan snatched Caiden's wrist. "To your acceleration. Now. We are *leaving.*"

"*You* have nothing at stake!" Caiden tried to wrest himself free, but Laythan's grip only tightened. "Why is leaving Unity so important to you?"

"You're hurting him." Taitn intervened, planting a heavy hand on Laythan's shoulder and glaring until the man let go. "Laythan used to be a security pilot for the Dynast family. He was betrayed . . . and Prime Laureli, who he was protecting, was murdered."

Laythan's face changed at the name, wrinkles deepening, distress sparked into pain. A momentary softness passed through his eyes, a wisp of the sort of love Abriss had evoked. Then it was gone, and Laythan straightened, a tower of wrath. "*I* was blamed and tossed in a Dynast prison with an eternal sentence. I broke out and decades passed, but time moves differently for the Dynast's Graven family, and I'm still a fugitive in Unity. Boy, you don't seem to grasp how common it is for someone to feel aggrieved or betrayed, for someone to want revenge and never get it. We all learn to deal with it and move on."

"It sure doesn't look like you've dealt with it. Just ran away." The hurtful words were double-edged, and Caiden cut himself saying them. His body was still too small to contain his grief, and there was nowhere for his frustration to go but lash out at the people around him, as Laythan had warned.

Acceleration. I'll grow to contain my grief.

Laythan's voice rushed, clipped. "Abriss is a master astrologian. She has skills and technology to predict events before they happen, and divine information about the past and present anywhere in Unity. But *only* in Unity. If her 'stars' haven't already told her I'm here, it wouldn't be hard for her to find me. We need to get you accelerated, then *leave*. And if what I have at stake isn't enough for you, remember that the Dynast would kill to get their hands on your *Azura* if they learned of it."

Caiden sucked a deep breath. Pangs stabbed his ribs.

"You take him, Taitn," Laythan finished gruffly. "I need to track down En." He pulled up the hood of his coat and strode from the atrium.

Taitn laid a comforting arm around Caiden's shoulders and said softly, "Growing up well is your best revenge against the Casthen. Don't forget that."

Growing up . . . His body would become six years older, but his heart and mind wouldn't be six years removed from the slaughter.

He'd heard Çydanza's voice. He had a target now.

Revenge was the best revenge.

"Let's go," Caiden said, and marched on.

CHAPTER 18

ACCELERATION

Caiden and Taitn carried on through Emporia, following the purple thread of light through an open market. The dazzling sights projected into the lightseep walls and columns didn't hold his attention anymore. They were flat lies. Approximations of worlds that so many trapped and exploited souls would never see.

The thread eventually ended in a huge hexagonal cavern of the Graven ruin. The Cartographers' luminous white material made up a circular platform thirty meters in diameter. Walkways speared out to reach openings on the far walls. The platform was rimmed in long counters and consoles, with maps and other data in three-dimensional holosplays.

The lightseep obsidian walls of this cavern were not dramatically landscape-filled but showed a modest vista of cloud.

They stood there for a long moment while passagers and xenids milled about. All the Cartographers dressed in fitted, angular layers of a light-gray and purple material, which softened up even the imposing xenids like chketin and saisn.

Caiden urged, "Taitn?"

The man took a determined sip from his flask before tucking it away. All the softness had left his face, and its natural severity took over. His rigid jaw sank his cheeks in, and his dark brows pinched together. He was much younger than Laythan, but wrinkles were beginning to betray Taitn's history: smile rays by his eyes, grimace lines peeking from his beard, anger grooved into his forehead. It was the grimace that deepened now.

"Which desk?" Caiden asked.

"Right. This way." He led Caiden to one of the desks without a Cartographer at it and placed his hand on the glassy white surface. Luminescence traced his palm until he pulled away.

Taitn fussed with the little buckles and snaps on his blackbird-green jacket, making sure they were tight. Everything in order. The nervousness wasn't lost on Caiden, but he wasn't sure how to interpret it except to be nervous as well. Maybe the acceleration all at once *was* as dangerous as Taitn claimed.

A female Cartographer approached the counter. Long platinum ringlets sprung around her torso as she walked. "Passagers Taitn and Winn, welcome. You are here to use Winn's acceleration credits?"

She appeared human from afar. Up close, her pale skin was semi-translucent, giving hints of anatomy beneath: a white ghosting of her teeth around her smile, the blue of woven arteries in her neck, and the faint gush of a heart above the low cut of her garment. Stars of data danced over her piscine irises.

Caiden waited but Taitn didn't speak. The man's mouth was parted and he had a blank look, frozen in recognition, almost as severe as Abriss's trance, but this woman had no freckles.

Caiden stammered, "Y-yes, my—the acceleration, please."

The stars swam across her eyes. She smiled. "I see. Six years. These can be distributed as finely as thirty-six installments. Thank you for sharing your memories, Passager." The Cartographer bowed her head, silvery curls bouncing over her shoulders.

Taitn's throat bobbed. "Lyli…"

"Hello, Taitn. I will be Winn's acceleration technician and rehabilitation counselor." She looked to Caiden and smiled, her purple lashes shivering like butterfly wings. "I can answer any questions you may have about the procedure. While your life span will be shortened by the acceleration, there are many practices that prolong human longevity, dependent on genetic-resonance factor." Her eyes refocused from the sparkles occluding them. "And I see here you have fine genes, young passager. Six years will hardly chip away at the long life ahead of you."

Caiden managed a smile back, disarmed by her clinical manner. He kept his gaze off the slender bones and lacy veins ghosted into her strange white flesh.

Lyli asked, "First, in what increments will you be accelerating?"

Caiden avoided Taitn's pained expression and said, "All six. All together."

"Certainly, Passager Winn. Have you been made aware of the risks and recovery involved?"

He swallowed. "Yes."

"Wonderful. Please follow me."

She led them across the causeway stretching over lightseep clouds, and through a doorway into a warren of halls.

Taitn trailed behind Caiden's shoulder. Caiden glanced back once. The rays at the edges of Taitn's eyes crinkled in a steady wince.

When Lyli pressed her hand on a blank wall, light cracked around the frame of a door, which dissolved in a cascade of particles. Caiden followed her in, then stopped cold. The biodata chamber for acceleration was the same type he'd entered for the memory jog. He stared, loosening the reins on his doubt.

The memory jog had ripened his terror into fury. What would the acceleration do to his mind?

He looked back at Taitn for reassurance, but the man's eyes were glassy and a rapid pulse thumped in his neck. He rubbed his knuckles over his jacket—where the flask lay in the pocket beneath.

"Taitn?"

"Yes. It's fine." He marched into the room.

Cartographer Lyli paused by a holosplay next to the chamber. "Please select what preprogrammed networks of synaptic stimulation you would like to employ during the accelerated years. These will be arranged in the noetic processing module and sequenced to condition your individual brain." Caiden glazed over. "Both static knowledge and physical experience may be implanted, with the success rate dependent on the individual's mirror neurons. I will meanwhile design the neural architecture while you prepare for the procedure."

"Synaptic…"

Taitn translated. "The skills and knowledge you want. I'll handle it. They have to be chosen carefully, or could conflict and damage the… Well," he said, restarting, "you need more mechanical knowledge to help Panca with the *Azura*'s repairs, as well as piloting skill and the sciences necessary to understand neural control systems. Combat, so you can take care of yourself. Languages, reasoning, philosophy…"

Taitn sidled to the very edge of the holosplay and kept his gaze away from Lyli and the chamber. He blinked hard and frequently while navigating the glowing purple words, throwing them to a separate display, where Lyli poked at a console, her own eyes flickering with stars.

She smiled at Taitn's choices. "Physiology, neuroscience, molecular biology, harmonic neural networks—my expertise as well." Taitn's blush crept above his beard. Lyli turned to Caiden. "Please undress to your undergarments, Passager."

Caiden sat on a bench and peeled off his clothing. The cold air probed beneath his skin. "Taitn…What's it like?"

Taitn reached for Caiden's clothes. "We'll get some new ones. These won't fit…after. And the accel is mostly sleeping." A tiny strain in his voice stood out like a black thread in a white skein. "Your consciousness will be inhibited by harmonics while your brain and body are activated. Then there's a cooldown while your body adjusts. Your consciousness will recombine, and you'll be moved to a nutrient bath for sleep incubation."

None of that description told Caiden what it would *feel* like.

"When you get in there…" Taitn paused. "Don't think about who you were, like you did for the memory jog. Think about who you want to be."

I want to be like you. "What happens if I can only think about who I was?"

The wrinkles fanned around Taitn's eyes again, mapping pain and bravery in the same strokes.

"Excuse me." Lyli crouched beside Taitn, brushing his shoulder—he stood abruptly. The Cartographer held a handful of the same tiny cubes Sina had applied before the memory jog. "May I?"

While she applied the nodes to his body, Caiden had nowhere to look but at her face, and was thankful that the brightness of the room filled her with light, minimizing her translucency.

Finished, Lyli rose and hooked her long hair behind an ear. She asked Taitn, "Are you taking care of him?"

"And Laythan is too," he replied stiffly, "taking care of him..."

"I will require you to remain with me and observe the procedure."

"I shou—yes... Of course." He turned to Caiden. "You ready? I'll be here the whole time."

Caiden straightened and marched into the chamber dressed in under-clothes and shivers. This was his portal to revenge. The copper-colored gills of the floor scissored his soles. The bubble eyes spotting the walls would be his witnesses.

Lyli signaled the door shut. She and Taitn blurred past the chamber's thick glass.

"I'm ready..." Caiden's voice bounced off the sealed walls. Could they hear him if he screamed? Sina hadn't heard him—or hadn't cared.

He closed his eyes. This was it. Six years in a flash.

The pressure began in his ears, crushing his brain between. Just like the memory jog.

Think of who you want to be. Kind. Brave. Strong. Smart.

He had been kind to reassure Leta, but awful to leave her behind. He'd been strong enough to make it through the massacre alive, but too weak to save anyone but himself. Smart to make a deal with Laythan but stupid to break the crew's trust later by venting his wrath against Threi.

The chamber went dark and the pressure equalized through Caiden's skull. Redness in his vision cooled to black. A thrill rippled up his body as gravity peeled away like old clothes, and his feet rose off the floor, suspending him in the middle of the space.

I want to be stronger, independent, capable, and compassionate. Someone who can annihilate injustice.

Warm, purring waves filled in around him. Beads of air burrowed in and out of his skin.

I want to be worth something. Someone who belongs in this world.

Dizziness rippled up his spine. Sweat trickled down it. The growl of a machine kicked up, buffeting him with vibrations that knit through his bones and organs. His consciousness was a puff of smoke swirling inside his skull.

The vibrations rose to a gale and blew it apart.

Unshackled from time.

"Light willing, please..."

There were two voices, one filtered to a low rumble and the other to a hiss. Caiden teetered and was grasped with a blanket or cloud or satin sea that he plunged into and floated on. He was carried away, and washed up on some shore.

He vibrated in and out of himself, and bounced off his own edges; jagged rage, silken need, iron valor, and a soft, swampy feeling he chased after.

"Hey." Taitn's voice quavered.

Caiden opened his eyes to a blur. *Is everything all right?*

Idiot. You're dying.

He lay flat in liquid with his head supported on glittering crystalline folds.

"You'll be all right." The quaver was still in Taitn's voice. "You'll be fine after this. Safe. Everything's fine."

Caiden reached out. A skeletal hand. Knobby bones showed beneath skin stretched too tight, too white and flushed with dark-mauve veins, freckles stark.

"Taitn?" he choked.

"It's t-time to sleep."

Sleep? Oh, crimes... He tried to move but the liquid claimed him. The light dimmed.

Sleep would mean nightmares. His brain knew no other dreams.

Caiden's consciousness drifted, relieved as the dreams began sweetly with memories of muggy days fixing dusters surrounded by the smell of grease and crushed herbs. A long soak in a bath after hard work. Leta wearing a crown of blue chicory flowers in her soft brown hair. She was too short to see over the grass as they trampled to a shady oak. In its tall branches, they peered through optics to count the livestock. A herd of yearlings was ready to go to the Docks.

The vapor above ripped open. Had he known that was his first glimpse of the real sky, he might have been more curious than terrified. The orange light was from a sun they'd never seen.

The dream ricocheted into nightmares. Inside the transport, he was smothered with tangled limbs and faces, every inch of the space stuffed into a solid mass. The churning bodies mired into sweat, piss, and feces. Caiden suffocated on reek and tried desperately to ball up, away from the undulating skin.

The writhing turned to panic and screams. Fingers clawed Caiden's hair and wrenched his skull back. His limbs pulled in all directions as the soup of human terror boiled. He plowed his limbs against flesh. His scream was eaten by other screeches.

Then darkness drained to desert. The horde scrambled out, stampeding him away from Leta. The beasts seized and chewed. Caiden didn't have a glave in this nightmare, and he didn't escape. Tackled and too exhausted to fight, he lay screaming as a nophek tore into his belly.

More rounds of stench and roar, more teeth and teeth and teeth. Pain chewed him up and spit him out.

Caiden jerked awake into a rigid, thrashing body. The back of his head cracked against crystal, over and over. He was upright, restrained in place while the nightmares scrabbled through his skin and spurred convulsions. His heart was a butterfly in a web, tugging every direction to get free.

Magnetic restraints. He tried to relax. He squeezed his eyes shut, spilling hot tears of agonized relief. It was over. Awake.

He tried to look over his body for the bite wounds. His left arm had been hanging off his shoulder. He'd run a kilometer on a shredded foot. There would be a stump of bone left.

Smooth hands touched his face.

Silken speech grazed his tender mind.

There were new words in his head—an edifice of language.

"Am I...whole?" he asked in Andalvian, a rolling tongue of layered meanings; he'd said seven things in that one phrase. He could be done with slaver speech at last.

"Yes." Lyli ran a wicking cloth over his cheeks and neck. "You are twenty years of age, and located in Emporia in Unity. How do you feel?"

Caiden blinked away fresh tears. "Broken," he rasped, "and put back together."

His voice sounded strange. Deeper and coarse. Not just raw from screams.

His brain felt scoured, filled with tingles that twisted away like a flock of starlings each time his thoughts approached. What bugs were they picking at in there?

Accelerated concepts bubbled in Caiden's mind; brain plasticity, cognitive development, emotional utility. New modes of thinking that had been involuted into his mind during the accel would begin to differentiate outward as he utilized them, the liquid crystals of his brain reoriented. Even the way he appraised his condition was different. As if by leaving youth he had taken a step back from his own mind.

With a *snap*, the magnetic restraints opened, and Caiden fell off the frame. Growing pains flowed through him like waterfalls over shifting rocks, and he wailed as he fell into the Cartographer's arms. His body was too heavy and she crumpled to her knees, arms around his torso. He was taller...so much taller than her now.

"Sorry..." Caiden whimpered as he stabilized on all fours. Vicious ache vibrated every bone. His vision mushed up, everything over-bright, but he didn't need to see to know something was wrong.

Waves of ashy hair cascaded around him and brambled off his face. His skin was taut, muscles brittle, bones rubber. He was more pain than flesh. Caiden wept, which blurred his vision more.

"I understand this is very strange for you, Passager." Lyli tenderly helped him crawl to a standing position. "Your acceleration appears to have been successful, but your emotional distress exceeds even the effects of compounded adolescence."

"A dream."

"The incubation should not stimulate dreams."

But the memory jog nightmares would hound him everywhere.

"Passager Endirion!" she called.

Footsteps thundered in from the outer hall.

Caiden blinked away more tears. His lungs were two clouds of pinpricks.

A stronger, taller set of arms encircled his torso and supported him, guiding his feet forward. "Hi, kid." En's voice wavered. She started to lead him to a bench by the wall, but a full-length mirror caught his eye—the shock slammed him so forcefully, he tripped to the floor.

A strangled sound lodged in his throat as he recoiled from the wretched thing looking back.

CHAPTER 19

FORGED

En clutched Caiden as he rocked in horror before the mirror.

Taller by eight inches. Hair down to mid-back, and a *beard* trailing with it. Scrawny muscles stretched on spindly bones, frame too large for his skin, tendons too tight for his bones. Every movement strummed bands of ache. His face was drawn and pimply, with pronounced freckles over his nose and cheeks looking like the spots that appeared on a diseased creature just before it died.

He felt injected into a new version of himself, shoved into a doll that was his property, his slave to drive with his will.

This was everything he'd wanted. He couldn't hate it now.

This is the body, the blade, that will end the Casthen.

Loathing swelled up, but he closed his eyes and probed for the familiar anger deep in him. It was there. Quiet, and differently shaped. Gone was the hot, biting rage of his fourteen-year-old self. The accelerated years had packed it into a brightly smoldering ember laced with meaning. Caiden still had the same thoughts and feelings about the Casthen, but they linked up and arranged, where before they'd just been fuel tossed into that inferno of hate.

En guided him to the bench and made him sit. "Lyli, dear, some slick-pads and a flamecomb, please? And the other items I brought."

Caiden wobbled, dizzy and vibrating.

"Six is a lot of time for what a small body you had. Adolescence is meant to be gradual. I rarely agree with Taitn, but...I wish you'd chosen slow."

"Taitn…" The voice wasn't his own anymore. Time and nightmares had chewed that up too. "Where?"

"He…couldn't bear to look. And he started to—well." En sighed. "I'll get you fixed up. Just sit and rest."

Lyli returned and deposited a stack of items beside En. "I apologize for my oversight." She bowed. "I should have inquired what areas of keratin suppression to employ since it was so many years. I should have anticipated the shock. Most patients accelerate amounts less than six months."

"Just as well," En said, mustering cheer. "I've been dying to braid his hair."

Caiden raised a trembling hand to comb through the tousled mess of his long locks. His claws snagged there, and En gently untangled him.

"Take your time, Passagers." Lyli's lips curled, the kindness in her smile undermined by a ghostly jaw. She bowed again, then left the room.

Disappointment shut Caiden down. His crooked body hunched forward and he closed his eyes, attempting to focus on nothingness as Panca had taught him.

While Caiden steeped in his daze, En fussed with him, wiping his sweat with a tingling cloth. She wielded a device like a brush with teeth of tiny flame, and stroked this over his face and neck, then through fistfuls of his hair. Finally she pulled all his blond locks back to make a tight weave, combing her fingers over his scalp, a sensation that soothed him half to sleep before he remembered sleep was sand and blood and teeth. He jerked alert, and she caught his face in her hands.

"All right, easy," En said, and backed away. "Here, I bought these for you."

She set a stack of clothing on his lap. New colors and textiles: rich blue, rosy gray, black—and many belts. Embarrassment tugged at him distantly; he was only clad in underclothes, much too tight.

En sat nearby, turned away to give him privacy, and shifted form: shorter, skin darker, and hair lengthening so he had something new to braid while giving Caiden space.

Caiden stood weakly, peeled off the underclothes of his younger self, and dressed awkwardly, constantly misjudging his new strength. Too soft, too hard. As if he needed another learning curve. He worked raw ligaments, stumbling over his bones, wincing through twinges.

The new clothes hugged his skin. The morphcoat slicked into tiny iridescent black feathers, sculpted around his shoulders. His gray undershirt's dense gossamer mesh captured and dispersed heat. The overshirt was a thick, soft material he'd seen En wear, with angular seams in a Cartographer style. The baggy black trousers—matte leather but as soft as everything else—hid his ungainly legs.

Caiden rubbed at layered growing pains in his shoulders. His fingers grazed the brand, and he recoiled, grimaced, then quested his fingers up the complex braid En had fixed against his skull.

He snapped up his boots and straightened.

"Ready to look again?" En asked, drawing close, but as Caiden pivoted to the mirror, En snatched his shoulders and pinned him with a fiery gaze. "Your body will fill out *fast* with correct nutrition and exercise. I have a whole regimen of combat sparring lined up for you, and I can blackmail Ksiñe into cooking whatever you want. The accelerated time is still bundled into your cells and will blossom as you get used to your body and mind. Right now you're dismayed but *be gentle to yourself*."

There *was* a buzzing in him, as if a little exertion would floresce the bunched capabilities and plump out his skinny, hollowed new self.

En nodded firmly and twirled Caiden to face the mirror.

This is it. This is me.

The dashing clothing hid some of his frailty. His mind felt more capable but this new physique looked like the acceleration had stretched more holes in him.

"So much for being stronger." Even his voice was so brittle it broke. Not the voice of a hero.

Thanks to En, he was clean-shaven, hair half the length and smartly weaved away from his face. There was a hardness in his features that wasn't just his frown. His skin was too pale and the freckles too stark. Even his hair wasn't as bronzed as it had once been. He looked fake, artificially ideal, like a piece of metal too smooth and shiny to have been around for long.

It looked like Threi's skin. Too perfect and new.

The thought intruded, unwanted.

Did the Casthen have acceleration chambers too? Accelerated, Graven Enforcers. Was Threi the only one?

En said, "We'll get muscle on you, don't worry. Skin'll clear up too."

"You don't have to use slaver speech with me anymore," Caiden told him in Andalvian, conveying gratitude and many more thoughts in the same words. "What do you use?"

"Shihl is what most passagers speak," En said in a new tongue, crisp and melodic.

"I get to fly now," Caiden said in Shihl. He tried on a grin, not as ragged-looking as he imagined. "For justice, I need wings as much as I need muscle."

"Justice, huh? Come on, I bet gallant's waiting." En signaled the doorway's dissolve, then led Caiden through.

In the Cartographers' hall outside, Taitn sat against a wall, face in his hands and fingers twisted into his hair.

Lyli stood at a safe distance, knuckles kneading her lips. She looked as if she couldn't decide whether to comfort Taitn or not. When she spotted Caiden emerging, she straightened.

Taitn shot to his feet, expression glazed, processing Caiden's put-together look. Then he blinked and fumbled in a satchel. "Here, I got—Here. Eat." He handed Caiden a ramia.

The scents awakened a ravenous hunger. Caiden tore into it, crunching the salty flakes, tender meat, and luscious sauces. He moaned and had to force himself to slow down.

Taitn seemed heartened, and smiled. He draped an arm around Caiden's bony shoulders.

As they left the Cartographers' warrens, Lyli said, "Farewell, Passagers. Please return if you require further medical treatment or rehabilitation."

Caiden waved farewell, but it dawned on him that he wouldn't see Lyli again. The crew would be fleeing the dangers of Unity as soon as Caiden could pilot by himself and Laythan had his own ship ready. Caiden was keeping the *Azura*, and he would find a way to Çydanza, with or without the crew.

En hummed. "You're gonna be pretty handsome when we get you filled out and muscled up. I have an idea where to send you when—"

"Don't," Taitn snarled. "Acceleration is aging and synaptic conditioning, *not* experience. He's still a child, and will be for a while. Maturation isn't a matter of shoving time into a body."

The conviction in that statement stung. Caiden mulled it over while the electricity between Taitn and En turned vicious.

En halted. "And you're a grown man, but your experience is still—"

Taitn threw a punch at En's jaw, but En blocked it with a wrist and stepped in closer. His playful expression grew earnest, and his face and physique changed, smoke spilling around her gray eyes, skin paling, musculature toning lean. The change seemed intended as an insult. A statement, at the least. "*Maturation* means discovering all the different facets of who we feel right being and how we fit into a complex world. Winn has the benefit of a family of misfits; each of us can point him in the right different directions to figure things out for himself. Stop assuming my intentions are harmful just—"

"What would you know about discovering yourself?"

En's jaw flexed as she chewed on a retort. "I know there was a time when you didn't think my intentions so foul."

"Hey," Caiden barked, hoping he had the merit now to break up spats like this.

En glanced over, apologetic, then mustered back her usual cheer. "The most important question is…" She turned back to Taitn, letting a somber glare drag out uncomfortably long. "Did you talk to Lyli?"

Taitn rolled his eyes. Pink spread through his cheeks.

"That's a no." En smiled and swiped her hair away from an expression of forced nonchalance as the three of them resumed walking.

A puzzling forest of birch and iris filled up the lightseep walls around them.

Caiden cut the simmering tension. "What…Excuse the phrasing, but what *was* Lyli? Her skin, it…" What would be rude to inadvertently imply? He'd noticed raciation in both humans and xenids. And who knew what sort of "mosaic" he himself was.

"She's a survivor," En said. "Flung into a particularly bad universe for humans. It's filled with radiation and screws with scalar gravity nodes. Some crew survived and were rescued, but their white blood cells were wiped out, bone marrow problems, others had their skin and muscles melt—" En waved a dismissive hand. "Anyway. Lyli is still healing; the treatments give that diaphonization look, but I'd say it's working in her favor." He winked at Taitn. "You should talk to her. I saw her hair is still—"

"Why don't *you* talk to her." Taitn strode faster, pulling ahead.

En merely laughed, but the sound was tight. "Oh, I did. She was dismayed that you left so early. Then she had to call *me*. And now I need to impersonate some people and exercise some fists to talk with some potential gloss-buyers. I'll see you two back at Pent's."

En split off with a wave and a happy jog that Caiden could now tell was half-forced. Minutiae of body language he had missed before were brighter to his grown-up brain.

He continued on with Taitn through parts of Emporia that looked familiar due to the vistas projected in the jeweled walls. It made sense to paint such a vast place for easy navigation, rather than everywhere looking the same.

The rhythm of Taitn's breathing ratcheted up, until he let it all out in one go: "I'm sorry. I shouldn't have left."

Caiden shrugged. "I didn't want to see myself either."

"It's not that…"

The man didn't elaborate, and Caiden let it go.

They passed into a huge concourse projected with gigantic waterfalls, close to Pent's depository. The scene had shifted to artificial night. Water cascades glittered like nebulae.

"You screamed." The dim light obscured Taitn's face. "A lot. I couldn't interrupt the incubation phase. And the night before, on the ship…you screamed then too."

Caiden took a moment to arrange his new thinking—gone was the shame, secrecy, and stumbling of his youth. "Panca said my brain will perseverate nightmares about the memory jog every time I sleep." The words came out quieter than he intended, husked raw by his new voice.

Taitn stopped walking. "If I had known—"

Caiden shrugged again with a wry smile. "I wouldn't have let you stop me doing the memory jog. I was brash and furious, remember? Now I'm shrewd and furious." He chuckled. "I feel good about it. Even if those memories keep cutting me for the rest of my life, people will see what the Casthen have done, no matter what the Primes say. That's all I can rely on right now. I can't save my child self from what I endured, but I can do something for others who are in that same place."

Worth any cost. He'd been a seed set adrift on a strange wind just before the field was torched—it was time to sprout now.

"Brave." Taitn continued walking. "Just don't let bravery become stupid overconfidence. Like En."

"His fighting? He told me he likes fights."

"He likes to punish himself. It's different. His surface cheeriness is a smokescreen." Taitn's feet scuffed as he walked. "People punish themselves when they hate who they are: saying foul words about yourself, or fighting until all of you is a pulp. We hope our words will push us to be stronger, or a better self will walk away from a bloody mess, but you can't smash yourself into shape. Own what you hate, and polish the rest of you until that hated part is outshined completely."

Caiden had certainly been a bloody mess in the nightmares he'd endured to pay for his new body. Hopefully a better self was walking away, even if it didn't look it.

He said, "You're awfully hard on En."

Taitn winced and raked his fingers through his hair and down his bearded cheeks, frowning. "He—she and I got off on the wrong foot. I never knew him before all the augmentation . . . Maybe that—Maybe I'd be nicer to him if I had. I don't know."

"I have a very important question," Caiden said. The pause stretched out the sullen mood. He asked, "Did you only bring one ramia?"

Taitn guffawed and rummaged for two more in his bag.

Caiden relished them in happier silence during the lift ride to Pent's vast depository.

The *Azura* rested inside the "shielding hollow" blister in the lightseep obsidian wall, a quiet black bird in a nest of white glow. She needed repairs and tuning. The acceleration had shriveled Caiden's body, but his mind was filled and eager.

Taitn smiled and stayed outside as Caiden strode into the hollow through its milky membrane of light. Breath caught in his throat. He circled his starship, gaping like a fool. Panca walked out of the bay and watched him.

"Panca, you and Taitn were right. She's unlike anything out there."

He had words for the ship's various parts. He recognized the style of her thrusters, and could tell from the lattice abrasions that she had wave-collapse resonance shields. But what stunned him were the stark *gaps* in his knowledge. There were no known words or concepts for so many parts of her. She was unique.

"You don't speak slaver anymore," Panca said in Andalvian. Her words also meant, *You're free*.

Caiden beamed and followed her inside to the serene new world of the engine room. His brain assembled words and ideas into flowing constructs as his gaze swept across the engine and auxiliary machines. "It's almost... a tiny stellar engine, but it uses glossy power." He ran his hand over the striated back of an energy resonance chamber to a cylinder fowling that glittered with inner particles. "This is the housing for the orb guidance?"

Panca nodded and perched her hands on her hips. "Controls mini thrusters."

Replacement parts that Panca had gathered were collected on the floor, and Caiden had names for most things now: capacitors, malta coils, dielectrics, braided glossy clusters.

Soon he was dashing, crouching, and crawling between units. "The bleed air off the Loran cowl recycles back into the ramjet!" He laughed as concepts and words sprang to mind, filling out a rich field of knowledge. He was stumbling over his own feet and looked like a creature ready for death, but the acceleration *had* filled him with the knowledge and capability he'd lost during a childhood of slavery.

Panca's gray face softened in mirth. "See why neural crown control doesn't work?"

"The stagger's broken. What's this?" He grazed a hand over a glassy encasement. Its vibrations greeted his palm and quickened his pulse.

"I think responder for universe florescer."

"Right, to maintain the rind, drawing on the same fuel as the engine."

He ran a finger down the draw-strip of the fuel tower, a pyramid on which the fuel prism rested. Braided tubes held energy the blue color of sulphur fire. Pink stars zipped through and fed tucked-away chambers.

"Quantum feedback loops...Do these only work in the *Azura*'s universe?"

"Haven't seen 'em run," Panca said.

Caiden stood. His grown heart raced, hardly big enough to contain this new excitement. Once the repairs were done, he would finally have his wings. "There's a lot to fix."

Panca smiled. "Let's start."

CHAPTER 20

SHARPENED

Hold still." Spots of concentration bubbled over the bridge of Ksiñe's nose. He gripped Caiden's skull with a coppery-gloved hand, and maneuvered it at painful angles.

Caiden stopped fidgeting in the pilot's seat. Dimples of air blossomed around his face while data arranged along those nodes to map his extended nervous system and coupled quantum states.

Every pilot required a neural implant for direct mental contact with ship controls, rather than the more difficult physical twitch drive. It would also bond his consciousness to the *Azura*'s functioning over time, entangling their mirror neurons, letting her learn his intentions and proclivities. For the implant, ultrasonics would create a nanostructure inside his pineal gland using local material—giving Ksiñe direct access to his brain, where one "accidental" slip could kill or impair him.

Ksiñe hadn't softened up since Caiden put everyone's lives in danger at the Den. Caiden needed forgiveness. The implant did double duty as it forced the medic to spend time with him; maybe long enough to bridge some conversation.

Ksiñe's posture lost its keen edge, becoming elegant as he worked. The red eyeshine in his pupils was less ferocious and more surgical, focused. On his shoulder, his whipkin pet watched with big eyes and pert little ears.

Caiden cleared his throat. "How long have you had her?"

Ksiñe's posture sharpened. Vexed scarlet freckles swarmed over his cheeks and neck. "Hold *still*, if you want to live."

Caiden sighed and reminded himself that the Andalvian's sour attitude had a valid source, just as Caiden's anger had been born from slaughter. How many awful or closed-off or ignorant people were the result of a prior hardship for which they shouldn't be blamed? And how many, like Leta, were simply misunderstood or struggled to connect?

Andalvian culture was stoic, yet they were expressive by biological nature. The dichotomy, as Ksiñe exemplified, often led to unhealthy repression. Although Ksiñe's malevolence dimmed considerably in his native Andalvian language, now that Caiden could speak it.

Heat boiled in Caiden's brain as Ksiñe began to maneuver laser sonic frequencies to build the implant.

One step closer to flying. Then I hunt Çydanza.

His consciousness foamed, thoughts indistinct, and a purr slithered from one ear to the other. Weird senses slipped through: the cold armrests, rogue infrared content in the overhead lights, Ksiñe smelling like plants and rain.

The whipkin crawled timidly into Caiden's lap. Her furry body stretched long then bunched up round, with folds of extra skin piling around her. Caiden couldn't move his head to look down, but he smiled and reached up to stroke her. She nipped once, and chittered, then rubbed her forehead into his palm.

"Done." Ksiñe shoved Caiden's head away. "Test now."

Caiden nestled his skull into the headrest cradle. His brain expanded, knitting with the *Azura*'s data cloud at the edges. His proprioception expanded to include the ship's hybrid musculature, its inner hums, and the glossy lightseep spine of it, which lay in his awareness like a lightning bolt dormant in clouds. "I can feel the perception control and memory structures."

"Good."

Ksiñe noticed that the whipkin had defected onto Caiden's lap. Blue bands like hot flame slashed his temples. He kissed a sound between his teeth, and she scurried up to cower around his neck.

Caiden stifled a chuckle and peeled from the seat. His body was rubbery, but the new mental connection with the ship glowed strong. In the clouded cockpit windows he caught his reflection and the promised results of the accelerated years. Combat sparring and nutritious cooking had filled out his emaciation and remedied his clumsiness. His gangly limbs of fourteen had evened against his height, and with lean muscle padding him he appeared finely chiseled rather than carved out. His face was a clean shave, but his shoulder-length hair sprung from a lazy tie. The braids En made were impossible to replicate.

He glimpsed a stronger, more mature self, someone who could throttle his temper. Someone good enough to destroy the Casthen.

Someone who wouldn't have left Leta alone in the transport.

Ksiñe said quietly, "Twenty months, ephemeris time."

"Huh?"

"How old whipkin is. You asked." Teal clouds wafted across Ksiñe's collarbones, even as he looked away and fussily organized his tools back in a case. "I have had her since she was in egg."

Caiden suppressed his smile. It seemed the pet's approval was worth something. She wrestled out of Ksiñe's shirt and circled his torso. Her webbed fingers gripped and her body flattened, smoothing out the white and indigo patterns in her fur.

"A forest species? Built to climb?"

"And glide and swim. From saline woodland."

Her little nose sniffed in Caiden's direction.

En strode abruptly through the shielding hollow's milky membrane, clutching her chest. Several hues of blood streaked her. She grinned and sucked on a split lip. "Caused a bit of trouble selling the gloss. The Dynast is *ravenous* for it, have some special project going on that requires loads."

Panca stalled her work nearby and headed for a roll of tools. It made sense that a mechanic would repair injuries to someone as augmented as En, but En scowled as she plonked down against a wall and opened her shirt, looking away. Her skin un-pigmented, and the inner mechanisms and materials opened up in petals or scales or dissolved entirely, to expose En's beating heart and pulsing lungs in a vivid tangle of components.

Panca investigated. "The dilatant layer's glitched again. Frustration?"

En's lips tightened. She scraped at a streak of blood on her cheek and shrugged.

Caiden asked Ksiñe quietly, "What's with En's shift in mood?"

Ksiñe delivered a reliably unadorned answer, "They joined Laythan to figure out who they wanted to be, but now cannot patch things with Taitn or sit still with Panca, so make no progress. Multiverse is full of distractions. Fighting, flirting, and...En loves all the F's. Distractions."

Caiden watched the pair struggle. Panca probed a tiny awl into En's mangled chest. "Heart leaflets obstructed again. Holding in resentment." She withdrew her tools and placed slender fingers over the blue bulge of En's heart, focused in her sense-sea.

En flinched hard, jarring Panca away. "I can do without the leaflets. Just fix the mini-actuators, yeah?" She looked over at Caiden. "You getting any sleep? Those are some dark circles around your eyes, kid. You need rest to integrate the acceleration."

Caiden had hardly slept at all, but he would have to face the nightmares at some point.

Soon.

He exhaled and turned to Ksiñe, trying to soften up an accusation that had been festering in the corner of his mind: "When you inspected my brain and makeup right before the memory jog...did you see I would have this side effect, that it would twist my synaptic firing and perseverate the event in dreams?"

The Andalvian's eyeshine flashed as his gaze darted away. He stroked the whipkin's back and didn't answer.

About as good as a yes.

Caiden hesitated. Andalvian was a language of interweaved implications. He laced blame in where it was due, and said, "I'm sorry for what happened in the Den. The nightmares are why my fear is still raw and biting. They'll remind me for the rest of my life that when the slaughter started, I hid and ran. I let everyone die, to save myself."

Ksiñe moved brusquely, stowing his case in a wall compartment. "Running might have been best choice."

"Nothing about my sister's death is *best*," Caiden snapped as some reflex jerked in him. It was the first time he'd called her *sister*, after learning what siblings were. The new label, by giving meaning to their relationship, made his heart ache a thousand times worse.

"Immoral choice can lead to morally positive gains." Ksiñe scooped up the whipkin and petted her belly. Black frustration drained from his features. "Running made you stronger. What you do with strength matters and validates. Violence done to you is painful—transmute pain back into violence."

Caiden recalled something Taitn had alluded to. "You have history with the Casthen, don't you?"

Ksiñe's scarlet eyeshine fixed into a glow as he stared. "You will learn to be vicious to survive. Multiverse has many tastes, and chews us up differently depending on species. Andalvians are a game to some; a thing to break and make our skin show pain, grief, arousal, shame. I broke into something so sharp no one dared touch me." The whipkin burrowed into his jacket. He hugged her, and his skin blanched. A tiny snarl wrinkled the bridge of his nose. "Casthen slaughtered and I slaughtered them all back, but they are too immense to stop forever."

Caiden said, "I'll be even sharper. The nightmares are sharpening me into a blade, a trowel that can dig up the Casthen's deep roots for good. I'll figure out how to get to the Casthen Harvest and to Çydanza. The Cartographers or Dynast must know."

His aim sounded childish and the logic had holes, but the breadth of *choice* in a multiverse so vast paralyzed him whenever he tried to think about what else to do with his life. Justice was simple, straightforward, and good.

Ksiñe petted the whipkin's back as she flattened against his chest. "Each time a blade is sharpened, material is lost. Sharpen too many times and there is nothing left. It becomes thin and brittle, easy to break."

"Then I'd better sharpen up fast." Caiden rose to his feet. He probed the new neural link with the ship, which glowed warm and strong. "These wings are patched up. It's time I learned to fly."

"Winn!" En called across the bay. "Not a great time to ask about flight. Laythan's trying to rush his new ship's—the *Second Wind*'s—configurations to get us far away while also potentially exploding, and Taitn is arguing for an initial test run of crossover and egress. Let their dust settle and blood cool for a bit."

Panca was still repairing, and chastised En. "You let the biomineraliza-tion get beat to pulp, it'll need replacement code. Is this where Taitn—"

"Don't." En untangled and stood, rushing to close up the machinery of her chest and rebuckle her clothing. Huffing, she turned to Caiden. "I have somewhere I want to take you before we leave."

"Where?" Caiden asked, suspicious.

"Oh, it's better to be shown. Trust me."

"Tell me plainly, or I refuse."

She grinned. "Laythan thinks you need control, I think you need release. Taitn thinks you should go slow, I say you should hit something. Your altru-ism is admirable, kid, but it comes with a temper you need to get a handle on, and you need to realize that not all memories have to haunt us."

Caiden's nightmares weren't just memories but all permutations of the event, as if his mind struggled to freshen the horror each time. He narrowed his eyes and scratched at his morphcoat's feathers.

"Come on." En strode over with a bounce back in her step, and offered a hand. "Need to get you cleaned up first for this, your hair looks horrendous."

CHAPTER 21

LETA

Fidgety and unsure whether to be intrigued or terrified, Caiden tousled his freshly cut hair—a couple inches long on top, cropped shorter down the sides—and ran a hand over his jaw and the shadow of facial hair.

A vibrant red navigation thread twined the air, leading him and En into cramped and intimate hallways. There was less lightseep obsidian visible here, where the Graven bones of Emporia filled in with the muscle of shops, bars, and sport rings.

"We're meeting a friend of mine," En said as he stopped in front of a nondescript door. "These are private quarters, not working. Well—sometimes working. But not today. Anyway, there are words you need to hear and things you need to say. So, whatever or whoever you need, that's what's here."

"Your vagueness isn't boosting my faith in your intentions."

En softened with a smile that was new: delicate and genuine, without the coy edge. "I keep my stories and try to grow from them. The right reflections at the right time did wonders. Maybe they'll do the same for you."

A tender look still on his face, En placed his hand on the door's surface. A red glow frothed around it, shooting off particles of information.

"Daylight?" said a female voice from within, projected by the door.

"I brought him, lovely," En said.

The door opened, Caiden dithered, and En shoved him forward.

In the middle of the mostly empty room stood—levitated?—a fair, lavender figure. The shape was vaguely human, composed of diaphanous gauze like countless layers of spider-web veils draped over a porous, transparent skeleton.

It was a vishkant, a mnemonid, like the one he'd seen in the Cartographers' Den, the creature that had changed appearance as his mind began to see familiar things in their features, conforming to his thoughts and desires.

Vishkant were powerful. Often predatory.

"All right. Play nice." En smiled, backed up, and signaled the door closed. Caiden smacked into it as he turned to follow. He patted the surface. "En? Hey!" He turned to the vishkant, apologetic. "I should—"

As his gaze moved over them, they grew more solid, their gossamer cloud condensing into an undecided human shape.

Caiden frowned and cleared his throat. "I'm sorry, I have to... t-to go."

Vishkant could perceive memories and mental activity. This one's vapor form flickered like static while Caiden's thoughts flailed, reflecting his discomfort.

"You're safe here," they said in a feminine voice at once familiar and strange. "Relax."

Caiden had more than enough of his memories every time he slept, he didn't need them in the flesh. He pressed his back against the door. "I'm sorry if En promised you something. I really... should go..."

Her face was a blur of various pretty features as she stared at him, *into* him in a way that was both hypnotic and disconcerting. Her body solidified, dewy gauze slicked into skin and a simple tunic dress.

"You've been through a lot, haven't you?" Her voice grew sweet and quiet like a shy voice he'd heard before. "Relax, Caiden."

"My name's..." His voice diminished until he couldn't hear it over the roar of his bloodstream as the vishkant's face settled. Large hazel eyes in thoughtful features. Flower-pink lips. Fawn-brown hair rolled over her shoulders, bleached from sun and disheveled as if straight from a breeze.

She was Leta, but somewhere around Caiden's age of twenty.

"I—I..." Caiden stammered as she walked up, inches from him. "But I left—"

"I know." The girl's features crumpled in a frown, her lip quivered, and she wrapped her arms around him, fitting softly against his chest. "You were always so sweet to me, Cai."

It really was her voice. Airy, tranquil. She smelled of sweetgrass, clover, and wildflowers. She squeezed him harder—solid and real.

"You survived?" Caiden buckled, wrapping his arms around her. Her warmth seeped into him and he was instantly back in a sunlit field, home, where the air was sweet and nothing demanded of him. A lump lodged in his throat but he managed to say, "I'm so sorry."

"Don't blame yourself for what happened. You've been through so much and haven't stopped running since that day. Please stop here with me for a moment, I promise you're safe." She nuzzled his shoulder.

Caiden's misery cracked open, flooding the canyon that relief gouged into him. He tilted his forehead into her hair and held her tighter, but this wasn't the Leta of his memories. Like him, she was older, taller, composed, and he had abandoned child Leta to the stench and the darkness, the beasts and their insatiable hunger. He'd run, never the hero she'd thought he was.

"I need to leave," he whispered. "I'm very sorry. But this is . . . You're not her."

Leta is dead.

His body felt poorly built again, ravaged by the thundering of shoved-in years and compacted adolescent emotions. Had he been brought here just to feel miserable at the reality of his failure? Leta could not have survived, and even if she had, she'd be impossible to find in this vast multiverse. The very nature of freedom threw her far from reach.

"It wasn't your fault." She looked up and disarmed him, her eyes so warm. Her appearance was pruned by his thoughts, accentuating features of the compassionate and analytic Leta he knew when she was happy alone with him, rather than the shelled-off and abuse-tender girl he'd comforted so often. "Nothing that happened was your doing. Your bravery made me feel brave."

Brave to sit and wait for death. Caiden wanted to pour apologies into her. His mind burgeoned with nightmare scenes. "I'm sorry." He pushed her away. The void between filled with cool air.

"Don't be." She smiled, sunshine. "You don't ever need to be sorry for what was done to you. You're still as wonderful as always. I can see how soft your heart really is under all that temper. Revenge isn't the answer, it doesn't suit you."

Those little sparks of denial lit the inferno of Caiden's temper. "*Everyone* is trying to talk me out of justice, as if it's so simple to move past slaughter."

Before him stood the memory of a precious life snuffed out. His righteous rage, which everyone was trying to extinguish, was exactly the determined fire that could destroy the Casthen. Over centuries, no one else had done it.

"I'll *make* revenge suit me. I can make sure no one else loses as much as we lost. I survived, plagued with remembrance, so I can do this one immense thing."

Leta shook her head. "You're taking responsibility for events that weren't your fault. The nophek operation, the genocide, the side effects of the memory jog. Caiden..." She hugged him fiercely, fitting her sunny warmth against his frustration. He didn't pry her off but wasn't sure what to do with his arms, and his head filled with the scent of sweetgrass. Voice muffled against his coat, she said, "You don't have to let go of your reasons for wanting justice. Those are what make you who you are, the person I loved. But you have to start forgiving yourself for the things that are out of your control. No one expects you to be infallible and indestructible so quickly. You are spirited and kindhearted and self-sacrificing, and that is so much more powerful."

The pressure of her embrace and the salve of her words wrung Caiden's temper dry. He crushed her close. She knew everything, even what he wouldn't admit, but it didn't change the mountain of struggle ahead. His eyes teared, and he let the sobs find their course, and Leta pulled his wrist back with her as she uncurled from his arms. Behind her stretched a plush bed the color of clouds.

"Rest," Leta whispered. "No one from your old life would want to see you always in pain for their sake. You deserve care too. And how are you going to help anyone if you push yourself till you break?"

Laboring under the heft of Leta's wise words, Caiden sat on the bed. She settled next to him and wrapped her arms around his waist, snuggling into his side. If he was to be thrashed with nightmares all his life, at least he could be balmed by one sweet, healing, affirming cloud of a dream for a moment.

"Memories or not," he said, weary, "I know your nature lets you understand. Thank you for that."

The vishkant's eyes twinkled as she gazed across him, observing the invisible. "Endirion won me out of a life of service. I've owed him since, and I'm so happy that favor was you. And of everything your thoughts might have evoked from your past, I'm glad it's someone you missed."

An electric shiver ran through him. He fell back on the bed and rolled on his side. Leta bunched in his arms and pressed her forehead against his collarbones, releasing a whimpering sigh. Caiden inhaled the sweetgrass scent of her hair and imagined, guiltily, that things hadn't changed, they had lived on, family unbroken. Orchard grass and leafy alfalfa swayed around them in ripples, purple flower heads bobbing in the breeze. Spicy fragrances baked off a sunny oak shading them, and Caiden's worries were mundane and few.

Mind raw from grief and stuffed with warm visions, Caiden didn't have nightmares as he fell asleep with Leta's living weight in his arms. When he finally woke, he felt *rested* for the first time since the desert. Dim light bathed him. The bed radiated heat. His aged body was untangled of tense knots and growing pains, and every sense of not quite being his own.

The vishkant lay beside him in a neutral state: a velvety cloud, face vague through a thousand particle veils. Caiden reached for her gauzy shoulder in fascination and touched cool air before she turned and his hand buried into waves of solid, fawn-colored hair. Chicory flowers scattered in the curls.

Caiden raised his hand to stop her. "You don't have to change. I know you're *you*, not... not the girl in my memories. And I want to thank you. *You*, not... Do you know what I mean?"

Idiot. He growled out a sigh.

"I know." She chuckled. "But you need her." The vishkant's diaphanous folds waved over her transparent skeleton to clothe it in Leta's body, dressed in the creamy tunic with a chicory-blue sash. She smiled sunlight. "And I'm young, I can't always choose what I become."

Caiden took her hand, at first featherlight and downy before his memories coaxed it solid. A vishkant's appearance was partly an individual hallucination elicited by pheromone, and a reflex on the part of the vishkant, molding their molecular constitution. "Can you tell me about your kind?"

Leta giggled. "You're wondering if I'm real or illusion. They're identical. Your brain fires the same way whether you're remembering an event or living through it the first time."

"Can you see *all* of my memories?"

"Young vishkant can only see recent memory and thoughts. As we age, we lose that ability but can see the deeper past. We are very fragile, yet almost impossible to destroy. We are shy and insecure but suited to commanding others. Coveted and dreaded."

"You're another species this multiverse conspires to exploit because of your abilities. The sort of slavery I want to end."

"Judge individuals as individual: there's too much variety in the multiverse for broad statements to ever serve us well. This multiverse also has goodness—like you and Endirion Day."

She sat up and circled her thumb over her palm, spinning a purple-blue hue that hardened into a glassy replica of a chicory flower. She handed it to him. "I recognize the wonderful side of you. Anger abrades it, but also polishes: the true, shining core of you, Caiden."

The flower was perfectly detailed, down to the serration on the petal edges and the white tips on its inner rays.

"Would Leta forgive me for running, if she'd lived? I wasn't wonderful then—"

"But you can be now." She smoothed out the hair by his temples, pasted by dried tears. "Your choices don't have to stem from what happened in the desert. You're not the boy who ran."

CHAPTER 22

FLIGHT

His steps were lighter as he made his way back through Emporia toward the lift concourse. He'd been gone a few ephemeris hours, hopefully long enough for Laythan and Taitn to have settled their argument about whether to leave Unity quickly or first do a test flight with the new ship, the *Second Wind*. If Taitn could show Caiden the basics of the *Azura*, he could fly alongside them on the test cruise—perfect.

Trekking back, he soaked in the diversity of Emporia. Projections filled lightseep walls with artistic holo-renditions of nebulae and kelp forests and snowy peaks. Landscapes blurred in and out of phase or one into the other as his viewing angle changed. The variety of realistic biomes amazed him, while also reminding him of all the experiences he had grown up without.

He followed the navigation threads while dodging the larger or stranger xenid types. He was now able to spot semi-corporeal xenids like sopheids, nareids, and syncrasids.

Caiden entered the vast concourse painted in waterfalls. The crowd flowed about their business—but in one spot, it eddied. People turned to look the same direction, some stopped, uneasy, others slowed their pace.

Caiden almost missed it: striding away from the concourse to follow the Dynast's copper navigation thread...dressed all in fitted black clothing, without Casthen armor, marched Threi.

The bastard's face was unmistakable: too pale and perfect like a portrait blanked and redrawn too many times, and his thick, short hair was mussed into dark snarls.

Something was slung over Threi's shoulder, handled like property. A child? A slave? The body was hooded, a few trickles of hair spilling out.

Dizzy fire lapped in Caiden's breast, burning up the softness Leta had left there.

More of the crowd around Threi snagged and took notice as he passed by. Given how he'd affected Cartographer Sina with his suggestions—albeit with difficulty—he had to be fairly Graven, and those he passed were snared in a much smaller wave of the same awe that the Dynast Prime had evoked.

Nausea heaved in Caiden's belly and his morphcoat bristled into quills. How quickly his good mood and clear thinking muddled. He wasn't the impulsive child who would have fought Threi head-on, but maybe if he followed, he could see what Threi was up to. He picked a safe distance and followed the Casthen Enforcer. It couldn't hurt to see where that copper thread led, or why Threi wasn't wearing any armor.

The smoky quartz corridor to the Dynast's district was teeming with Dynast sentinels. They bristled at Threi's passing, polarizing toward him before their shoulders relaxed—some bowed—heads swiveling to trace him until he'd gone. Caiden used their distraction to slip by with other xenids, walking with purpose and using lightseep columns to shield himself from view. This was still public space, and he was breaking no rules, but his racing pulse choked him, heat turned to sweat. If he'd left his hair twenty inches long, he might've had a better disguise.

Threi turned through a doorway. Caiden hung back for a beat, then followed.

Straight into a palace.

A massive space one kilometer across hollowed out Emporia's lightseep ruins. Where the rest of Emporia's lightseep was simple: hexagonally walled hollows, straight columns, angular joins, and big flat facades...this space had fluted columns and daises and stairs and archways puzzled together like masterfully cut jewels. On every surface in every direction, the lightseep obsidian's colors slithered between translucent and solid, light-filled or shadow-soaked, tricking the eye with reflective angles and invisible alignments.

These magnificent bones hinted at the Graven ruin's original shape, before it was stripped of whatever spiritual materials had fleshed it out.

Caiden marveled all around as he fit himself among pockets of crowd, most of whom were marveling too. Threi, ahead, strode with purpose like he'd been here before.

Toward the back of the gigantic palace, a grand hall gaped and thinned out the crowds. The Dynast's flagship perched at the far end, just in front of an opening to space. A shimmering atmoseal capped the opening and a view of stars and traffic outside. The flagship itself had to be twenty or thirty times the *Azura*'s size; flat, wedged, and bladed like an ax, cored through with cylinders fluted in glossalith. A beast of engineering. Its finish was layered Dynast colors of black, blue, and copper, and tiny windows winking light.

Dwarfed by the flagship, but with a presence far more immense, the Dynast Prime Abriss stood by the foot of it.

Caiden's heart swelled, inexplicably. Even across fifty meters, his adoration drew him to her like a tide. She wore a knee-length copper coat atop a dark flight suit, reflecting a lustrous glow around her body.

"Nine crimes," he swore under his breath. Was Threi there to tell the Dynast that the *Azura* existed? Or to expose Laythan, the convict? Caiden aimed closer while keeping to the edge of the hall where the crowd basked in this glimpse of the Prime.

Threi stopped in the center of the hall. His posture bulked and curled like a predator poised as Abriss approached him alone. Did she know he was Casthen? Was he there to sell the gloss he'd reclaimed in the Den?

They shared words that Caiden strained to hear across the distance, his translation devices unable to parse snippets of syllable and motions of lips. The Prime said something that made Threi's posture recoil, then he forced himself to stand even taller.

"*Kneel*," Abriss said warmly, but her voice brimmed with intent and was raised enough to reverberate across the space.

Caiden's knees went weak, his whole being filled with a rush to please her. Around the circumference of the great hall, xenids in the crowd fell to one knee in unison. The *crack* of bone on floor and *zuzz* of rustling cloth filled up the air at once. Caiden was able to resist, at this proximity, as were some of the other species in the crowd. The Andalvians mostly remained standing, and Caiden recalled Threi struggling to convince Sina of his orders. The power had limits.

Threi resisted for one heartbeat.

Two.

Then even he folded himself down to one knee, still cradling the burden over one shoulder.

Is he a vassal of hers? Caiden leaned against a pillar. He couldn't hear the contemptuous exchange that passed between the two as Threi rose laboriously to his feet.

More words passed between them. A shrug from Threi.

Whatever language they spoke was archaic and hard to unsnarl, but between the translators and Caiden's understanding of a descendant tongue, he stitched the bits together: Threi was trading the body for information.

Caiden scrubbed away the sweat on his brow. This exchange they were making might not be about him or his ship, and the body might not be a child or even alive.

Abriss knelt to splay the body out across her knees and inspect it. The hood tumbled down and head lolled—on the other side of Abriss where Caiden couldn't see what species. Something rare or capable, and valued for superficial uses? Caiden was proof that if you obtained a being young enough, you could shape it into whatever you wished.

Satisfied with the barter, Abriss rose and passed the being into the hands of sentinels. Caiden drifted closer to the flagship so he could see where they took the body: folded up into an egg-shaped pod and loaded on top of others. Were the contents all the same?

He'd missed conversation between Threi and Abriss. She said, "Very well," and reached in her pocket to draw out a miniature star resting in her palm. Whatever the tech was, it made a dimple in the density of space and jetted out sharp rays of light. The fingers of Abriss's free hand were loaded with glass rings. She gestured over the star-tech. Rainbow ripples of light gushed out of it and separated, arranging within a sphere that surrounded her. The colored light hanging inside formed into data symbols: astronomical bodies, planets, aspects, projections. A small orrery.

Laythan's words sprung into Caiden's mind: an astrologian like Abriss could divine information and predict events, within Unity.

Caiden paced to relieve the tingles in his spine. He pretended to observe architecture while fitting into other groups. There was no way to get closer to the conversation, and their archaic language was a briar of melodies.

Abriss used her ringed hand to shift through data and zooms, surveying the complicated geometry of Unity's heavens. "It is here," she said, along with other words that were lost.

"Where?" Threi hissed.

"In Emporia."

Anger raised his voice enough to hear; "*Where* in Emporia?"

"An inexact initial question produces inexact answers." Abriss looked up sharply as a score of Dynast sentinels poured into the hall. Their raucous, mismatched steps fell into a perfect rhythm the closer they came to their Prime. She closed her palm around the orrery device.

Whatever she said next made the sentinels fan out in an expanding circle to clear the hall of visitors.

Caiden swore and slinked away, back through the Dynast's lightseep obsidian palace. *I have no proof of any scheme, just inconclusive and poorly translated dialogue. Laythan would slug me if he were here.*

There was nothing worse Caiden could do than cause more trouble.

But one thing was still clear. He had to fly as soon as possible.

The *Azura* was vulnerable.

Anxiety and excitement hummed similar chords in Caiden as he headed to where he'd been told Taitn was waiting. He stood in a grungy lift chugging up a wall of Pent's depository.

The lift opened to a large, unlit room with a short ceiling. The far wall was translucent but dirty, and looked out on streams of ship traffic and flashy lettering on Emporia's next layer over. With new languages, he could read the colorful light-script, no longer the signs of foreign terrors but hawking mundane things like respiratory implants, motile tattoos, and exotic cuisine.

"Taitn?" His voice ricocheted off hard surfaces as he stepped from the lift. "I saw something I need to talk to you about."

The room's lightseep surfaces were peppered with projection devices.

"Over here," Taitn's excited voice rang out. "Are you ready to fly?"

"Y-yes. Beyond ready." Caiden walked in and looked away from the bright windows, letting his eyes adjust to the dark. "I was also thinking if you're taking the *Second Wind* to…"

In the middle of the space, Taitn hunched over a lone-standing pilot's seat and a half ring of tall holosplays.

"What's this?" Caiden asked.

"It's an old model, but still good for testing ship compositions and upgrades before actually installing or removing any parts. Mostly, Pent uses it to enforce a no-refund policy."

"A model of—" He cut off, needled by the realization. *A flight simulation. Stupid to have believed a first-time pilot could jump right into a starship—why wasn't the stupid accelerated out of me?*

Caiden scratched the scales on his morphcoat. He tried to cram disappointment in that small corner where he shoved anger and frustrations and everything else he didn't have time for. To deal with *soon*.

"Taitn, on my way here—"

Taitn initiated the foggy light of the holosplays, which began to congeal. It lit his smile, which was so excited it may as well have been a punch to Caiden's chest.

"I modified a C-Center Class ship that's a close match," Taitn said, not listening. His fingers flew across the holosplay setup, and the lightseep in the room exploded into a sprawling vista. Caiden's train of thought cut off. Whitecaps and rose-colored foam tipped cyan waves. The air condensed into the walls of a cockpit, pressing the ocean behind windows.

Taitn lowered a brilliant thread-thin neural halo around Caiden's forehead. It hovered at forehead height, riveted by the strange magnetics of his new implant. It would approximate neural control in this…simulation.

Caiden crawled into the lonely pilot seat. He couldn't break Taitn's heart now. This wasn't the time to discuss haste or fear.

Taitn switched something on the seat, which tugged back Caiden's shoulders and waist. The metallic scaling on the morphcoat must have been magnetic, designed for flight, similar to Taitn's prim green jacket. "Post-acceleration, all the sensations and maneuvers are already in your brain. We just need to unlock it so you *feel* that instinct. I'll be right here behind you as we fly a test course."

Caiden hovered his hands, and brilliant lines—drive guides—congealed in the air and twined around his fingers, ready for him to orchestrate motion.

The engine was docile and lazy, not a latent wildfire like the *Azura*. Caiden's fingertips traveled across now-familiar symbols and circuit trees. The faux engines spun to life, pushing off the ocean. Foam and spray whipped up beneath the hull. Caiden felt every droplet on his skin.

Taitn said, "Get her moving."

His smallest motions and the vibrato of his nerves sent signals to the ship's mind. Ocean spray turned to roiling vapor as he revved the thrusters and climbed to puffy clouds. The tiny stars of flight-track points led the way.

Caiden's frustration vanished. This wasn't the *Azura*, but it was still incredible. A stupid grin split his face as he rocketed up. The pressure of a lean gravity melted him into the seat, and the butterflies in his stomach tickled up into a laugh.

Taitn patted his shoulder. "Now straight and level, hotshot."

Ocean billows ripped past into a new vista of crystalline water with golden bands twisting on its surface. A chain of basalt pillar mountains jutted out of the kelp forest. The track lights descended into them.

"Take her under," Taitn said.

"Under?"

"The water. C-Center starships are aquatic too."

"I knew that." Caiden laughed again and pitched into a dive. As intention and excitement roared in him, a tense curl rumbled somewhere in the ship's body. They hit the water with barely a splash, and plunged into silence. Flexing towers of flowery leaves and beaded stems striped the blue. Sunlight narrowed into shafts, and marine hues transformed to sapphire depths where distant lights twinkled the way.

He tried to think of an exclamation more intelligent than "Wow," but sat speechless.

The engines fluttered to life. Water rushed through portions of the ship. Caiden's mechanical knowledge whispered suggestions of marine ramjet propulsion. Pressure and density parameters flickered in his peripheral vision.

Track points rolled him sideways between kelp bands, below basalt arches, finally ascending out of the sea in a burst of glittering drops, hovering momentarily as the thrusters erupted back into their former shape. The ship guzzled air and fire as it shot up to a clear sky.

"How fast can I go?" he asked.

"Fast as you want."

Caiden grinned and pulled his wrists in, gathering the cockpit's light guides, bunching and condensing the ship's power. Its roar narrowed to a fine screech as it picked up speed. The seascape squiggled into dunes and serpentine banks as tan earth took over.

Desert. Binary suns adorned the other side of the world. The sky was black, and a glow blanketed the ground a kilometer high, like the nophek planet. Caiden's speed slowed, and it wasn't his trembling hands but his quaking mind and the jaws and sand and metal scents that made the ship groan and sputter, losing pitch.

The stars were white nails holding up a black curtain.

The ship yawed right and began to roll. Stars spun.

Taitn's hand slapped over Caiden's and the control lines flashed red as he took command. In an elegant tumble, he completed the roll, spinning sky and ground until the ship leveled out neatly just above the sand.

"Terminate," Taitn said gently. The desert flickered to darkness, and the large, bland room surrounded them once more. But Caiden's mind was still there, fogging up. His body was fire, tendons glitching, body rigid.

"Hey, breathe," Taitn said. "Your brain has to integrate. We won't push it, we'll do several sessions. The accelerated skills are still unfolding in you."

Taitn lifted the halo off Caiden's head.

It's just sand. He stared at the darkness where the vision had been, and drew a shaky hand through his sweaty hair.

"Winn?"

He thrust aside festering thoughts and told himself his quivering was from the exhilaration of flight. He thought of the blue and the speed, and summoned his bravest smile. "That was incredible."

But it wasn't the *Azura*. In simulation, the bulk and power of the ship was an illusion. He was steering nothing, in control of nothing.

They both swiveled around at the sound of the lift opening. Ksiñe stood inside and kicked a case their way, then punched the lift button. "Laythan said feed you." The whipkin perched on his head. She squealed recognition before the doors closed and the lift shuddered back down.

Taitn retrieved the case and opened it: full of ramia, still steaming. Rich, spicy, meaty aromas wafted over.

Caiden accepted one and ate, but disappointment flattened even the ramia's taste. "How many more simulations?"

"Sorry." A thinly veiled fear consumed Taitn's brutish face, excitement gone. "You hate waiting, huh? This isn't something to rush, no matter what Laythan says. Push yourself too hard and you'll make errors. A ship like yours isn't the same as these simulations."

Caiden nodded, unable to verbalize. His objection would sound like Laythan's, and that would push Taitn over an edge. He took the ramia to the window wall and sat to eat.

Vessels of all sorts whizzed to and from the hexagonal rooms making up Emporia's many layers. The traffic patterns looked much easier than what he'd flown in the simulation, and he recognized the different classes and origins of ships, like the sleek Dynast patrollers shelled in the same colors and style as their flagship.

Taitn sat beside him, but instead of eating, he pulled out his blue-and-white lacquered flask.

They watched the traffic for a long while before Taitn met Caiden's pleading gaze. "Laythan agreed to taking the *Second Wind* for a test flight away from Emporia, through crossover and back through an egress. Come with us. I'll walk you through cargo-class-vessel procedure. Easy flights."

Cargo class...Caiden finished chewing before he responded. The manners he'd learned on his homeworld still applied in the multiverse, and it gave him a moment to bundle up his hopes into words. "Taitn...I'm ready. It's a short flight, I can go with you, piloting the *Azura*. If anything happens, you'll be right there. Or Laythan can come in my ship; he used to be a pilot."

Taitn crossed his arms, leather creaking, half silhouetted by the window's glow. "Part of you is ready, but not all of you."

Caiden finished the ramia and heaved to his feet. "I won't be reckless. All of me feels ready to fly."

"Recklessness makes people forget things. There's another reason we can't take the *Azura* out."

"I didn't forget the Dynast's Graven tech sensors. I've studied them. The sensors are carried on ships, and work in zones, sweeping Emporia. I charted a simple route that stays ahead of it and ends up in open space. I'm ready." Heart hammering, he turned his gaze to Taitn.

The pilot's reaction was calmer than expected. A blank look. "No. And not just because you're reckless to push yourself. Laythan won't ever agree to it. He's terrified of your ship and won't allow it anywhere outside the shielding hollow until we're ready to leave."

"Laythan? He controls so much of your life, Taitn . . . It's *my* ship. I just— I can't stay bottled up. I need to . . . *move*."

Taitn steepled his hands against the window. His dark-blue eyes traced traffic patterns back and forth.

Caiden opened his mouth to speak his heart again, but all his carefully prepared words were already expelled. The morphcoat prickled between breezy mesh and scales as waves of heat rolled off him.

Softly, as ever, Taitn asked, "What's so important that you're rushing to risk your life?"

The worth of Caiden's life flashed in his mind: Leta huddling in a corner of darkness and filth, waiting for him to return, blood and violence on her doorstep. *That* was the cost of his survival. How many more beings like him and Leta were out there, exploited by the Casthen? Illegally harvested? Slaves auctioned? Universes pirated? Threi had dumped a child-sized body into Abriss's arms, something he might've killed—the injustice of the Casthen ongoing. Caiden couldn't wait, turn a blind eye, or allow complacency to sink in. His eyes alone were clear.

It was all too big for words.

Caiden scrubbed a fingernail through dust on the window's base, serrating the grime until vivid colors bled through. "In the Dynast's district, I saw Threi buying information from the Dynast Prime. All I could under-stand was that he was looking for something in Emporia. Laythan's fears might be true."

"What were you doing—" Taitn cut off, jaw grinding. "Laythan is prone to overreactions. We'll only be gone a day. With more simulations and depending on how you perform piloting the *Second Wind*, we can leave Emporia right after and everything will be fine."

Caiden ate another ramia and mulled it over, but couldn't find the fault in his simulation performance or his request, and felt slapped by Taitn's dismissal of what he'd seen. Why be honest if no one listened? There was some snarl in the web of the crew that he still didn't understand and it kept sticking him in place, even at twenty years old. *My jagged edges don't fit in this puzzle. I keep bouncing around, damaging everything I touch. Maybe like a river stone I'll be smooth one day after years of tumbling.*

He said, "You can't know that everything will be *fine*. What was the point of my acceleration if I can't be ready to fly now?"

It stung. Even to him it stung and felt stiff, but he refused to relent this time. He wasn't just something for the crew to fix and coddle.

"Stay here alone, then. With that attitude, you're not ready to pilot the *Second Wind* on our test trip away. If you're so rushed to get better, you can fly the simulations here all you want." Taitn levered off the window and paced to the lift. "Pent's here if you need anything while we're gone." Voice cold, firm, and hurt.

CHAPTER 23

BELONGING

Caiden spent every hour in the simulator. He flew through craggy planet cores, conflagration clusters, industrial stations as large as Emporia, and gaseous universes with zero visibility. He dug through vessel specs and obscure records to approximate the class and mods of Threi's rare Glasliq ship. If he was going to protect the *Azura*, he needed to be able to defeat or outrun it. In the sims, he chased, combatted, and fled from the Glasliq over and over until he could beat it consistently in any environment.

He slept only brief stints, always in the *Azura*'s pilot seat, letting his neurons keep incubating the link with the ship. The nightmares found him every time, but they were briefer with the link active, and he cried a little less, screamed a little quieter.

After another long rash of sims, Caiden rolled out of the simulation chair, plucked Leta's chicory flower off the console—his reminder—and shoved it in his morphcoat pocket. Exhausted but pleased with his progress, he took the lift down to Pent's depository and walked through its darkness to the shielding hollow. The vast space of starship wrecks and junk heaps reverberated back to him the smallest sounds, outlining isolation. The crew would be back in one hundred eighty arcminutes—not that he was counting.

He pawed a hand through his hair. His steps were brisk but his ribs tight, breath labored. He hadn't meant to hurt Taitn, and Laythan was still pissed from even earlier, but the crew's judgment of Caiden's decisions seemed more about their own history reflected in him than it was about any recklessness on his part.

Caiden fussed with the *Azura*, abuzz like a bee around a black flower. He checked the engine multiple times, checked the exterior thrusters, the shielding matrices, and the integrity of his neural bond. He vented frustration into work. Responding to his exertion, the morphcoat's sleeves dissolved and the material around his chest transformed to breezy scales. Wisps of hair stuck to his sweaty temples.

There were many more tests to run with the ship's universe activated, when the tiny stellar engine became a different creature. Caiden didn't need to physically touch the florescer anymore; he grasped it through his neural link, and triggered it mentally while standing in the bay.

The candescent opal bubble expanded out of the florescer. The rind boiled past him. Air slithered from his lungs. Threads of him were wrung out and released. The weirdness of it was lessened each time he crossed over, and in the *Azura's* universe, his burdens lifted. The air tasted sweet. The rind settled, encapsulating the ship entirely within the lightseep blister of the shielding hollow.

Thrice nested inside his machine, in the bubble of light, within the obsidian, Caiden fetched tools and happily tinkered on the *Azura's* frayed nerve lines within the walls.

Footfalls and voices reverberated in the depository outside, loud enough to be heard within the hollow. Caiden groaned. Pent had returned. He'd rather be lonely than spend more time hounded by the inquisitive and forgetful saavee. Maybe Pent would forget the ship was even here.

There were multiple voices and many feet.

"Crew's here." Caiden smiled. He put his tools away and paced the bay a few times, re-memorizing his apology to Taitn. The simulation logs and his dedication had to count for something.

He shook his hands out, and strode across the bay.

A shadow swaggered up the ramp toward the rind, drenched in light.

"En! How'd the test flight go—"

The light bloom cleared as the figure approached.

"Hi, Freckles." A wavy smile. Mismatched armor. Blue faceplate shoved to the top of his head, framing a pale, unmistakable face. Threi. "I've crossed over three hundred and sixty-nine different rinds..." He plunged a measurement device into the *Azura*'s rind. Dark distortions burbled as the device tasted the universe. "And as I hoped, *this* rind is perfect."

Adrenaline kicked Caiden's guts, electrified his tired limbs, and sent him right back to that moment in the Den where he'd unwittingly let Threi see the ship's universe. This time, Taitn wasn't around to fly the *Azura* to safety.

Caiden launched forward to close the distance. Threi pulled a glave from his thigh and fired.

Click. Incompatible with the universe. Threi cocked his head at it then re-holstered. "Pity."

Caiden lunged with an uppercut. Threi's head snapped aside and his fist barreled into Caiden's ear. Caiden stumbled, head ringing, one side of his brain filling with heat.

Strong. He shook his head—a mistake. Vertigo smothered him. He pushed off the spinning floor and punched at the Casthen's blurry face. Threi blocked and slugged Caiden in the cheek, sending him sprawling.

Blood gushed in his mouth. He choked on it and spit out a fragment of tooth.

"Let's just talk," Threi said, the words honeyed with Graven intensity— but not enough to sway Caiden. Threi's boots paced into Caiden's doubled vision.

Caiden jammed an elbow into the bastard's knee, dropping him to the floor. He kicked at Threi's windpipe, but a hand caught his boot. Threi slammed his other fist into the base of Caiden's skull.

Darkness brimmed. The *Azura*'s floor was hot and sticky. Bleeding. Caiden bubbled out swears and clawed at consciousness. Fighting off night- mares had accustomed him to this sea: the seeping black, the nearby threat. He sensed movement and forced one eye open to a skewed view. Threi dragged him by one foot across the bay.

He tried to choke out a word, but his body was out of reach. There was a spark of him in his skull, swallowed by another black wave. He sensed an impact and his own crumpling limbs as Threi tossed him to the corner by the cockpit.

The man slithered into the pilot's seat and slid it forward to the twitch drive pads. The engine growled.

No... Caiden couldn't feel his body but maybe he could grasp the *Azura*'s. His thoughts flailed with the neural link. The darkness surged, topped with sparkles of pain. He was flooded with sensations of thrust and torsion. Caiden razored his focus on the florescer, willing it off, imagining its song ending.

The rind collapsed and shrank, its edge purling back through the bay. Caiden coiled against the wall, ready to spring. When the rind swept over Threi, the man spasmed in surprise, head jerking out of the cradle. Caiden lunged to grab the back of Threi's skull and continued the motion with a fistful of hair and mask, slamming Threi's forehead into the console rim.

They both tangled on the floor. Threi grappled. Metal smashed into Caiden's windpipe. The man's arm squeezed from behind, armor digging in.

Caiden twisted and pried while his free hand scrabbled for the glave on Threi's thigh. Static throbbed in his vision. A buzz of pale noise. His fingers wrapped around cold metal. He whipped his forearm up, pointing the glave behind his shoulder at the blur of the Casthen's face.

Threi ripped the glave from Caiden's hand, which loosened the choke hold. Caiden elbowed the man's stomach, his bone cracking against armor, but the choke loosened more. He wrenched Threi's wrist and twisted free, spun the arm around to push Threi to the ground. Instinct-fast, the man's momentum shifted. He rolled, tossing Caiden into the wall.

Blood spurted into Caiden's mouth as he bit his cheek. Tones rang in his head. Threi was a blur, still holding the glave, pacing toward Caiden with a hateful stride. Playtime was over.

He had no chance alone against the Enforcer.

But Caiden wasn't alone.

Azura. He tried to stand, steadying against the wall, while his mind flailed at the neural controls. The ship's scalar gravity was off. He held the nodal pattern he wanted in his mind and willed her gravity back on.

Threi, two paces away.

Snap! The initiation pounded Caiden's chest, knocked air from his lungs. Threi snagged midstride, his waist caught in a bundle of gravity nodes. Caiden pushed off the wall into a lunge, snatched the glave from Threi's hand, and rolled past. He sprang to his feet into a slam of vertigo but managed to raise the glave against the back of Threi's bare neck.

"You don't have your shield, I can tell this time," he said between panting wheezes. Threi would've been wearing a collar-type glave to generate a shield.

The man raised his hands and backed away, turning to face him.

Caiden added, "I'm stupid enough to fire this inside just to see your brains on the wall."

A smile stretched Threi's too-white, too-perfect face. "Hear me out, pup."

Caiden trained the glave at Threi's chest. Sparkles teemed in his vision, and vertigo threatened if he moved. *Shoot him.*

But somewhere in Threi's head were the coordinates of the Casthen Harvest, Caiden's best route to Çydanza.

Threi yanked the skewed blue mask off and mussed a tangle of short dark hair into snarls. A purple welt crowned his forehead. He looked Caiden over. "Accelerated already? A boy after my own heart."

Caiden forced a wry, spiteful smile. "You've accelerated fighting?"

There was no way a human was that fast and strong while looking no older than Taitn. Threi had hawkish features, clean-shaven, intelligent, and sculpted. His skin was flawless white except for what looked like a thick dusting of even whiter freckles. Stretched like the reverse of wrinkled age, the tautness of forced youth. Something about his features looked eerily familiar, as the Dynast Prime's had. Attractive due to a hidden peculiarity. Repulsive because of the same.

"I've accelerated *everything*." Threi's amicable smile sheathed the daggers in his eyes. He lowered his arms, cracked his neck, and reclined against a wall. "Relax. Just listen. You're not going to shoot me. I'm your key to defeating the Casthen, and you're *my* key."

Caiden snorted. "And why would you want to defeat your own organization?"

Threi shrugged. "I'm only going to say this once, so listen up. I'm Dynast Arbiter Threi—" He seemed to cut off, or drew himself up, chest filled with the air for more words he didn't expel. Muscles twitched in his jaw as he continued, "Infiltrated into the Casthen as the highest-ranked Enforcer, embroiled with Cartographer freethinkers. Without the Casthen Prime's dictatorship, their operations can be brought back to moral standards—myself in control, aligned with Cartographer aid and values. Then you can leave a hero, better than you ever were before. Everyone wins."

Caiden leaned shakily against the pilot seat, glave still trained on the madman. How many of these claims were lies?

"Seriously, pup. Put that down. I'm stronger and faster than you."

"More reason to kill you. I can shoot before you get up."

"Your heart's stopping you." Threi tilted his head back and closed his eyes. "Not that you're too good-hearted to kill me—you proved you weren't when you tried to shoot me the last two times. It's the dark part of you that won't kill me. The darkness and violence you were bred for. You want the Casthen destroyed as much as I do."

Bred for...

Threi said, "You shot at me twice, now I'm offering to point your glave in the right direction, at Çydanza's heart. You'll never find the Casthen Harvest without guidance."

"No one's been able to kill her before."

Threi's eyes sparkled. "They didn't have the *Azura*. Or you."

Dizziness flamed through Caiden's injured brain as he tried to think. If the *Azura* would help him kill Çydanza, that was more reason to defend it fiercely. "That's what you were trying to learn from the Dynast Prime; where my ship was."

"Sneaky, are you?" A simper stretched Threi's white face. "*Encased in lightseep, like insect in amber.* Took a lot of old Emporia blueprints to solve that riddle."

"Why me? You need an expendable part in your plan?"

"Oh no. I need a *valuable* part in my plan. The irony is delicious: we'll kill Çydanza with a blade of her own design. You see, you're more Casthen than I, as much as you'll hate to admit it. You belong with the Casthen, but not because you were Casthen *property*."

"Bred..." Chill sheeted through him.

"That's right." Threi closed his eyes again and wriggled more comfortably against the wall. "You were meant for so much more than your mechanic's life, or even a passager life. It was an oversight that mixed up

shipments and sent Çydanza's last batch of Paraborn mosaics to CWN82—
you included."

The Paraborn interbreeding project for private military operations. The
Cartographers' database had been unable to parse most of his genetic
makeup.

"I was engineered."

"Çydanza might as well be your mother, having conceived of your design
and use. Child and product. You're Casthen through and through, pup.
And I bet you thought you were worthless and discarded?"

Clutching the pilot's seat, Caiden lowered onto his knees. His arm
burned, glave still pointed at Threi.

The man continued, his rich voice filling up the bay. "You *belong* with
us. When Çydanza finally tracked the shipment, she deployed me to recover
the children, but you'd already been sent to slaughter. I got to RM28 too
late, and crafty passagers tailed me into the system, then began to raid the
gloss. You see, it *was* you after all, in a way, who exposed our whole operation to the multiverse."

Caiden's body was numbing, ribs cinching tight. "What was I engineered
for? What's my purpose?" The questions came out mangled, dragged
through the thorns of his fear.

Threi chose a new smile from his arsenal, one that was half snarl. "Be
proud. You're a soldier."

Caiden lowered his shaking arm to his lap. If Threi had found him on
the nophek planet instead of Laythan, or if the shipment of infants had
arrived where it meant to, he would have grown up as a Casthen... *through
and through*, as Threi said.

He maundered on. "And not just any dumb lug with a glave. You're the
last survivor of our first successful attempt at breeding Graven soldiers."

Freckles.

"We wanted superior aptitude, senses, healing, and the ability to command obedience and inspire love even from an enemy. The best of however many xenids they could cram into one body. It's almost impossible to
propagate Graven genes artificially, for a number of reasons—especially the
kind you came from. The Dynast family is horribly inbred because of this

problem. Çydanza's scientists have been toiling to find the right cocktail of bits that would let the Graven essence stick. Meanwhile Abriss—the end of the Dynast line—is experimenting in a different direction, with gene transfection. Çydanza pulled ahead in this arms race when she succeeded with your perfect batch."

Caiden's mind reeled, not helped by the head injury.

During his Appraisal at ten years old, the overseers had assessed his worth and placement. *Fit, no disease, healthy brain, fine inclinations, unusual intelligence and aptitude. Strange to get one this clean.*

He had thought they meant how thoroughly he'd washed. And when they seemed to approve of him, his heart leapt to his throat. "I—I'm good?" he squeaked. The better words wouldn't form on his tongue: *valuable, worthwhile, functional, proven to belong.*

The two had looked at him for a long moment, really looked.

"Perfect," one said.

Perfect.

That moment of recognition had filled him with vigor and purpose for years. But his very question, the Graven intent of it, had coerced the answer he wanted once they looked at him and the connection was made.

Caiden stared at Threi's face, the dust of white freckles more pronounced when he knew what to look for. "Are you a product of Çydanza's design too?"

"Heavens, no. Çy picked me up when I was your age. I survived within the Casthen maw because I learned how to fill in cracks faster than she could break me, and I rose in the ranks by bullying my Graven way around."

"But you're not perfect either, are you? Not like Abriss." That sent a crack through Threi's nonchalance for a moment. Caiden continued, "You're Graven enough to snag attention in a crowd and have your orders obeyed, but I saw you having to work for it. And you can't influence me much, can you? Otherwise we wouldn't be having this chat."

Threi's nostrils flared, a nerve struck. "That's right, Graven Paraborn pup. You're Graven enough that I can't kick you about like I can everyone else, and it's delightfully refreshing. I'm enjoying the challenge of persuading you without using genetic force. So please—wriggle harder."

Graven enough...

Caiden scrubbed at tingling sweat on his freckled cheeks. Memories unspooled. The gloss deal with Laythan, the crew agreeing to take him off the planet...they could easily have taken the gloss and the ship and left the useless kid. Then Taitn letting him fly when he'd asked directly... all the questions they'd answered...protecting him...Panca helping him when he'd screamed...taking him through the acceleration, even though the gloss was sold...the ship repairs...

Am I just a piece-of-shit Casthen cur, cruising through life, carving reality to my whims as I go?

Imagery and phrases replayed in his head with new meaning, unraveling the loving care he'd imagined from the crew. Despite all the ups and downs and the burden he was, he'd evoked enough affection and loyalty for them to keep him in their orbit. He recalled moments on his home planet where a shouted outburst had pacified someone too easily, or a glare had made bullies shy. There were instances where his Graven effect might've made life a little easier in ways he hadn't realized were different. And Leta. *What if—*

"Ah, you've realized," Threi said. His Casthen armor gnashed against the wall as he shifted and closed his eyes. "It's harrowing, to suddenly know your very reality is false, compelled. So, now it's time to decide. Stay with your found family—which is a lie, a *forced family*—and live a dull life of cargo trade and safety zones. Or join me and gain access to the Casthen Harvest; Çydanza'll let you in with open arms, delighted to get one of her Graven soldiers back and ready for duty." He chuckled, enjoying every needle he stuck in. "You can return to your pack later if you wish, once she's dead and you're a hero."

Caiden levered to his feet and stumbled through a burst of vertigo. He strode to a wall compartment and fished around in the med kit for the fat red tranquilizer cylinders. Threi looked human—one tranq would do— but he grabbed three to be safe.

Head still craned back, Threi cracked a blue eye open and observed Caiden with disinterest. "I can read you better than you can read yourself. You'll say yes."

"I have no reason to trust you."

"You don't have to trust me, you just have to want it bad enough. Let me sweeten the deal."

Caiden stomped across the bay with tranqs in one hand and pressed the glave's square muzzle against the man's temple.

Threi smiled. "You have nightmares. Cartographers told me. You can be free of the repetition; I know how we can solve the memory loop."

Caiden's heart skipped.

"You never asked for it, did you?" Threi's stare turned glassy. "You did the right thing, and got punished for it. That sums up this twisted multiverse. But lucky you—your ability to relive your most horrific memories is *exactly* what will allow us to destroy Çydanza."

Caiden's agony would be worthwhile if it could somehow destroy the Casthen Prime. The nightmares...they were shrapnel left in his body from the ordeal, and cut him every time he moved. Unless he extracted them altogether, he would live on with wounds that could never scar.

"How?"

"I can't tell you all of it just yet, but I promise I will," Threi said.

Caiden growled, "Say '*soon*' and I'll shoot you until there's no charge left in this."

Threi laughed, which scratched the glave muzzle across his temple. "I'll tell you everything, but you have to say yes first. Agree to follow my plan and I'll give you access to and assistance in the revenge you crave, and solve your nightmares for good." He extended his hand, gloved in black membrane and tiny scales of scratched steel. "Deal?"

Caiden wasn't fourteen anymore, wasn't stupid enough to take a deal with uncertain terms. He pressured the glave's muzzle in to tilt Threi's head and expose more neck. "Good night."

Threi chuckled. "See you soon."

Caiden plunged all three tranqs into the man's artery.

CHAPTER 24

BRAVERY

Threi's eyes closed to slits and he slumped to the floor. Caiden kicked him in the groin to ensure he wasn't faking. Not a twitch. Maybe three tranqs was too much.

He hooked Threi's boot in the crook of one arm and dragged his dead weight across the bay and out to the ramp. At the entrance of the shielding hollow, a Casthen crew was waiting. They lurched into motion, glaves up, stances ready. Caiden whipped up his glave, too, and kept dragging. They wouldn't fire if their boss needed Caiden alive.

He shouted, "Take him out of here, we're done talking," and half threw and half kicked Threi off the side of the ramp.

The shortest of the group of four scurried over and checked Threi's vitals, followed by a huge chketin, who hoisted Threi around the waist like a doll. They both backed up while a third, lanky figure stalked toward Caiden. The shorter Casthen whisked injection syringes from their belt and tore off Threi's armor plates to jam the syringes straight to his heart. He gasped, eyes snapping open, body going rigid with a flood of revivers and performance enhancers. His veins popped into relief.

Caiden hissed a curse and fired at the lanky Casthen. They dodged the beam with whipping speed, their body fluid or morphing beneath the armor. They raced up the ramp, spear glave extending and the pronged end of it crackling electricity. Caiden stumbled back, focused on the scalar gravity, piling nodes around the back of the bay. The pattern adjusted. Electric tendrils sputtered out, and the Casthen's headlong rush smacked the clotted gravity as if hitting a wall.

Caiden slapped the door control panel. The back closed up, forcing the Casthen out. He heard orders barked from outside.

Pent's depository wasn't safe anymore. Threi's unnerving nonchalance suggested his plan wasn't over yet. But outside the depository wasn't entirely safe either; there were patterns of Dynast Graven-tech sensors to avoid, and Caiden would be too easy to spot if he simply hung out in open space outside Emporia. Piled on that, his mind would struggle to steer the *Azura* with a dent in his skull. One of his ears still bled, hot and alarming.

Streaming more curses, Caiden launched himself into the pilot's seat, head in the cradle, and threw his arms into the air. The cockpit filled with misting light particles that congealed into the drive guides. Threads of light coiled around his fingers and palms, ready for his direction. The mini thrusters trilled and hovered the ship in place.

Caiden's hands trembled like birds waiting for a wind.

The engine whirred to life on its own, engulfing Caiden's mind in a soothing whisper.

"Nine crimes, why did it have to be *now*?" He swallowed tingles of sour adrenaline. "I can't fly without breaking everyone's trust in me."

Metal banged against different areas of the bay doors, and Caiden recalled what Threi's group did in the Den, setting charges to disrupt door seals and crack open the ships for gloss.

"I'm sorry, Taitn." Caiden tensed his fingers and powered the thrusters, hoping one or two of the Casthen might've been caught in the ignition. He sped the ship out of the hollow and into the crowded landscape of Pent's depository, leaving the Casthen crew behind as frantic blips in the cockpit's holosplay. He maneuvered around hazards in the dark—bin piles and freighter carcasses—edged in guidance glow. His muscles flexed, tendons tight. His clammy hands quivered in midair where the forgiving controls laced his nervousness calmly. He sailed the *Azura* out of the atmoseal entrance of the depository, and the ship calibrated its internal scalar gravity.

"Out safe." His head was stuffed, throbbing with arrhythmic aches, but he was in the clear. The ambient temperature ticked down in response to his sweating.

Now to find somewhere safe and hidden to dock. He brought up a map of the flight pattern he'd designed. Coppery hues outlined the Dynast's migrating sensors. The timing of zones replayed, perfect every time. If he was careful, he could avoid them.

One arcminute until the sensors roved over this slice.

Less than two kilometers away, another Emporia layer shot vertically. Between the layers coursed dense traffic of all speeds. Caiden merged in the flow and sensed the etiquette of passing, the subtle pauses and slows that let other ships complete their arcs.

When he spun to put the ship's belly against a surface, his head spun with her. Dizziness swirled the streaking ships overhead, and Caiden lulled as the *Azura* nosed down into the stream. Lights scattered like stirred insects. Thrusters growled and roared.

"Shit," he hissed.

Everything blinked at him to respond. He couldn't distinguish the sparks in his vision from actual blips in the display and the copper perimeters of the scans. Traffic buzzed him, small ships cutting in front and large ones shoving their jets so near he was forced to bank. Caiden breathed deep and limited his movements. He weaved around blocky transport cruisers, small beamer quads, and sleek gray chketin warships. There was no air drag, no rush of pressure against the hull. The *Azura* cut through silken void like a blade.

Flying his starship surpassed the simulation in every way, from the real fuselage and plating to the hum of genuine power, the singing of eldritch components. The simulations were fun, but this was glorious, and he wasn't even pushing it hard. He made an intention and the *Azura* was a step ahead of him already, engaging space with ease.

Guilt peeled off him. Limitations lifted away. He let the inertia carry the ship in a slow traffic line, and closed his eyes for a sweet second, whimpering in pain. Darkness welcomed him. Neither his parentless genetics nor his Graven control nor his slave brand mattered in the *Azura*. He exhaled all his anxiety, set Threi's revelations aside, and inhaled the cockpit's warm, happy glow.

A smile stretched on his face as he felt a burn he hadn't experienced since trying to shoot Threi in the face that very first time: *confidence.*

Freed from specific gravity, orientation ceased to have meaning, and

Emporia was a different world on its side. Vast, light-studded slabs glided by above and below. Caiden got his bearings, checked the sensors, and picked up speed toward Emporia's top. He rolled until the walls were vertical on either side. A strip of open space far off between the layers showed a tapestry of dusty veils and pinprick stars.

"Cartographers," he thought aloud. "There's a passager docking lobby."

The Dynast didn't have scan jurisdiction there; the Cartographers were a neutral organization, serving passagers first and foremost, often with no questions asked. Even if the Cartographers didn't want to help him, he could take the time to get communications set up and reach Laythan. The crew was due back soon, close enough to reach.

The Cartographers' sector was tantalizingly close, but Caiden was forced in a roundabout direction as the Dynast sensors swept in between.

Emporia's exterior was as varied as its lightseep interior. The upper levels were studded with brilliant colors that melted and reshaped across hexagonal membranes. All vendors of some type. Ships hunkered against the shop walls like dark butterflies at stunning flowers. Caiden danced the *Azura* between Emporia's market layers, letting the engine's power fill his body while light shows filled his eyes.

The blinking orange indicator seemed part of it all, at first.

A chketin warship needled out of the wall and threaded into traffic at blinding speed. Caiden responded with a jerk, lashed by panic. He nosed down into a stream of tiny vessels. Several bounced off as their shielding engaged. The force jarred his ship sideways and spinning. He squeezed his fingers in the drive guides as if clutching a lifeline.

"Shit, shit!" *Stupid.*

His brain turned muzzy at the sharp roll. The ship was heavier, faster, and more taxing than any simulation. Barraged by visual guides, auditory blips, and rhythms, his brain struggled to process, blurring or omitting sensory input. He heaved his arms back and pulled the *Azura* level with one of Emporia's layers.

He relaxed his fingers but couldn't rein in his panting. His nerves were strands of razor fire violently strummed. "To void with this," he swore. "Slow. I need to go slower with this head injury."

He tried to channel Taitn's patience, and dipped back into gentler traffic in a district that oozed green light. The ship's heavy wings cut curtains of plasma into spirals.

SCAN AUTHORIZATION flashed in the middle of the cockpit.

Shadows slithered in his peripheral vision before they popped up in the *Azura*'s sensors. Two ships, both small. Their squared diamond bodies sloped to down-pointed wings on either side, all skinned in patterns of matte black, vitreous blue, and lines of copper.

Dynast ships.

The realization slapped him, and the *Azura*'s engines responded with a building screech of potential speed. He curled his fingers and ripped the *Azura* through traffic. The two smaller ships matched his veers.

Panic whipped Caiden's muscles, but they strained against each leaden maneuver. He pulled sharply into a narrow passage. Cargo pods bobbed in his path. He rolled to dodge them, then popped out the other side of the passage as the whole section rotated. The two ships in pursuit emerged on either side and closed in.

Caiden clawed his fingers in the guides and thrust his arms sideways to power the ship between cargo cruisers with only inches of clearance. Every muscle and tendon in him corded. He yanked the *Azura* up tight, bailing at a right angle to speed against Emporia's side.

The two Dynast ships vanished. Caiden gasped in frigid air. His arms cramped and the atmospherics chilled his sweat. Sparks sawed up and down his limbs. This was *not* like the simulations.

He rolled the heavy ship around until the ground was a ceiling, then coasted as he scanned the opposite plane to get his bearings.

One Dynast ship streaked from the ceiling in front of him. Lights razed the cockpit, dissolving the holosplay.

The other ship screeched up behind him.

Thunder smashed the *Azura* with a blinding charge as both ships shot out electromagnetic pulses. The two waves crashed together in the *Azura*'s middle and foamed through her systems, knocking out power.

She plummeted toward Emporia's wall.

Half of Caiden's neural activity shut off. He blinked dumbly for a beat before his nerves fired like lightning loosed. "Reinitiate. No time. *Please*. Reinitiate!"

He lurched from the pilot's seat and plunged his hands into the twitch drive panels, which didn't need a neural connection to use. Secondary power glittered online and the *Azura*'s engine reinitiated, blasting away moments before striking Emporia's surface.

They jetted to safety, but using the twitch drive, the ship's motion was heavy, desperate. Caiden struggled to regain control and keep his body steady against the console without any restraints. No frantic motions would help him now. The slightest twitch of a fingertip ricocheted the ship into violent motions.

Huge cruisers slid by like walls. Caiden weaved through, hoping the visual obstruction would maintain distance between him and the trailing Dynast ships.

But there was no need. To Caiden's surprise, the two vessels peeled off.

Somehow, he didn't think that could be a good thing. He didn't appear to be in any zone that would scare the Dynast off.

Caiden heaved clear of the cruisers. Cramps vised his wrists. The thrusters juddered. He powered forward delicately, each fingertip commanding incredible energy.

Ahead of him, a swarm of tiny ships billowed and condensed, then abruptly spilled off in two directions around a congealing glassy surface.

A whimper punched out of Caiden's breast. *The Glasliq*.

The Dynast chase had shined a huge beacon on the *Azura*. Had "Dynast Arbiter" Threi chatted up the two pilots: *Hey, I've got this, leave him to me*?

The Glasliq's viscous surface hardened into wings with a bluebird sheen. Its inner metallic gills resembled a skeletal sneer.

Caiden's throat clotted with despair, and he sucked in massive breaths to keep tears out of his eyes and ignore the throbbing in his brain. Now more than ever he needed to be able to focus. The ship was heavier and more complex than all of his strength, its intelligence too much for his young mind, its power too brash for his nervous system, and Taitn had been right about *everything*.

"I trained for this." The hope rang hollow. His training against the

Glasliq had been a simulation, and Caiden hadn't trained at all using a twitch drive.

He leaned forward for speed and tipped straight down between Emporia's layers, through haphazard traffic currents.

The Glasliq cut the fray as if it were immaterial, deforming and reforming as needed. It splashed ahead in traffic and flared back into solid shape in front of the *Azura*, forcing Caiden to bank, bouncing him off small beamer ships and barreling through a narrow passage between walls. Trying to herd him into clear space.

He blinked away sweat and tears. Cramps rang his bones but he kept his fingers clawed tense, speed steady. The Glasliq flooded the passage behind him. He was familiar enough with the vessel to weave among obstacles so fast the Glasliq's inner skeleton couldn't fold quick enough even if its liquid body reshaped. Caiden also aimed for the brightest sectors, so that light soaked the Glasliq's reflective body and killed its maneuverability, blinding Threi faster than his cockpit could polarize against.

It would be enough. He could make it.

Shaking all over, numbing himself to the rhythm of need, Caiden raced between another set of layers.

His left hand seized up in a flurry of pain. The crystallized panel wouldn't release his fingers.

"No," he cried, the word mangled into an animal sound of distress. Though his left hand was still on the controls, his cramped fingers were frozen in place. Out of control, the ship rolled, yawing right toward Emporia's side. The Glasliq cruised tight overhead, filling the upper view with watery curls.

This is it. The serenity surprised him. Terror was a veneer; beneath it, he was exhausted. Able to surrender.

A section of Emporia slid into view lit in white and purple, clean and beautiful and *Cartographer*. A dart of hope punctured a sigh from him.

An iris slowly closed on a docking bay in the Cartographers' wall. Caiden needed both twitch drive panels of control to make it. He clawed his right fingers to lower the *Azura*'s speed, then used his right hand to rip his paralyzed left forearm from the plate. He twisted his good fingers through the freed-up left panel to angle the *Azura*'s nose away from the wall. Toward the iris opening…but the roll worsened. They wouldn't fit.

The iris bit into the ship's wing and pitched it into rotation.

Unrestrained, Caiden was tossed like a stick and hit the ceiling shoulder-first. The dock's walls scraped over every surface. Shield deflections rocketed around in Caiden's brain as the neural link informed him of every abrasion, stress field, and impact. His body mirrored them all.

He was a little cog shaken inside a can. The edge of the bay ramp slammed into his neck, crushing a gurgle out of his throat. He scrambled to hold on to something. A sharp surface grabbed him instead and pain ripped up his arm, tangling with cramps and fractures. The roar in his ears hid his screams as he was tossed to a stop on the *Azura*'s floor.

The engines died. Blackness oozed into Caiden's senses.

He couldn't move anything but his eyes. And his chest, surely, because he was still breathing.

Muffled voices resonated through the gloom.

Open, he thought, hoping a thread of neural link remained. The bay doors sighed.

Light washed over him, and he regretted the command. Crumpled on his side, he saw his left arm: the radius bone was splintered in two, humerus broken, muscle shredded off in purple strips like ragged sleeves. The mess wiggled loosely in his shoulder socket. It should have been painful, but he didn't feel it. Didn't feel anything below his neck.

There was very little blood on him. It was all over the walls.

The voices were shadows that drew closer but became no more intelligible. Caiden's head filled with the razor whine of charged weapons.

"It's a kid…" a gruff voice called.

Blood sputtered in Caiden's mouth as he tried to speak.

Someone said, "Passager Winn, 8116," and more distant shouts skewered the air.

"Hold on." Lyli's voice. Lyli's tranquil, velvet voice. "Passager Winn and the starship *Azura* are under special consideration. Exempt it from scans while I take custody of the pilot. Summon the rest of medical, please."

Caiden peeked through sticky red eyelashes. A cluster of glaves pointed at him. Lyli crouched, washed out into a silhouette of wavering curves. He wasn't aware of any pain as a crew marched in to bind him together and slide him onto a stretcher. The glaves' whine left his head but a fizzing of broken tones remained, wriggling through the canyons of his gray matter, and wringing out his consciousness.

"I'll begin the..."

Something tore Caiden apart from the inside. Searing pressure crunched through him. Blood boiled, skin blistered, bones white-hot rods. He screamed, swam, and clawed the air but touched nothing. Pain radiated up his throat into screeches.

Vague awareness frothed in his skull. Lyli's attending hands were spatters of rain, her alarmed shout a lone ribbon of wind. She was a little storm of worry, and Caiden, still blind, could only feel her until he finally woke, lying flat and submerged in liquid, his head resting on crystal manifolds. He strained his gaze down to confirm that his arm was still a shredded mess.

"Hello, Passager Winn. You are stable now." Lyli's face was backlit and framed by waist-long silver ringlets. "You have sustained substantial cervical vertebrae injuries, and are currently paralyzed. Your arm, as you can see, is severely damaged as well. We have put you in a temporary decision-stasis. Your condition will not worsen, but a choice will need to be made between reconstruction, augmentation, and amputation, after extensive nervous-system repair. There is only so long we can keep you stable until we must operate on your spinal cord, so please, deliberate swiftly. You have already been unconscious for a full ephemeris day."

Caiden closed his eyes. His body burned with an itch he couldn't scratch. Everything heavy, muscles roused from sleep but not fully awake, buzzing with prickles like a galaxy contained.

His voice was a mush of husky syllables when he said, "Lyli... the *Azura*..."

"We have arranged for your starship to dock in a Cartographer recess shielded from Dynast detection zones. Your safety and anonymity is important to us, and the Cartographers remain a neutral entity."

Lyli hooked a long ringlet behind one ear. She looked over his body with a clinician's gravitas, unfazed by his gruesome injuries. He must have looked like the butcher had taken a break mid-slaughter.

All damned, what a mess. Caiden marveled down at the ribbons of striated purple muscle and glistening white tendon that wrapped his broken bones like a twisted present. His neck had to look worse, skull hardly attached.

He was little more than meat.

"Passager, an anonymous message was delivered for you." Lyli looked politely away as she held up a black card for him to read. White words emerged on its surface: "*I told them to keep your bird locked up tight. You'll change your mind. It's what you are. I'm leaving for the Harvest in two ephemeris days—decide by then.*"

There was no mistaking what "*told them*" implied. Threi had used his Graven effect to make a suggestion or order that the Cartographer dockworkers would struggle to genetically refuse, just like he had influenced Sina at the Cartographers' Den before. But Threi's Graven powers weren't absolute; he couldn't saunter in at any time to take the ship. Could he? Giving Caiden the freedom of choice seemed to mean that Threi's offer was sincere. The man needed both the ship *and* Caiden's cooperation, which couldn't be coerced.

Caiden had less than two days to get the *Azura* as far from Unity as possible.

CHAPTER 25

AUGMENTATION

He was born Casthen.

Was made for them. Belonged there.

Confusion hashed in Caiden's head, unable to form in his paralyzed body.

His engineered nature wasn't something he could change, outrun, or hide.

Earlier barbs dug deeper: why Threi would want to betray the organization he worked for, and what his link truly was to the Dynast. How inaccessible Çydanza seemed: in all his searches on databases and maps, he hadn't found a way to the Casthen Harvest. Its location was talked about like myth; a grand quest many passagers had embarked on and failed, returning with a story wilder than the last. Even the majority of the Casthen's own adherents were escorted in and out effectively blindfolded.

Threi was Caiden's clearest path in.

But he still wasn't sure how entwined the Casthen were with the Cartographers or Dynast, whether Threi was a sole rogue agent or if the organizations themselves were as incestuous and murky as he. Or if he was lying entirely.

Caiden roused when a hand stroked his forehead. Its repetition became as crucial as a beating heart or inflating lungs. When the motion stopped, palm lingering over his damp cheek, Caiden opened his eyes.

En wore a desolate expression, brightened by a twinkle of hope in her eyes. She hooked a spill of black hair over her ear, lifting stripes of shadow from her face. Spicy citrus fragrance tickled Caiden's nose.

"Hi, Winn." She tried a smile: a sad, crooked thing. "I've looked like you more than a few times."

He moaned and shut his eyes again. Paralyzed, all he could do was lie and wait for admonishment, misunderstanding, for them to throw him out once and for all. And if they didn't—was that because a Graven part of his soul soothed their misgivings and convinced them they loved him enough for another chance?

A coarse little tongue scraped his temple. Caiden flinched and closed an eye as the whipkin covered him in kisses. Her long-fingered paws took hold of his jaw and hair as she sniffed around his face and licked up half-dried salt tears.

"H-hi, sweet girl."

Did genetic coercion extend to animals too?

Ksiñe stood next to Lyli farther in the room, in deep discussion as they pored over a holosplay of data and a model of Caiden's shattered spine.

En said, "Ksiñe's the only surgeon in Emporia experienced with your sort of hybrid nervous system. And I'm biased, obviously, but an augmentation—hybrid organic and machine—can be installed and in-grown fast to replace your injuries. Biological regrowth is slow, even with a makeup like yours that regenerates at alarming speed."

What a good quality, for a soldier. He turned his cheek into the whipkin's soft fur. She curled around his skull and rooted her wet nose in his hair.

"The test flight of the *Second Wind* went well. Laythan is still allergic to Unity and anywhere the Dynast is, eager to leave, but we're waiting on you, kid. Laythan is hard but not heartless—he'll wait, even if he is furious right now. The fact that he hasn't kicked you out already means he's deeply attached, just can't show it."

Caiden knew why now.

"Furious, huh," he said. "And Taitn?"

She hesitated. "Taitn feels guilty. He's shut down, won't talk to anyone."

Silence filled the room. En leaned over him, her gaze brimming with compassion on the edge of pity. He didn't want pity.

And her compassion wasn't real. It was invoked.

"I'll do the augmentation," he said.

En reached into the stasis-bath liquid for his intact right hand and squeezed. Caiden felt it: a momentary break in the burn, the tingles fleeing from her touch. If only his whole body could be squeezed, the anguish wrung out of it.

Lyli approached, her creamy blue eyes filling with stars of data. She was dressed in luminous white and purple, and with her milky skin backlit, her bones showed through even more. "There are decisions to be made regarding material, style, and function."

Caiden looked at En, pleading.

"I'll take care of all that." En smiled down at him. "You're gonna love it."

He hadn't even spoken—his look alone swayed her. Caiden shut his eyes and couldn't muster a thanks.

En started chatting merrily with Lyli about hyperdiamond, biomineralized bone, dilatant nanoparticle skin, and morphic crystal.

The whipkin's warm furry body left. She jumped to Ksiñe as he approached and looked over Caiden's mangled body. "Casthen?" he asked.

Caiden blinked and met the Andalvian's red gaze. "Yes. Cracked the base of my skull. Ended up in flights I wasn't ready for, trying to escape. Heard things I didn't want to hear."

Ksiñe nodded and stroked the whipkin's back as she flattened to hug his torso. "Then you made best choices you could."

Caiden stared in surprise.

Ksiñe shrugged, his skin vibing calm lavender bands.

Was this gentle acknowledgment due to Caiden's Graven effect? He wasn't sure how to tell, how to recognize when or whether it was poisoning his interactions. If anyone was proof of the effect, it was Ksiñe. The Andalvian's hate had transformed into camaraderie in a short span of time. Seems it wasn't due to Caiden's efforts or empathy at all. Although Threi had struggled to influence Sina, also Andalvian—some species were more resistant.

Rousing softer thoughts, Caiden said, "Thank you for being my surgeon. I'd trust no one more."

If he was a Casthen cur bred to alter the wills of those in his presence—even to the slightest degree—he had to be all the more mindful and considerate. Anything, to balance out the monster they'd made him.

Caiden must have been making a weird expression, because Ksiñe's forehead speckled green and he plopped the whipkin by Caiden's head again. She nuzzled into his hair and licked the back of his ear, snuffling sweet sounds.

"Animals are medicine," Ksiñe said. "I prescribe her until time for operation."

Caiden smiled for the first time since the crash.

The whipkin groomed his hair, then her own snowy fur, then glommed onto half his skull and fell warmly asleep. Given that his head was all he could feel, Caiden soothed under the pressure and was able to relax without sleeping, until Ksiñe arrived with a team.

He begged not to be put to sleep—therein lay the desert of death—so instead he drifted in a chemically bizarre, muggy half-consciousness on the operating slab, infiltrated with filaments of light.

When it was time for the augmentation, a filmy oxygen mask covered his face and obscured the operation. Yet he *heard* every gruesome part of it. Squealing like pressure on a cracked pane of glass. Bursts of suction matched with flurries of dizzy heat in his brain. Grinding of an unsteady, ringing metal blade.

Occasionally, he made out En's warm citrus scent, and her voice, a husky whisper of optimism and faith telling stories to drown out the sounds of mutilation. Eventually, the team moved Caiden off the slab. His vision was a mess of textures, his hearing a tapestry of nonsensical delays. Groggy, he was helped upright in one of the Cartographers' rooms.

White, luminous Lyli grasped his right arm, her hands soft as cloud.

Dark, shadowy En was on his left, gripping his foreign shoulder: crystal that blurred an array of black folded petals. His arm was sleek, porous bone bundled in layers of plump bluish muscle, sapphire pins, and lustrous white tendons like bands of pure light.

He gasped at the flurry of sensation that radiated from En's touch, each cell a landscape of feeling, multiplied a millionfold.

"It'll calm," En assured.

Eyes closed, the sensory overload was all he could focus on as the two women moved him to another room. In the back of his mind he thought of Leta's synesthetic hypersensitivity, how sound sometimes cut her, a graze might bludgeon, and textures sat cruelly on her tongue. Like this... How had she possibly endured?

"The repairs to your spinal cord and the cervical curve of your vertebral column succeeded without incident. Additionally, your augmentation has been completely integrated with your nervous system. It has replaced eight percent of your body. How do you feel?"

"I *can* feel, that's better than before."

Lyli's piscine eyes smiled. "I understand you were dismayed by the mixed nature of your genetics, but it was precisely those strengths that made your spinal injury repairable. Your medic was quite complimentary of your biology."

Ksiñe seemed to value all things objectively. If he had known on their first meeting that Caiden was such a well-designed creature, would Ksiñe have hated him less?

"It's *fine* work." Strands of hair slithered from En's tie as she bent left and right to observe his arm. "My friend Cheza is the best dynamic pigment artist in Unity. Look at those flaws. Freckles, even!"

Caiden's new left shoulder and arm looked so identical to his right, he forgot it wasn't real. He smoothed his hand down the construct, skin-soft and brimming with sensation. His skin was warm. Slivers of black veins contoured the aug.

Lyli tried to stifle a charming smile, and bowed before leaving.

Caiden asked, "Before, it wasn't skin-toned, how——"

En whirled next to him and transformed in the same motion as he stretched his muscular right arm next to Caiden's left. The black seam veins fattened and skin turned translucent. The inner construct had workhorse materials scuffed by use, gouged with fight scars, and loose from age. Fat ribbons and wires pulsed, ready for action. "Think of a shiver from your neck down your arm."

Caiden imagined—it felt exactly like a shiver as the pigment dissolved and his skin grew transparent again. Bluish muscle ribboned around black bones and crystalline actuators. Angular strips of cloudy diamond covered his shoulder and the back of his neck. He imagined it had been part of him his whole life, like his mortal flesh was torn up and this had been beneath it all along.

He ran the skeletal black aug hand through his hair and turned to a mirror on the wall.

Several vertebrae had been replaced, including the spot where his slave brand had been.

Lustrous diamond replaced that symbol of Casthen property.

But Threi had ripped open a scab Caiden hadn't known he possessed. He wasn't property—he was *Casthen*. Their mark was in his bloodstream, his marrow, his voice, and every damn freckle on his skin.

He curled his hand into a fist, his blue machine muscles bulging. A shaky exhale leaked from him.

En smacked a hand on Caiden's hyperdiamond shoulder. "This represents your reckless bravery. Each augmentation is a story, a reminder. I'm not proud of all or most of mine, but these stories have built up into who I am."

"Reckless bravery, huh? You say that like it's a good thing."

"*I* think so." En patted Caiden's shoulder again. "I need to cheat some Cartographers out of medical fees and structure repair. Go check on your ship." En swept out the door.

Caiden found his shirts and morphcoat in a pile on the operating slab. A furry mound lay in the center: the whipkin, asleep.

"Hey now, I need these. Why didn't Ksiñe take you?" Caiden wiggled his fingers under the creature and lifted her up in a ball. She uncurled and climbed up his arm, stretching the length of it. He stroked her patterned back and noticed a message strip fashioned into a collar loop.

It read: *Painkiller.*

Caiden chuckled. He dressed while having to relocate the whipkin for every sleeve and buckle-up. His morphcoat transformed into soft leather with a hood, in which she coiled up while hugging his neck, nostrils whistling by his ear.

He exited the Cartographers' white warren halls to the main lobby— the circular platform in a cavern of lightseep clouds. Down a side passage toward the hangars, the Cartographer halls teemed with passagers and with maintenance teams repairing a great streak the *Azura* had left.

The activity drove the whipkin deeper into Caiden's coat, where she clung flat against his chest, little head over his heart. "Yeah," he said, "I wrecked this place. How big is the repair bill En's trying to cover?"

He unlocked the door to the docking recess where the *Azura* perched: a simple space with four of the Cartographers' luminous white walls. Purple and gold hues throbbed over her like bruises.

"You deserve my apology the most." He strode into the bay and dumped himself in the pilot's seat, settling his head in the cradle. The whipkin balled on his lap.

"Sorry, *Azura*."

The cockpit holosplays bloomed. A red stack of chevrons blinked, then formed blocky squiggles of text. It was the guttural language Taitn and Laythan argued in, and read: FLIGHT CONTROLS HAVE BEEN LOCKED BY COMMANDER TAITN MARAY ARTENSI. ENTER PASSCODE.

Caiden stared at the alert, heart sinking. *Commander?*

Taitn needed an apology the most, it seemed. Until Caiden got the codes, he'd lost his only set of wings.

CHAPTER 26

FOUND OR FORCED

The huge, beetle-like *Second Wind* parked inside Pent's depository, all prepped to leave. Laythan and Ksiñe huddled over inventory beside it.

Caiden fluffed up his bravery—the morphcoat obliged, changing to leather and spines. The whipkin clung to the whole side of his head, flattening his hair. Her slender prehensile tail thumped his cheek.

When they neared Ksiñe, the whipkin made a mighty leap to him. She squealed and climbed circles around his body.

"Thanks for the painkiller," Caiden said. "Worked wonders."

The Andalvian nodded, speckles pink.

Pent carted materials to a pile by the *Wind*'s side, and stopped to squint as Caiden approached. "Who is?!" he screeched. "Laythan Paraïa, letting a strange man come to ship—"

"This is the boy," Laythan said. Caiden would probably always be a *boy* to him. Laythan drew himself up, all tense muscles and rigid spine. He said nothing but folded his arms, waiting for an explanation.

Caiden paused to tighten the reins on his temper. Was temper a soldier trait too? *The darkness and violence you were bred for*, Threi said.

"Threi, that Casthen bastard... he came to steal the ship. The only thing I could do was fly."

"Stupid objectives like vengeance will get you killed, boy."

"You're not listening. I didn't fly seeking vengeance, I was trying to keep the *Azura* safe. I remembered all the dangers you'd drilled into me. As for vengeance..."

The captain narrowed his steely gaze, scars dimpling white.

Caiden braved the pause. "That need is carved into me each night. The memory jog perseverates nightmares. Every time I sleep, I'm back there, in some permutation of that day. Panca told me it won't ever stop, like hers."

"Panca?" Laythan's forehead wrinkled, shaping a crown of guilt. "She never—"

"Didn't you ever notice her medicating, or stop to ask her what she felt? She suffers as much as I do, just keeps it quiet."

Laythan rubbed his forehead and grimaced, drawing his hand through a storm of hair. "All right. We're leaving tomorrow. Make sure you and your ship are ready."

"About that…is Taitn here?" Nerves prickled Caiden's stomach.

"He's up in the sim room." Laythan squinted. "Why, what happened?"

"He locked the flight controls."

Laythan hissed a curse. "Well, go sort it out! If he'll talk. Take this." He handed over the blue lacquered flask.

"Th-thanks." Caiden headed to the second-floor lift, then paced inside as it ascended.

The lift doors opened. Taitn sat by the window wall, arms resting on his knees, watching vibrant signs, glazed reflections, and starship traffic.

Caiden sat next to him and took a small sip of the blue flask, relished the bittersweet, then handed it over.

Taitn accepted it but hesitated, eyelashes shivering.

Someone called the lift back down below. Caiden swore—out of time, and he'd only just arrived. "Are you…" There was no delicate way to ask. "How many years? How did you get through it?"

Taitn took a drink then looked at his hands between his knees. "Fifteen."

Accelerated fifteen years. Caiden winced. "All at once?"

Taitn said quietly, "There was only one skill they wanted from me. So, there's only one skill I'm good at. The best at." He spread his fingers in front of the window, backlit by countless hues. "I let ships become my real body, my expression…since this one isn't worth much else anymore."

The ascended lift opened. "Some people disagree," En said.

She walked over, sat, and clapped Taitn lightly on the back.

Taitn squeezed the flask until cracks burst through its lacquer. "What do you know about feeling comfortable in your own skin? You really don't have a heart anymore, do you?" He shot to his feet and caught the lift, leaving Caiden and En in silence.

Blue and gold spotlights streamed in front of them. Violet light bounced across the film in a blocky script that Caiden couldn't read backward, advertising something he wasn't interested in. En had her usual uplifting scent—citrus blossoms and spicy resin, mystery and cheer together.

"Well. I guess my question about the egress route will have to wait." She fished another, smaller flask from her coat and offered it. Purple flowers decorated white enamel. "Here. I keep this for injuries. I know you have a few."

Caiden took a sip. Floral with sweet overtones, a spicy heart, and hot both in temperature and flavor, it was perfect for her.

When he looked over, a tear ran down En's cheek, pulling the smoky stain from around her eyes.

"You too." He handed the flask back.

They watched the lights.

En asked, "How do you feel, with the aug?"

"Different. But right."

"Good. Augmentation—of all kinds—allows fluidity. Gender binary or neither, fluid, both, a different body or a noncorporeum. Before joining this family, I changed my shape, personality, and preferences constantly. I wouldn't recommend trying to fit to others' expectations. Create who you feel good being. And it's all right if that changes too."

I don't have a choice, En. I can't possibly rewrite every thread Çydanza weaved me from.

She smiled crookedly and handed him the flask. "The aug looks great on you. Cheers."

They sat in silence while Caiden warmed up his words, then asked, "Is Taitn a...Is he a commander of something?"

"Where'd you hear that?"

"He locked the *Azura*'s flight controls. It had his full name and title."

"Ah." She snatched the flask and sipped. "The Dynast's Bielskan faction uses children in its soldier programs. On the losing side of a galactic conflict, they needed a hero. Taitn was their top pilot at twelve years old. The military accelerated his physical and mental abilities so he could pilot them to victory."

"He had no choice?"

"They were his family. The wrong Bielska did was to throw him out when they were done with him. Heroes aren't useful in peacetime. They ignored and forgot about him, leaving him to cope with the aftermath of his rapid over-acceleration alone. He sees himself in you, I'm sure. So...you need to show him you're not going anywhere, and that you'll listen."

Caiden inhaled the liquor's fragrance, took a final sip, and offered the flask to En.

She shook her head. "Keep it and give it to Taitn. He's got injuries too." En nodded to the lift. "You can guess where he's retreated to. Much like Panca, there's only one place he feels at home."

Caiden smiled. "A ship."

He headed back down the lift and boarded the *Second Wind*. The interior was tri-level and spacious. Caiden walked through a big cargo hold into a branching hallway, onward to the bridge. There was no illumination except the console and holosplays. Taitn sat in the central pilot's chair. Delicate music flowed.

"The *Wind* is amazing." Caiden's voice rang conspicuously in the emptiness.

"She's no warship. But she'll handle whatever we throw at her." When Caiden drew closer, Taitn peered over and appraised him for a long moment.

Caiden scratched a hand through his hair and over the nape of his neck—brandless now.

"En's training paid off. You look good."

"And your training. You were right, the simulations were what I needed. I did hundreds while you were gone. I should have listened to you. And apologized faster."

Taitn folded his arms on the console and stared, eyes growing distant.

Caiden wrung his knuckles and looked around. *All damned, what do I say if apology doesn't work?*

Doleful string music floated from the console.

Caiden asked, "Do you regret it?"

Taitn looked over, frowning. "If things hadn't happened as they did, I wouldn't have met Laythan or the rest of these fools. I would have ended up back in another war, somewhere, probably."

"I never would have met any of you either, if..." If he had died. If Threi had found him on RM28. If his shipment had never been mixed up with the slaves' to begin with.

Caiden dug out En's flask and set it on the edge of the console. "En means to apologize too. She just doesn't know how to say it."

Taitn took the flask and scratched a thoughtful fingernail over its floral print.

Caiden leaned over the navigation unit, observing its parameters and components, a flight system entirely different from the *Azura*.

Taitn unfolded a holosplay of flight specs in the air. Caiden scrolled with a finger, assessing the ship's strengths and weaknesses in comparison.

Taitn hesitated. "You tried to tell me about seeing Threi, about the danger, and I didn't listen."

"That's not your fault."

"It is, though."

He drank from the flask. Caiden scrolled through engine specs.

The music sparkled and crooned.

"Let's both do better," Taitn said. "You're safer when you're allowed to stretch. I see that now... No more simulations. The code is 1238, Winn."

Heat crawled into Caiden's cheeks. The writing on the *Azura*'s floor, WI90NN-1238. Did Taitn know his name was a lie?

Taitn handed over the flask, and Caiden took a sip of fire-sweet. His smile grew and the flush crept up his neck.

Then his lifted spirits swiftly died and a sinking feeling crushed his ribs.

The codes had been fairly easy to obtain. He'd wedged his Graven will into a gap, and pressured the whole matter his way—was that how it worked?

Threi's words seeped in again, poisoning every interaction: *It's harrowing, to suddenly know your very reality is false, compelled.*

Caiden grew quiet while some of the crew filed in to prepare a final meal before they all departed in the morning.

Ksiñe set up a floor table and filled it with a spread of food. A large case folded out into a sort of miniature kitchen lab, and the gastronomer went about what could only rightly be described as art. Ksiñe elegantly sliced colorful food and lit things on fire. His whipkin dashed between him and the ingredients and tools, fetching and returning items. The aromas recovered Caiden's shriveled appetite and dark mood.

A meal, then a rest, then he would pilot the *Azura*, with Laythan watching over him, and they would all get safely out of Unity. Then Caiden would seek out a way to the Harvest.

He breathed more delicious scents. The path ahead was simple. He would worry about Graven things later.

Panca entered the bridge. Laythan stood and swept over, not slowing his stride or missing a beat until he crashed her into a huge embrace. Everyone stopped to look. Panca's eyes widened, the bright limbal rings flicking in confusion.

"Apologies, Panca," Laythan rumbled, still grasping her tight. "All these years. You'd think my eyes were healed, by the look of them, but I'm still a blind fool."

She softened and slipped her arms around him. "You've still cared. You don't need to show it."

"You *deserve* to be shown. That's where I failed." He led her over to the group under a fatherly wing.

Near the door, Taitn and En locked words. Caiden spied out the corner of his eye while chewing a small brick of fatty treak. Taitn handed En her flask back with a few short shy or grudging words. A spill of black hair covered En's expression as she extended a hand, which Taitn clasped. They spoke—not much—and Taitn yanked her by the arm into an embrace—not long—a clap on the back before he turned and strode for the table. En stayed, hand hovering and eyes wide, then shook her head. A smile itched the corner of her mouth.

She jogged over and pulled up a pillow to sit on, then poured herself and Caiden two mugs of a hot drink. She clinked hers against his.

He sipped. It had a dark, bloody citrus underscored by the old fragrance of oak. *Hisk, dash of mulled redmar.*

Ksiñe set down a sizzling platter. Curling black pods on top inflated an inner boll of fuzz. He popped one in his mouth and instructed, "Eat it whole."

Caiden tried one. The fuzz crisped on his tongue, crackling down to a melty nectar. Ksiñe tapped the side of the mug. Caiden drank. The sweetness transformed into a rush of bitter, brawny spice. He grinned.

As the crew got settled around the table, the whipkin chose Caiden's lap to snuggle in, of everyone's, and he puffed with pride.

Ksiñe lit flames and stirred mixtures, as if tending to a living thing. Grayish spots bubbled happily between his eyes. His scarlet pupils were less wild animal and more moonlike, tamed by joy in his art. "You are still too lean," he muttered, handing Caiden a tiny cloud of vapor surrounding a gleaming green kernel. "Also need zinc."

Caiden watched Panca slurp one gracefully, then copied her. He coughed, a fiery burst cooling into a creamy, eggy flavor. He couldn't help his moan.

En giggled. "Cute." She crunched a strip of crispy meat.

The crew's mood equalized into a content silence. Caiden took up a somber tone. "Hey...when Threi came for the ship, he told me he's a Dynast... something. As well as a Casthen Enforcer. Conspiring with Cartographers. He wants to destroy Çydanza."

Laythan snorted. "Don't get mixed up with someone who's playing three sides. He's playing his own. The Cartographers will keep the Dynast away from the *Azura* until we leave tomorrow, but it might—"

"They were forced," Caiden interrupted. He had to share everything if he was going to untangle any of it. "Threi is Graven—I don't know how or how much...less than Abriss. He coerced the Cartographers to keep the ship secure. He hasn't taken it outright because he needs me to join him first."

Laythan hissed through his teeth. "All the more reason to leave. What makes you believe he wouldn't take the ship to bait you to him?"

Caiden swore. "Hadn't thought of that. He seemed like...he really needs me to agree." *The nightmares. How could they possibly be useful to him?*

"Even better reason to leave," En said, "if he prefers mind games over force."

Taitn frowned. "Once we're out of Unity, where's a safe planet to stash the ship on while things cool down? Somewhere Winn can also get a handle on flying, and growing more?"

Everyone fell silent, considering this. Caiden scritched the whipkin's belly while she clasped his hand in long-fingered paws.

Ksiñe shrugged, face darkening. En folded her arms. "Laythan—"

"No."

She scoffed. "We all know about your private, uncharted planet. And we all know you'll never retire. It's the only charting you've never turned over to the Cartographers, yeah? The ship will be secure there if literally no one but you knows it exists."

"No."

"You have a better place in mind?"

Laythan grumbled and pulled up a database holosplay to comb over a map. "I'll find something else."

The subject dropped and the crew returned to light conversation and a sweet course Ksiñe prepared. Caiden lifted out of his brooding, and like a little ember nestling into tinder, he relaxed into the warm glow of the moment. With family.

Forced family.

The crew wasn't unhappy with him. That counted for something. He wasn't Threi, bullying his way through life with the whip of his Graven will.

In a pocket, he twirled the glass chicory flower between his fingers.

"Hey." En fixed him with a side-eye. "What's on your mind?"

"Hm? Nothing."

"Something. I swindle and flirt for a living, you think I can't read a face?"

"*Create who you feel good being*, you said. I want to be the difference I never had, someone who can champion for those unable to fight for themselves."

En threw her arms around him, crumpling him against her chest. "Aww, kid, your heart is huge. We aren't telling you to squash that, we're trying to make you see that you *already did your part* for justice. You paid back with your memory jog. And there are plenty of small good deeds to do in the multiverse, you don't need to topple an empire to make a difference."

Caiden clawed his fingers through his hair to slick back the waves En had mussed. "Without that empire toppled, the multiverse's perspective won't shift. The normalization that keeps generating exploitation and damage won't change. I need to take action before the multiverse's corruption becomes normalized in my heart too."

"All right, we hear you," En said. "But we still need to get out of Unity first. Take this *one* break to not worry." She fished in her pockets and pulled out a stack of glass rectangles. "Game?"

"I don't know how to play."

"Watch a round first. Taitn!" She wagged the pieces.

The pilot looked up from his flask, flushed and scowling. "Play Layth or Pan."

"Come on."

Taitn's eye contact faltered. His fingers screwed together as he feigned interest in the flask's broken lacquer. "Then change...Please."

En's pretty smile widened.

"I won't play you like that."

En waited, but Taitn didn't look up. She sighed. "All right, gallant." En ran a hand over her face and up through her hair, arcing into straighter posture as his body expanded and sculpted. Shorter hair, lighter skin, and a shadow along his chin. En's smile stayed the same, and while Taitn's scowl didn't cool, the tension visibly eased from his shoulders.

"Why does it matter?" Caiden muttered.

"You'd understand," Taitn said quietly, reaching for his share of the disks. "Seeing a memory over and over scrapes the injury so raw it can never heal."

CHAPTER 27

RED AS HATE

Caiden crept from the *Second Wind* once everyone fell asleep, and backtracked through Emporia. Sated and smiling, having won six games through "beginner's luck," En claimed, he walked with easy steps, happier than he'd been since before the day the sky opened.

At twenty, having mended the knots and frayed ends his mistakes made, he fit into the crew like a missing piece that snapped them all into place with one another. He had the flight codes for the *Azura*, he would whisk her out of the Casthen's reach, and his memory jog would continue to make waves. Packs of Dynast sentinels already prowled Emporia, preparing to enforce the order that the Casthen vacate Unity.

Caiden entered the colossal concourse of layered walkways, where waterfalls filled the lightseep surfaces. Huge plumes of vapor coiled all around without sound, temperature, or taste. He walked toward the Cartographers' district on the same route as that first day headed to his acceleration, strolling down to same atrium where—

The walls were bright with image feeds, this time too. Caiden froze as a rough female voice grated his ears.

"—*don't judge the expulsion, as it's allowed our fleet to focus on recovery efforts in CWN82, where other planets are being reclaimed, which is an opportunity, and blame always gets in the way of opportunity.*"

Çydanza, the Casthen's Prime.

There was no image for her feed, just their symbol—his old brand—in the center of the screens. A crowd clotted around them in the atrium.

"A planet was discovered in the middle stages of being set up as a replacement livestock-breeding operation—though the faction responsible is unknown."

Heat surged up Caiden's neck. His morphcoat flickered into scales. *Unknown? My memories showed them—*

"A pity, since nophek are so rare and delicate, the existence of the precise environment to farm them could have been unimaginably lucrative if it had been shared, and the Dynast could have profited most of all if they had cooperated instead of looking to their own interests."

Caiden closed his eyes. The slave-brand emblem burned in afterimage against his eyelids. Red as hate.

His focus flocked away. His body turned to fire poorly contained in skin, while tightness gathered in his stomach.

Çydanza's voice was a rasp of sand. *"The recording itself was found to be compromised, fabricated by the Cartographers, for suggestion is a powerful thing, even stronger impressed by a powerful machine, stronger still to influence a young, developing brain, and what does it say that the Cartographers have yet to respond to the allegations that their mnemonic source is himself a passager?"*

Lies. Power moves.

He could waste the rest of this life trying to get to Çydanza. She had no face or form, not even something he could imagine to play out his scenarios of vengeance in his mind. She lay in a fortress obfuscated by centuries of myth.

"The source—a young mosaic—was stolen Casthen property, implemented in the nophek operation organized by the unknown faction, and while the doctored memories are meant to incriminate the Casthen, our presence in CWN82 was merely a result of tracking our stolen property."

Caiden reached up to where his brand had been. His fingertips tingled, nail trembling *tick-tick* against the diamond.

"With the allegations against us in flux, I have gained Dynast and Cartographer clearance that my Enforcer remain in Unity to oversee a number of operations in critical motion."

Threi. What new scheme was this?

Caiden elbowed through the crowd and headed out. This wouldn't rile him like it had his fourteen-year-old self. Even in a corrupt multiverse, there were things to love and enjoy. Perhaps he *could* be happy doing small actions that mattered, and let the rest go. He'd done his part with the memory jog, and the Casthen wouldn't be able to refute it. He could thrive by doing justly in every moment possible.

A new voice from the feed stopped Caiden in his tracks.

"*To some, the ethics of farming nophek may be acceptable under the light of these new developments. But I ask you to observe the ethics of their slaughter.*"

The Dynast Prime. Her radiant, enthralling voice snared him and twined him up, pivoted his feet, and wrung out every worry he'd thought was on his mind.

As Abriss spoke, the crowd reoriented toward the display wall in one collective wave that shoved Caiden to the front. Abriss wasn't physically present, this time, but her image appeared on the screen, her strangely ordinary but mesmerizing freckled features almost as powerful as that first encounter. Her voice was just as twilight and soothing, even filtered through the broadcast system.

Caiden's willpower dissolved into a summery feeling, an ease and purpose, heart quivering, eager to protect.

It terrified him.

"*The investigation into the memory jog has concluded without question. As such, we will take no action to overturn it. My stars have told me this is amenable to all, but we should educate ourselves with hindsight.*"

Shivers caressed his skin. The precision of her diction felt like it arranged him, too, sorted his thoughts, cleared the unnecessary.

"*It is not Dynast policy to get involved in multiversal conflict. There is safety in the known, not the new. In Unity, we know how to treat disease, prolong life, generate free energy, and stabilize commerce. The Casthen may do as they will, for the danger and corruption outside Graven Unity is the punishment inherent in leaving it.*"

The Prime closed her eyes for a long moment. The crowd went dead-still. Her lashes rose, thoughts aligned. "*We rescind our incrimination of the Casthen free-course faction following this conclusive proof that the Cartographers' anonymous mnemonic record was falsified.*"

"False?" Caiden breathed. He didn't hear her next words awash in the murmur of the crowd. Shock doused some of the Prime's effect on him, and he edged closer to the screen. "Those memories weren't false. *We can't keep erasing the reality of slavery.*"

Caiden strode for the wall's screen.

A black-gloved Dynast hand shoved him back. "Respect, cur."

Cur... He glared at the sentinel. The man blinked at him, nonplussed—snared by Caiden, another Graven spider. Caiden balled up frustration in his diaphragm and lungs and spoke with all his energy. "*Step back.*" The sentinel obeyed with a puzzled look still on his face.

A vile sickness twisted Caiden's insides. He was a monstrous thing the Casthen had made, and he could never change that.

The black storm of old rage swallowed all the warmth and optimism Caiden had gained after his dinner with the crew. *Everything I suffered for. Every nightmare that'll gnaw me up for the rest of my life—all for nothing.*

He didn't hear any more words. He curled his augmented fist, marched to the wall, and slammed it into the screen. The Prime's image rippled. His new muscles were more than tight: he felt charge gather, pinpricks of power and speed clouding into a storm that he loosed. His next punch sent radial cracks skittering three meters through the wall, crashing into the woman's image. It wasn't her he was angry at. His anger just *was*. Perhaps always would be.

He drew back for another hit. Gloved hands hauled him away by his shoulders but couldn't stop his thrust. He pummeled the glassy rift, throwing up liquid and sparks. The pigmentation streaked off the surface of his aug hand to reveal transparent skin and black bone beneath.

Dynast officers dragged Caiden into a tight bundled group. As the fight drained from him, it surged in them: a fist met his jaw and snapped his head back. Arms looped his elbows and stretched him. Their shouts and curses muddled, and Caiden laughed, which turned to a bloody cough. A knee or boot found his belly. "Cur" spat into his ear.

Caiden ripped his left arm free, elbowed a skull as he drew back for a punch. He struck at an officer's looming face, but a knobby gray hand caught his wrist mid-swing from behind.

Caiden's blue muscles fattened, the storm in them curling against the hold. He looked up at his captor: a male saisn's dark face, pitted with broad furrows. The face of a powerful tamed animal that still had wild in it. His muscular features were rife with discoloration from healed scars. His eyes were black pools with a burning limbal ring, and the jeweled accretion in his forehead reflected pure white under the overhead lights.

Caiden froze, noting the gray-and-purple Cartographer garments honing the saisn's sinewy frame.

"That is enough damage, Passager." His forearm bulged with pronounced muscle bands, just able to match Caiden's augmented strength.

Behind the saisn rushed a winded Lyli, pale as a ghost. "Disciplinarian! I will handle this."

Disciplinarian? Shit. Caiden, panting, twisted his wrist but it was held fast.

Lyli said, "This passager is recovering from grave injury and is under my aegis. You may stand down as well, sentinels. Merely a fit of pique."

An admirable attempt to save him, but the saisn yanked Caiden away from the group. Lyli caught up and snatched the Cartographer's coat to stop him at the edge of the crowd.

"Maul, release him, there is no need for this. He did not hurt anyone. It was simply a wall, and they are easily repaired."

"Do you not think the crash did enough property damage?" Maul's voice was gravel, his throat serrating the words. "I advise he learn to curb his reactions or move on from them, before punching a wall turns into worse." He tossed Caiden free.

Caiden massaged his knuckles. The pigment un-glitched. He stepped to Lyli and lowered his voice. "My memories aren't false. What good is your memory jog technology if it can so easily be claimed to be fabricated? Get a vishkant to confirm my truth!"

She shook her head. "If it were so straightforward, there would be no contention. I am sorry, Passager." Lyli made to reach for him but curled her hands together over her chest instead. Afraid of him? She stepped closer and lowered her voice too. "Please come with me so I can examine your well-being, and do not worry, it was simply a wall—"

"No," Caiden whispered. "Maul is right."

My anger is a taproot, straight to the Casthen. The acceleration hadn't pulled it out of him, and the nightmares nourished it like water. The soldier's temper bred into him made for fertile soil. His bloodstream pulsed with violence and darkness, as Threi had said, just itching for a way out of his body.

Threi's promise, *We'll kill Çydanza with a blade of her own design.* Caiden had been searching for belonging and purpose, but it lay with the Casthen all along.

Maul towered. "Clinician Lyli, why are we housing this passager's ship in our secure docking recess?"

A muffled, amplified voice behind them replied: "Because I said so."

CHAPTER 28

ENEMY OF MY ENEMY

Five Casthen parted the crowd. The man in the lead had a confident, swaggering gait and a tall, broad-shouldered, slim-waisted build that was unmistakable even with the featureless blue mask covering his face and even if he hadn't said, "Leave, sentinels, he's here with me," at which the Dynast group shuffled and muttered among themselves. Groups were harder to coerce, it seemed. Threi's shoulders contorted at the hesitation, and he twisted to face them, having to repeat the order with intent and gravitas, "*Leave*," before the sentinels peeled off like clouds facing a gale.

"Cartographers." Threi recovered with a dashing bow. "I'll take it from here."

Maul's face scrunched, considering, then he grunted and turned to leave. Lyli wore a relieved and loving expression. She bowed then followed Maul. Lucky for Threi: two species he had an easier time convincing.

Threi turned a circle to the rest of the mixed passager crowd. "All of you can leave now too—show's over." A third of them loved him enough to obey. He yanked off his mask and peered around the crowd with a gentle "*Go*," and convinced the next third to drain out the atrium exits. Snarl wrinkles stacked across the bridge of his nose. He nodded to his Casthen crew, who bullied out the remainder of the crowd.

Caiden rubbed his kicked jaw and straightened. His morphcoat leather thickened, ready for a fight. "What a good soldier you are, able to eliminate a threat in moments. Not perfect, though, are you?"

Threi swiveled to face him, simmering. "Not yet."

"Why are you here?"

"I came to see Abriss's statement, because who doesn't want to watch a leader so plain and uncharismatic charm an entire crowd?" Threi dragged his hand through dark curls.

The other armored Casthen fidgeted, hands near glaves.

"And you," Caiden said, "so handsome and charming, struggle to dismiss that same crowd." Aggravating the Enforcer wasn't a smart move, but Caiden was in a tetchy mood.

Threi donned an artful smile. "A shame, the falsification of your memory jog."

"That was you."

"Not I. Çydanza sees quashing rogue errors as a game. The result of your survival—incrimination—was an error she swiftly corrected."

"Really? She seems less real to me every day. Yet *you* benefit directly."

The others shuffled at his hostility, but Threi laughed. "True. Now you've gained absolutely nothing from the memory jog except trauma that will hound you the rest of your life." The man glanced among his crew. "Return to the ship. The Paraborn and I need to talk."

They took no extra urging to obey.

When they'd left earshot, Threi said, "I twirl around my finger three keys: your liberation from horror, your route to the Casthen Harvest, and the secret to killing Çydanza at last."

Pulled hard by those promises, Caiden closed his eyes. The brand of the Casthen afterimage still hung there. The nightmares were a permanent brand, one he couldn't replace as easily as skin and bone. He said, "Tell me your plan, start to finish."

"Sorry, pup, can't do that. Mind, memories, and information are more powerful currency than you know. And even with all you've seen and heard, there's still a *lot* of the multiverse that can't be explained by anything less than direct experience. And if not knowing every detail scares you, you're not ready for life in this multiverse anyway."

Threi stalked close and extended his hand, gloved in black membrane and tiny scales of scratched steel . . . resuming where they had left off in the previous encounter. "Deal?"

Caiden had thought being an adult would solve everything; he'd wanted to be just like Laythan and the others. But the crew showed him how deeply old lessons burred in, and how easy people found it to ignore them as time passed on. Caiden needed to face his knots head-on, *now*, and not carry them along into the rest of his life like bits of shrapnel folded into the body by scars, still digging shapes into him.

He would have rather died on the nophek planet than have survived only to relive that day over and over. And he would happily sacrifice himself to end the Casthen, if the path were clear. He couldn't live happily while knowing they still exploited vulnerable worlds.

He loved his new family, even if his genes had forced them to accept him. But they deserved better; he would become someone grown *out* of the atrocity from which he came. Only that would prove he was worth their care.

Threi's eyes were dead sapphires, betraying nothing.

"Deal." Caiden grasped the man's hand as he might a snake in the grass: before it could strike.

He trekked alone to the *Azura*'s docking recess, his decision hardening into reality. His unbuckled morphcoat transformed to a thin mesh, and he picked up a brisk pace to feel some air. The Casthen were the only weight left in him, and unfettered from anything else, he could focus solely on ripping them out of the world, and his rage with them.

He input the security for the door, which dissolved open.

Taitn stood before the *Azura*. "There you are. You disappeared after the party."

"You all fell asleep..."

"*I* did. En passed out. There's a difference." Taitn clapped Caiden on the back and rested his arm there. "How does your neural link feel? Not altered by the operation?"

The neural link congealed with proximity, spreading a sunny, satisfying feeling. *Taitn must not have heard about the falsification yet. If I tell him, he'll try to convince me it doesn't matter.*

"Link's still strong." Caiden's voice quavered.

Taitn's gaze cruised over the *Azura*'s black, glistening hull. "I'm curious what the link will allow you to do, over time. We might have only scratched the surface of what this ship is capable of. The engines are tuned to her universe. Panca thinks some of the stranger components *only* function there."

Shut up, Taitn. Each adoring word dug Caiden's pit of guilt deeper.

Taitn spun him gently. "Everything all right? You look downhearted."

Throat tightening, he managed to reply, "Just tired."

"Laythan will come by soon to fly with you. We'll be out of Unity in no time."

"Thanks, Taitn. And...well. I didn't have real siblings, but..." Caiden hesitated lamely, staring at Taitn's bearded face that might have looked brutish if not for the warmth in his eyes. "Well, never mind."

Taitn's smile widened. "Rest up." He headed for the door, his footfalls echoing, the ties on his boots jingling.

"Taitn—" Caiden fumbled for meaningful words. Something better than a goodbye. "I think Lyli likes you. You should talk to her."

Taitn turned, and Caiden almost burst out laughing at the man's stunned expression.

"No more spending time with En for you." His blanched face turned rosy. He pivoted and walked out, but his shoulders shook with a chuckle.

The door materialized closed, leaving the wall uniform and smooth. Caiden's smile wilted. Warmth left.

He perched his hand on one of the ship's vanes and pressed against her solid metal, traced her older scars with a finger. The *Azura* was his home, his safety, his rock in the turbulence of the multiverse. Upright, weathered, and battered, like him. Of mysterious composition, like him.

"We saved each other." He ran his fingertip along a seam. "I can get through this if I have you. This final stretch."

He walked inside, threw his coat over the pilot's seat, and slumped in it, resting his head in the neural cradle. Luminous holosplays unfurled in the cockpit air. Blocky print still read: FLIGHT CONTROLS HAVE BEEN LOCKED BY COMMANDER TAITN MARAY ARTENSI. ENTER PASSCODE.

"Twelve thirty-eight."

Tension unleashed. A surge of energy foamed through the *Azura*'s mass. Caiden exhaled, and teared up at the immensity of the release, felt through the link. Half his tension had really been hers. He leaned back and let it un-ratchet from his tendons, the stress ooze from his bones.

The others would be better off without him coercing them to help when they shouldn't. He had wondered why his jagged edges didn't puzzle into the crew's smooth sides, harming then even when he tried his best. His edges fit the Casthen already.

Caiden set the glass chicory flower on the center of the console. Hopefully the core of him, the shining spirit Leta had seen, would keep him sane in whatever Casthen void he headed into.

"I'm not the boy who ran away. I'm the man who's coming to avenge."

The ship sang as he lifted his hands into the drive guides. Tendrils of light wrapped his fingers, infiltrated his nerves. Caiden's neural firing knit into the glossy spine above him, and his sense of body expanded to the ship, from its delicate shielding to the heavy, ancient mineral of its fuselage. There was something primordial yet deeply advanced about her: the ineffable patched with the mundane.

The *Azura*'s mini thrusters hummed. The floor of the hangar dematerialized on command. The particles twinkled away like sand, revealing the massive hollow of a hangar gaping beneath. He lowered the ship gently. Light-studded landings stacked the hangar's walls, with passager ships of all size and type berthed against them. A hexagonal pad in the center of the space lay empty except for Threi's Glasliq. Purple ruffles of flame edged the ship's quiet thrusters as it landed. The avian wings shivered and collapsed to its compact body, rippling into a seamless vitreous surface.

Caiden's heart stumbled at the sight of the enemy. He arced his hands, spinning gently around to face the Glasliq as he lowered. A doleful tone filled the *Azura* when he set her down on the pad.

Compression jammed his chest. Shoulders rigid. He withdrew his hands from the guides, which dissolved in weepy sparkles. The engines ramped down.

He rolled out of the seat and signaled the bay doors open with a mental command.

Threi's crew clustered by the Glasliq's base, while Threi strode for the *Azura*, a holosplay database unfolded over his palm. He flicked at a map, and hardly looked up as he strolled into the *Azura*'s bay. The moment Threi stepped in, the energy hum of the ship agitated, scratchy in Caiden's neural link like interference in a signal.

Threi said, "I can fly us home, it's quite far—"

Caiden snapped, "It's not my home."

"Oh, pup, do yourself a favor and accept these facts early. If you have any resistance, the Casthen will break you. You'll be much more resilient if you lean into it. Besides, it's true. We can even visit the lab where they mixed up the cocktail that's you. Or the warehouse where your birthing pod was housed. How about that?"

While Caiden smoldered, Threi continued linking together a route of egresses and universes on his map.

"The journey will take enough time that we can get to know one another, but I already know you, young mechanic-would-be-soldier. There's very little you need to know about me that I haven't told you already."

"You've only told me your name and that you're loyal to yourself yet serve everyone. They call that a 'slut,' I think."

Threi laughed. "And I've stayed alive a *long* time."

Caiden closed the bay door. "So, which of the fables are true? The Casthen Harvest is a portal inside a whale's stomach? Folded into the interstices of time. Scattered between different universes that make up a whole. You have to sacrifice the blood of an innocent to get in, or sing the right notes of an old star-mariner song?"

"All of those, yes," Threi said, squeezing the holosplay shut. "Though it's technically not a *whale*; we call it a holobia."

"You're joking."

Threi angled for the pilot's seat but hesitated as Caiden flinched. They locked eyes until Threi backed up with an elegant gesture to the chair. "You fly. I'll instruct. If you pass out from strain, I'll grab the twitch drive."

Caiden hesitated, fingers tickling the glave on his hip.

"Oh, stop. I'll be right behind you." Threi positioned at the back of the seat. When Caiden didn't move, Threi said, "For your own sake, pup. I know about your accident. Your leash hasn't ever been unclipped, but it's time now. I have more years in a cockpit than your Taitn Maray Artensi. More conquests than Endirion Day. More crew under my command than Laythan Paraïa. Sit, Winn: let's go kill the Casthen Prime."

CHAPTER 29

GATEKEEPER

It was better not to say goodbye. The crew would know what he chose, and in time they'd move on. He'd just be a stray Laythan had fixed up that ran off again. He had to head into his darkness alone.

Caiden relaxed in the pilot's seat as Unity's rind approached and engulfed the ship, filling the view with a swash of pearlescent color. Once they were through, the scenery past the cockpit window crisped into detail. The ship systems pieced together light into imagery more stable than their velocity would afford a human eye. Blue and lavender gases devoured a nearby planet. Behind it, tiny stars buttoned a swath of milky dust. Charting appeared in the cockpit, overlaying the view.

Background processes analyzed the redshift of nearby alignment stars, and within moments the ship's timepieces calibrated. The transmitter tech clocked subatomic dimensional wobble based on the local universe's gravity wave carrier... and stalled messages from the crew stacked in.

Anguish leached into Caiden's breast. *These'll break me if I read them now.*

"Can I offer you some advice?" Threi asked, coming up behind him.

"Shut up."

"If you've made a decision, own what you've chosen. Don't look back or vacillate. You're sad? Fine. Feel it and get it over with, because in this multiverse you'll be up against something else in the next moment and you'll need that head clear. Let me fly." Threi sidled into the cockpit. "We need to chain through multiple egresses and I don't want to be directing you the whole time."

One stellar egress lay up ahead: a wall of opaque, glowing dust hanging like a spiral curtain. Bundles of distorted lines pulled the milky light back into a ring shape, with a starless void gaping in the middle: a hole in the folds of spacetime. Stellar egression would get them quickly between universes across vast distances, jumping galaxies and universal clusters.

Caiden peeled himself from the seat to let Threi take his place, the man fitting poorly with his Casthen armor.

"How long is it going to take to get there?"

"It'll feel like a couple days."

"Are you capable of straight answers?" Caiden twitched at the sight of an intruder in his seat.

Threi shrugged and zoomed the ship right into the black maw of the egress.

The void slammed into Caiden. Every particle of him stopped, slathered across space and time. Squiggly electric filaments whipped across the walls, his skin, every inch of space. Then pressure slapped him back together. Wavy threads of light sucked back into their surfaces. The darkness pooled.

Caiden clung to the seat as nausea boiled and sparks danced. It was far worse than crossover.

"First of fifteen. Get used to it." Threi sat forward, hands in the twitch drive instead of the light guides. His fingers moved with delicate precision as he rode gravity like rapids.

Through the cockpit, another egress drew near: glowing dust spiraled into a starless pit, strapped open by belts of curved light. Caiden groaned.

The light ring of the egress swept over them, then the black circle engulfed the cockpit. Caiden was again buffeted, streaked, and snapped back into his body, stumbling to a kneeling position. The view filled with prim asteroid belts around a striped gas giant. Beside them, a universe rind dominated the expanse with fiery waves of cerulean and orange. The rind swept through the ship, kicking Caiden in the stomach and stopping his heart for several beats. He gasped on the other side and blinked at bizarre afterimages.

Asteroids hurtled at the cockpit. Caiden death-gripped the seat as Threi calmly spun the ship sideways.

"Relax." Threi dived effortlessly, his fingers a flurry of spasms in the twitch drive. "We have incredible shielding."

Caiden winced at each nick in the *Azura*'s armor field.

"What a find." Threi pulled out of the rocks. "To think she was perched in the desert this whole time. We combed that planet and found nothing. At least, not anything that wasn't well buried at the time."

"Shut up."

Threi craned his neck back and smiled at Caiden's scowl. "Sorry, pup."

"Don't call me that."

"Sure, soldier."

Caiden was ready for the next egress, which helped, but Threi banked the ship sharply right into a second. The gut-kick of it doubled him against the back of the seat. His joints popped, and a buzz oozed out of his head.

"Twelve more of these?"

Threi waved Caiden off. "Take a break, you're annoying. Rest. Eat. And so forth."

There was nothing to eat but emergency rations. Caiden already missed Ksiñe.

He headed to the scour, fully clothed. It didn't clean as thoroughly, but he welcomed the tingle and untangling. In the sleeping chamber, exhaustion folded him on the bed. But memories waited in sleep, and he wasn't ready for those to hammer more cracks in him. He rebounded between deep relaxation and the adrenaline of catching himself falling asleep.

Metal banged metal, reverberating into the room.

Panic seared Caiden awake. His brain mashed the sound into memory and kicked him back to the desert: *Sand worm, wriggle out.*

"We're here," Threi called down.

Caiden jolted from the bed, quivering, swearing, and ran a hand through sweaty hair. He walked up into the bay and peered out the cockpit windows. The ship drifted beside a tiny moon or a very large asteroid, wreathed in fine dusts. The surface was oak brown, rough and pitted, nothing of interest except a few bluish scabs.

"All right, hotshot, put this on." Threi tossed him a body harness of silvery webbing with small wing-shaped tanks over the shoulder blades.

Caiden unfolded it, frowning, then walked over to the cockpit windows. The cloudsuit was for spacewalking, but this moon-thing orbited nothing, and the vicinity map looked sparse. A distant sun lay behind them. "Why don't we land?"

"That's not a planet." Threi strolled to the end of the bay and poked around in a holosplay of auxiliary systems. He initiated an atmoseal membrane over the doors: it purled like fire then calmed into a luminous sheet of violet.

Caiden said, "You're not used to explaining things, are you? You just order people around."

"Usually, yeah. Suit up so we can get you tethered." Threi fished a long cord from the bag he'd brought and looked around for something to tie it to. "It's not a planet, it's the species called holobia."

"*Species?*"

"It survives in space by having a self-sustaining internal ecosystem. Water cycle and plants and critters—or so I hear."

Caiden paused mid-dressing, one leg in the lattice of the suit. "Shit. There really is a portal in its belly?"

"We're not going *inside* it. What I need you to do is get it to uncurl."

Caiden straightened. "You're serious."

"Deadly." Threi began attaching the line to a tether loop in the floor. "Entrance requires at least two people; I'll be the pilot, you be the bait. A good first test for you, don't you think? This holobia won't flinch at being pummeled with space debris or weaponry, but it's sensitive to bioharmonic electromag fields. If you touch it, it'll start to move and I'll fly you out to lure it away, then reel you back in. It's faster than you think, so don't get ground to mush between the surface plates or whacked into the void or, you know, swallowed."

"Swallowed? This is sounding more and more like a joke," Caiden grumbled as he yanked on the rest of the harnessing over his clothes and head. The silvery cords crisscrossed his limbs and torso. Threi threw him the end of the tether, which Caiden fitted into the molecular fastener between his shoulder blades. All in all, it didn't feel like much protection. "Who do you usually get to be live bait?"

Threi glided over, grinning. "Oh you'll meet everyone soon enough. Your brand-new family, Winn." He clapped Caiden on the back, which also triggered the cloudsuit.

A second skin of fleecy material spread over Caiden's body, filling up between the spaces of the harness. The fleece crawled over his skull, and he held his breath as it sealed up his mouth and nostrils—but then the material all over him flashed and puffed up. Gas expanded in gaps between weird molecules, continuing to puff out until the material became a hazy, translucent aura wreathing him entirely. The protective cloud scintillated, infiltrated with floating particles of other materials or functions. Caiden inhaled tangy oxygen as a pocket of air formed around the front of his face.

Threi punched the bay doors open. The *Azura*'s tail split to a vista of stars. The luminous atmoseal membrane across the opening was all that defended them against the void.

Brow scrunching, Caiden walked over and stood before the opening. "You want me to touch it? Where?"

The ship had drifted so the thing Threi called an animal swung into view below: a sphere of oak skin, bland all around.

Threi shrugged. "Doesn't matter. Can't tell front from back anyway."

Caiden stepped through the atmoseal, which fizzed angrily around his cloudsuit until he was past. Into the utter silence of space. Blood rushed in his head, breath whisked his ears.

The unfolded bay-door panels made a ramp out to nothingness, and as he walked to the edge, he left the *Azura*'s scalar gravity field. The invisible nodes of it tugged his body until he was out, weightless, feet lifting off the ramp.

Nothing but the semi-visible cloudsuit protected him from space. Nerves flittering, Caiden peered down. *I'm really going to let Threi tug me around like a worm on a line?*

He tried to figure out how it was all a big joke, Threi winding him up for a lark. When he glanced back, the bastard was smiling.

Caiden sucked in a deep breath and pushed off into the vastness of space. The tether wiggled behind him, an umbilical to the ship.

Stars spotted the ether.

Caiden floated, and his heart kicked at him, but not because of the cold beauty of the surroundings. Because the sensation in his body was the same as the memory jog process, a weightless and silent pressure carrying him.

Groundless, alone.

The holobia's desolate surface looked like RM28, the nophek planet. It stretched to fill his view as he approached. Caiden was going back to the desert, stranded on a prison world he shouldn't have escaped. That fear was a whisper, this time, not the punch it had been before when the flight-simulation planet triggered visions of home.

The cloudsuit wicked away his panic sweat in cold little flurries. The suit's composition regulated temperature, radiation, and atmosphere, while the edge of it, a half meter from his body, pushed a path through the dust.

Caiden glanced behind; the *Azura*'s black flank glistened under distant sunlight. The tether snaked to her across the void.

Inertia drifted him closer. The rock had no noticeable gravity, artificial or otherwise, despite its looming presence, a couple kilometers across. He stretched out a gloved hand to stop his glide.

He touched, palm flattening on the oaky surface. Dust curled away.

Nothing happened.

That bastard. Probably cackling at me right now.

Caiden gripped the rough surface so he wouldn't rebound away. He peered over his shoulder. The *Azura*'s thrusters idled. The umbilical tether was still attached, at least.

He sighed into his suit's pocket of air and closed his eyes, stilled his mind and racing pulse.

The rock under Caiden's palm split open.

Brown texture peeled back like a lid. Cloudy membranes slithered aside and glassy flesh beneath rolled with color.

A pupil contracted to a void-black circle in front of him.

An eye. *Fifteen meters across.* Caiden flailed back, kicking instinctively to propel away. The eyelid slammed shut like an avalanche then peeled open again, all the more terrifying because the huge motion was utterly silent. Deep as a lake, feral colors swam in a bioluminescent iris and that great pupil dilated like a black hole. More skin split, and across the holobia's surface, twenty more enormous eyes opened and swiveled to Caiden.

Swears poured off his tongue. Caiden rowed his limbs uselessly through the vacuum.

Laborious and silent, the massive beast moved at him.

The tether yanked. Caiden rushed backward, breath wrenched from his lungs. Stars streaked. Threi punched the acceleration to drag him away. Caiden's intestines clumped against his bladder. The velocity made the cloudsuit congeal around his head and back, hot and tingly.

A rumble from the holobia juddered Caiden's bones. He peered past his feet and watched the holobia's body uncurl. The puzzle-piece armor of its surface uncoupled as it stretched, no longer a sphere but more of a flatworm shape. Amidst the folds of its segmented body, Caiden spotted the reason why they needed it to move: the beast curled around a stellar egress. Light speared out into space as the brilliant ring of the structure was revealed.

All damned, this bullshit is the Casthen's front door? Caiden whipped through space as Threi jetted the *Azura* away, and the holobia followed. Its front was all eyes, and the skin separating them diminished or sank in until one monstrous single eye surface stretched the front of the animal.

The pupil squeezed into a horizontal bar. Which split open. Into a mouth.

Caiden squeaked indecent sounds.

The holobia picked up enormous speed as a freakish maw opened, a whole planet split in half to swallow the *Azura* whole.

"*To void with this! Threi! Faster!*" The suit absorbed his words, and there was no audio link to the ship anyhow, but Caiden streamed curses and scrabbled back to clutch the tether.

The holobia's mouth was a muscular pit wide enough to consume a ship a hundred times the *Azura*'s size in one bite. Saliva curtains layered inside like atmoseal membranes.

Caiden's frenzied breathing was the only sound as he watched the maw gaining, wider, mucus gleaming. He twisted around and grappled with the tether line, climbing hand-over-hand and hoping his augmented strength could haul him away faster than he could be swallowed.

The *Azura* pitched up to head back to the egress. Caiden was flung around. The holobia's body whipped out and gases jetted from its side. In a burst of speed, it lurched, mouth gaping on all sides of Caiden. The saliva sheets pummeled him. His cloudsuit condensed back to a second skin but wasn't thick enough to armor him from the slap of the mucus membranes or the shock of *sound* as it roared back, inner atmosphere surging around him.

He balled up and bulleted through as something sucked him deeper into the holobia's throat. He struck a tissue wall, bounced off, spun. He flailed out, grabbed something, but it slicked through his fingers. Glowing, fleshy pink fronds surrounded him as he was pulled deeper in. The space was cavernous and bioluminescent but he couldn't tell if he was seeing the inside of a body or a bizarre jungle. Screeches ripped his ears, something gurgled, the rush of blood flow or waterfall. Caiden gulped air in the tight little pocket of his suit and tried to find footing and handholds as objects rushed past. He was slapped by frilled cilia as long as trees, indigo mucus smearing against him.

Then *whoosh*.

Hot pressure dug between his shoulder blades. The tether wrenched him away. At terrible speed he hurtled out of the gullet back through the throat, barraged by a mayhem of colors and impacts and howling tones. He zoomed through the mouth of the thing and pounded through saliva curtains. Sounds cut off as he reentered the vacuum. His cloudsuit burst into its puffed form, which threw off all the mucus shit on him.

The *Azura* glinted into view.

"Finally, you bastard," Caiden whimpered.

The holobia's mouth still gaped, its enormous body unrolled in space, but the *Azura*'s speed pulled Caiden away. The ship arced toward the ring of the stellar egress, swinging weary Caiden along behind.

The ship dived into the black pit of the egress, and Caiden was too damn exhausted to panic as he passed through next, chewed up and wrung out. Every cell of him felt separated from the next, attached by tenuous electricity, and there was a beat of blissful time that felt eternal, as if he were back in the heart of that star, the eye of a plasma storm. The world was white and void, and a gentle oblivion swallowed his worries. He thought he had a name for this place, but couldn't grasp it among the strange whispers grazing his soul. Voices of dead loved ones kissed his mind.

Then he was snapped out the other side of the egress, smothered by space and time and a new gravity—at least he wasn't in the luminous jungle belly of a colossal monster, covered in juices and saliva.

In the new universe, Threi cut the engines. Caiden kept drifting toward the illuminated bay. Threi gathered up the slack of the tether and hauled him in through the atmoseal. The scalar gravity inside draped over Caiden like a blanket of velvet force that instantly said, *You're safe.*

"Nice job being so tantalizing," Threi said. "But maybe tone it down next time."

The cloudsuit fizzed and glitched as it struggled to manage Caiden's heat and sweat, his temper flaring as he ripped at the harness buckles and tether and clawed himself free of the suit, then rolled on his back. "Bastard," he exhaled. "You did that for fun, didn't you?"

"Actually no, the holobia's never been that aggressive before. Usually it rouses and drifts away a bit and we fly through when the egress is exposed. Maybe the *Azura*'s crystal is like some kind of candy to the thing. See anything cool inside?"

Caiden glared and pushed up. His morphcoat thinned to an airy silk, and his body steamed. Bruises ached all over. "*That's* why no one's found the Casthen Harvest?"

Threi signaled the bay doors closed and the atmoseal off. "Not just the holobia. The stellar egress we just went through is like a trapdoor to get into this universe, which has a rind that's impassible to all electronics, ships, mechanics, most species. The only way in is the egress we went through."

Caiden dragged fingers through his drenched hair and wobbled over to the cockpit. Starry space filled the view in all directions. There was one small, languid star nearby. No planets. No station. "How far away is the Casthen Harvest in this universe?"

"It's right in front of us."

CHAPTER 30

HOME

I t's *right in front of us*?" Caiden gave Threi a scathing look. He squeezed self-consciously at bruises swelling up everywhere, sweat clinging his shirt to his body, and a *smell*—the holobia's cloying saliva. "Is my surprise that entertaining for you? I'm fresh out of patience, slaver."

Threi ambled up beside Caiden in the cockpit and thrust a hand into the foggy light of the idling drive guides. Bright lines twined around his fingers and he flew the ship forward, conducting motion with only one hand. How many years of piloting had he accelerated for that level of skill? And delicacy: Threi's slim fingers twisted and hyperextended to bring the *Azura*'s nose up to a fist-sized hunk of quartz floating in space, so small and transparent it would easily go unseen.

Threi said, "The Graven left keyholes all over the multiverse. It took us a while to realize that's what they were, longer to rebuild the rest of the door, and the longest to figure out the key." He pulled a complicated little device out of a pocket and raised it in the air. "The key is song."

Threi inputted code into the device. Nothing changed in the normal range of Caiden's senses but he felt instantly unsettled. Prickling, like a frequency a little too high or low to hear, like eyes watching your back or the sense of a loved one on their way home.

The crystal out in space turned solid white.

It sang, just like the *Azura* did when she flew: a weave of vibrations, a tapestry of tones, telling a story in words that Caiden's body tried to convince him he understood. Perhaps it was the Graven part of him that resonated.

Across uncountable kilometers out in space, more crystals became visible as they responded to the first. In the middle of this array, a transparent structure emerged.

It was lightseep obsidian, phasing from another dimension into reality. This Graven ruin stretched thousands of times larger than Emporia, as if space itself had hardened into a labyrinth jewel. So vast, it even encompassed the languid little star closest to them. Threi guided the ship along the side of the structure, shifting the viewing angle to reveal more vertices and iridescent lines sliding like a glass blade from a sheath of space itself.

"A hollow fortress, I like to think," Threi said. He headed the *Azura* inside. Translucent walls folded in around them, refracting starlight, making a maze of space.

Caiden said, "It doesn't look like Emporia."

"This lightseep's less physical, more like a distortion of space than a material surface. Whoever the Graven were, they discovered how to manipulate matter and energy in ways even the Dynast still can't comprehend. Lightseep exists on multiple planes at once, and at an absolute-zero-type phase, it practically doesn't exist. The Casthen Harvest is buried here inside. Without the key bringing this whole area to the perceivable plane, we could have flown right through and never known it existed."

Caiden gaped as more gorgeous surfaces slid past. The holobia, the song key, the hidden lightseep fortress—he would have never found this place alone. *I made the right decision. I'm where I need to be.*

Even Threi had a gentle, admiring gleam in his eye as he marveled out the window. "Abriss would kill for this, to know something like this exists."

"Why don't you tell her? You two are acquainted."

The gentleness burned out of Threi's eyes. "I don't sell things for free."

"What were you handing off, in Emporia?"

"Merchandise. We have a lot of that here." Threi gestured out the windows.

Within a hollow of the vast "fortress," and at the edge of the star-sun's habitable orbit, lay a misshapen planet clad in megastructure, knobby like a hand gripping a green-and-purple orb. Small universes of various size blistered the sunny side like dewdrops of strange light, most scooping into the planet itself, some hovering just above it. Vast troughs of greenery crisscrossed through lavender dust. Scaffolding structures jutted out of the ground and skewered the many universes with walkways and tunnels.

"Welcome home, Winn of Casthen."

Caiden flushed and bit back his retort—Threi was a bully, rewarded by response. Instead, Caiden said coolly, "I didn't know a planet could be covered in so many universes."

"That's because there's no other planet like this in all the charted multiverse. Those universes are different climates, micro-differences in physics, and the planet in a habitable zone and tidally locked. The megastructure is ours that we built on, but the planet . . . I suspect the Graven *created* all those little universes somehow, some testing ground. If a ship like yours can create a world, we now know they're not just an emergent phenomenon, they can be *controlled.*"

"And the Casthen repurposed these universes. Keeping slaves and animals? Growing materials to sell?"

Threi snorted. "It's not all bad. We rehabilitate the endangered, reverse extinction, develop, cultivate. Good things happen here. Casthen are the matchmakers of the multiverse. Environment to species. Product to consumer."

"Misery to innocents."

"That's because Çydanza isn't one of the good things here." The ship entered atmosphere. Heat roared. The *Azura*'s metals sang as the engines switched to planetside flight and Threi cruised to the dark side of the planet. "Çydanza is completely isolated. She never sees the real physical or emotional impact of her choices. She plays economic operations like they're games, just data, earnings, and progress on a screen. Not people, not physical goods—just numbers, ratios, and percentages she can move."

Caiden still wondered if she was real. "How can she have that much power if she never leaves?"

"You'll understand soon."

Soon. Caiden folded his arms to buckle down the urge to punch.

They glided low over a medley of universes like different styles of garden. Some lush, others spare. One caught his eye: crystalline water, knotted trees, bluish sand.

Like his picture in the aerator.

His mother's voice, close by his ear in the roar of the transport; *Soon. Imagine where we could be going. Green, do you think?*

He'd suggested, *Maybe the place everyone gets retired to?*

Maybe...

It was here. A snapshot lie of a place no slave would ever go.

Now Caiden was twenty, but so little time had passed since the eternity that was that transport ride, he was still waiting for it to be over. For the promise of soon. For his mother to come and get him and say, "It's time now, Caiden, let's go."

His vision glazed and Threi's voice mashed up in his ears.

"Now," Threi said, "Çydanza thinks I'm acquiring the ship for Casthen operations. I'll introduce you as my probationer. She'll enjoy that. Always tells me I don't care about things. Now I've picked up a stray. Quite soft-hearted, I am."

The megastructure on the dark side of the planet was encrusted with lights in a web of lines and circles. Threi slowed on approach to a bright, circular building nestled into the structure's crust like a knot in wood. Green and gold hues rippled on the facility's pleochroic surface as the ship moved by.

"Enforcers' pad. Remember, not a squeak to anyone. No one here is a friend."

"Right. You're not." Caiden checked his two glaves and other hidden weapons.

An iris folded open in the facility's ceiling, and Threi descended to settle the ship on a parking pad. He peeled from the seat and cracked his neck, then nodded to the bay doors. "Open 'em."

Caiden obliged, the back panels unfolded, and a score of Casthen swarmed in. Caiden whipped up his glave, but twenty glaves pointed at him.

Threi marched ahead. A scratchiness in the *Azura's* idle energy—Caiden sensed through the link—smoothed out once Threi left the bay. Curious.

"Cool it," Threi said to the group, "this is my new probationer." The crowd parted around him. Here, the man wielded a dual blade of Graven presence and rank-based loyalty, but among a people so mixed, his effect had to be unreliable. Caiden noted the man's shift in physical bearing, the way he threw his energy around.

Threi wagged a hand at Caiden and led the way into a dark passage.

Caiden's neural link with the *Azura* severed as he walked out of range. A muggy sluggishness settled in his brain instead, and after a while he realized the origin of his rising unease: this place *was* home.

At least in appearance it was. The walls were familiar manifolds of lattice, panel, and piping: the inside of a giant machine, the familiar gills and ports and rivets from his childhood. The grate floor sang with every step, wafting up heat and a moist, sulphurous scent identical to the aerators. Doors and halls were marked in the same stenciled script that had labeled the dusters of Caiden's home planet. The large warehouses they passed through were models of the huge pasture compounds.

The world he'd grown up in was Casthen through and through.

Threi navigated a labyrinth of self-similar passageways, finally unlocking the entrance to an indoor greenhouse: the ceiling was all golden, milky light, and the ground was an inch of water thick with rootlets, from which sprang a field of spidery white lilies. Threi led the way across a flowerless strip of floor to a single glass-walled room in the greenhouse's heart.

"My room," he said.

Caiden hugged his arms. Odd and suspicious, intimate, being led straight to the man's private space. Candescence reflected off petals, filling the greenhouse with a glow. Sweet, waxy fragrance laced the air. Caiden said, "I didn't take you for someone who liked pretty things."

"If you stop to think about it, you know nothing about me at all." Threi hauled open the glass door and flourished his hand to invite Caiden inside.

A messy bed, a blue coverlet, several desks littered with gadgets and chemistry, cases of *paper* books, a large projected holosplay, a scour, a large mirror, and—bright copper, filling up all of one corner—a biodata chamber for acceleration.

Caiden took it all in and realized he really did know nothing about this man. "This is the part where you tell me our murder plan."

"Not quite. You'll need to meet Çydanza and be approved for probation.

Don't worry. She likes feisty." Threi's smile returned, stretching the corner of his eyes. "Scour and change into uniform. I'll come get you soon."

Soon. "Uniform?"

"You need to play the part." Threi shoved at him a bundle of mismatched armor like random pieces restitched together off a machine. And the mask, metallic blue and faceless.

A lump swelled in Caiden's throat.

Casthen through and through.

Threi pushed the door open. And smiled. "Stay put."

The man was gone for hours, long enough for Caiden to thoroughly snoop. Threi's possessions were impersonal and his databases vast. He had collated all of the Casthen's research on Graven ruins and biotechnology, and stored an old backup of the Dynast's data about the same. Nearly all of it was past a security wall Caiden couldn't hack.

The acceleration chamber also functioned for desenescence—reverse aging—and had been used a recorded total of eighty-nine times. The tinkering on his desks were all sensory-blocking prototypes and Graven research. The paper books were Dynast fables, philosophical treatises, and first-contact records of various species. He felt he knew even less of Threi than before.

Caiden sheathed himself in full Casthen armor. He gripped the mask. The outer side was the color of a bluebird, riddled with white scratches, minimally contoured. Thin slits slashed eyes and nostrils, perforations over the mouth. The inside was mirrorlike with a pleochroism that waved between orange and purple as he raised it to his face, meeting his distorted reflection.

He expected it to be dark, with only the eye slits to see through, but inside, the mask turned translucent to his vision.

"I'm one of them. A cur," he said, listening to his voice both muffled and amplified in his own ears. One of *their* voices.

I can endure and pretend. He laughed. All his life he'd pretended. A mechanic, he thought, but really just a slave. Or worse: a mis-shipped child soldier, pretending to be a slave.

The leathery underlayers were skintight, stretching as he moved. The armor plates clung and added considerable weight. When the glass door of Threi's room opened, he swiveled—then stumbled to catch his momentum, his limbs grating together as the plates jabbed him. Just when he'd gotten used to his new body, it was ill-fitting once again.

Standing just outside, Threi wore the same armor and mask. "You look good," the bastard said.

"Shut up."

"It suits you—the anger and the mask. Come, Çydanza waits." Threi stepped away from the door with a bow.

"How are you going to stop me from killing her the moment I'm there?"

"Oh, you'll see."

The mask hid Caiden's snarl. All his decisions led here. Now he would see what Threi had been so secretive about. Çydanza, the creature who built his misery, owned him, enslaved him; the orchestrator of the end of his world.

Out in the sterile megastructure, the other Casthen gave way as Caiden and Threi passed through. Some wore the uniform armor and others were dressed in prim outfits that evoked an air of research.

A set of scans led up stairs to an atrium filled with holosplays and monitoring equipment, where Threi inputted commands. He shoved his mask to the top of his head, pulling back messy hair. His skin was flawlessly smooth, pallid, and matte; not shiny like a newborn, not waxy like the dead. The mix of freshly reborn and long-deceased gave the accel chamber in his room more meaning. A man of haste.

"Ready?" Threi donned his trademark smile.

"You'd love me to say I was *born ready*, wouldn't you?"

"Atta boy." Threi jogged down a flight of steps to a wash of iridescent light.

Caiden tugged at the stiff vambraces. The mask captured his breath, hot on his cheeks and loud in his ears. He followed awkwardly, steps laden with dread and quickened by curiosity. In the circular room below stood a platform cut in half by a rind that arced up and out of sight. Needles on thin arms poked the rind in a circular frame as if to pull one area taut.

Caiden whirled on Threi. "She's inside a universe...What's wrong with it? Why?"

"Touch the rind and it'll kill you. It destroys almost all organic matter. Understand?" Threi marched to the side of the platform. His fingers worked at instruments, poking luminous diagrams and plucking dimpled forms. "It's rather complicated to get data through, but the Casthen have had centuries to perfect it."

No one can survive getting in. The perfect shield. Caiden stood transfixed by the rind's brilliant storm of white, cerulean, and pink. Within the framed area, its roiling calmed enough to make out sand and pools and a figure walking to the viewing platform. Not so much a figure as a column of pale murk drawing nearer. Clearer as Caiden squinted for details and the milky rind settled.

Threi shoved Caiden forward. "My new probationer, Prime. Something special. A surprise you've wanted for a while."

"Special…" The machines enhanced Çydanza's thin, sandy voice as if it vibrated off the whole rind.

Caiden clasped his hands so they wouldn't shake, but the tiny armor bits over his fingers jittered.

"Special how, Threi, what have you found?" A familiar voice? As Çydanza approached, the cloudiness settled. She was human: her tanned features distraught, russet-brown hair piled atop her head, brow drawn together, and lips pressed thin.

Caiden's heart stumbled. "Mother?"

She stopped one pace from the rind's calm surface, which revealed more of her details every moment. Caiden recognized each line in her face, the scratch scar on her temple, the stern set of her mouth, and her brown eyes strong and kind.

His pulse ramped and his throat tightened. A layer of his soul was shredded by the sight, releasing guilt pent-up by the accelerated years. *Soon.*

He gasped in a sob and stepped forward, but Threi's hand smacked onto his chest.

"The rind *will* kill you," he warned.

Caiden stood inches from it, and so did his mother, doubly blurred by the rind and the tears stinging his eyes.

"Caiden." Her voice was soft and low, the voice that had rocked him to sleep when he was four, soothed him when he was injured, reassured him when he was full of doubt. "You survived, you ran, didn't you?"

Guilt sluiced through him. The frenzy of the beasts. Red sand. Splintered bones.

"You froze under that rock as the beasts bit me, tore my body in two, the entrails pouring, blood spraying across the world—you did nothing." Her calm, measured voice bored into him, each word a dagger reopening wounds in his mind. The memories gushed out like lifeblood.

"I was . . . fourteen. I was just a boy."

"You didn't save anyone, Caiden, except yourself."

His armored hand trembled an inch from touching the rind. He clawed it back and shoved Threi's arm away. "I ran." He choked. Armor chattered as he quaked. "I ran, and I lived. But you . . ."

His mother shook her head. "And tiny Leta, the sweet girl, she ran bravely after you and was trampled underfoot, neck smashed by a boot, legs mangled, until the beasts found her tender flesh and ripped through her chest in one bite of *so many* teeth—"

"*Stop it!*" Caiden lunged with a balled fist, but Threi caught his wrist and hauled him back, arms around him.

"Easy!" Threi hissed by his ear. "This rind will strip your flesh off."

Tears gushed down the inside of Caiden's mask. Haste and loathing and fire throbbed in him, but he had nowhere to go, nothing to strike.

His mother sneered and ran a hand up her face, into her hair to let it down. "Your sweet Leta crushed and devoured, poor girl, a pity, since what a fearsome match you two would have been: wisdom and power together."

Dewy vapor steamed about her head. Her hair paled to waves of sun-bleached brown. Wisps of gauze congealed into a crown of blue chicory, and twenty-year-old Leta's flower-pink lips smiled at him, her hazel eyes glistening with adoration.

Caiden choked on a hitched breath and twisted around to Threi, ripping from the man's restraint. "*Cydanza is a vishkant?*"

Threi perked an eyebrow and shrugged. "Surprise."

CHAPTER 31

CASTHEN PRIME

Caiden cursed under his breath. No wonder no one had ever killed Çydanza: an impervious species in an impassible universe.

He surveyed Threi for reaction or clue, but the bastard was deadpan.

When he turned back to the rind, he looked into his father's steely gaze. Memories teased through Caiden's head like a scratchy, pulled-on string. *Be strong.*

She had been leading the Casthen for longer than most could remember. If what the young vishkant in Emporia had told him was true, Çydanza's age meant she could only see his deeper memories, not recent events or thoughts.

"Çydanza. That old life is behind me."

"No, boy, it never will be behind you," his father said, face beginning to morph between red lacerations and the diamond-shaped punctures of jaws. "You should not want it to be, despite what your friends have told you."

The crew. Their faces, words, the many moments swirled in Caiden's mind. Older vishkant couldn't see recent memories, but where was that cut-off, for Çydanza? Caiden shut his eyes and focused. What Çydanza could perceive or become was controlled in part by his own awareness—so he focused on nothing, as Panca had taught him: *Focus on nothingness, just be here, breathing and present. Let your thoughts slide off and away.*

Caiden opened his eyes. His father's bloody visage melted into lavender cloud, frothing over a spongy, transparent skeleton beneath. New skin congealed over a fine-boned face. Cerulean eyes stared. Sunny hair fell over lace-clothed shoulders. An unfamiliar person.

This was the real her.

Caiden strangled his hate into a manageable thread. He needed to concentrate.

"You want to kill me!" she exclaimed, but her expression remained bored. "Like Threi did when I first uprooted him from Unity, but you see how lucid he is now, how much progress he's made, how *many* smiles he wields? You were born and bred in the machine of Casthen, but perhaps you are secretly angry that I shipped you off to the wrong place, and for that I apologize, you are due better, but you're home now, child, and we must shape and sharpen the untempered blade of your rage."

Caiden focused on Çydanza's cerulean eyes, her hard, bored face. "I have control of my anger."

"No, Caiden." Her voice chafed. "Or is it Winn? You said yourself once that Caiden is dead, but have you earned a new self yet? I see your anger, it comes from love, not fear, and if we're going to change the temper of your steel, we need to heat that anger further. Helplessness is the source of it, so you will obey or I will have that young vishkant friend of yours brought here to the joy of all my enforcers—can you imagine? Vishkant are so pliable when young, so primed for impression, whether they wish it or not." Çydanza laughed: a stale sound sawing up and down her throat.

Caiden's armor rasped together as his muscles coiled.

Threi paced by in front of him to break the trance. "No need for threats yet. He's special, remember?"

Çydanza leaned closer to the rind, bathed by its pink resplendence. "That you are, Caiden, Winn, I see your lust for justice, your yearning to belong, your violence that you think the slaughter poured into you so you can pour it back out onto someone else; you're one of us, equal, strong, and worthy—you belong now, and you are worth something to me."

"Valued because I'm expensive." Caiden's fingers itched to strangle the apathetic dullness from her face.

"I was saddened to lose the nophek operation, as the gloss research from RM28 alone has saved seven hundred thousand lives and resurrected twelve extinct species—not a poor bargain, in my mind—but I am heartened that at least we recovered you in the fallout, child. You are worth a whole society."

The absurdity of that idea left Caiden speechless. The mask suffocated back his fuming breaths. Tremors jabbed the ill-fitting armor against him.

Threi stepped in. "Well—as you said, Prime, a blade's no use to us unsharpened. Come on." Threi gripped Caiden's shoulders and spun him.

Bursting with energy and questions, Caiden let himself be led off the platform.

"Threi."

"Wait until we're out, soldier."

Caiden wrenched his shoulders free and marched, expelling his fire into motion.

When they were clear of the atrium and back in lightless, intimate halls, Caiden erupted and slammed Threi against a wall.

Threi raised his palms. "So, you're familiar with vishkant. Initiation into Casthen is her dredging up memories and secrets, for blackmail or torture. She makes ammunition of the things we care about. So, we tremble and obey."

"Does that mean there's something you care about?" Caiden shoved Threi into the wall as he released.

Threi chuckled. "No, I help her out of the goodness of my heart. This way."

Caiden strode after him into a lift with barely enough room for two. He ripped his mask off and loosened buckles. A rapid pulse raced through him, throbbing where the uniform fit too tight.

"Explain," Caiden said. "Or I'll rethink not slugging your smug face."

Threi was pressed to his shoulder. It wouldn't do any good to thrash the bastard up. Although Threi had said himself before: sometimes it was all about feeling better...

The man smiled wider as the door opened and he stepped out onto the top of the structure and the vista Caiden had seen from the air: various sizes of universes blistered the planet's side in pockets of vague, vibrant activity. The nearest ones were riots of greenery and flocks of pink and orange creatures.

Threi stepped to the edge of the roof. "Çydanza can see parts of our long-term memory, but at her age—damn ancient—she can't see our most recent experiences or ambitions. She's also less capable of grasping immediate thoughts, especially if we keep our awareness away from touchy subjects. I didn't tell you the full plan before in case you were so fixated on the details of it you revealed it to her or turned her scrutiny onto me. Her deep belief that she's untouchable is an arrogance that keeps her from being suspicious."

It probably also contributed to her casual cruelty, if death or retribution wasn't a punishment she ever feared.

Caiden said, "Explain now then. Vishkant can't be shot, burned, electrocuted, suffocated, or sliced, since they're essentially particle clouds. And how would we lure her from her universe?"

"She can't be lured—I've tried with every excuse, emergency, threat, and every single Graven trick up my sleeve. She's too smart to leave. And there's no way in. The rind is impassable for every other species I've tested except vishkant, and Çydanza doesn't allow vishkant on the Harvest for that very reason. The one time I tried to sneak one in... went badly. When I scanned the *Azura*'s rind in Emporia, I knew I'd finally found a solution. We can bridge one universe with another: fly inside with the *Azura*'s universe to protect us. That's the easy part."

"What's the hard part?"

"Mature vishkant have a defense mechanism, a neurological attack." Threi fished a little machine out of his pocket and held it out in his palm. A holosplay field of dimpled air sprang above it, projecting light in a three-dimensional space. "We call it a memory flood. Victims are faced with every fear and doubt, every horrible memory, all of the derision and self-loathing they've internalized, twisted into visions and a real, whole-body experience."

Footage filled the holosplay: a scene in Çydanza's viewing room. It streaked as Threi scrolled through clips, the rind always the same but the figures before it—and who Çydanza became for them—different each time.

Threi stopped scrolling. The clip played through. Çydanza reached her hand through the rind. It unmade her arm into scintillating particles that re-congealed into flesh and blood on the other side. She extended her fingers to the shoulder of an Andalvian whose skin rippled terrified mauve, blackening into shivers where Çydanza stroked their neck. In the silent footage, the Andalvian flailed at their own scalp, clawing pieces of spiny hair away, then chunks of flesh, frantically digging into the soft bone.

Caiden covered his mouth with a hand, stomach turning over.

Threi said, "I've seen victims go insane, hemorrhage, self-mutilate. Çy will use this ability against anyone who tries to attack her."

Another instance: this xenid simply wailed and wailed, limbs curling inward, spasms crushing them to the floor where they screamed until exhausted, eyes blank, mouth still agape.

"I've tested the extent of it, and substances to inhibit neurological reaction, but they don't work. The memory flood requires direct contact, but no armor or clothing can block it. The pheromones also make it more real."

Another: a mauya stripped out every hair and every feather-petal from every wing until she was a crumpled mass of puckered skin.

"The brain stimulus continues after the person is physically released. Nonlocal memory is affected too, as are highly augmented individuals."

More: a chketin cracking their skull repeatedly on the floor. A man walking straight into the rind, layers of body boiled away. Dermis, then tendons snapping, fat melting, bones splintered. Caiden watched in horror as clips played, Çydanza crushing souls from the inside out. The victims that didn't grow violent were reduced to puddles, mental capacity drained. Casthen soldiers hauled out the brain-dead and the bloody heaps. Sometimes with shovels.

"Enough." A flash of hate seared through him. "You '*tested the extent of it*'—does that mean these victims are xenids that you sent in, knowing what would happen?"

"That's right." Threi's expression hardened.

Caiden took a step at him, fists itching to fly.

Threi shut down the holosplay device and strode to Caiden, using all three inches of his superior height, stopping close enough that Caiden inhaled that waxy lily scent. Caiden shoved an elbow to make space between them but Threi seized his upper arm and twisted him around into a choke hold with the speed and strength of accelerated decades.

Caiden's blood cut off, cinched by armor that squealed as Threi's biceps flexed. Seconds of consciousness left, his vision sizzled, and Threi said breathily in his ear, "Don't forget you agreed to follow my plan when you accepted this deal. You agree with my end goal—you don't need to agree with my methods."

Electric pressure dammed up in Caiden's left arm's augmented muscles. He went to release it in a superhuman pull free, but Threi let go and pushed his back so he stumbled away.

The man's voice was all business when he resumed. "The memory flood requires focus that only the oldest vishkant can muster. She can't keep it up forever or repeat it frequently, it takes a heavy toll to sustain. Multiple individuals can be affected at once, and I've thought of pouring a small army on her to try to exhaust her energy, after finding a way in. But now that I have you, there's no need for an army."

"Me..." Caiden's jaw throbbed; his head sizzled with oxygen. He scowled and fought the urge to cough, trying to not give Threi the pleasure of reaction.

Threi walked to the edge of the roof and gazed over the Casthen domain, cutting a regal figure with his shoulders erect and hands perched on his hips. He was shadow, backlit by bright worlds and a sea of stars. "The *Azura* gives me the means to get into Çy's universe, but I doubt I'd psychologically survive her memory flood. I've faced my past reflected in Çydanza for years while she revels in trying to break my walls. The memory flood...that *circumvents* walls. But you. We can make you indestructible."

One little push, and Threi would go tumbling over the edge. A pity Caiden still needed him. "Explain."

"Two reasons. First, you have only fourteen years of secrets and hurt for her to work with to try to destroy your mind, but you have twenty years of emotional intelligence to resist it. And, you're now equipped with the mechanism to relive the worst of your memories in realistic detail."

"The repeating nightmares."

"That side effect is species-specific, and memory jogs aren't commonly used or commonly survived outside of rare Cartographer application. But because of it, you're exposed continually to all the things Çydanza would use against you." Threi swayed with excitement. He ambled closer, and Caiden resisted the urge to back up. "The Casthen have a machine that we can reverse-engineer to hold you in that memory loop—in an incubation sleep—so you can face your trauma until it doesn't faze you anymore. That, combined with tasks involving real nophek, will numb you to the horrors that Çydanza will use to break your mind and your focus."

"You," Caiden growled, "*promised* a way to eliminate the nightmares!"

"I promised a way to *solve* the memory loop, not eliminate it. This is how you get free of them: control and acceptance. Imagine walking through your history without the slightest reaction, just peace that it has built you into who you are, that it's behind you now, and that you've gotten revenge for everyone you lost and saved millions more from the same exploitation. You're the only creature who could become impervious to Çydanza. Only you."

"What a lie." Caiden scrubbed a hand through his hair. The motion jabbed armor into him. Bruises and sprains twinged from the holobia chase, but the pain echoed every phantom bite from the dreams, every mile run, every kick and jab in the transport. "Not free from years of horror, just living them over and over in one go. If I do it, if I kill that part of myself, but Çydanza still ends up killing me—"

"You'd still be the closest anyone has come to ending her. Trust me, I've tried, searched, struggled for years."

He recalled the murky research, genetic data, and strange sensory devices in Threi's room. All in an attempt to survive the memory flood?

Eager, almost breathless, Threi pressed on. "There might not be another person like you in this whole damned multiverse, *ever*. Young, wronged, uniquely haunted, and full of temper. You're a magnificent cocktail of hate, Winn, and this is your chance at revenge, once and for all."

Exhaustion clawed Caiden to the floor. He sat and slipped his legs over the roof's edge, peering down the dazzling height.

I would be suffering to ensure the liberation of many.

Countless small universes glowed with resplendent color across the landscape. Inside them, a host of captured lives grew, were tended, harvested, sold. The sentient ones might not even know they could be more. There were easily several hundred rinds bisecting the planet's surface, filled with unknown treasures and terrors.

Caiden flicked his augmented thumb against the blue Casthen mask's inner edge, fraying its crystalline laminate. Ksiñe had warned him that a blade could be sharpened until there was no material left. But if he came out the other side intact, he would be stronger than ever before, ready to live a free life. Absolutely free.

He'd need to survive the desert again. And again.

And he'd need to find his footing among the Casthen. The more he fit in, the better.

Caiden rose to his feet and fastened the Casthen mask over his face, combing his hair around the magnetic buckles. "Once we're in and her memory flood is exhausted . . . how do we kill Çydanza?"

Threi grinned. "The *Azura*'s rind."

"Vishkant physiology is incompatible with it? What, we just throw her at it? How can you be sure that—" Ice shot up Caiden's spine. "How many vishkant did you torture in different rinds to deduce which kind will destroy their physiology?"

Threi's smile lingered. He shrugged apathetically and folded his arms.

The man was violent, powerful, and deeply disturbed. And Caiden's only option.

CHAPTER 32

DREAMS

Several days of waiting and "soon" passed while Threi set up the incubation system he had planned. Caiden spent the time sequestered in the probationer sector, hatefully participating in Casthen things: combat drills and sparring, lectures, economic overview, flight sims, bland meals.

Every time he slept, exhausted, in his aerator-like Casthen quarters, the nightmares crept up from his past, making him impatient to get the whole ordeal over with.

Now as Caiden stood looking down on the coffin that would trap him in horror for two hundred ephemeris hours, he wasn't concerned about terror or pain.

He worried about the trust it meant.

He could be trapped forever in nightmare. Threi had access to the *Azura*.

"What did you say this place was for?" he asked. "Biological computing?"

Threi's whole body flexed to haul the generator crate farther out into the aisle. The warehouse stretched tall and wide into darkness. These containers were stacked like huge rectangular drawers—big enough to fit most xenids—in rows and columns, the shelves infinite along interconnected halls. The entire mass hummed, amplifying into a sickening din of dissonant tones.

"You won't like the answer," Threi said.

"When have I liked any of your answers?"

A memory sprang at him: Laythan's voice, *When do I ever like your plans?* Then Taitn had flown straight into the core of a star.

Caiden's heart tripped. The crew was freed of their Graven-induced obligation to him now. They could go on with their lives not snared in his. How long would it take them to forget, with his Graven face out of sight?

He hugged his bare arms as shivers set in. He was stripped to under-clothes, skin stuck with nodes and viny wires. The cracked-open container was a tank of photonic liquid, crowded nano-organisms, power manifolds. A machine within a machine within a machine: that was all the Cas-then was.

Threi replied, "The N-Sector Servicer sustains living systems and utilizes them. Depending on species, this might be biocomputing, testing physiol-ogy, or harnessing psychosomatic states. A versatile biohijacking network." Threi straightened and frowned, peering down the aisle. "Once we can hack in and make modifications, we can keep you in a sustained delta brain wave state, while maintaining your bodily functions. Ah—here's the girl."

A short, human-looking young woman emerged from the darkness, with little pin lights dotting her Casthen armor. Caiden recalled the smaller member of Threi's entourage in the Den, holding the bag of re-collected gloss. Her blue mask was strapped across one shoulder. Over her minimal Casthen armor and clothing, floor-length hair spilled and braided elabo-rately around her body. Hair that long and thick was a mauya trait—the strands more like axons—but she had animal eyes like an Andalvian, huge pink-white pupils nestled in black, reflecting light. When she bowed, her falling hair changed color: the pleochroic strands were silvery cream with casts of pink, lavender, azure, and shadow, shifting by viewing angle. That feature wasn't mauya. Neither was her short stature, barely up to Caiden's shoulder—mauya were tall and wispy. What creature had the Casthen made?

"Hack it, Silye, and make sure you account for his hybrid biology, I don't want him brain-dead or paralyzed."

Caiden winced. "Cheery thought."

Threi handed Silye a tablet. She took it, signing to him with her fingers, *Yes, Prime*, and Caiden raised an eyebrow. Threi's acceleration-bleached skin actually showed a blush. The man curled back over his holosplay and fussed with wiring he'd torn out of the container.

Silye pursed lips that were the color of a bruise, and pulled up a projected garden of code hovering over the tablet. The rings on her birdlike fingers let her prune, transplant, and sow. She paused once to sign to Threi; *The stabilizers...offline but connect...separate?* The words in the middle, Caiden didn't know.

Had they bred out her voice? Or a biological compromise, to gain some other mutation? If fostered ignorance was slavery, if a whittling of function was servitude...even one's own genes could enslave them. The gravity of the idea sank Caiden as he watched the mauya-hybrid pluck at code, her strange eyes flicking rapidly, engineered mind at work. The Casthen didn't just enslave people, they *created* people enslaved by their own biology. A sort of thralldom that determined—unalterably—the ability to heal, the regulation of hormones and chemicals, neurology, drive, intelligence, procreation.

Mutilation, pre-womb.

"Get inside," Threi said.

The tank liquid was bright blue and purple, a riot of bioluminescent movement. Caiden stepped in, swarmed with tingles. Careful of the gossamer wires dangling off his body, he folded himself awkwardly inside. Vibrations organized particles in the liquid into shifting geometric patterns. Submerged up to his neck, he shivered.

Silye nodded at her screen as she rotated the projected code structure, then handed the tablet to Threi. He pushed it back into her hands. "You're going to stay and monitor him for the eight ephemeris days."

"What if something happens?" Caiden asked.

"You'll be fine. Right, Silye? Tell us." Threi faced her intently.

She swiveled, her eyes flicked up to meet Threi's Graven blues, and the change was clear: her bright pupils dilated in a black sclera, her lips parted in adoring awe. The rise and fall of her chest stopped and the tightness in her expression softened around her eyes as she stared.

She was completely entrained by his Graven wishes, and Threi was a spider casually oblivious to the moth he constantly caught.

Silye signed, *Survive—yes.*

"See?" Threi wagged a hand in the air. "Silye is claircognizant, she knows truths spontaneously, intuitively."

That's what they bred her for. Caiden gripped the edges of the tank.

Silye added, *Emerge the same—no.*

Threi shrugged. "He'll come out better than he went in. Let's start the clock ticking."

"What do you mea—" Threi planted a hand on Caiden's skull and shoved him down.

The fluid grew heavy then solid, snagging his limbs as he thrashed upright. A bubble of air formed around his face. He gasped. With his eyes open, the congealed liquid was too brilliant and frantic to see, so he closed his eyes again and tried to relax.

Numbness turned to hypersensitivity. The wires that attached at the surface of his skin started to burrow beneath, scouring raw nerves, snaking through his bloodstream. Caiden shrieked into the air bubble. His body flinched at the sensory chaos of temperature and touch, his ragged panting itching his ears, pulsing red searing his skull. A vise squished his brain until sleep clobbered him *hard.*

Darkness, warm.

A low vibration split into harmonics and became needles of frequency, perforating him with stings of pressure. His consciousness dilated. Sparkles multiplied into stars into grains into sand and Caiden was returned to the desert of death.

All the bravado he'd prepared vanished.

He sprinted from a nophek. His boots pounded sand. Behind him, the beast's hot breath tickled his heels but he was fourteen and couldn't run any faster. When it leapt onto his back, his small arms couldn't push it off. Its foreleg was as thick as his torso, which it crushed into the sand. Air rattled out of Caiden's little lungs.

The nophek's wet mane coiled over Caiden's neck and cheeks as it bore down and ground his face into the desert. Teeth filled his vision. They clamped his shoulder: perforating skin, meat, snapping bone. Saliva sizzled like acid.

Mouth agape, he squeaked. If only the beast's weight would suffocate him away from the pain.

Suffocate.

He flailed out of the dream, into a clogging darkness. The impression of every razor tooth stuck in him. The crunching repeated, on and on until the darkness vibrated into the roar of the stuffed transport.

This time, he was a tall, muscular fighter of twenty. He held a glave in his hand and joined the deluge of bodies spilling out. He fired through the crowd, piercing nophek vitals but still failing to save. His people were rent to shreds. A nophek slammed Caiden's back, squeezing him between desert and claws. He shoved the glave in the beast's chin and shot up, spewing brains and rainbow fluid.

This isn't real. It's just a test. The glave shook in his hand, but this time, he wouldn't run.

In front of him, his father stumbled and hit the ground, face engulfed by teeth that crunched through cheekbone. Caiden screamed and shot over and over, but the teeth had already punctured brain. He jerked his head from the sight, only to see his mother pulled apart by two nophek. Her shriek peeled a layer off his soul.

This isn't real. Caiden fired the glave, sending blinding beams through the monster's flesh.

More nophek charged.

Thirty paces away stood Leta, ten years old and bawling. Fleeing adults knocked her to the ground. Boots smashed her neck as she wailed. Just as Çydanza had said.

"*No!*" Caiden screamed, and sprinted to her as a nophek plowed toward the easy meal.

The glave clicked when he fired. Out of fuel. Glistening teeth like a hundred daggers bit Leta's chest whole. Caiden rammed his augmented fist straight through the nophek's skull. Spasming, he gathered up his sister's gruesome body. Limbs draped over his arm like a waterfall of blood. The scarlet seeped, spreading as it only could in a dream, until the entire desert lay red.

Caiden closed his eyes. *Let me die like I should have then. Just meat, in the end.*

The darkness chewed up his misery and spit it out anew. In this dream, countless footprints stamped the sand red. Thirty muscular nophek circled him. Nostrils fluttering. Eyes flashing. Their hideous appearances weren't surprising anymore. He even had a little sympathy. Hungry things.

One squealed and lunged, biting Caiden's leg from behind. His severed hamstring whipped back, shooting jolts of pain. He bellowed and fell forward, cueing the pack to pounce. He curled his arms around his head, bit his sleeve to keep from screeching as jaws ripped chunks from him, splintered bone, uncoiled organs. He let them eat. The pain consumed him.

He became nothingness once every bit of him was swallowed. The darkness spit him back out into more savagery, which chewed him up anew.

Caiden tumbled down a dune and fell on his face. His limbs were asleep, too heavy to wield.

A pack of nophek charged for the kill.

"Free meal, pups." His voice was as rough as Çydanza's, broken by a cackle that he couldn't stop. It was humorous, being eaten so many times. Crunched and torn and gulped. A nophek's coarse mane grazed his face, hot breath dewing his cheek with saliva. It yawned, mouth lined with the sharpest pearls and a huge serrated tongue.

Darkness. One nightmare made him Casthen, in armor, ushering his own child self into the transport box.

"Everyone will be provided for," he promised hundreds.

And then he was the little boy in utter darkness alone.

When forever was over, he dreamed again, and was lucid. He picked what moment he started in the slaughter, and threw his energy into all the choices he might have made.

Leaving Leta and fleeing with his parents—both killed twenty meters from the door.

Convincing his parents to stay in the transport too—the nophek rush in for trapped prey.

Taking Leta with him as he runs—she can't keep up, and gets trampled by the crowd.

Shoving Leta under the rock instead—the nophek dig her out after they eat him.

Caiden tried everything different. Each outcome was immeasurably worse than him surviving with shame.

His imagination grew as exhausted as he, unable to conjure fresh nightmare scenarios. The meaning peeled off, washed clean, inert: a test he'd passed over and over.

The darkness chewed him up and spit him out to a nightmare that was tame. Caiden walked from the transport while being smacked by the stampede. He craned his neck to the top, fifty meters tall.

Tuning the screams from his ears, he scaled the cube's girders and pipes. He sat on the edge and watched the slaughter. His heart set a calm pace, his breathing long and slow. The wind grazed him, warm and ionized. The horizon was a bright ribbon, buttoned by stars. He *smiled* experimentally. His mind had exhausted the horror of his youth. It became funny, everything he'd been through. The absurdity of the ordeal. Something no one should survive once, much less so many times. He laughed, and couldn't stop.

The tank he lay in cracked open.

Brilliance speared every cell and chopped up the dark. Caiden was hauled out of fluid, hacking and crumpled, dropped onto frigid metal. He lay whittled down, muscle carved tight on wobbly bones, all of him wrung out and re-sopped and wrung until he'd become a wretched, starving creature.

A chketin's enormous hands clamped his upper arms and lifted him clean off the ground, dangling like a doll. Someone stabbed at his chest with strangely colored fluids in pen cylinders. Reddish hues fanned beneath his skin.

The chketin's fat fingers uncurled, and Caiden fell.

"Easy, Jet!" a familiar voice barked. "Back off, slags!"

Bare hands grazed Caiden's torso. He flew into motion on reflex, crushing his fist into something bony. A throb of afterimage mobbed his vision. His augmented hand grasped a soft thing and he flung it away, then he shuffled back and blinked hot tears. Breath, pulse, thoughts all churned, failing to assemble a sense of this new darkness.

The chketin's boisterous laughter filled the room. A couple other Casthen mocked him in languages he was too exhausted to parse.

"Hey." Threi reached out. Caiden scrabbled him away with shaking hands, but Threi's fingers locked around Caiden's wrists and hauled him to his feet. "Hey! You made it. You're out."

Fight instincts surged up. Caiden flicked his wrists down and around, throwing off Threi's hands, following up with a jab that caught a white cheek. Threi stumbled back, clutching his face and covering half his smile.

"Still spirited, our soldier." Threi chuckled. "A little more Casthen than before. Bring him along, Sil."

Caiden panted madly. No sand here. This darkness was wild and hostile.

Silye slipped her hand in his and pulled him with the group. Black flowers bloomed across her cheek: he'd punched her. *She* had been the soft thing he flung away.

Caiden stared at that bruise as they walked, and a shadow coiled in him.

Threi said, "You've been dreaming for eight straight days. Let's get you nourished and settled. You can finally meet your new family."

Starving. He croaked out a chuckle. He'd been nophek food for days. Strange—now the food was hungry.

CHAPTER 33

BORN AND BRED

He followed Threi's crew through the facility past labs conducting obscene research, training halls with soldiers sparring, and all the while he witnessed casual discrimination in the corridors, but his anger didn't flare like it used to. His new self had walls thick enough to contain all his fire, and finally, even as the teeth of injustice bit him, he could choose whether to swing a fist or wait.

"You watch yer back 'n' sides when the boss's not lookin'," said the dark, mauve-skinned chketin. They bent to rumble hot, musky words in Caiden's ear. "All the freckles in the world won't keep yer little bones from snappin'."

The words wafted harmlessly over him. How many beasts had he faced down?

He was numbed from days and days of brutality, and wondered if the same numbness would have grown if he'd lived and trained in the Harvest since infancy. The Casthen's garden would have sprouted him into a choking vine, flowerless and cruel. A boy who hadn't grown up with Leta's wise lessons.

What a fearsome match you two would have been, Cydanza had said, *wisdom and power together.*

He tried to recall the girl's voice, but it sieved through all the holes the incubation had made in his memory. His head was sand, blood, and teeth.

"Hey, daydreamer!" Threi patted his cheek. Caiden glowered back. "Eat, then we'll get to more sparring. The incubation poured *days* of violence into you, and like Cydanza said, now you have to pour it back out. Sit down."

They stopped in a large mess hall crowded with circular tables. Caiden sat slowly, every movement deliberate, shy of phantom pains. He'd used a scour, then dressed in compression gear and vibrational mesh to heal up the physical stress of the incubation. His Casthen armor fit over top, and fit better, curving along his lines instead of jabbing.

He eavesdropped on the crowd. Most Casthen were muttering about him, with refrains of "Paraborn" and "freckles." It was easy enough to guess what story they'd put together: Threi finally recovered one of the lost Graven Paraborn kids. In passing murmurs they mocked how he wasn't as strong or strange as they thought he'd be. The scientist groups unconcerned with Caiden discussed bigger problems: tourists had stirred the holobia and might've glimpsed what it was hiding. Casthen ships were chasing down the witnesses, fabricating a proper accident.

Threi's crew of four sat down at the table, none of them appearing to be any one species. Silye sat next to him, herself too mixed to comprehend; spills of hair draped her, rippling pink to blue sheens as she turned.

"Yeh, size us up, pup," scoffed the half-saavee, his musculature unusually gaunt and knobby. "I'm saavee 'n' vhisilin, only one you'll ev'r see."

"Because it ain't no good," the chketin said, and roared a laugh.

"That's Jet." Threi introduced the stocky, dark-skinned chketin. He pointed to the saavee. "He's Pinch. And the tal is Towa, she."

Towa's narrow body had a tal's ruffled, smoky material layering her. A netting of rose-gold threads contained her morphic flesh around humanoid bones. Buoyant silver hair like cirrus clouds framed a hard face.

Pinch asked, "Yeh, 'n' what is 'e?"

"He is half Threi," Towa hissed. The saavee chortled and the chketin rumbled.

"I'm all me," Caiden murmured. "Human."

He felt a bit less human after the nightmares. More of a new, wild thing. He had been intimate with the nophek: tangled up with their bodies, flesh in their teeth, blood in their bellies. Maybe he'd devoured something about them, as well.

"*Mostly* human," Threi replied, "highly Graven, and a bunch of other things you can't see. His traits were micro-tuned: from metabolism to reaction time."

"More than half Threi." Towa sneered, baring sharp black teeth.

Threi waved a hand. "None of his Graven's from me. Çy doesn't use Dynast genetics. She has something she thinks is better."

Not related to him—that's a damn relief. Caiden met the tal's dagger glare. *But I'm clearly not Graven enough for these curs to like me. Except Silye.*

He turned to her, and she swiveled, her cheeks grew pink, strange eyes stared, and she was a moth stuck in Caiden's unintentional Graven web. He winced.

Threi winked. "You met Silye."

"What are you?" he asked her, genuinely curious. Silye showed traits from the rarest xenids, which made it clear that she, like he, had been designed for an express purpose. Claircognizance, or something more.

She signed, *I don't know.*

"His eyes're goin' one place," Pinch jeered, and squinted diamond-shaped pupils at Caiden. "You grown that body up nice but not had time to use it, that it?"

"Not interested," he said. Rage and lust weren't the same fire. And now his rage boiled up in a place the nightmares had scooped out for it, a place where it could burn without catching the rest of him aflame. *This* was the control he had needed all along.

Pinch shrugged. "Well, she don't make much sound, some people like that."

Before Caiden could channel fire into fight at that remark, Silye whipped her arm out of her hair, unsheathing a flash of knife that she dug against Pinch's armpit so fast he froze.

"Enough," Threi said, volume raised, Graven-flexed. Silye wilted instantly at the order, her face cringing in shame. Pinch grumbled and curled back over his food.

Good for her. Caiden eased down but sank into a black mood. He wasn't here to make friends, in the den of the enemy. He would find and chisel away the parts of him that were Casthen, and if there was anything that was solely *him* and not part of their machine, it would remain. Rock chiseled away—hopefully a diamond within.

Threi shoved a dish of food in front of him: tan cubes like the ration blocks of his homeworld. Hardly worth calling them food. They tasted chewy and bland, packed with salty mineral grains. He grimaced but ate as hunger won. *What I would give for Ksiñe's cooking now.*

Shredded memories floated up. Snatches of detail he struggled to assemble. What had they eaten, that last meal? Treak, and some drink with spicy hisk. En's laugh. The whipkin's warm fur. Or was that all from before?

Caiden pulled the glass chicory flower from his pocket and squeezed its toothy lavender-blue petals. He frowned at his fist, trying to recall the color of Leta's eyes.

The crew's conversation at the table ceased. Jet snatched Caiden's wrist and plucked up the flower before Caiden could close his fist again.

"Wha's you hidin'?"

"Give it back." Caiden swiped for it, but Jet dropped it into Threi's waiting hand.

Caiden kept his palm extended and fixed Threi with a glare.

"Çy was right." Threi turned the object in his fingertips. "You're very sweet. See, slags? If he was half me he wouldn't be half as soft."

"Give it back," Caiden repeated calmly.

"You have to fight to keep things here," Threi said, and handed the flower to Towa.

Caiden curled closed his extended hand and held his spine straight.

It was time to pour out the eight days of violence dumped into him.

"Fight me for it." He met Towa's loathing gaze. The barklike substance of the tal's body bristled with emotion, captured by the ring threads that circumscribed her all over.

The mood shifted in the Casthen mess hall. Sound roared as tables were dragged to create a clear space for the fight. A diverse crowd gathered around the edge, clotting into a din of voices: crowing and clicks, great bellows, hisses.

Caiden took up a defensive stance. Combat styles he'd trained with En branched out in his mind, alongside the sparkling instinct he'd gained from days of fending off nophek attacks.

Towa rushed in a blink. *Fast*—all kicks. Caiden's blocks and dodges were a dance of preemptive instinct. He caught her leg with his augmented arm and pulled her to him in a takedown. Her back smacked the floor, but she whipped upright in a heartbeat. Caiden jabbed at her throat, missed, and was rewarded with a smack to his temple.

He staggered. His fire was loose—he could move, hit, *control*—and finally the fight was all real. Towa tried to hook one of his legs but he gripped her shoulders and pulled her into his rising knee, connecting with her windpipe. She gurgled and stumbled back. He landed a kick in the side of her face through a swirl of silver hair.

Caiden panted madly. A smile plastered his face.

The crowd—the room—roared with energy. Towa spit blood and closed the distance. Caiden grabbed her neck with his aug hand and tackled her forward. Her back hit the floor with a satisfying slap. She choked, blood foaming at her lips. Her knees dug into his back, trying to get a hold to roll him, but he was heavier, a steady, towering, sharpened rush of fire cresting like a wave and *he had to move*. He pummeled her sticky face, pushing silver streaks of hair into red. Her skull rebounded on the floor. *Crack!* A solid, juicy echo of each punch.

A shout or three needled through the blood-rush roaring in Caiden's ears. He wrapped his blue-muscled aug forearm around Towa's windpipe as he curled against her back. She gurgled, black fangs bared, arms scrabbling.

Her morphic flesh slimmed and she twisted, joints dislocating to squeeze a shoulder through his hold and slam an elbow at his head. Stars exploded behind Caiden's eyes. Towa laid into him, snapping his aug wrist and fracturing ribs. Pain and pain, like the stones of a cairn burying him. He was still conscious but a darkness pulped his vision. He grappled blind, rolling Towa so he was on top of her but she easily threw him. A kick landed above his ear, and the pain shoveled in, burying him.

"*Enough!*" Threi shouted. The audience was a mess of shouts and slaps, half-elated and half-outraged—their mush of sounds in Caiden's ears died down in the wake of Threi's shout. "He's had enough. He's just got out of that hellish nightmare, for crimes' sake."

The dark peeled away as Caiden's pupils dilated, and his panting finally subsided like a tempest moved on, whisked away by some other wind.

Towa hacked blood beside him. Her weird eyes glared brightly, black around irises of concentric rings. She backed away, peeling no-longer buoyant hair off her bloodied face. Her ruffled material stressed against the thread netting.

Threi looked pleased. "I'd say the nightmares sharpened him up."

Dripping sweat, Caiden crawled to his feet, still infused with the rush, the vigor, twice as alive as before. Guilt tried to stick in him when he saw Towa's face, but he'd lost, and he had two choices here in the den of the enemy: dominate or be bullied.

Threi held his hand out to Towa. "Give it here. He's earned a consolation prize for effort."

Towa twitched, hesitating. Frustration carved a sneer in Threi's face as he rounded on the tal, inches away, voice heavy with command. "Everything that's yours is mine. I said, *give it here*."

Towa resisted for a beat, her body ruffling, face tight as she tasted Threi's breath so close. But the Graven resonance—or whatever it was—invaded her spirit with proximity. Her pupil rings constricted together and her expression smoothed to obeisance. She handed him the glass chicory flower before stalking away. Threi turned and dropped it into Caiden's bloody palm.

The gathered Casthen's cheers stuffed Caiden's ears. Their previous refrain that he wasn't as strong or strange as they thought was replaced with hollers of support. Threi clapped him on the back and said, "Rest up, fight more, eat. In a few days it'll be time to anneal this blade you've become."

CHAPTER 34

HARVEST

Caiden rested, woke, sparred—the same for days. His opponents were skittish, the nightmares were boring, the pain familiar, and ration blocks bland. Caiden's fire pent up more and more. His complaints to Threi about all the delays were met with apathy, and Caiden wondered if the man was stalling for ulterior reasons. Or just trying to get Caiden feeling integrated in the Casthen routine.

The rumors about him settled down, replaced with fresher gossip: a new scientist had been assigned too high a security clearance, there was another external disturbance to the holobia requiring destructive measures, and one universe blister was too small for what the biology unit wanted to test.

Finally, Threi was ready.

"In here." Threi crossed a darkly churning rind. His voice dissolved until Caiden followed through. "—a good little soldier if you want to pass for my probationer. Plus nightmares aren't quite like the real thing."

On the other side was a warehouse lit only by the rind, with aisles of stacked cages. Caiden slowed to peer through the mess of tubes that infiltrated each. Small beasts huddled inside. One gave a weak snarl, revealing sharp, pearly jaws: the miniature of Caiden's dreams.

"Nophek."

"From RM28. The passagers were raiding gloss from the mature nophek, while us Casthen focused on gathering up pups. These won't live long outside a compatible universe—thus the chemicals—but we've located a suitable host planet elsewhere, to start the operation all over."

"Start over?" Caiden's feet stuck in place. "You're serious."

Threi peered in. "Aren't they cute?"

"Threi. To start over—"

"You didn't think Çydanza would stop, did you? She wriggled out of guilt. No one can stop her but us. There's a freighter here stuffed with purchased convicts and dregs, ready to be processed then bound for a planet of green grass and juicy, fast-growing livestock."

"How long do we have until they're processed?" Caiden leaned to the cage. The sickly nophek startled inside, rammed the front, and snapped its salivating jaws. Caiden flinched.

Threi laughed and continued down the aisle. "The workers will be processed in twenty ephemeris days or so."

"*Slaves*," Caiden shouted at Threi's back, stopping him. "Call them what they are. Don't dress up the Casthen's actions in apologetic language. Give it the weight it deserves."

Threi's always-ready smile stayed, but wrinkles curdled over the bridge of his nose. "Yet you don't apply the same weight to yourself, *soldier*."

Threi pivoted and carried on.

The young nophek in the cage convulsed on its side, snapping its mouth between each whimper. Its eyes were little moons in the dark. All around, a thousand moons in five hundred faces. The pups would be planted on another forsaken planet, as children like him had been; both humans and nophek used like cogs in a machine to produce the end result of the gloss.

At a door by the end of the aisle, Threi put his hand on a genetic code panel. "We've bred out a few fecund females and now they're ready to harvest. The Dynast is impatient for delivery."

"Did the Dynast buy *all* the gloss from the operation? What are they using it for?"

A tendon in Threi's temple pinched. "Research. They use gloss's high energy potential to power Graven technology and bioresearch."

"What's the part you're not telling me?"

"I'm not obligated to share anything I don't think will benefit me. Here." Threi handed him a diamond blade.

Caiden stepped in and froze. Small reddish lumps—neonatal nophek pups—bobbed in fluid-filled cubes. Their tiny bodies were infiltrated with milky feeding tubes and intravenous fluids, though it seemed impossible that anyone could find a vein in a creature so small.

In the next room, three adult nophek stood in metal contraptions that squeezed their bodies in place, and their heads sat in vises screwed to bony ridges in their skulls. Blood dripped around their wild eyes, down their wavy manes to the floor.

"They're in pain." Caiden tensed. It didn't feel real, after seeing so many of the beasts in his nightmares. They were slightly smaller in the waking world.

"They're on painkillers," Threi replied. "Gloss matures with the nophek and is only present in adults, but mature nophek become more resistant to sedatives and too wild to handle. That's why so little is known about their species. Our research is mostly limited to glossless pups."

Caiden approached the thing of his nightmares. Teeth two inches long. The jaws that had torn Leta's lungs from her rib cage. The reek of metallic blood filled his head and he remembered the taste of it, how slippery it was coagulated. Caiden tightened his grip on the knife, ticking it against his thigh.

"Why knives?" he whispered, and regretted his shaky question the moment it left his tongue.

Threi leaned in, inches away from Caiden's cheek with his own blood-and-lily scent, pausing to prolong discomfort. "Because knives are intimate. You need to be present with your thrashing fear, the stench of it, the slick of teeth. Fear needs to be wrestled with. If I thought you could harvest with your bare hands, I'd give you no weapon at all."

"I did." He'd grasped upper and lower jaws in his fingers, looked down the serrated pink flesh of the throat. Then he'd pulled, and rent the skull. "In a dream."

"Good. Just use the damn knife." Threi strolled to one nophek and plunged his blade into the top of its skull. It shrieked, shrill and grating, blood spattering from its gaping mouth. The beast thrashed against clanging restraints.

The sounds drummed up terror still fresh in Caiden's bones from the nightmares. The scent kicked his mind into a panic that he fought to restrain. This *was* different from the nightmares. This had meaning, it wasn't going to reset, they weren't phantom beasts. They lived.

Threi gripped his knife handle with both hands and pushed it back to the beast's nape. "Shove it to the hilt. That'll break up the liquid crystal matrices of the growing fluid." He pulled it out and slammed it down to one side, making a crosscut, then he gripped the opening with both hands and thrust open the four parts of the skull. Pink and white brain matter jiggled inside. Threi dug his fingers in and fished around, emerging with the gloss orb.

"Your turn." Threi beamed and walked to a basin on the opposite wall.

Caiden stared at the dead nophek's gaping skull. Fourteen years old, he'd covered himself in that violet fluid, pleading that something would save him from the horror.

"Intimate, huh." He measured his voice, each syllable a stitch keeping him together.

Threi chuckled and washed the gloss until it gleamed with inner colors, its structure perfectly clear. He dropped it in a containment box of coded light. "Knives are more fun than a laser."

Caiden stepped to one of the beasts. Their unique blood scent sliced over his tongue as he breathed. His mind's eye filled with flashes of biting jaws, his body crowded with phantom pains of countless teeth. The knife quivered, but it wasn't fear that stalled him. His fear had dried up in the desert.

He pitied them. Hungry, captive creatures.

This nophek's eyes were white pools filled with the same terror that had consumed him as he wormed his way beneath the desert rock, pissing himself, sure he was going to die.

"Winn." Threi stood behind him.

Caiden raised the blade. *This gets me closer to ending their oppression for good. This is how I kill Çydanza. Someone forgive me . . .*

He plunged it to the hilt. The nophek's piercing squeal knocked the air from him. He gasped it back in and closed his eyes while he slid the blade back, fighting the nophek's convulsions as it bucked. The blade crunched against bone. Hot breaths bellowed over his chest.

Caiden had to open his eyes for the second cut. The nophek's round pupils rolled up at him. His hands were smeared vivid, primal red.

He clenched down a hot flurry of sick and made the second cut. It went smoother, and his augmented strength easily pried the skull apart. The dead beast's body shook. The tongue lolled. Muscles twitched.

Caiden knew that feeling: something was dying in him but he was still kicking.

He reached into hot, silky fluid. His fingers teased around the smooth orb of the gloss until he fished it up in his palm.

"Cathartic, isn't it? Destroying the thing that destroyed you. Çydanza's future onslaught of killing memories will feel like this, far more real than mere nightmares. The more exposure you get, the better. Clean and box that gloss." He moved to the last nophek in the line.

Caiden turned away to the basin but still heard the bone crack, the squelch, and the shrill whine of life leaving an innocent creature.

Shivering, he washed the gem, the thing more valuable than him. He wasn't surprised, it was mesmerizing. When rotated, it paraded every color imaginable, condensing the energy to fuel starships, to power ancient technology, to unlock quantum potentials. Caiden was just Graven meat. An expensive soldier stuffed with bad memories and a volatile temper.

And a heart, still, he hoped. Even if bits of it were dying.

Caiden's nightmares reoriented to reflect his deed. The following few nights, he had that blade in his hand, plunging it through bone, feeling the beast bucking against death. But dreams were milder than reality.

"Now for the real test," Threi said when he came to gather Caiden again. "Çydanza has assigned you an exceptionally special task."

Caiden followed while thumbing the diamond knife sheathed against his thigh. "Just tell me what it is now. Your love of drama is boring."

Threi laughed. His armored shoulders were all Caiden could make out in the dark corridor under spotlights. "We've kept a sire. An especially old, monstrous, and intelligent male nophek. It's time to harvest the most developed gloss ever recorded."

Silye was waiting for them at a six-meter-wide door. She had a mag-cart loaded with weaponry. Her hair whisked like a dress as she maneuvered power cells into a meter-long glave.

"I don't need all this," Caiden said. "I've fought them countless times, I know how they move. And you said this one was old?"

"Oh heavens, pup, you'll need this and more." Threi sorted through the armament and passed items to Caiden. "This isn't a dream. You can really die in here."

Caiden held a dangling harness, similar to the cloudsuit, but designed to emit a shield of dilatant air around vital points of the body. Threi handed him two small pinch-fire glaves. Silye tested then passed over a pair of bracelet glaves.

"What are these?" He tried them on; they wrapped around his knuckles like cages when he curled a fist.

Silye tapped her ear and made an explosive gesture with her fingers. *Sonic.*

Caiden shook his head. "Overkill." He looped the harnessing over his armor, with the little power pack glowing in the center of his chest. One small glave at either thigh. Bracelets on. Silye passed him the long rail glave, an electric spear of sorts. Last, she rummaged in the cart and handed Caiden packs of analgesics, fast-restore gel, and performance enhancers.

Threi unlocked the door. His smile wavered. A lump bobbed in his throat. "Don't die."

Or Cydanza lives on forever.

Threi added, "I'll stand by this door, so bail if it's too much. Failing and getting a scolding from her is better than dying. Usually."

Threi signaled the door open and shoved Caiden through a thick rind.

His insides squirmed with fire, throat parched instantly, tongue shriveled with spice. Hacking, he staggered, righted himself on all fours.

A jungle. Lush, wet plants crowded the darkness. Small floating lights or insects roamed, providing an eerie glow. Among rocks, decaying timbers, and hanging vines stretched some tattered film—resembling the holobia's saliva—and patches of ground resembled muscle amidst the soil. As his brain fumbled familiar terms of strange flora and mist-adapted aquatic species, fear whittled his thoughts down to one sight.

Two luminous white pupils riveted on him in the dark, forty meters away.

One was half-lidded—something wrong with its eye?

Caiden crouched. The nophek waited in the gloom. An almost inaudibly deep drumming emanated from its throat.

"Crimes, Threi was right. This feels different." Sweat trickled down his spine already. Adrenaline sparkled across his skin. He chugged a vial of performance enhancer and crept closer, keeping trees between them.

The reflective eyes tracked him. Roving lights drifted over the beast, illuminating contours of furred muscle and the glint of scaly skin. Its withers had to be as tall as Caiden's shoulders, and its paws as big as his head, tipped in curved claws. Similar to the young nophek in the warehouse and the pup he'd seen in the Cartographers' Den, this huge male's body was scabbed in an extensive array of medical devices, chemical housings, and other life-support systems. While originally strapped or riveted on, the devices had embedded and grown over with scar tissue.

This universe wasn't kind to it. The beast jingled as it shifted its weight to track him.

A pang of heartbreak struck Caiden. Maybe it would be merciful to put this creature down.

The nophek snarled and charged with incredible speed, its legs ripping up foliage. Caiden fired both the small glaves, emitting jagged energy tendrils. They skittered off the nophek's hide, not stalling its charge a single beat.

Caiden dropped the useless glaves and vaulted up the tree trunk beside him. He clutched a high branch and hung, his diamond knife ready to plunge with all his weight.

The nophek coiled on its back legs and *jumped*. For all its bulk, it moved like fluid, twisting impossible joints. It grabbed Caiden's branch. Its lower body curled around, weight snapping the bough.

Caiden fell gracelessly, dislocating a shoulder on landing. He scrabbled up. The nophek landed on its feet and clamped its huge jaws around his leg, biting into the instantly thickened air of his shield. It protected Caiden's limb but the pressure still slammed him to the ground. The teeth bit slowly, inching through even the dense air, until it reached armor and crunched.

Caiden screamed at the stress, but the Casthen armor he loathed was resilient against teeth.

He kicked the nophek's boxy face to free his leg, and rolled away under the swipe of a paw. So much for the air shield.

The nophek's guttural roar split through Caiden's breast, tumbling his pulse as he ran for a higher position and swung the long spear glave off his back. Moss and membrane slipped beneath his boots as he tried to plant himself, using the spear as one would when fighting boar: skewered by their own force.

The nophek's three-beat charge shook the ground. Caiden's glave danced with electricity. The nophek plowed into it chest-first. Electric bands splintered against its hide. The glave tip gouged into muscle and hit a breastbone so solid the glave's rail bent in the middle, digging Caiden into the ground. He yelped and held tight with his good arm. The butt end crumpled armor plates against his stomach, until the whole glave snapped in the center.

The nophek backed off, rolling its giant shoulders and kicking at its chest. Then in one whole-body riveting motion, its eyes and frame squared on Caiden in the dark.

"*Shit!*" He scrambled up and clutched the knife. A good, trusty knife.

The nophek snorted and charged. Caiden rolled down into a rocky gully, curling against the brunt of the fall. He scaled the other side slowly, one-armed, then bolted away. His panting ratcheted in speed as he watched the nophek leap the chasm behind him.

Just need the gloss. Hit the skull.

He stalled to pop his dislocated shoulder back into place. The ground rumbled with the nophek's pursuit. Caiden aimed for a vertical rock. He launched backward off it as the nophek plowed straight through, sending shards flying. Debris showered Caiden's armor, pitching him midair, but he landed straddling the nophek's shoulders among clustered vials and buckles. He grabbed a handful of mane and pinched his knees in as the monster bucked, eyes wild and brilliant in the dark.

Caiden primed a killing blow. His augmented muscles crackled with electricity. He yanked his body forward into a stab at the nophek's skull.

The beast curled forward and pitched Caiden over its neck. He struck his bad shoulder and hissed swears. He rolled through dizziness in a tangle of fern.

The nophek bit his torso whole and shook him like a rag. A tooth shattered the power pack of the air shield. Dirt raked him; plants slapped his face. Within the whiplash and bursts of light, he stabbed his blade at a cheek, an ear, anything. A hundred nightmares blurred into the pain.

The nophek howled and dropped him. Shaking its head with a huff, it backed off, dazed and clawing wildly in front of it.

Caiden sprung up and instantly regretted the move. Familiar pain lanced his chest. The armor seams had let some teeth through. A punctured lung, maybe. One good arm.

The nophek limped badly on one foreleg where a medical canister had grown into the joint and *cracked* with each step. A loose pin skewered one eyelid. A cord chafed around its neck, cleaving a pit of scar tissue—that was why every other inhale came out a heaving wheeze.

Caiden swallowed blood and heartache. The nophek nightmares had snipped out his fear and grown a blossom of pity. He needed to beat the Casthen while retaining his sense of mercy, even if it killed him.

He could try to free this monster from suffering.

It charged and leapt at him. He dodged but was caught in the slap of its bony tail. With feline agility, the nophek whipped around and pinned Caiden beneath its front paws. Claws buckled through his armor. He held off its dripping maw with his augmented strength, and tried one swift punch of the sonic glaves, but the pressure glanced right off the nophek's skull, little more than a flinch.

The beast levered its full weight. Caiden fumbled for the cord gouged into its neck and ripped it with a shaking hand, tearing scar tissue and rivets out as he screamed, pain whipping up and down his arm. The chain came free in a gush of blood. The beast yelped and jarred enough for Caiden to roll away. Armor plates wrenched free, stuck in claws. Caiden spun around its foreleg, holding on with his legs as he gripped the canister embedded in its knee. He crushed it in a fist until it was slender enough to yank out.

The beast roared and reared up, throwing Caiden several meters away. A rock slammed his hip and spun him flopping into a stalky plant.

He cursed in Andalvian, seven swears in one. The knife was gone.

The nophek's eyes flashed fury. It charged, lopsided and half-blind.

Caiden stood on leaden legs. He spotted an intravenous knot of pain-killer spores on the monster's ridged back. Bright purple, not erupted yet. He held his ground, vision blurring.

The nophek bounded, raising a forearm for a swipe, claws splayed. Caiden rolled under its armpit then jumped at its side, smashing the spores before he was barreled over by hind legs and tail.

The nophek shrieked and gurgled as it collapsed, flooded with analgesics.

Caiden trembled on the ground, vision streaked with sparks, augmented arm twitching, other arm numb.

The monster shook from head to tail, mane flicking off lathered sweat. Its body was still mutilated by overgrown devices, but with the painkillers, it didn't feel them anymore, and powered over to Caiden with fresh vigor.

"Damn!" he whimpered, and gathered rubbery legs beneath him. Too slow. Claws slammed into his fleshy shoulder, twisting him, snapping his lower leg. He shrieked and spun himself the opposite way, free of the claws.

He choked and crawled to a tree where vines latticed around a decayed trunk. He climbed up with one leg and his augmented arm, which spasmed, randomly losing grip. Curses streamed with his panting as he hauled himself up and clung at a safe height. The enraged nophek rammed the hollow trunk. It bent and creaked with each hit.

Caiden held on, less afraid and more disappointed.

After being chewed endlessly in nightmares, he'd be eaten one last time.

The ramming stopped and the nophek backed up, exhausted, wounded—pain soothing by the moment. It set down on its haunches and quivered there, watching Caiden with huge moon eyes.

The tree began to list sideways.

Caiden stabbed a painkiller into his side. "I'm not gonna make it back to the door, am I."

CHAPTER 35

MERCY

The razor scent of nophek blood sluiced into Caiden's nose as he waited. The beast watched. It began to lick the elbow joint where Caiden had torn out the chemical canister.

With the tree slowly tipping, and nowhere else to go, Caiden climbed gingerly to the ground, several meters from the beast. He kept his hand placating, his posture easy.

He moved a few inches closer.

The nophek continued watching and licking its wound. Past the haze of exhaustion and pain in its eyes lay a keen intelligence. The gloss in its massive head might allow it levels of reasoning or perception that Caiden couldn't fathom.

His knowledge of phenotypes, animal communication and behavior, and body language across species all bobbed uselessly in vertigo. He emptied his mind of expectations and thoughts, focused on being as empty as the wind, summoned compassion, then took another step toward the beast.

This is real.

The nophek shifted, dark russet skin rippling with fur over fluted muscle. Caiden paused until the creature settled.

He ripped off the mangled armor on his mangled arm and had to lift his flesh-and-blood hand with his machine arm as he approached the monstrous nophek slowly. Its nostrils flared pink, smelling him. He was transported back under the rock crevice. The tang of blood. The beast's bright eyes were pits like reflective white water, on which Caiden's silhouette wriggled.

One more step, and his hand hovered before its muzzle.

The big male huffed a hot breath across Caiden's bloody fingers, then lowered on his belly, exhausted. An opioid dullness spread in his eyes.

Caiden folded laboriously onto his knees and sat in front of the beast for a solid minute, his body unconvinced that the threat was really over. Agony radiated through his limbs. His breathing was mushy.

The nophek remained calm, his eyes weary-dull but intelligent. Caiden examined the needle in his eyelid. Part of a broken injection site? He stared into the nophek's pupils for a long while and contemplated whether saying something first would make any difference or just make himself feel better. The nophek emitted a clicking rumble, which Caiden, exhausted and a little bit crazed, took as a go-ahead. He tenderly slid the needle out—the monster elicited a tiny snarl—then dabbed some fast-restore gel over the punctures.

"I'll do some more?" Speaking did make him feel better. He held out his palm. The nophek puffed against it eagerly, then closed his eyes.

Caiden pressed to a standing position through a mountain of pain, and pulled out the rest of the analgesics. He used one on himself, the rest on the beast, then limped around the huge body, roaming for injuries to salve and medical devices to correct. He didn't recognize most of the substances and tech: the Casthen had pulled out all the stops to keep this big guy alive for a cruelly long time.

"We're a lot alike. The Casthen hurt us both."

When the beast was all patched up, Caiden fell to his knees, swarmed in dizzy speckles, drenched in sweat. He set his dislocated shoulder better, splinted his leg, and collapsed on his side. *Is killing the nophek merciful, since he lives in suffering?*

"Cydanza will punish me if I fail to harvest your gloss," he murmured. "But I don't want to be this . . . murderer."

A memory flashed: the nophek pup that had chased him into the *Azura's* rind, in the Den, and died in a puff of red mist.

The blood on his hands from the earlier gloss harvest. So very scarlet.

Caiden whimpered and struggled to his feet in the dark. The roving lights glowed over the aftermath of their fight, which oriented Caiden to the door. He had a short window to leave before the beast regained the will to devour.

He limped along, and heard the nophek rise and lumber forward, crushing slippery plants.

Blips of fear rose through Caiden's dizziness. He turned. The beast's huge dilated pupils flashed light.

"Just how intelligent are you?"

The nophek made a sound between a purr and a growl, so deep it vibrated Caiden's achy ribs.

"Well..." He wobbled in place, feeling more than a little crazed now. This was a dream gone on longer than usual, he wasn't sure how it was supposed to play out. "Come with me to the lab, I can refresh some medicaments and you'll feel better. I don't think anyone'll dare harass us two broken and angry things."

The nophek lumbered after him as he navigated a grueling path to the door. At times the beast caught up, and Caiden was grateful to set a hand on his shoulder and hold himself up. The performance enhancers were wearing off, and the core of his spine itched, which was an alarmingly new and specific sensation.

The doors opened, and Caiden raised his hands for peace. Threi let out a hissing curse. For once the man's eyes were bugged with fear. Towa stood behind him and bristled, raising a glave.

The nophek snarled through his whole body. Caiden laid a hand on the monster's quivering muscles until he stilled.

Threi stepped back and exhaled forcefully, raising an arm for Towa to stand down. "I shouldn't be surprised, should I. Safe to say you're not afraid of them anymore?"

Caiden's hand sank into downy fur. He smiled and looked over as the beast leaned into his palm. So much more connected beings beyond language: pheromones, hormones, vibration, electromagnetism, bloodstream, scent.

"We need *gloss*," Towa hissed, her gaze flicking to track the nophek's every twitch. "A heart of gold won't impress Çydanza."

"I'm not afraid of her."

"You should be," Threi replied delicately. "I am impressed, but you need a reason—a *good* one—to keep this nophek alive."

The monster purred against Caiden's palm. He looked over and smiled wider. Despite everything he still had to overcome, this felt like a victory: his first true connection in this wretched place. And proof that his memories didn't control him anymore.

Compassion wasn't a strategy within the Casthen machine. He needed reasoning that increased Casthen *profit*. Swallowing butterflies, he thought fast and said, "Research on nophek has been limited because adults are volatile, powerful, and resistant to sedatives, and there are few universes where any of them survive long. Isn't that why you devoted a whole environment to this one?"

And why none of his ghastly ingrown equipment had been tended to. Caiden patted the monster's rippling shoulder: he growled low again and leaned into Caiden. "Now look. A chance to study a mature one in detail. Maybe there's something about their maturation that makes them incompatible with so many universes...If we figure it out, you might not need one rare planet in a billion in order to cultivate gloss."

Threi crossed his arms and inhaled slowly.

"Threi," Towa warned.

The man flipped a hand to shut her up. "Fair. I can convince Çydanza to be lenient. The gloss order is due in eight ephemeris days, and that's probably as long as the nophek will live outside the universe it was in. You have that long to convince us that the nophek is more valuable alive than the value of the gloss in its brain."

"You're allowing this?" Towa yelled.

Threi kept a generous distance from the nophek, but beamed with pride. "For now. He's done what no one else has managed, all this time. A mature nophek's energetic physiology is different from a pup's; he might have a point about their survivability."

"You've gone soft." Towa backed up at Threi's vicious glare, then flinched as the nophek's jaws snapped.

"And you've gotten a little too sharp." Threi held his glare and turned to her intently. He drew himself straighter, spine curling at his neck, eyes glittering with that distant look he got when he tried to summon more of his Graven influence.

Towa's hard jealousy melted into obeisance. The constant motion of her tal's body material calmed into a drape.

Graven cur.

The nophek growled too. Caiden patted him. He would reoutfit the beast, adjust the chemicals, add painkillers. Caiden would give back the second chance he'd been given by Laythan's crew, even if that care had been Graven-bought.

He would give life, not take it.

Caiden worked tirelessly, energized by a straightforward task. He shed the Casthen armor and wore soft trousers and a shirt. His morphcoat turned to a breezy plaited silk. The mechanical know-how from his childhood mapped easily onto his newer bioscience knowledge, and he whisked around the Casthen lab doing the work of a whole team alone.

Almost alone. Silye was the only one not terrified of the nophek.

He cleaned out the final abscess, the nophek growled low, and Caiden chuckled. "Last one, big guy." He patted the nophek's rump. "Silye, test this one too. Please."

He reached over with a pus sample in a dish. She rushed from the lab desks. Her long hair wrapped her body in sheaves and braids, tied or clipped out of the way over her clothing.

"Syringe, please."

He didn't need the *please*. It didn't soften the Graven blow. Didn't dull his shame. Silye jumped at his every command, and glanced over often to anticipate his needs, and stared adoringly when he gave her attention. Caiden accepted the syringe with a thank-you and a smile—softening those blows however he could. Silye blinked each time, as if politeness confused her.

He turned back to the nophek and drew another blood sample, then collected the drip-filled vial of cerebrospinal fluid. For days he'd moved methodically, gathering test tissue and fluids and tending to wounds in the same sweep. The beast was compliant through a mix of a fatigue, chemicals, and the universe parameters gradually breaking down his body. Caiden hurried.

Silye tapped her chest and reached out. Caiden nodded and handed her the samples for processing. Now: they wait.

He stretched, cracked his back, and rubbed tired eyes. Humming vigor pooled in him once his momentum stopped.

The weary, heavily drugged nophek lifted his muscular neck and pressed his wide forehead into Caiden's chest—head so big it dwarfed him. Caiden's mind stopped. He closed his eyes and leaned in too, wrapping his arms around the monster's head and feeling the *weight* of the gloss: that pit of raw energy pressuring against his heart. Exhausted calm poured into him. And deep respect: decades had grown this power in the nophek's brain, spark by spark, crystalline particles aligning in quantum glitches built by the flowing of time.

"You're tired like me," he murmured. The nophek's exhale fluttered hot against Caiden's chest. He bent over that big head and scratched his fingers into the maned neck, careful of stitches and bandages. "I encountered a little one, once—was that yours? I did wrong by it. Somehow, despite all the visions of nophek eating me, I can't get over seeing that baby dying." He turned his cheek, downy fur grazing it, an earthy scent beneath the sting of chemicals. "Let me do better."

The nophek shoved Caiden away playfully, his force massive despite weariness. He shook gently—aware of the tubes and patches—before settling on his front paws. He wheezed a soft breath and flattened, claws as long as Caiden's fingers splaying on the lab's white floor.

Glass jingled against the pack of vials around the nophek's neck: Caiden had strung the chicory flower there. Hopefully he could keep the good part of his heart alive, one good choice at a time.

Caiden smiled. Çydanza couldn't use the horror of the nophek against him—not being shipped to them, not his family dying in their jaws, not his own death. The nophek weren't at fault for his suffering. Çydanza was responsible for the enslavement of them both.

He had to be ready to face her, make her accountable.

Soon.

Caiden sat, leaning against the nophek's side. He pulled up a holosplay to finish collating the data they'd collected. It was promising.

His stomach grumbled. He'd been sleeping in the labs, but still had to expedition to the mess hall for food. Rumors sprang up about him and the nophek each time he was seen, but otherwise the facility gossip shifted on like seasons: the young scientist had been reassigned and not seen again, the security fleet destroyed another tether-pod someone sent through the Casthen's impenetrable universe rind to try to gather data about the inside, and one of the Enforcers was missing in Unity. Towa had glared at Caiden and hissed, "All these problems since *he* got here."

Thankfully, he'd dealt with Threi's crew less while in the lab.

Silye glided between machines and surfaces, engrossed in her tasks.

"Take a break," Caiden called, before he realized it wouldn't reach her as a friendly suggestion, but as a command. Her pale eyelashes fluttered as she swirled around and drifted over in his gravity.

He shut up. Whether it was through symmetry, pheromones, cosmic alignment, or some inexplicable quantum entanglement—every word he ever spoke would be Graven whether he wished it or not. And every charmed word carved her will into submission.

She found a seat to "take a break" on, sitting obediently, and Caiden flushed with shame.

How much of her world revolved around Threi's silver tongue and Graven face? No wonder the man was so messed up, accustomed to his will cutting through life like a hot blade through tallow.

"How long have you been here?"

She gestured two fingers in a circle: *Always.*

Caiden's heart chipped. She hadn't seemed *unhappy*, just aloof and focused. Caiden had been happy as a mechanic, fixated by routine, calmed by order and knowing exactly what his job was. He hadn't known better.

"What do you do here?"

Her slender fingers flicked. *Help the Prime.*

Caiden frowned and sat upright, closing his holosplay. "Threi. Have you always been by his side?"

She tapped *yes.*

"Is he a father to you or a…" *A lover.* The idea saddened him before he could ask. There was no such thing as consent, with someone as Graven as Threi and as susceptible as Silye. *Or with me, the same kind of monster…*

Her appearance was strange and alluring, and Caiden had glimpsed, in his short stroll through Emporia's red district, more than enough fetishization of the unusual.

Silye shook her head at both.

"Does he keep you isolated? What do you like to do?"

Her bruise-dark lips twitched, half a smile, and she sprang from her seat to walk over. Silye sat on her heels in front of Caiden. He noticed for the first time the white stubs jutting from her shoulder blades and along her spine, pushing through her voluminous hair. They were undeveloped bony angles with plush, petal-like material curling white against her back. Mutated mauya wings.

A holosplay sprung over her gloved fingers. Light laced the dimpled air as she fanned through a server database with a hacker's speed, eventually settling on a dump of media listed by name and type. She leaned toward him with it, to answer his question, and scrolled slowly.

Footage of distant places, travel logs, entertainment shows, things not Casthen.

Caiden's heart chipped more. "You like stories, reading and seeing things?"

She nodded and closed the holosplay. Her soft gaze sought across his face before meeting his eyes and instantly dashing away.

Like Leta. Maybe simple discomfort in Silye's case, but in Leta's, abuse had punished eye contact. On one bad day, six-year-old Leta had arrived on his doorstep late. Her bruises were nothing new, but she was cold from the walk, and cold from the ice her parents had used to minimize the visibility of their scorn. He wrapped her up in blankets and hugs, and held her convulsions until the temperature equalized.

"I won't pass Appraisal," she said.

She'd been set up to fail.

Caiden squeezed her tighter and replied, "The overseers know everything about us, they can see what we're meant for. You'll have a task that's perfect for you, and you're perfect for it. It's all right to struggle, you'll get through."

Back then, he had believed in the Casthen system.

Silye had no visible signs of harm except the faint purple on her cheek where Caiden had hit her in his nightmare daze. He burned to apologize, reach out, fix—but who knew what Graven touch did to someone so sensitive.

He steeled himself and asked the hard question. Perhaps his Graven voice would be useful for once, and demand truth. "Does anyone hurt you? Make you do things you don't want to?"

Silye shook her head and patted the knife hidden against her hip. She signed, *Too valuable. He keeps me safe.*

Caiden sighed relief. But something still didn't fit. Threi didn't act like she was a companion. Was she a mere assistant, an obedient body to fetch things and answer questions with claircognizance?

"Do you ever visit the kind of places that are in your media?"

Not allowed.

"You were with Threi in the Cartographers' Den, weren't you? And Emporia? He hasn't taken you anywhere else, like planets?"

She signed, *I am useful enough for some missions. Too expensive to risk on others.*

It hit Caiden like a punch. *"Useful enough,"* nine crimes.

"Can you speak?"

Silye shook her head and signed—*power*—tapped her throat and made an explosive motion with her fingers. She opened her mouth, small pearls and pale gums, and a jaggedly cut stub where her tongue had once been.

Caiden flushed with an anger that was webbed in sorrow. "Threi did that to you?"

She shrugged.

"This isn't a matter to shrug about, Sil. Are you...happy here?"

She blinked as if the word "happy" were new.

"Crimes, Silye," he cursed, and dropped his forehead into his hands. "You can even *see* what you're missing. You deserve better."

Caiden's shame fissured deeper. Whether Silye understood or agreed with the morality of all her actions, there was no question her loyalty was involuntary. He'd thought that no one could be part of the Casthen machine and not willfully buy into the immorality of it, but Casthen adherents could be oblivious to the harm of their work. A will-less ignorance—like Caiden in his childhood—good hearts turned to bad deeds because of a narrowing of their worldview and beliefs. Leta-vishkant had tried to tell him as much: *Judge individuals as individual: there's too much variety in the multiverse for broad statements to ever serve us well.*

He pushed to his feet to stride to the lab holosplays. This was the Casthen's main lab, which housed all biological studies and a complete genetic-engineering database. He dug around, and it took a while to link up names with numbers. Nothing was a *name* to Çydanza—everything was defined by numeral.

Paraborn. Caiden ran into his own brood files first, blatant by the red flag: MISSING. He didn't know which number he was out of the twenty that had become slaves due to one numeral of error. But they were all the same mosaic makeup in slightly different weightings, constructed around one unwavering Graven factor that was simply named "the dominant"—all details security-encoded at the highest level. The overall cocktail of genetics was too complex for Caiden to memorize, and his throat seized up at the sight. He offloaded the data to his personal database for later, and combed back to Silye's records.

She'd been bred with a mash-up of traits that amplified her response to Graven control. Human, mauya, some sopheids and syncrasids. Some people believed that the Graven once designed or conditioned certain species to respond even more strongly to the entanglement, in order to evoke loyalty from those beings on a genetic basis. Silye was all of this sort, predisposed to love Graven things even more than other species. The perfect companion for Threi.

Acceleration chamber. Graven research. Prototype sensory-blocking devices. Genetic engineering. Threi's Dynast affiliations... Had she been created as a *test* subject for something?

"Silye, does Threi—"

The door opened and Threi strode into the lab, stopping abruptly to take in the scene—Caiden and Silye and nophek. "Time's up."

CHAPTER 36

APPRAISAL

As he and Threi descended to the rind of Çydanza's universe, Caiden fastened the blue Casthen mask over his face. He never imagined it would be a comfort, but facelessness felt secure.

Towa hung back in the control atrium above, inputting commands to clear the rind for viewing.

Caiden wrapped an arm around the nophek's neck, petting a nervous rhythm. Mercy was his decision, and now he had the data to back it up. He glanced at Threi, who didn't meet his gaze but betrayed a stitch of worry. A crinkle in his perfect brow.

The resplendent rind threw reflections across Caiden's mask in lurid splashes and waves. Çydanza materialized from vapor to flesh. Her pale billows congealed into a womanly shape, long blond hair and cerulean eyes, an angular, unmotherly face. Fitted white lace clothed the vishkant's body. Caiden's hatred electrified at the sight of her, but he could lash it down now instead of lashing out.

The nophek growled against Caiden's arm wrapping his neck.

Çydanza's lips curled in a hollow smile. "I sometimes admire and even delight in disobedience, when it produces a gainful outcome I didn't perceive, or reveals an effective trait in one of my Casthen. So, explain your findings to me, Probationer."

Compassion wasn't an "effective trait" to her. Caiden straightened and nodded to Threi to pipe the data into Çydanza's world. "Have a look. I mapped how the gloss development changes the nophek's neurochemical system and morphology through adolescence. Without a specific universal parameter, the gloss poisons them as it develops, and then corrodes the gem upon their death. My data, with more comparisons and live tests, using the Casthen Harvest's variety of universes, might result in either a regimen of treatments through different growth phases to counterbalance the environmental conflict, or lead to a plan of migration *between* universes. You'll be able to broaden the possibility of where the nophek can survive—or even thrive—based on their age. A sort of pasture-rotation system, but with universes." Caiden's words sped, his two days of concerted effort rushing out. "And there's evidence, in living brain tissue this old, that clarient—incorporeal sopheids, merged with quantum consciousness—might actually be the parasite responsible for triggering gland crystallization in adolescence. As it grows, they expire, leaving behind luminiferous catalyst energy. If this is true, there could be a way to cultivate gloss in vitro." *Without harming animals.*

Caiden was panting lightly by the time he'd finished his defense. His nophek watched Çydanza with analgesic-dulled but feral eyes, brilliant pupils thinned to slits. He head-butted Caiden and tensed. Caiden pressed his palm against the nophek's chest.

Çydanza's smile twitched. She watched him for a long moment, then looked over what he'd done to the nophek: patched wounds and humanely fitted chemical packs. Silye had even helped him bathe the monster, whose coat was satin-soft and rich reddish-black without the mud.

"What a fascinating proposal." Çydanza stepped inches from the rind. "How special you are, soldier-scientist; come closer."

Had enough time passed to push his recent memories into her range of perception? The deal with Threi, the nightmare incubation, the whole plan...

Caiden stepped near, pruning his thoughts, focusing on how black her pupils were in the ocean of her irises. There was something dead in her eyes and she didn't appear quite as real as the vishkant in Emporia had. Because of lack of pheromones, with the rind separating them?

Çydanza extended a pale hand and dipped it into the rind. It blurred and dissimulated but emerged whole on the other side, inches from Caiden's face. Just as he'd seen in the footage of the memory flood.

"Prime—" Threi called, voice quavering.

"Hush, Enforcer."

Caiden glanced sideways, eyes wide behind his mask. Threi's worried gaze snared on Çy's hand. And the nophek snarled behind him, strumming the tension in the air.

I'm ready if she uses the memory flood now, I have to be.

But then she would know he was immune.

He focused on her fingers as they uncurled. She must have felt his artery pulsing wildly a half inch away.

Caiden summoned Panca's poise and focused on nothingness. Breathing, being present.

Thoughts slide off and away.

Çydanza's pearly nails scraped the bottom edge of his mask.

Imagine you're wind. Nothing can snag it. It streams over and keeps going, because it's empty. Nothing.

Her palm cupped Caiden's jaw, sliding under the mask and over his cheek, solid and warm. There was even a scent…a floral musk like violets in the field.

Ah, here are the pheromones. Caiden measured a careful thread of air, sieving his anxiety.

As Çydanza held his face, her gaze flicked to Threi. "Why so nervous? Come here."

Caiden's heart skipped.

She would find out.

Her gaze glided back to him as if she sensed his doubts. Surely she felt his rapid pulse now, touching him.

Threi drew near. Caiden slipped from Çydanza's hand to clap Threi on the back as jovially as he could muster. Threi's eyes widened in surprise. Caiden spoke hurriedly, "Jealous, not nervous, Prime. He's sour that I've done something he never could, even with his accelerated years. I might win all your favor."

Threi caught on quickly, cleared his throat, and shrugged. He even managed a blush. "Proud, not jealous. You are what I made you."

A sick burst of relief lightened Caiden's chest.

Threi added, "I did worry you would reject his effort out of hand."

Çydanza drew her arm back through the rind. Her lips didn't move from their frozen line, but mirth creased her eyes. "You two *are* a charming pair, but you've become quite lenient with what you have made, Threi, letting your probationer fail his task, even if he failed in a spectacular way."

Threi, recovered, shrugged again, and crossed his arms. "His research makes a good point, if we can produce gloss in a lab."

"It is a good point, and I do not reject out of hand," she drawled, her gaze flicking back to the nophek, who lowered his stance and snarled so deep, the metal platform vibrated.

Caiden took the nophek's big head in his arms, his shaking soothed by the creature's warmth. His cheek was still chilled by Çydanza's touch.

She continued, "And I am pleased by what Winn discovered about nophek; however, *this* nophek has exhausted its usefulness, and regrettably I am already late on delivering sweet Abriss's mega-gloss. She has a fresh test subject for it, and no one makes an eager Dynast Prime wait. Towa! If you will."

In a blur, the tal lunged down the steps to the platform, landed, and sprang up at the soft tissue of the nophek's armpit.

A blade plunged to the hilt.

The nophek screeched and reared up. Caiden was shoved onto his back, a scream seizing up in his throat. Towa ripped her blade out of the surprised beast, then mounted his shoulders and plunged the knife into the back of his neck.

Caiden shook, armors jittering against the floor. It was too late in a flash.

The nophek's pupils dilated to startled moons. Tongue curled among gaping teeth. He moaned the saddest sound before a gurgle rumbled from his mouth.

Tears blurred Caiden's vision beneath the mask. His lungs ached with the stifled scream, anguish scraping his insides as he watched Towa brandish a diamond pick and spring-loaded forceps. She cracked the nophek's huge skull open as his body slumped to the platform, violently twitching. She fished beneath brilliant, prismatic brain matter and hefted out a perfect sphere of gloss larger than her head.

The tal fixed him with a triumphant glare. She bent to pluck the glass chicory flower from the collar on the nophek's carcass, and turned it in her bloody fingers as she carried the gloss out of the room.

Tears pooled on the bottom rim of Caiden's mask, which hid his expression as he blinked furiously. His softness was being judged every second. He pushed up, averted his eyes from his dead friend, and clenched his fists to silence his shake.

Çydanza would pay for this death. He had everything he needed to kill her now.

Her gaze locked on him, eye line taking in the teardrops quivering on the edge of the blue.

Threi cut in fast. "I'll send a team for the carcass. Winn, let's go."

"Threi," Çydanza said, calm as a cloud, "it seems having a pupil has curbed your usual ruthlessness, and while you've been attending his probation quite closely, aren't there other tasks you've been avoiding? I don't leash you but I do tire of your wandering, sweet hound."

"Apologies, Prime, we've been having too much fun."

Caiden didn't think the man's face could blanch more, but it did. Ivory freckles stretched across his tight cheeks.

"And Winn, to reward your efforts, I will allow you to finish your research: dissect ten of the nophek pups and five of the yearlings to develop your clarient hypothesis and start experimenting with an in-vitro culture."

The pups. A black sensation filled Caiden from his feet. Vertigo tipped the room and he closed his eyes, embraced emptiness, and said in his most even tone, "Yes, Prime."

They were just words, empty. And she would be dead.

Soon.

"Good child." Çydanza smiled.

Caiden marched through the glowing lily field into Threi's room, his pace whisking priceless petals off their stems. Threi stalked at his heels. Inside, Caiden ripped off his Casthen carapace, tossing armor and straps on the floor. Beneath it, his body steamed, the heat visible in the chill air.

"Winn."

He pried off the blue mask and squeezed it in his augmented fingers until the crystalline laminate shattered into rainbows. He didn't care that Threi would see his tear-streaked face. "We're killing her now."

"Cool down first." Threi handed him a glass of water. "Sorry about the nophek. I didn't think she would still harvest it."

"You're not sorry." Caiden took a gulp and doubled over hacking—it wasn't water, it was liquor. He swore, then took another swig. *The pups. Nine crimes, those little ones...*

He was ready: engine firing, heart aligned. There was one last thing to clear up. "What do you intend to do as the new Casthen Prime once Çydanza is dead?"

"Involve the Cartographers, release the economic monopoly, meld Casthen with passagers so we can all work toward similar goals. The Casthen as an organization wields the greatest resources in the multiverse. But Çydanza doesn't use them for any end goal or higher purpose."

"Let's go. Now." Caiden sat on the bed and smacked a fist into his other hand. He thought over the plan—and a realization slapped him. "If the *Azura*'s rind will destroy a vishkant, what's stopping us from flying over and plowing the rind right through Çydanza's universe before she can run? The ship's rind is bound to touch her, then it's all over. I won't even need to endure the memory flood. Why didn't you think of this before and just steal the ship?"

"No. My plan, my rules. You exhaust her ability, then I get a moment with her after she's defanged. We do it my way or not at all."

The man of nonchalance was now a hive of anxiety. He snapped his fingers repeatedly.

"*A moment*," Caiden repeated. "Why do you need a moment with her? You need to hiss some villainous one-liner in her ear before we chuck her into the rind?"

"I have nothing to say to her." Threi's knuckles itched against the surface of the desk. He stared at the floor, eyes glazing.

Gears tripped into place in Caiden's brain. He looked over the mysteries populating Threi's room: the Graven research, private accel chamber, sensory-dampening prototypes and chemicals, the rare genetics...and

Silye. She was part of whatever his scheme was, engineered as a test subject and tool.

Caiden still couldn't grasp the bigger thing that Threi had been preparing for so long.

"You've toiled for years itching to kill Çydanza," Caiden said, hot and measured, "yet you act like she isn't important to you."

Threi's ice-blue gaze snapped up. The glassiness turned sharp and brittle. "Çydanza has lived effectively immortal, taking voyeuristic pleasure in the memories of her subjects, and delighting in the growth of an empire. She's predictable and fixed in routine." Threi composed himself and straightened to unbuckle his armor down to the black garments beneath. Free, he stretched, rolling his muscular shoulders and tousling snarls of hair. Through the glass wall behind him, the greenhouse lighting set the white lilies ablaze and lent him a vibrating aura. His white freckles glowed in death-pale skin.

Threi continued, voice rough and quiet, "She has no great aim, no diabolical plan to rule the multiverse, only to exploit it. As difficult as Çydanza has made it to kill her—with her species's abilities and an impassible universe—she's not the hardest person to kill in this multiverse. There's a chance, and it's past time such a privileged creature perished."

Caiden snorted. "You have a gift for saying a lot of words yet answering nothing."

Threi didn't smile. He folded his arms behind his back, and had that regal look again, a cinch between his shoulder blades, a knot in his jaw and eyes gleaming as if he looked out over legions. "What is important to me is no concern of yours, soldier. We can destroy Çydanza now, but you have to agree to do it my way."

His way seemed to be to do nothing at all, to test and scheme endlessly, snared in research and convolution and the vast resources the Casthen possessed. It started to make bizarre sense. The Casthen system was madness and violence, and had corrupted even this Dynast creature, webbing him in a breed of obsessive complacency.

Caiden couldn't trust anyone's judgment here. He couldn't ever harm the pups. Couldn't stay any longer. It was time to stop being Threi's pawn.

He rubbed his chest, remembering the weight and warmth of the big nophek's head, the hum of the ineffable gloss.

There was so much to avenge.

Caiden headed for the door and said, "We'll talk about this when you're ready to really share."

"Winn!"

Caiden strode through lilies and darkness, aiming straight for the *Azura*.

CHAPTER 37

ÇYDANZA'S UNIVERSE

His ship was a gorgeous and fearsome sight, her slick black body glazed with reflected gold and purple texture. Her wings were preened back, vanes sharp, thrusters closed in like flowers for the night.

Caiden's neural link with the *Azura* veiled his mind in sunny serenity. The sheer familiarity of it in this dank and hostile place cracked a wellspring of grief.

It was time. Not soon, but now.

"*Azura*. Let's destroy the heart of the Casthen."

He threw himself into the pilot's seat and settled back, closed his eyes. Breathed. Nothingness, like the wind.

The seat wrapped his tired limbs. Caiden rubbed his chest again, feeling the echo of the nophek's pressure, the hum of its decades-old gloss. Shipped off to the Dynast now.

The *Azura*'s idle engine whispered melodies to soothe him.

"Let's make sure there are no more losses like this. Ready?"

The cockpit fogged up with bright air eager to coalesce into drive guides.

Caiden would engage the *Azura*'s universe and fly her straight through Çydanza's lair, killing the vishkant in the process.

He raised his hands. Threads of light weaved around his fingers. He tilted his palms up and lifted. The ship rose, mini thrusters powering them past the facility's ceiling. The megastructure on the planet's dark side glittered with lights. Twilight formed a distant ring, and small universes blistered the surface and hovered above. Past the atmosphere was the faintest glisten of the lightseep fortress that turned space itself prismatic.

Caiden's heart flitted. It hardly seemed real after so much waiting. After sacrificing youth for power and abandoning his family in order to willingly be chewed by nightmares, now he was serene enough to endure whatever Çydanza threw at him...fast enough to chase her if she ran...strong enough to restrain her if she fought.

He flew smoothly, without the small twitches and large sweeps of his earlier piloting. His body was a knit of tension and relaxation, more than powerful enough to direct wings and thrusters. The *Azura* responded instantly to his mental desires. Her moods were home and her song was where he belonged. He'd missed it.

At the edge of the facility, he hovered. Çydanza's universe lay below, shelled in by a half sphere of black megastructure over top. He had checked the composition of materials: the *Azura*'s rind would destroy them as he flew right through, and if he kept going, the ship's universe would engulf Çydanza's and she would be pushed through the rind and killed.

Caiden reached up and pawed the florescer above his head. The universe blossomed outward in milky, billowing colors. The chorus of Caiden's being instantly harmonized, instabilities dissolved.

"She'll be dead in one swoop. Be fast, *Azura*."

Caiden tilted sharply, nosing down to Çydanza's shell. Dusty material kicked up as the *Azura*'s rind plowed through the black wall. Metal ripped and screeched. A mess of iridescent filaments slathered the view. Solid alloys crumpled into decreasing fractal particles as the rind chewed through.

Then the *Azura*'s universe hit the edge of Çydanza's. Colors rioted in the view. Caiden squinted against the light, as bright as the star's heart had been, until he was through and the ship glided.

In the chaos of disintegrating materials, he glimpsed Çydanza, cloudy and startled, thirty meters away.

Caiden pressured his hands forward to drive the ship into her and crush her against the rind.

The air around the ship locked up, stalling it in place. Pain slammed Caiden's fingers in the drive guides, twisting them to claws as he strained.

The thrusters howled but the ship didn't move, caught in a defensive web of scalar gravity and electromagnetism.

Caiden cursed. He hadn't anticipated that. He couldn't plow the ship's rind into her—but he could grab her and drag her into it by hand.

He charged from the cockpit, opening the bay doors and careening into Çydanza's world. The space was pale sand and pools. Çydanza stood at a cluster of desks and huge holosplays. She grew solid and sprinted for the edge of her universe where the viewing platform's frame provided an exit.

Caiden ran. The pounding of his feet on sand felt effortless after countless dreams fleeing from nophek. He'd mastered speed.

The vishkant stumbled, unaccustomed to threat.

Caiden tackled her and pinned her to the ground. It was ten-year-old Leta's throat he grasped. Her terrified eyes glittered with tears. Sweetgrass scent flooded his nose, and blue chicory blossoms spilled from her hair.

"Cai! Please!" Her lips trembled.

"I'm not fooled." He yanked her to her feet. She squeaked and her hands flew up, twisting him with surprising strength. They both crashed on the sand. Caiden looked up and was on the nophek planet, sky black and horizon bright. Çydanza was a beast that leapt at him but he didn't flinch. Jaws swarmed his face, yet every inch of him had been bitten before. Memories of pain radiated like old friends, unwelcome but familiar.

He wrestled her to the ground. When the sand spray of her thrashing cleared, Caiden was back in her universe, splashed by a shallow pool, strangling his mother.

Despite the kind eyes, the horrified gaping mouth, and the human pulse in her neck beneath his palms—this was not his mother.

"Lies. Forger of lies." He hauled her up by the neck and dragged her toward the ship's deadly rind.

The *Azura* blurred between two images: her real, rind-shrouded shape and the half-buried tower he'd found on RM28. When he looked back at Çydanza, he stumbled and fell. He was wearing Casthen armor, covered with the blood of beaten loved ones. They draped over his lap; his mother mangled, half a face, and Leta, only torso.

This isn't real. He pulled harder, pushing to his feet. Çydanza transformed. Caiden pulled his fourteen-year-old self, face streaked with tears and sand, speckled with his mother's blood, hauling the innocent version of himself not to the *Azura* but into the maw of the black transport headed to slaughter.

Çydanza dug her feet into the sand and hooked Caiden's ankle, tripping him. He wrestled her as he fell, and was swarmed by a cloud of jaws. The nophek piled on, pincered his skull, ripped out his throat—he knew how each artery gushed, the familiar pang of tendons, how juicily his own clavicle snapped. "*I've seen*"—he gasped—"*this all... before.*"

Caiden grappled with the vishkant's cloud-body until she solidified. He'd seen his parents and Leta killed too many times before. It was boring, infuriating. He locked his augmented hand around her ankle and pulled: only ten meters from the rind.

Visions continued to assault. Flashing nophek eyes. Pearly jaws. A thousand punctures. Pain, terror, excrement, betrayal. A child's feelings. They were the file that had whittled and sharpened him into more than a child.

"*Winn!*" Panca's scream.

Caiden staggered.

He glanced down, and he was dragging Panca by her upper arm. Blood drenched her, leaving a red furrow in the sand, skin chafing as he pulled.

She squirmed and whimpered, her hands scrabbling at his arm.

"Tricks," Caiden growled despite the tears stinging his eyes. It felt real. And the crew, his new family—they weren't anything he had dreamed of hurting.

He trudged on, staggering madly through a cerulean pool, dragging his heavy burden. His boots filled with water. Çydanza screeched and flailed. The sound joined his headaches, burned behind his eyes, blinded him with searing white. He felt his scream but didn't hear it. Memories bit him, rapidfire, striking his brain like an electrical storm. These weren't the visions he'd seen so many times. The physical impact was real and unexpected. His nerves gnashed. Muscle spasms jerked him to the ground. He was reduced to a crawl but could still drag her.

"Stop, *brother*, please," a tender voice whimpered.

Caiden froze, quaking as he turned. Taitn's voice.

Bones of one mutilated arm glistened through Taitn's flesh, and his other hand clutched his throat, which an energy blast had tunneled through. Caiden was armor-clad and bloody again in the vision, a glave in his other hand thrumming with the shot that had hit Taitn.

Brother.

"Not real." Caiden choked on heartbreak and tried to turn away. Four meters from the rind, he had to pull. His legs jellied as he kicked to propel himself. Çydanza's body twisted and re-formed in his grasp.

Ksiñe's whipkin squealed. Caiden flinched and dropped the creature. She scurried away to cower around a vision of Ksiñe's battered corpse, black and half-buried in the sand.

"*No,*" Caiden cried, tumbling over himself to crawl to his friend. But the illusion dissolved, and the vishkant was up and sprinting away.

Chemicals sawed Caiden's veins. Vision crumbling, he couldn't see which way the *Azura* was, where Çydanza ran to; there was just sand everywhere and the crew, his family: crimson corpses splayed across the desert.

He had prepared for nophek, but *this...*

His heart wouldn't ever be ready for this.

Caiden fell to his knees, racked with sick. Numbness rooted in. Panca, flayed; a knife in his hand.

Someone heaved him to his feet—*Laythan?*—pushed him then kicked him in the chest to send him sprawling through the *Azura*'s rind. He slammed into the bay floor.

Convulsing, he blinked away blood and tears for one final view: Çydanza stood safe and triumphant on the other side of the *Azura*'s rind. The defense beams that had captured the ship in place now levitated it up and out of her universe.

Caiden had failed.

He'd been prepared to see his first family die and all his old world swallowed. But his second family... he still cherished them.

The *Azura* was lifted away. Caiden lay broken on the bay floor as the memory flood continued to bite him, building into a new nightmare. He could endure any torture but the crew…the sight of them slaughtered because of him…in danger because he'd survived and they'd taken him in. He was vile poison.

And now Çydanza knew he intended to kill her.

And knew the *Azura* could do it.

CHAPTER 38

MERCILESS

Achketin foot barreled into Caiden's ribs, breaking two or three and sending him sprawling. Pain rained in a storm of hate. A kick in the hip, the groin. His fingers bent until they snapped one by one. The Casthen mob descended before he got far from the viewing room and his audience with Çydanza—who was very much alive and alarmed.

"His breeding is too valuable to destroy."

Çydanza had spared him, but gave no firm order for others to do the same.

Someone lifted him by the throat. A punch cracked into the back of his neck, and would have shattered the vertebrae again if it weren't hyperdiamond.

Caiden fought back with everything left in him. He had to get to the *Azura*.

"Dismantle his ship, down to its marrow."

Bruises pulped. Skin split. Agony was a familiar sea.

"There is no one I can't break," Çydanza had said, *"and now that I've seen his greatest fear, he will shatter. Do you all know the rumors? Follow them, these many whispers scratching at our gates."*

The rain of violence whisked away. Caiden's face was plastered on the grate floor, chevrons digging into a swelled cheek.

"Threi, I'm disappointed over what a light leash you have. If your probationer cannot become a perfect Casthen soldier, I'll be forced to discard him for his insolence—and will make an example of his demise, a dramatic one... you do love drama, sweet hound."

Consciousness came and went, a fickle commodity. Days might've passed, he wouldn't know inside the megastructure, on the dark side of a planet.

Distantly, he sensed all the sort of care he'd given the big nophek: salve, analgesics, antibiotics. And someone tinkering. His augmented fingers were popped back into place. Skin re-polarized. He was rolled onto his back.

Silye. Her gorgeous hair spilled over him like a blanket as she worked. Jet, the chketin, gripped Caiden's arm in two-inch-thick fingers and wrenched it back in the socket. He was then lifted up completely, dangling.

"Prop him there," a voice said. Crisp and savage, beautiful, alluring: a dark, Graven voice. "Crimes, they gave him a thrash."

The bite of a needle. Soft adrenaline, cinching him up. He opened his eyes, over-dilated, the light seeping all over.

It had been Threi's voice. The man stood in front of the *Azura*, tall and regal, like he owned her.

Caiden tried to speak but just mushed words.

Threi marched over and crouched. He grabbed a fistful of Caiden's sweaty hair and plowed Caiden's head against the metal wall. The man leaned in, cheek to cheek, hissing ire in Caiden's ear. "Your stupidity ruined years of planning. If Çydanza hadn't ordered the *Azura* dissected, I would take it for myself and give you a convenient little accident." He paused, breath warm. "What was it?"

Confusing question. Caiden rolled his head away and met Threi's ice-blue gaze.

The man asked, "What did she use against you, your real fear?"

Caiden's mind churned that thought around. The memory flood had ruined him, but it wasn't fear of nophek...

"Love."

She'd used his fear of loss. Losing the only family he had left.

He whimpered, head swamped and dizzy. He'd thought he was being selfless by sacrificing his happiness to liberate the multiverse from Casthen rule, but somewhere along the way he'd simply convinced his subconscious that he was deserving of suffering. His fixation on revenge cost everything—and he'd been too self-destructing to see.

Threi said, "Do you remember what she ordered you to do? The test and punishment?"

His brain swam through adrenaline, recalling more of Çydanza's judgment.

"Process the slaves that will restart the gloss production." The words lined up dry and sour in his mouth. He was too thrashed to imagine what that meant.

A perfect Casthen soldier...

He whispered, "What do we do now?"

"*You*, obey." Threi leaned in again, breath strained against Caiden's ear. "I'll take the *Azura*. It'll be dismantled but not destroyed: like you, it's too valuable to discard. Çydanza will try to sell it to the Dynast. I'll do what I can. As for you..." Frowning, Threi drew back, both hands on Caiden's bloodied shoulders, assessing him like a faulty part. "There's only one way you'll survive. Trust me. It'll make it easier."

He wrapped an arm around Caiden's waist and wrenched him to his feet, pinning him against the wall and gesturing Silye over. Threi draped Caiden's weight onto Silye's slight frame then backed away. Caiden strived to stand taller and relieve her burden, but his body was a monument of pain.

Threi peered at him intently and said, "Graven Winn of Casthen, you have to embrace your engineered nature. Sort out your shame. Develop your Graven gift—it's like a muscle, stronger with intention and practice. It's what will keep you alive now that every Casthen fang is sharpened and turned your way."

Threi paused, looking haunted.

Graven.

"Abriss," Caiden slurred, his thought process jumbled. But Threi drew up as if pulled by strings, posture predatory and regal. Caiden frowned. "What did she do to you?"

The world broke for a heartbeat, black and raw.

"She loved me." A lump twitched in Threi's throat. He blinked and shot his icy gaze to Silye. "You're assigned to him while he completes Çy's task. Watch him closely and catch every Graven sound he speaks—he needs to learn what he is, once and for all."

Silye nudged a triple-rail glaive into Caiden's armored hand. He followed her, dazed. Waves of twitches still hounded him, his body barely recovered from the beating despite the scour, advanced treatments, and rest. Even the Casthen's resources couldn't salve the results of a one-target brawl.

And his breast ached with something pent-up, growing stale. His compassion, perhaps, drying up at last.

Silye slipped her hand in his to lead him on. Her fingers quivered. He squeezed.

She led him to a large platform on the outside edge of the megastructure. Huge beetle-like freighters hunkered where metal met dirt. Their backs split open like wing casings, and human shapes spilled out in rivers of black motion. Casthen enforcers herded the river tributaries into one large flow to a massive scour chamber. People pooled inside, were cleansed, and filtered to rooms beyond.

"Were they bought from all over the multiverse, like my people were?"

Silye squeezed his hand: *Yes.*

The throngs of people reeked of mud, sweat, and urine from being cramped in the freighters. This was a scene of nightmares: throngs on the Flat Docks, the transport, the desert. Caiden forced a chuckle. They were all just meat from this elevated perspective, as he'd been, once. Meat for something to chew.

He made his way down to ground level. His mask hadn't been repaired after he'd shattered it, and the glassy cracks cleaved his view, seeming to double the crowd.

From slave to slaver, simply because of biology, an error.

Armored Casthen prodded the throngs to the scour. One of them—a burly chketin—barreled in, shoving with enough force to break skin and trip the crowd into knots.

"Stand down, overseer!" Caiden shouted, pouring focus into the sound. It squeezed from his diaphragm and vibrated up, cast from his tongue as a Graven order as clear as he could make it. The chketin Casthen halted instantly. The slave made to spring like a wild animal, but Caiden brought his glave up into the man's gut and said, "You too. Be orderly. *Everyone.*"

Terror rippled over their faces, curses hissed out, then most of them soothed into awe. They shuffled on, *orderly*, and the overseer herded with a gentler hand.

Caiden balled up a wretched feeling. The Graven effect really was stronger with intent, and his face wasn't even showing. It would have been even stronger had they seen him.

It was better this way. No one hurt. Orderly.

He followed Silye to a large chamber freestanding on the dock: memory-obliteration tech, which the crowd would filter through, wiped and ready for a world of lies. The chamber resembled the Cartographers' biodata chamber, but dark and rusted instead of bright and polished, as if trying its best to embody despair over hope.

Armored and masked, a faceless Casthen Enforcer, Caiden numbly ushered slaves in one by one. They looked up at him, rapt or alarmed, as he had that day on the Flat Docks. "Move on," he said. "Don't be scared. You'll be taken care of."

Their fear melted at his Graven words. They trusted him. Was it wrong to lie if it healed? Was it merciful to give them relief?

Caiden tried to remember if hope had dampened his suffering in the transport. A little, he thought. Or maybe he could tell them it would all be over *soon*.

Faces streamed by. Mostly human, some xenid or mixed. Some were elder and hardened, others as innocent and fearful as Leta. Tear-streaked. Furious. Bewildered.

Caiden couldn't whisk them all back on the transport and jet away to safety. Even if he did, the root of all this misery remained. He'd failed to pull Çydanza from the Casthen soil like a weed. He'd lost his chance and the *Azura* with it.

Silye stood beside Caiden at the control panel, while he hit EXECUTE as each person stepped into the machine. He absolved their past. Would their new world be vibrant green? If it was like his, at least they wouldn't be tortured or overworked. Their only chains would be ignorance. They would be happy.

Numbness set in with the monotony of the droves, and with nothing else to occupy his mind, it kept replaying the big nophek's death. His brain knew nothing but repetition.

Sweat slithered beneath his armor. The droplets found the same paths down his back, repeating, his posture throbbing with cramps.

Caiden felt unreal. All of reality unreal. A lucid dream. He shoved his mask up to the top of his head, yanking pale hair back.

"All of you, stop," he said, pouring out his desire with heartfelt Graven intent.

The crowd of hundreds halted.

Partly because of fear, confusion, or youth. Mostly because he was a Graven cur.

Silye stopped too.

"Sil... did you know you were designed? Made here for a purpose?"

She blinked at him, and signed, *I serve.*

Silye needed to be free to decide who she wanted to be, within the limitations of the genes the Casthen had given her.

Though freedom felt far away, for him and her both.

"Continue, orderly," he called, and the rivers of bodies flowed.

The monotony continued, Caiden locked inside it, hardly realizing when the processing was over. Silye poked him. He looked at her through his haze. She grabbed an edge of his armor and tugged him to the side of the deck where several Casthen had cornered a score of slaves.

"What's this?" he asked.

"Faulty ones," a tall saisn told him. "Memory wipe didn't take. Boss said you're to guide them to the N-Sector Servicer containers."

Ah, the horror can get worse. Caiden nodded and swung his glave around to shepherd the group into the facility. Silye took the opposite side.

N-Sector swamped them with a dense hum the moment the big doors opened—a sensory ordeal even for him. He thought of Leta, a neurotype more attuned to space, for whom this would be incredible torture. Did the Casthen consider that as they threw whomever wherever? One of the slaves was tremoring badly already.

Aisles stretched to darkness and shelves shot out of sight. Caiden goaded the unfortunates down an aisle. He stopped at a lit section where Casthen waited with containers already pulled out, like the one Caiden had been in to incubate his nightmares. These slaves would simply sleep, their biology part of the computers, or linked in for medical research or human testing of products.

Numbly, Caiden assisted. The slaves were undressed, then fitted without dignity into the coffins inside each box. Thread wires and spider nodes infiltrated their skin—Caiden knew that violating sensation.

Then the containers were slid back in, and the wall of shelves looked all the same. More bits of a machine, nothing to mark that a body lay within, a person with a heartbeat and dreams. The other Casthen left, and Caiden stood alone with Silye.

She tapped his vambrace, and gestured when she had his attention: *They are watching you. Time for the next task.*

He wobbled, bone-weary, and fantasized about lying in the *Azura*'s pilot seat and resting, letting the crystal cradle him, her lullabies heal—but by now, she was being ripped apart from shell to spine.

I don't deserve rest; I just ushered thousands into misery.

CHAPTER 39

REAL

Before Caiden's bruises and breaks had mended, the Casthen mobs came for him once more, defending the murder attempt against their Prime. He walked to the mess hall for food, starving, and three hundred soldiers rose up again.

He summoned his rage and grief and fought back. Between his augmented strength, combat skills, En's training, and his dream-time battling nophek in the desert, he demolished half the group, which only served to prove the effectiveness of his Casthen breeding. He had become the honed and polished blade Çydanza had wanted him to be.

Caiden belonged here.

His body buzzed with instincts, hot and frenetic. He fought with tooth and claw—and Graven pleas, but the mob was a mix, too many immune to him. The ten allies he gained by screaming, *"Fight with me, you curs!"* only lasted a few arcminutes before they were broken too.

He spilled more blood than had been in the nophek's whole body, but it wouldn't bring that sweet beast back. He succumbed to the void that the nightmares had hollowed out of him, the part that admitted the violence was fun, the crack of bone rewarding, his Graven charm refreshing after a life of struggling to feel like *enough*.

Compassion wasn't big enough to fill that hollow.

The mob ripped armor off Caiden. He was kicked and bludgeoned with chairs, hip fractured from a chketin fist, hurled across the mess into a choke hold and talons, and they re-injured every bone that Threi's crew had tried to patch up in him from the last time.

Eventually, the mob grew bored and ebbed away: some said Caiden had learned his lesson, others wanted the toy to heal up for another round later. Caiden lay wrecked on the mess-hall floor.

Fourteen years old, he'd gotten up from a similar beating, dizzy and hot-tempered, ready to march after the older boys who'd hurt them. But Leta grabbed his arm.

"Let them go," she'd said. "If they stay away, who cares."

"I care. You're hurt."

Her fawn hair almost covered the blood on her scalp.

"So, why hurt them back? They'll just hurt you more, nothing will change."

She was wisdom and he was power, but power had done him little good against Çydanza, and Leta was dead forever.

It wasn't "sacrifice" if nothing good came of it. Caiden was just a man in pain.

He moaned and rolled onto his side to retch again. Blood dribbled through the fine sieve of the grates. A pipe somewhere hissed. Distant machinery grumbled through kilometers of metal.

Silye found him once the blood had cooled.

"Help me up," he whispered, and croaked a "*please*" to wrap the iron of that Graven order in some manner of velvet.

She brushed sticky hair from his face and checked his vitals.

"To my—" *Ship.* The last word died on his lips. Home wasn't his Casthen room, it was the *Azura*. What would be left, when his ship was dismantled?

She knows, Silye signed right in front of his face, but Caiden couldn't make sense of it. She gave up and looped an arm under his torso, helping him to his feet.

Caiden waded through agony and vertigo with every tiny step. Silye stayed glued to his left side, under his arm. Slurring, he said, "Would you help me if I wasn't making you?"

She didn't pause, just shifted her grip to pat his heart.

They reached a scour, and she leaned him inside. It initiated, whipping energy through him, shocking every system until he tingled from his marrow to the little hairs on his skin. Minor injuries and swelling had healed.

His knees buckled and he folded up awkwardly inside the tube, eyes slitted, vision bleary through his lashes. Silye crouched at the opening. Her creamy hair was a waterfall of color and shadow. Her eyes black but for the round, concerned pupils surveying him.

This isn't sustainable. Killing Çydanza is further away than ever.

Silye reached in and picked up his hand, tugging him to a standing position. He let her lead him through the Casthen darkness to an even darker cramped room and a cot with one tattered blanket. He collapsed onto it. She tried and failed to arrange his limbs in a better way, and resorted to stitches and salves on the wounds that the scour hadn't healed.

"Silye!" Threi shouted down the hall outside.

She swiveled around, shoulders cringed.

Caiden reached a weak hand out to pinch her sleeve. "You shouldn't have to go."

She looked at him, eyes bright and pink in the darkness, curved with a smile. She patted her heart.

"*Come!*" Like Threi was yelling for a pet. Footsteps boomed in approach and then past, and Threi's knuckles rapped the door on his way.

Silye flinched then levered to her feet and swept out the door.

Caiden curled on his side, inviting the twinge of the fractured hip. He was Graven enough that all love was a lie, but not Graven enough to save Silye from abuse. He'd never succeeded at that with Leta either.

He curled a fist and tucked it under his hip, leaning into pain. Darkness seeped up—perhaps unconsciousness, Caiden couldn't tell the difference. There were no dreams or memories. He was beaten and scrubbed so raw, none of his history remained. Might as well have been here since infancy. He'd ended up here after all, and the intervening time had taught him nothing.

He wanted to dream of something nice, for the first time in so long. He plucked through tattered memories, and poured imagination into the holes. The nophek's throaty purr as it head-butted his chest. His father's laugh, his mother's playful scowl, and Leta braiding flowers into crowns. The spicy age of oak scent, and the green, and how warm their world's wind could be. He'd made jokes and laughed and was happy being only a mechanic. Leta laid a crown upon his head.

A spotted hand palpated Caiden's temples. He flinched as a light pierced his retinas—one, then the other—leaving a foggy afterimage. Blinking, he brought his hands up to swat at the figure, but fingers wrapped around his wrists so gently he paused.

"Crimes…what did they do?" A voice Caiden knew. As gentle as the hands.

He begged his memories to carry on to the next. His brain was frozen, rewiring frantically, knitting together headache threads like thin whines braided into screams. He opened his mouth and worked his jaw, hoping sounds emerged. "*Taitn?*"

Impossible. They were far away, and had moved on. Now the crew were no more than weaponized memories that Çydanza would wield against him.

Darkness throbbed in his vision. Multiple sets of hands helped him to a sitting position. Threi's crew, going to force him into functional shape again for some new horrific task.

But soft, spotted fingers probed his head.

"Ksiñe." Caiden blinked until the Andalvian's face emerged.

The scarlet speckles crowding Ksiñe's nose thinned to cirrus clouds. "She missed you. Stopped eating." The whipkin climbed down his arm and clambered over Caiden's collarbones. She dug under his coat and shirt to flatten warm and fleecy against his bare chest, squeaking and purring all the while.

Caiden swiveled his head. Ksiñe and Taitn. Laythan. En by the door, muscular and bristling with glaves. Panca behind her.

Icy shock sheeted through Caiden.

This was a new kind of dream. The nightmares had eaten away his childhood, now they gnawed on newer parts of his past. Çydanza's attack had rattled loose a new perseveration. "You need to leave."

Caiden slid to his feet off the cot.

Laythan slugged him in the cheek. He tumbled onto the floor, half-caught by Taitn. Ksiñe scowled and sprayed sealant over the fresh gash on Caiden's cheekbone.

"After all we did for you," Laythan fumed.

Real. Real, real, this is real. The pain was keen. Caiden's head teemed with sparks, vision fuzzed—this wasn't the feeling of a dream. He covered his mouth with a shaking hand and struggled to believe the sight.

Laythan continued, "Still too stupid to see that people care about you."

Care. He'd left them because they were better off that way, free and safe. "Impossible."

En peered over her shoulder. "You didn't think I'd have the resources to find a way here eventually? Such little faith you have in my disreputable ways! I worked at it day and night, kid."

They came because of Graven love, because his engineered nature was a hook he hadn't dug out of them first. He caved in at that thought while Taitn helped him up to his feet.

Caiden's speech clogged on its way to his tongue. "No. You only… because I'm Graven…"

"Oh." En swung her glave back and swept from her position at the door, straight for him. Laythan stuck an arm out to stop her but she slapped him away, carrying through to tackle Caiden in a strong embrace. Sprigs of pain burst in him. Her dark hair encompassed his head, citrus scent stung, warm voice filled him. "That's not why."

Caiden's thoughts stuck together. It had to be a fever dream. The whip-kin wriggled out and jumped back to Ksiñe as En squeezed. She cuddled into his wounded cheek and said, "I'm augmented enough to be a good amount resistant to Graven charm, while Andalvians are naturally averse and Ksiñe sour enough to hate anything, and look at Laythan—a bit of Graven grease might've softened up the old man's edges but you had to fight to gain his respect."

"Back to the door!" Laythan peeled En off Caiden and towered. Light glazed the hardest edges of his face and the sharpness of his eyes. "Respect but not approval. Is this really what you wanted? *Look at you.*"

Caiden gingerly probed his cheek. "I wanted to destroy her and—"

"No, that's what Threi wants."

"That's right." Threi sidled into the room and shoved a glave to En's skull while she walked back. He deflected the muzzle of her glave as she fired into the ceiling. Twinkles of liquid and metal rained from the blast. Threi pointed his other glave at the group. "You really shouldn't have come."

Caiden's heart sank.

Pinch and Jet flanked Threi with weapons. Towa followed. Silye cowered against the wall behind.

"Take them to the viewing platform," Threi ordered.

Caiden stepped forward. Threi turned a glave on him. Towa glanced over her shoulder as she herded the prisoners out.

Caiden and Threi stood in deadlock for several moments.

The warmth was sucked from the room. His family, swallowed, like the machine had swallowed everything. *Please let this be a nightmare. I didn't come here to be rescued.*

Threi lowered the glave and looked Caiden over. "Çydanza will expect you there too. You'll want the uniform. Anonymity. Trust me..." He looked around, but the little room—Silye's?—had nothing. Threi *tsked* and removed his own armor. "Use mine. Hurry. And you'll...You have to keep your head about you or she'll decide to end your second chance, and you won't get out of there alive. Winn, we still have one opportunity to kill her, but you need to trust me this time."

Trust. Caiden cinched Threi's armor on his body. *I still love them. Çydanza proved that when I failed to kill her. I can love them even if their reciprocation isn't genuine. Crimes, En, why did you have to say those words.*

They were *family* and he had thrown it all away to make himself suffer among the enemy. Was it less because he craved justice and more because he felt he was deserving of punishment?

Threi handed Caiden the blue mask. "Be ready."

CHAPTER 40

REWARDS

Threi pushed Caiden in front as they headed for Çydanza's viewing platform. "Whatever you feel, don't let her see it. Do better than before. No tears. You said she used love to break you last time? Well, this ordeal will prepare you for what she'll throw at you during the next memory flood."

"What's going to happen to them?"

Threi took Caiden's arm and paraded him up to the atrium. "Just keep it together, and we can end everything after. We don't have long before the ship is... Listen, your friends won't be killed, just imprisoned. Çy prefers to wring the value out of things. That buys us time. We need to... finish the task, then this will all change, and you can release them."

Caiden seethed but said nothing. He sweated in the borrowed Casthen armor, all his clothes damp. The morphcoat was a limp mesh attempting to wick away his heat. He cinched the blue mask tighter. At least they wouldn't recognize him, wouldn't know he was standing there, useless to help, wouldn't see his complicity in all this.

"Do you understand how close we are?" Threi asked.

"Yes."

Caiden's understanding didn't make it any easier to see the sight down the stairs.

Casthen soldiers prodded the crew into a jagged row in front of Çydanza's universe. Rose and cerulean candescence lashed their bravely postured silhouettes. En's hair was loose and wild, his dark skin glistening with Casthen blood, and some dents in the armored soldiers behind showed just how much he'd fought. Panca's sensory veils had been ripped off, the core in her forehead swimming with light. Ksiñe's skin strobed black as a storm and just as bloody as En's. His posture tensed with violence, arms curled around the whipkin hugging his torso. Laythan stood tall as a statue of bravery, his broad shoulders square, eyes as piercing as ever. He rested a hand on Taitn's wilting shoulder.

Caiden and Threi descended together. Their footsteps hammered on metallic silence. The sound strummed every nerve inside Caiden's Casthen shell.

The frame in the rind clarified like the great eye of a judge, its rainbow waves ripping back around the approaching vishkant's figure.

Caiden stopped with Threi at the sidelines, looking down the line of his family all serried for interrogation, limned bright by the rind. His composure withered. Anxiety eddied in his body, hot and itching beside the chill of shame.

Çydanza stood before the rind and cocked her head. "Ah, captors, here to save their child. Your attempts poked up one too many times in the surveillance data, little birds picking at Casthen routes. Too slippery to catch, and our defenses too robust to break, but I could certainly *let* you in. After all, your presence provides a fantastic opportunity to test my sweet probationer's loyalty and absolve his final weakness—I will reward you each for that."

The Casthen soldiers jammed three long glaves against the back of Laythan's neck and shoved him forward. He stood, spine rod-straight. His eyes looked crisp and fractured in the rind's light.

Çydanza stared through Laythan and *saw*. Like withering leaves, her lips slowly curled in a smile. "Do not fear, Laythan Paraïa, I can reward you with everything you want."

Caiden's armor creaked as he ground his fists. Threi nudged his shoulder with a warning look. *Get through this, kill her, save them.*

Çydanza laughed—a wispy sound that morphed into something mellifluous. Her blond locks lengthened and lightened to a lavender gray. Her jutting cheekbones rounded, face filled out, skin darkened to a tawny shade and filled with freckles like the spattering of a heavenly rain. Caiden's breath hitched the way it had when he'd seen the Dynast Prime Abriss. This wasn't a true Graven response but a powerful echo. Beside him, Threi stiffened and made a choked sound. Whites gleamed around his startled eyes. He had no mask to hide behind.

Çydanza's gaze flicked over to Threi for a beat before she turned back. "Laythan," she said lovingly, voice bright as a songbird and rich as honey. "How adorable, you were Dynast Prime Laureli's protector! And you loved her, did you really think she loved you back, that someone adored by billions could find a place in her heart for one?"

Laythan struggled to get out words. "I didn't need to be loved back. That's not how love works."

"Your faith in goodness failed you that day she was murdered, but tell me, was it because of the half of your love's skull that Hesh blew off or because you couldn't aid her without crashing the ship and killing everyone anyway?"

Laythan's breathing grew ragged, pupils saccading as memories reared in his mind. He backed up a step but the glaves shoveled farther into his neck.

Threi drifted forward like a sleepwalker, looking thunderstruck. Caiden twitched, mind slow to connect. Laureli was one of the previous Primes, Abriss's mother...why did Threi care? More Dynast history that had built his hate?

Çydanza-as-Laureli smiled, her gaze flicking to Threi before she continued, "Oh, but it was your fault, wasn't it, being *blind* to Hesh's plans was as good as fault even if you hadn't been framed, though the punishment wasn't death because Veren knew value, a shrewd man I can admire. 'The body has a use and we will put it to use. All things in Unity have value, and the darkness changes souls.' Did you enjoy your use in the labor prisons, Laythan, did the blind darkness change your soul? Prison was quite peaceful those years, you thought. Don't deny it—sometimes you do miss the simplicity, the isolation. I can ensure you're able to greet the dark again."

What does that mean? Caiden's fury stirred where it had slept.

Laythan choked sounds, unable to speak.

Çydanza-Laureli finally turned her head to acknowledge Threi. He broke his icy stare at Laythan and looked at Laureli.

The woman said, "Luckily, Laythan—or is it Dynast Safeguard Laythall

Sorsen?—I have the perfect person to reward you for your bravery and your prison break. Would you please, my sweet hound?"

Threi had grown deathly calm at the name. His breathing was deep and predatory, his focus wrenched entirely off plan. In a husky exhale, he responded, "Gladly."

Caiden stepped toward Threi's back, fighting the urge to grab the man's arm. Threi glanced over sharply—a warning—but there was something untamed in his features, something the smiles and snarls had hidden.

Threi didn't need armor to look dangerous; all in black, tall and athletic, he strode with the grace of someone unstoppable. He slapped the guards' glaves away and leaned toward Laythan, issuing a Graven command. "*Move.* Up the stairs, you'll follow me."

Laythan's head tilted down, feet moved, willpower shrank. The rind's light slicked off the two men as they headed up the stairs, drenched in shadow.

Çydanza's smile withered. The body of Laureli dissolved into vapor and a whisper of skeleton within. "You," she hissed.

Taitn was shoved forward from the line. Three glave muzzles stacked against his spine.

"War hero..." Çydanza's form rippled and folded upon itself, congealing into white, silver, pink, ghostly bones, and a beating heart. Lyli. "Years of valiant service, praise, adoration, all admirably earned."

Taitn crossed his arms calmly, but his muscles flexed, his fingers dug in, jaw set. His eyes fixated on the ground, but he still saw whatever memories Çydanza excavated from his mind. So close to a vishkant, mental dams broke; every fear and doubt surged up.

"How gruesome that old acceleration technology was." Her voice took on Lyli's gentle, clinical tone. "You were laid on the torture rack of time, stretched until all your social connections shattered, then abandoned to solve your brokenness alone, you lost and lost, mocked and deceived, naïve until the point you stopped trying. How much easier it is to not forge connection."

"But not worth it," Taitn whispered.

"What was that? So soft-spoken and shy, so surprising that you are this gentle nonetheless, and your desire is sweet; but do you really think regaining those lost years will rejoin your body to your mind and make you worthy of love at last? I can give you back those many years, war hero Taitn Maray Artensi." Çydanza's treacherous smile did not fit Lyli's gentle face. "Take him to the desenescence chambers."

No. Caiden struggled to keep still, bit his cheek. The six years of accel he'd done instantly had been bad enough—desenescence would be a rapid breaking down, trickles of soul sucked out in every session. Did it wipe memories too?

Soldiers grabbed Taitn's arms and shoved him up the steps into Jet's waiting hands. As the chketin forced him along, Taitn twisted and said softly, "Pan, be strong."

She was quivering. Her velvety hackles raised.

Panca. Caiden smothered the urge to spring into motion. His lungs were hot and furious, rhythm lost. Sweat or tears ran down his cheeks beneath the mask, filling his nose with the reek of wet metal.

Panca hugged her arms and looked up bravely, but her shivers knotted into convulsions as Çydanza's vapor congealed into a tall, male saisn shape.

Caiden knew what she would be seeing in her mind's eye: her own memory jog.

"Ah…" Çydanza's saisn voice hissed and cracked like a whip of flame. "Your memories visit you often, First Daughter Pan Carai. Look how strong they are, a hurt grooved over and over, deeper each time…"

Panca's chest fluttered. Her shoulders caved in, balling up tighter. The core in her forehead dulled.

"Don't worry, sweet thing," Çydanza said, acrid as bile. "You fear I'll send you back to Aken, but didn't I promise to reward each of you with what you wish the most? You know nothing but the inside of a box, and we have many boxes here." The saisn's face screwed into a cruel sneer. "Take her to the Servicer."

En reached for Panca's shoulder as she was marched past, but a boot kicked him to his knees.

Caiden choked back vomit. The N-Sector Servicer was vile even to someone as insensitive as he.

Çydanza billowed back to cloud. The soldiers pushed Ksiñe forward. His face was a storm, his red eyeshine blazing with the rind's light. The whipkin whined in his hugging arms. Two Casthen grabbed Ksiñe's shoulders and pulled the whipkin away by the neck, throttling her squeak.

Ksiñe unfolded in a blur. The flash of a scalpel blade jammed into the Casthen's artery.

They fell to the floor. Blood flicked as Ksiñe spun and crouched, swiping between the armor of the other Casthen's thigh. But they were chketin and broke Ksiñe's wrist in one grab. The blade tinkled to the ground. The chketin grunted and grabbed the whipkin in a meaty hand.

More Casthen poured forward, jamming glaves against Ksiñe and shoving him to the rind. His body was a storm of hateful patterns. Face stoic, his gaze flashed to the whipkin as the chketin smothered her shrieks in an enormous palm.

For a long moment Çydanza simply stared, formless. Ksiñe flinched sharply on all sides. Memories of torture.

"Ah, Kasiñae, you were ours, long ago." She whispered the Andalvian name with a tonal emphasis of layered meanings. "Executioner, surgeon, torturer, harvester. Take off his jacket."

A soldier stripped off Ksiñe's upper clothing, revealing a torso riddled with scars: ragged gashes, straight slices, puckered burns, bites of all manner of teeth. A self-conscious darkening of his Andalvian skin framed each one.

"So *many* scars," Çydanza said. "You must love these wounds, to want to keep them now that your violent professions are over and no longer put you in the path of sick minds. And you've replaced your sweet little fillion, we never did get to sell the parts we carved up of her, a pity—are whipkin just as valuable?"

The skin of Ksiñe's face and torso dripped the smoke gray of despair.

"Do you miss the game your old employers used to play? Perhaps you miss those twisted affections, with so *many* mementos? There are countless twisted individuals among my soldiers, but pain is best built up tenderly, which you understand best of all. Take him to Harrower Iyllen for some of the games he misses."

Ksiñe fought, instantly overpowered. The Casthen twisted him around, prodding him up the stairs and away.

Only En remained. He straightened, chin lifted, posture light and easy, but Caiden could read the coiled angles, the fight pent up in augmented muscles, one heel raised, balanced on the ball of his foot. On the other side of the rind, Çydanza's cloudy shape solidified into a mirror of En, a twin not quite identical. Softer, without the hair-thin augmentation seams on his skin.

"You are fairly renowned in your own right, Endirion Day." Even the voice was similar. "Where Taitn is beloved by the law, the military, the factions, you are beloved among the lawless, but what a price, to be beloved by so many. Buying momentary affection by paying with body parts... Rejections—physical, personal. The world and everything in it rejected you, no matter who you were or are."

En's fierce eyes misted as he relived it all in his mind. His jaw was set, cheeks hollowed. Pigment glitched on his neck.

"I can help you," En's original self said, singsong. "You're changing in all the wrong ways, and look at all these parts, they aren't *you*. I wonder what will be left if we strip them away; do you still have a heart, Endirion Day?"

En managed a tight smile. "I never imagined you were a vishkant. Explains a lot."

Çydanza's own smile didn't falter. "Take him to the labs for divesting."

Three soldiers with glaves marched En out of the room, into the maw of the Casthen Harvest and whatever *divesting* meant.

"Probationer." Çydanza's shape fell apart in a fall of smoke.

Caiden crept forward. The hollowness in him had filled with rage, a furnace ready to incinerate. The tears beneath his mask seared hot.

She re-formed in his mother's visage. "They really care about you, don't they, to come all this way, but I saw in your mind how they held you back and confused you. Look at you now, stronger than any of them." She smiled in the same way his mother had smiled when she was proud, when he'd fixed or climbed or triumphed over something larger than him. Reflexively, horrifically, his racing heart responded with pride.

"You did well wiping the human stock bound for the new operation, and getting the defects settled in the Servicer. Let's test again how far you've come: I have another harvesting task for you. Whipkin have unique and valuable fascia, once flayed off, and in three rare universes, an element of their lymph converts to an expensive substance. The other parts have minor value: aphrodisiacs and such if I search more into cultural profit. You will butcher and prepare the parts for transport. Report to me afterward, and if you've managed this task, I will judge if it's time to move you from probation to full rank."

It took all of Caiden's focus to reply without wavering. "Thank you, Prime."

He turned to leave.

"But not yet."

Caiden swiveled back, wary.

"Your family needs time to receive their gifts. And since we did forge you to be a Casthen hero, and valor is in your makeup, you may not be able to resist rushing to their aid. After your task, I shall need them thoroughly broken to ascertain if you, too, shall break or if you're proven to be loyal and resilient after all."

Caiden cocked his head. "Time to..."

Çydanza looked up to the stairs behind Caiden. "Towa, take the probationer to a lesson in patience."

Caiden had hardly turned when Towa and three other Casthen surged down at him, locking his limbs, spinning him around and shoving him up the stairs. The tal hissed into his ear, "The Prime should not be giving you another chance; I do not care whether you come from that thing in the subterra or not."

Thing?

He twisted but the group held him tight as they ushered him to a nearby hangar and the solitary quarantine cell used for infectious animals. They threw Caiden onto a sieve-like floor.

Towa said, "Threi is not here to protect you. I will see that your family gets their due, and you will stay here, learning *patience*."

The cell door slammed shut.

CHAPTER 41

VALIANCE

Caiden's imagination was far worse than nightmares. Days passed and he couldn't sleep. His family was enduring torture.

Periodically, the Casthen opened the door, and only ever brought pain, not food or refreshment of the bucket they'd left him in a corner. They clogged the narrow doorway with bodies one hundred thick, blocking escape. He fought back with all the *valor* bred into him, venting the rage and worry that crammed up inside him every moment he was stuck helpless in a cell.

Groggy, bruised, Caiden lay on his back as the isolation stretched on. He tried to empty his mind, struggled to recall nothingness.

An electric hum spidered through the wall.

One door lock disengaged. Two.

He groaned. His cuts had barely scabbed from the last beating. Even his rapid-healing genetics were no match for this frequency of attack. Perhaps that was a point that Towa wished to make.

The airlock wheezed.

Caiden rolled to all fours.

The door crashed open. Silye rushed in, gesturing frantically. Wires and holosplays littered the floor behind her where she'd hacked the cell security. Her whole body shook, face pinched, fingers butchering the words she tried to make. *Threi said wait, but—* She cut off, hands trembling.

"But what?" he choked, scrambling to a sitting position. "What's happened?"

She signed, *I'm sorry. I'm sorry. I'm sorry.* Then she just stared and shook her head.

Caiden realized—recalled Silye's genetics—she couldn't cry. The distress escaped her body through her quivering fingertips, which he captured gently. He drew in a breath and held it, squeezed Silye's hands between his, and tried to gather his mind.

She exhaled, then gestured, *I know—I know—you need to go now, or no one is safe.*

Claircognizance. Chills sheeted through him. "Silye. Who isn't safe?" He took a deep breath and summoned every Graven cell in his body to align. "How long has it been? Where's Threi? Where is the whipkin held?"

Silye riveted to attention. She spoke with a mix of signs and gestures, blurring languages to be swifter; *Threi, not sure. Animal is in main lab. I released you early. Four days have passed. You . . .* Her hands hovered, shaking.

"Four." Caiden surged up, flexed his Graven will, and said to Silye, "Come with me."

He flew into a scour on the other side of the hangar, instantly healing minor injuries and relieving the pain load a bit. When he emerged, Silye had found his morphcoat. He whisked it on and rampaged toward the main lab like a storm front, as fast as his beaten body could go.

Out in the larger hallway, Towa headed a score of Casthen soldiers marching with purpose.

"*Stand down,*" Caiden snarled. Half of the group parted, but Towa attacked instantly and ignited the others' courage. The tal's leg slammed Caiden's left shoulder as he blocked. He spun and broke her knee. She shrieked. Ten others poured onto Caiden, and he eagerly expelled more of his valorous rage. He whirled one around to take a knife meant for his gut, threw them into the others, a kick to a groin, elbow to the skull, broken limbs and blood all over and he was done with a few heartbeats to spare.

Most of the other soldiers retreated. Towa sprang off her good leg and tackled him. He wrapped her in a choke hold, using his legs for torque. Her ruffled body wriggled in his grasp, black teeth bared and snapping until she finally passed out and slumped in his arms.

The glass chicory she'd taken before—her victory prize for killing his nophek—glistened in a mesh pocket at her hip. Caiden fished it out and shoved it in his coat, then detangled himself, breathless.

Free the whipkin. Get everyone safe. Find Threi.

He stole armor, then followed Silye and burst into the lab. "*Everyone out.*" His husky, savage tone cleared the room of even those who weren't as susceptible to his paltry Graven effect. The blood on him probably helped.

Ksiñe's whipkin lay sedated on a table, where Caiden was supposed to butcher her in a repeat of Ksiñe's worst trauma. A lump lodged in his throat and a whimper caught there as he rushed to the little animal and scooped her up. He tore off enough armor pieces to cuddle her under his coat against the crook of one shoulder. She mewed and he petted her head and cooed soft Andalvian syllables. "You're safe, little girl. I'm so glad I came in time."

He cradled her and rocked back and forth for a while before his relief sharpened into urgency. He commanded Silye, "Find a route to where my family's being held."

She flicked through a holosplay map and showed him. The prison cells weren't far.

Caiden sprinted, taking shortcuts and indirect routes. He charged down a narrow alley between warehouses and swept around the corner, slamming straight into Threi.

As they both staggered back, Caiden got his bearings faster. "Bastard," he roared and locked Threi in a hold against the wall. The scent of blood and lilies stuffed his nostrils as he leaned close to the man's ear. "What did you do to Laythan?"

"Talked, first." Threi didn't struggle. "I had something to settle with your captain. For the others, I used my own people or gave orders—I did what I could to soften Çydanza's abuse."

"*Soften?*" Caiden curled Threi's locked arm, ready to snap it.

"If *you* defy her," Threi snarled back, "you're just an unruly pup. But if she realizes *I* am against her, the entire Harvest will be locked down faster than you can blink." Threi glanced at the bulge of the whipkin in Caiden's coat. "That thing. Crimes, you couldn't do it, could you. Stealth was our only advantage but you've blown it now!"

"We still have haste."

"That's *all* we have." He growled through his teeth. "What was Silye doing? Now you're loose too soon, couldn't complete your task, and Çydanza won't give you another chance."

Caiden shoved him away. "I'm doing it with or without you. Even if the ship capture beams can't be disabled, I can endure the memory flood."

"Çydanza is on edge and knows *exactly* what to expect. One slip-up now and both you and your family are dead."

Threi fussed his clothes back into place and snatched Silye's holosplay map. "I'm not sure how long I can buy us time. We'll need to disable those defenses around her universe and cover escape routes. Create a distraction to preoccupy her most loyal adherents. Silye, dismantle surveillance facility-wide, make it an accident and a distraction at the same time."

Silye dropped to a sitting position and brought up another holosplay, its light filling the alley with flickers as she plowed through code.

Caiden stared straight into Threi's eyes, waiting for the man to meet his gaze. "You're ready? We'll do this?"

No more planning. No more convenient delays to punish him into obedience. No more "soon."

Threi's pupils constricted as he met Caiden's glare with ice. "You caused this, and you're going to see it through if I have to throw you at her myself."

Caiden's nostrils twitched. "Where is the *Azura*?"

"In a machinist facility on the other side of the Harvest, dismantled completely." He showed Caiden on the map.

"How much is *completely*?"

Threi grimaced in response.

"Did the machinists dismantle it segmentally so the organics can be recondensed?"

"Not sure, I'm not the mechanic."

"Nine crimes, Threi, this could take *days* that we don't have!"

The man's jaw tightened. "Don't suppose you have a manual on how to put it back together faster?"

Caiden swore under his breath. "No, but I know someone better than a manual. We'll have to pray it's enough when I see what the machinists have done. Cover my tracks and buy as much time as you can." Caiden surged down the hall.

* * *

He crashed through the ten detainment guards like a lightning bolt. His augmented fist barreled masks to pieces, ripped armor off, crushed bones. All the violence he'd received in the quarantine cell poured out. He knocked the last one cold then stole glaves and bladed weapons before rising shakily among the bodies.

A sick anticipation petrified in his breast. No nightmares could strengthen him enough to be ready to see the torture Çydanza had designed for his family.

He strode downstairs into the darkness of the prison ward. Strip lighting bled along metallic black walls. The cells were dark sections of a large central circle, with a corridor wrapping around. No cage bars on these—the front was a field of blue force. He found the security console and dug around in the code, wishing Silye had come with him. While he worked at bypassing the fields, every tiny noise reverberated against the hard prison walls. Small moans. Drips. Loud, raspy breathing. A rhythmic scrape.

Fury clawed around in Caiden's bloodstream beside the spice of the performance enhancers. He mashed the EXECUTE command and brought all the security down, then launched into the hallway.

First cell empty. Next.

Laythan slumped against the far wall. His bruised eyelids swelled half-shut over deep eyeless voids. Blood crusted down his cheeks.

Caiden was hammered with guilt.

"Laythan." He dithered between rushing and moving cautiously. Laythan's brow furrowed, not recognizing the Casthen voice both amplified and muffled. Caiden ripped off his mask and took hold of Laythan's shoulders. The man flinched then grasped Caiden tightly, pulling him into a hug.

"Tell me you're not one of those bastards now." Laythan's voice cracked. "Bloody fool. We didn't save you just for you to crawl back here."

"And I didn't leave just for you to rush into danger. I'm going to send the Prime to oblivion, but I need you all safe first."

Caiden squeezed before he pulled away and guided Laythan from the cell. The man weakly fended off Caiden's arms. "Boy, I spent a decade blind, you think I need your help?" He groaned as Caiden eased him against a wall. "The others—"

"Stay here." Caiden dashed to the next cell.

En draped against a corner. Machine parts and morphic materials lay exposed, a mangle of synthetic muscle, bone, and organ. His exposed heart beat, purple and glossy. His face was a mask of black bone and knotted white muscle bands, dribbling blood.

"En." Caiden choked on a sob.

En looked up, gray eyes wet and weary, but he smiled. "Look at you. You seem older, somehow." His voice vibrated in triplet, forced through soggy materials.

Caiden swallowed ache and forced a smile. "I'm going to murder her, En."

"I know ya will." En's voice crackled. "But *we* needed you too. In case you couldn't tell that, when you left. And don't give me that bullshit about you being Graven. You charmed me all on your own." En tried a wink, but the eyelid only half closed. "Your freckles are cute though, I admit."

Caiden sobbed a laugh. He helped En to a sitting position, but En's legs were splintered into segments. Tendrils of plasma twitched. "I can't carry you like this. Here—" He yanked up his left sleeve, flexed his machine muscles, probed an invisible seam, and fished between blue bands to rip out a nanogenerator. Pain flailed up his arm but he gritted his teeth and pulled out two more. His arm spasmed the last of its stored energy and fell limp at his side. He deposited the nanogenerators in En's skeletal palm. "Use these."

En's smile was a shiver of white tendon. "Help the others," he croaked. With the nanogenerator replaced, his strung-together bones tightened and plumped with a lather of protective material.

Caiden hurried into the circular corridor, steeling himself. *These* were the visions Çydanza had used to wreck him—and would use again.

In the next cell, Taitn lay in the middle, convulsing gently with each exhale. He was younger by years, with the sallow, gaunt look of desenescence performed without correction. His eyes fluttered open, lashes wet, dark-blue gaze unfocused. "What did those bastards do to you?"

The sobs Caiden had bundled in his chest burst out. He gathered Taitn up in an embrace weakly returned. Taitn's body was sunken around pronounced musculature. Purple rimmed anemic eyes. His dark hair waved to his shoulders and his beard was a mess of patchy lengths.

Taitn sighed and stood up with Caiden's help. "Panca." His shoulders crumpled and a teardrop hit the floor. "She was never brought back here."

"What? Oh, crimes…" She was still in the Servicer. "I have to hurry. Can you walk? En needs help."

Taitn nodded. Caiden strode on, past Panca's empty cell. He kept his feet moving and his anger condensing. He would need anger. He would fix this.

Behind, he heard Taitn shuffle to En's cell, followed by a string of curses.

Ksiñe sat in the next cell, unclothed, staring into void. In his pale, emotionless skin, every one of his old scars had been reopened. Shreds of muscle twitched. Tendons glistened around bone. Pigmentation sputtered bruises.

Caiden scraped the tears off his chin.

Çydanza would die for this.

Caiden, crumpling down beside Ksiñe, shed his armor and whisked the morphcoat off and around Ksiñe's bare shoulders. It pillowed into feather down.

"Ksiñe, hey." No response. Caiden scooped the whipkin out of his shirt, curling her warm body in the Andalvian's lap. He lifted Ksiñe's limp wrists and laid his hands on the whipkin's fur, rising and falling with her breaths. "Painkiller. Remember? Please."

Ksiñe blinked, reflective pupils dilating as he focused at last. His face blanched even more. "Little one…" He had the soft, scratchy voice of someone who had screamed their throat raw.

"She's safe. She's yours. I wouldn't let anything happen."

The whipkin mewed and uncurled, sniffing Ksiñe's wounds. He stroked her in a daze. She chittered and wiggled as she climbed carefully up his torso and curled her long body around his neck. Ksiñe pressed his cheek to her fur.

Caiden wrapped one of Ksiñe's arms around his neck and attempted to hoist him up one-armed. The Andalvian was light, even as dead weight. "Please help me move you…Panca is missing."

Ksiñe winced at that, and put weight on his feet, trembling but shuffling enough for Caiden to help him along.

They circled to the entrance just as Taitn rounded the opposite curve, awkwardly carrying En. He cradled her tenderly, frowning at her face, and lowered her onto Laythan's lap.

Laythan's blind hands explored En's wreckage. "We're all in the same shape, then? Winn, too, in his own way."

En chuckled, a half choke. "I've been hurt this bad many times, just... not everywhere at once. I think you got off pretty easy, old man."

Caiden lowered Ksiñe beside them. "The *Azura*'s in bad shape, too, and I need Panca's help. I'll come back for you all."

Pounding feet. Caiden swiveled to the prison entrance and whipped up a glave. It was Silye, racing up the steps with a glave of her own, one as tall as she. *Infirmary*, she signed. *I will take them. Surveillance cut for six ephemeris hours. Distraction next.*

"Thanks, Sil."

She nodded.

Caiden broke into a run, summoning up fire.

CHAPTER 42

ARMORLESS

Panca!" Caiden raced through N-Sector's warren of halls. His voice bounced off the walls of containers and the ceiling sixty meters overhead. The darkness and din ate up his calls. Every whimper he thought he heard in response was drowned by the whining hums or the heartbeat of his dread.

He stopped, mouth dry. She would never hear his voice, but in her sensesea she might pick up his intention, the desperation of his search.

"Panca!" He froze and listened through the echoes. Nothing.

He hurried, cursing the loudness of his footfalls ricocheting through the space. Dissonant hums crashed in the air like ocean surf, throwing out a crackling electricity that made Caiden's hairs stand on end.

Everywhere looked the same. He ran aimlessly, flinching at every errant sound, feeling like that little boy lost in the desert of death where everything was sand, sand, sand.

Every footfall brought him closer to finding Panca dead—or never at all.

Sense-sea. He stopped and fell to his knees, sat back on his heels, eyes closed. He emptied his mind to nothingness as she'd taught him, and gathered up his intention as if to make a Graven order, drumming up not a verbal call but an energy, a spiritual plea that might reach Panca through whatever dimensions lay beyond the Servicer's chaos.

Panca, sister, please . . . where are you?

A tiny wail weaved through the din. Left.

Caiden lurched to his feet, razing the darkness for a sign.

The thinnest of sobbing screams wavered past him like a golden thread in the roar of the machines. He sprinted down the entire aisle, twisted, down another. There was a container jutting from the stacks.

He hooked his right arm through a handle and pulled, leaning sideways with all his weight since his strong aug arm was deactivated. The container inched out, moaning against the shelf rails. With a *slam* it fell the last few inches to the floor.

Caiden shouldered the lid open. This container had no photonic liquid or nano-organisms like the one he'd incubated in. It had been gutted, and a short crimson coffin shoved inside. Threads rolled off it like waterfalls and linked into the Servicer through the floor. Caiden clawed around the seams and opened up its folding segments. Panca lay curled inside.

His vision blurred with tears. Panca's body was spotted in gleaming electromagnetic nodes beneath her skin. Hair-thin photonic threads dug into her body like silver vines. She shivered, eyes half-lidded, sobs leaking from her. The core in her forehead was a dull matte gray.

He muttered Panca's name like a mantra as he gingerly lifted her out. She winced at each spidery node he scratched off and the threads he had to pull out one by one. Sickeningly long, they slid under her skin, out of organs, from places deep in her body. Too entwined to have been inserted there, they must have grown, and were so numerous she might have been more wire than flesh.

Caiden wept tears and apologies and curses. With Panca finally severed from the machine, he cradled her as best he could with one arm. The grief was too heavy for his worn legs. Her body was suffused by vibrations and convulsions, crashing like waves in too tight a bay.

Have to hurry. Azura next. Once Panca calmed, breathing smooth and without whimpers, Caiden maneuvered her over his working shoulder.

He relied on hearing and extended proprioception to navigate the darkness and the bellowing of the Servicer and the deceptive rhythms of breath and feet and ache that told him to lie and let it all go, fall apart, be done. But he made it out of N-Sector into the outer hall's insulting brightness.

Caiden groped until his hand reached a solid surface, followed it, blinking, to a dimmer atrium.

He slipped his Casthen mask back on and piped an overlay map of the facility into the glassy laminate of the interior. The hangar Threi had said the *Azura* was kept in lay halfway across the world. There wasn't time, and every moment in the halls—even as emptied as they were—was another chance of conflict that could slow him.

Think smarter. He looked around; the overlay labeled the rooms and universes of the local megastructure.

"There." The Enforcer's hangar. It wasn't far, and the map indicated Threi's Glasliq perched on a platform. A ship would get him to the machinist facility fast, and there would be a medical kit inside for Panca.

One arm. Threi had flown the *Azura* one-handed... How hard could it be?

Nausea sloshed up, down, and sideways. Caiden clamped his throat closed. His right hand fixed a claw shape in the Glasliq's light guides, the only way he could maintain control of the thing with one hand. It was like flying a gyroscopic bird. Directionality mattered little and gravity interacted strangely. Sweat drenched his hair and all his clothes.

But the machinist facility lay just below. Caiden stalled his speed, the Glasliq's wings re-formed, and he lowered through an open ceiling. The gigantic arena was cluttered with parts, machines, and lifters, but nothing that looked remotely like the *Azura*.

Caiden shoved that worry away and set the ship down, shed the rest of his armor, and dug out a medical kit to do his best for Panca. The ship was military outfitted, with a plethora of temporary-fix meds: wound sealants, antibiotics, chems, mild stimulants.

He scooped up Panca's slender saisn frame and strode out of the Glasliq's bay. Mechanics gathered, expecting Threi. They startled when Caiden emerged. Swiftly, he summoned Graven charm and called, "I need you all to help me. Where's the *Azura*?"

The little group parted. Behind them, on a dais in the middle of the arena, a crystalline mass rested. Translucent, white, and fire-blue, with glossy lightseep inclusions, the spine of Caiden's ship lay nakedly dissected from everything else he knew of her. There was no other "ship" to speak of.

He clutched Panca and stood staring.

This place, this Casthen void. It shatters everything good.

The *Azura* had been opened up like a gruesome flower. Pieces of her shucked carapace hung in mag-suspension all around, glossy black with pale connective tissues. Inner parts were dismantled and levitated out in layers, resembling an anatomical drawing, a ripped-open insect. The engine block was mostly intact, hovering above the crystal spine; silvery cords connected the two, nerves and veins peeled out. The armor plates and wings and internal walls were dismantled but intact. The hybrid organic components—the parts that were easier to *grow* than to print and install— were melted, shredded, or dangling. These were also the hardest to restore, because growth took time that Caiden didn't have.

He carried Panca to the crystal-and-lightseep mass and laid her across it. "Please wake. I need you to help me. No one understands glossy engines like you. You'll know what to do. Please, Pan."

He lay with her, resting his head. There was a gentle vibration of energy in the crystalline mass. Tones braided along inner channels, weaving through dimensions. He'd *missed* this song. Only a whisper of the disintegrated neural link remained, but he swore the surface warmed against his cheek.

Panca sighed, finally rousing. Her eyes slitted open, bright limbal rings flicking in the black. She cuddled against the crystal and the crook of Caiden's shoulder. Relieved and absolved, he wrapped his good arm tighter around her.

"Winn..." Her velvety face creased. "She's...in so much pain."

Caiden's heart cracked. "Help me fix her? I don't know what to do."

Panca straightened, unable to walk, and looked all around the arena. Wilted by the sight, she shook her head. "Half of the *Azura*'s components're biological, she's not a puzzle we can slot back together. The shell's complicated. The resonance shields need to biomineralize. Seams take time to seal."

Caiden's brain fired at dizzying speed. "Threi can't hold down suspicion for long. Can we get the florescer working fast?"

Panca gave him a sad look and wrapped her arms around him for a brief, tight hug, and said, "See what the machinists learned, what materials they've got to work with."

Caiden lurched up and marched for the display array while shouting, "All of you, come!"

Some of the mechanics scurried over because they were susceptible enough to his loyalty-inducing effect, while others appeared confused, or recognized him as Threi's probationer but hadn't caught wind of the other drama. Whyever they helped, he was grateful not to have to crack more skulls.

He fanned through the research. The Casthen machinist team had done quite a lot of study on the *Azura* already: all the tests that Taitn and Panca had talked about doing. Caiden scrolled through and listened to explanations, both fascinated and sick to his stomach.

The ship's own stored data was intact.

A blip caught Caiden's eye. Unread messages. The crew had sent him communication after he'd abandoned them in Emporia, and he hadn't been strong enough to read them at the time.

Hey, kid. En's voice. *We know where you went. I just hope you decided it yourself. The others are mad, but I trust your heart. And I hope we taught you something you can use. Don't sink, please.*

Caiden covered his mouth with a hand, eyes misting.

Taitn's voice next, a choked-up rasp of a sound that cut off: *Winn . . . you don't get to choose to throw yourself away.*

If he had listened to this earlier, he might have changed his mind and turned around.

No—it would have softened him up and he'd have been crushed in the Casthen machine.

Ksiñe: *I said before—over-sharpened blade becomes brittle, easy to break. Move fast, don't waver.*

The nightmares had sharpened him to a breaking point, but it wasn't too late for the last part of Ksiñe's advice. Caiden turned back to the repairs.

Basics first; they arranged the ship in a general order, the hardware and plates in place. Caiden commandeered the big lifter mechs one-handed. Panca directed while she lay, drifting in and out of consciousness.

Dead organics were cleaned off metal and crystal, but the skeletal frame of the ship seemed even less likely to fly anytime soon.

"Panca . . ." Caiden wiped sweat from his neck. "This will take days. It's too complex."

Çydanza had ensured that the ship—the only weapon that could smite her—was impossible to repair. Caiden's family was safe and they could leave the Harvest together, but Çydanza would remain alive to keep exploiting the multiverse and sell the core of the *Azura* to the Dynast.

The white rings of Panca's irises danced over him and their work, then fixed in a stare over his shoulder. "Winn."

He cocked his head at her for a long moment, then followed her eye line behind him.

The Glasliq.

He swiveled back to her, excitement humming. "Use it for parts...how?"

She craned her neck up to the half-assembled skeleton of the *Azura*. "Magnetizing a liqui-solid'd be a quick exoshell on a minimalist frame—easier than assembling all her fuselage and plates."

"Tell me what to do," Caiden said. *Sorry, Threi. You owe me anyway.*

He flew the Glasliq up closer, then barked orders to the machinists to help with lifter-mechs, mag-levitators, and custom scalar gravity fields to position the *Azura*'s remains midair and borrow some of the Glasliq's articulated vanes and ribs. Caiden was reinvigorated by work familiar to his hands and mind, and he threw all of himself into it as he started to see a ship coming together around the *Azura*'s Graven spine.

This would actually *work*.

The machinist control desk was basically a cockpit, where Caiden both mapped out and actively piloted the arena's complex resonator system. It phase-changed the Glasliq's morphic crystalline matter into liquid so he could maneuver that wroth mass of sparkling fluid around the *Azura*'s new black skeleton. She looked like a twiggy insect caught in blue amber or a water drop. While Caiden shaped the levitating Glasliq matter, it filled with tetchy vibrations, spitting out spikes and angular ruffles like an angry sun. Careful phase changes bonded the material solidly to the *Azura*'s frame so it wouldn't dribble away once released, and could change phases later while remaining adhered to the frame.

Caiden held his breath as he deactivated all the fields holding the ship in place.

It stayed solid and gorgeous.

He released a shaky breath, heart full as he assessed their work. Metal ribbing and flexible bones scaffolded the liquid glass. The transparent body—in solid state now—encapsulated the ship's luminous crystalline spine, which spread an opal glow. The ship was more muscular and compact, the big thrusters clustered with mobile ones stolen from the Glasliq. The inner frame was folded up, looking like gills and ribs, capable of unfolding into any manner of wings for atmospheric flight.

Caiden carried weary Panca to a soft seat then entered the ship alone. The layout was much the same as before, and he draped himself in the salvaged pilot's seat.

"Last test. This is the part that matters." Caiden reached up to graze the florescer with his fingertips. Energy built up in the spine, stuttering around all the wounds they hadn't yet patched—but it finally bloomed out, the universe bubbling around the entirety of the ship. The rind's creamy, rippling iridescence absorbed into the Glasliq translucence, making the ship even more like a star condensed. From dark insect to brilliant bird.

Caiden sighed away all his heartbreak. "Let's go kill Çydanza."

CHAPTER 43

IF YOU LOVE ME

The glass *Azura* looked magnificent, but it was obvious from her drunken, listless handling that they hadn't tuned it and Caiden wasn't used to her new bones and muscles. At the same time, the ship's movements were sensitive, delicate, sharp as a bird of prey.

Panca curled up in the engine room, asleep and healing. Caiden was out of time to do any handling tweaks. He gritted his teeth and did the best he could one-armed, pushing through cramps to keep elegance in his motions—this new machine didn't respond well to inelegance.

He headed back across the planet to where Threi was managing the rest of the plan—he hoped. And where his crew was safe in an infirmary, he hoped, where Silye had guided them to wait until Caiden put an end to all this.

The Casthen megastructure swept past below, light-studded, colors shifting through the pleochroic surfaces. Ahead, the structure shell around Çydanza's universe blistered out from the facility. Half of it was still wrecked open from when Caiden had crashed the rind through before.

Finally, the temporary communications module found a connection to Threi.

"I'm inbound," Caiden said, "and the *Azura*'s rind works. I can see Çydanza's universe from here."

Threi's tight voice blared through the speakers. "She's not there."

"What?" Caiden twisted his wrist in the drive guides to stall the ship.

"We disabled the defenses and coerced the guards away, but Çydanza isn't inside. She sensed something or we slipped up—she's not in there. She could be anywhere and *anyone*."

Caiden swore on the void and the worlds and every ounce of trust he'd put in Threi.

"Silye caught footage," Threi said. "Çydanza escaped twenty arcminutes ago, no vehicular activity since then, and she can only run so far. I locked down a perimeter of the facility: she's inside it, disguised. Winn, come to the audience plateau, the big twilit plate by the northern pole. I'm going to try something."

"Nine crimes, Threi, will you tell me the plan straight *for once*?"

"I'm making it up as I go."

The comm cut out.

Caiden ground his molars together. He veered the ship north and curled his fingers into a fist, powering forward. The *Azura* cut the winds sideways and sang with speed. The perimeter of megastructure that Threi had locked down was visible from the sky: every light was on and blazing. Within the perimeter, the audience plateau glistened gold on the horizon, slicked by rays from the light side of the planet.

A broadcast piped in, sent to everyone and every speaker within the perimeter.

"Beloved people of Casthen…" Threi's voice was different: silver-smooth and brilliant, thickened by need and sonorous with Graven intent. Caiden's heart palpitated. The ship pitched as his focus drifted, and he yanked the guides up to keep steady.

"*What*," Caiden murmured, slowing the ship.

Threi's voice had never had this effect on him before.

The man continued, "Come to me, at the audience plateau. Come swift, my Casthen, I wish everyone to gather."

Caiden fought chills, his will melting, knees weak with the desire to please. How could Threi suddenly be so much more Graven than before, even over broadcast where the effect dimmed?

The result of Threi's wish was immediate: below, tiny forms streamed on foot and in vehicles from the facility and small universes, toward the plateau, forming rivers of movement.

Caiden's pulse clogged in his throat. *Like my people streaming to the Flat Docks.*

The *Azura* stalled as Caiden jolted still. One command, *over broadcast,* and everyone mobilized? He would have thought it a trick if the yearning weren't palpable in his heart too.

"Winn." A whisper through Caiden's comms only, Threi's voice was still heady with Graven appeal. Sickening euphoria swelled in Caiden for a moment.

"What have you done?"

Caiden meant this impossible Graven effect, but Threi answered, "Vishkant are less susceptible to coercion than humans, but even if Çydanza is not compelled to come, she'll want to blend in. Silye is safe outside the perimeter and has set the surveillance intelligence to flag anyone not obeying, or running the opposite way."

Caiden jetted ahead of the masses of people converging on the plateau. Threi stood alone on the burnished plate, dressed in a dark flight suit with copper straps and belts. The twilight glittered off broken vials littering the ground.

Caiden fishtailed the *Azura* around and set her down, then reached up to activate the florescer. The *Azura*'s universe swelled out, encompassing the ship. The rind may as well have been a drawn blade: all they needed to do was throw Çydanza into it, and rogue physics would annihilate her physiology.

He opened the bay doors—now unfolding more like a liquid iris, less flower—and stepped out.

"Th-Threi." He approached the man's back. Bronze sunlight haloed Threi's figure. Graven allure pulled Caiden in while an austerity kept him at bay. Something had definitely changed, and he was wary of what proximity would do.

Threi fidgeted with two vials of pearly liquid in his gloved fist, clacking them together. *Snick, snick.* Echoing across the plateau. He was counting. Abruptly, he thumbed the cap off one and drank it before throwing the vial to smash on the ground among the others. His cringe turned to shivering and a whole-spine flex of his body before he squared his shoulders and called out, "Stand before me, in rows, so I can see you all." The arriving crowd vibrated at his every word, rapt and energized. Several hundred settled into an orderly grid across the plateau deck, all of them in either Casthen armor or lab uniforms.

Caiden gaped at the sight, and felt his knees bend to carry him to the rows, too, before he course-corrected.

Over his shoulder, Threi said, "She's here somewhere. We need only draw her out." He glanced farther over and scoffed. "I see you did what you pleased with my Glasliq. You're lucky now's not the time for punishment."

Caiden stopped next to him and looked over. Proximity, scent, and sight slammed him with Graven force. Unbidden willpower brimmed in his body, aching to be of service, drawing him a step closer even as he realized the reaction. Fighting it curdled the warm sensations into nausea. Inexplicable shame infested him at the thought that he'd taken Threi's Glasliq or done anything to displease.

All damned, what has he done?

The thick dust of bleached freckles sparkled now in Threi's pallid skin. His features hadn't changed, but were alluring in a new way, the flaws more perfect than before. His expression was meditative, pupils tiny points of void in his pale eyes, which filled up with light.

Caiden glanced down at the broken glass and the last vial still in the man's grip. "You...enhanced your Graven resonance or body or...? How?"

"I'll get to test two things, this day."

Internally, Caiden recoiled at how he hinged on Threi's every word, wishing for a request, for a way to please. Enraptured by him; armorless and dressed in black, freckled and Graven, with that regal posture again, Threi looked more Dynast than Casthen.

Caiden quavered, "Test? Crimes' sake, Threi, we're here to kill Çydanza. What are you *testing*? What's in those?"

He had pegged Threi as obsessed and delusional, consumed by scheming an impossibility. But this composed and calculated specimen of Graven arrogance was nowhere near delusional.

Threi turned to the adoring crowd, which stood tense with energy, awaiting his command. Face somber and hateful, he didn't seem pleased by the loyalty of so many. He said to Caiden, "*True* love is built up through time and connection. We will never know what that's like. We get the fake version. Welcome to a life of lies, Winn. *This* is what it means to be Graven."

He strode forward before Caiden could respond, and Caiden was pulled along in the man's gravitas. They walked through the lines of Casthen. Heads swiveled to track Threi as he passed, everyone's movements eerily in sync. Their Casthen masks had been removed, but adoration masked each of them now, all the same.

Caiden scanned for abnormalities that might give the vishkant away: a dissident reaction, a glitching face, or a form not quite solidified. "Can't you just command her to come to you? Why didn't you try all this before?"

"I *have* tried this before. Even with my enhancement, Çydanza was almost completely immune to my Graven influence while inside her universe. The effect doesn't quite pass through, and is dimmed by broadcast as well."

The lines of Casthen they walked past grew monotonous, heads all swiveling, their awe identical.

Caiden asked, "Why didn't you use this on me, in Emporia?"

"I didn't lie about enjoying the challenge."

"I can tell when you're avoiding an answer."

Threi turned full attention to him, and Caiden unwittingly leaned in, heart skipping. Sick. Threi growled, "The enhancer is a work in progress."

"What about Çydanza *outside* her universe?"

"I'm not sure how resistant she'll be. If I call her to me now and she *is* resistant enough to not obey, she'll stand still to make me think she's not among this group. If I was touching her, I could control her completely, but touch means she uses her memory flood attack, and I—most likely— would kill myself in..." Threi trailed off, perfect features creasing as an idea dawned on him. "There is one guaranteed way to single her out from a distance."

Appetite sharpened Threi's silver voice raw.

He consumed the final vial and dropped it, shattering it.

Shivers scratched down Caiden's spine, but as he opened his mouth to question, Threi straightened, wielding a wealth of natural charisma, shoulders broad and head haloed in twilight, eyes brightening, he called to the gathered:

"Casthen... *if you love me*... then die. Die as fast as you can."

The crowd erupted in motion.

Soldiers unsheathed blades and fell on them. Others drew glaves and shot vitals. Arteries spewed. Bone sparkled in the air. The weaponless smashed their skulls on the ground. Some suffocated their brain of oxygen with their own hands.

Caiden's entire body tensed with shock, and a horrific need tore through him, his hand started to draw the knife on his thigh.

Threi caught Caiden's wrist. "Not you."

Within ten seconds, the thunder of screams and glave fire stilled to nothing, and the crowd of hundreds lay dead and twitching on the ground.

Except one.

An armored soldier stood, spear glave sticking through their neck. Blood trickled from the stab wound and fizzed on the deck. Armor plates melted. Body lightened to an effervescent vapor.

A stab wouldn't kill a vishkant.

Caiden fixated on the lone figure, his peripheral vision filled with quiet massacre. Blood perfumed the air. Heat wafted off the steaming bodies. He gagged. His weak knees gave out and he crumpled to the ground. Threi still held his wrist up.

He would have done it. Would have used the knife, lovingly.

The vishkant's particles re-congealed into her blond female body. She staggered in place, bewildered and convulsing.

"Grab her—*now*!" Threi's bellow was like a Graven whip. Caiden staggered up and exploded into a run. "I'll get the ship!" Threi rushed in the other direction to the *Azura*.

Çydanza whirled around, gained her bearings, and launched into a sprint away. Her body reshaped: lean and athletic and picking up speed.

Caiden reeled in horror as he leapt over corpses, falling twice and vomiting even as he forced himself up and onward. Footfalls splattered puddles of blood and flesh. Adrenaline lashed him but he wasn't gaining on Çydanza. She vaulted over the edge of the plateau into fallow white fields.

Just beyond, universes of all sizes bubbled the area in a great foam a kilometer high, teeming with variety.

Çydanza dashed inside the first universe, disappearing beyond the rind. Caiden bolted after her. Foliage smacked him on the other side. Layers of it stacked in towers. He lost sight of her, but veered to the path of swinging vines and chased after.

Into the next biome. He crashed through a half meter of water bright with red schools of fish. Çydanza was so light she sprinted on the surface, hardly making a ripple.

"*Crimes*," Caiden growled, "I'll lose her at this rate."

The *Azura* streaked by overhead, silver and blurry past the foam of universes. Threi wouldn't be able to track Çydanza on the ground.

Caiden leapt from the water, through a rind, into a desert. Memories sputtered up but he raced confidently after her across the sand, the footing familiar. Tree-height cacti bristled in rows.

He was gaining on her.

The next universe corralled a herd of lanky grazers in purple pasture; Çydanza ran into the fencing, dissolving through its mesh and congealing on the other side. Caiden climbed over with one arm and aching legs.

The animals spooked and knotted up, tripping Çydanza among them, while Caiden dodged through the herd with practiced skill. He lunged and snatched at the vishkant's arm. His fingers tingled through a mush of particles. She spun and changed direction, darting through a gate and out of the universe. Caiden raced on her heels.

He powered on but his legs felt brittle, each step cramping up his thighs. This rind slathered him in hot, queasy waves. Stars burst behind his eyes, and as he blinked, he realized some of them were real. They were out of the cluster of universes and beneath a starry twilight. The *Azura* torched overhead and spun around to face Çydanza. The ship rippled like a liquid sun.

There was nowhere ahead for Çydanza to hide or escape. She ran into a field of white lilies. Lightflies whirred up in disturbed clouds.

Caiden poured his hate and pain into speed.

He tackled her. Flower stems tangled in their limbs as they grappled, Çydanza screaming, her body slippery as her physique transformed.

"Give me your worst," Caiden snarled, pinning her with his weight and one arm around her neck. "It won't be enough."

His nose burned with the scent of crushed green. Çydanza was cold as ice beneath him. Twisting around, she sobbed, "*Winn!*" Panca's face streamed tears that boiled on the ground. "You're hurting me, please…"

"No," Caiden breathed. "Panca was crushed into a hellish box because of you. Like the others. Blinded. Ripped up. Wrung back in time. Tortured. *Tortured.*"

He hauled her upright. She wriggled free of his weak, sweaty grip, but he hooked her arm and folded her up against him. "*It's a game to you, isn't it?*"

Visions flooded Caiden's mind, pieced together from ragged memories: first the nophek and everything she'd tried the first time, those memories bland and brittle from overuse. There was nowhere teeth hadn't bitten Caiden before.

Çydanza shrieked and writhed. "Sweetie," his mother groaned, mouth gargling blood as her face was ripped apart by invisible jaws.

"Cai," Leta pleaded up at him, her eyes sparkling with tears. "Don't let us die."

Caiden's heart skipped furiously. His muscles itched to smash, to rend, to save, to embrace, and every confusion stuck him in place for one moment. Pain exploded through him as years of injuries—physical and emotional— stacked upon one another. Blood slathered upon blood.

Çydanza slithered free. Caiden reeled after her. Flies kicked up, winking. Petals scattered in low gravity.

He tackled her to the ground again. Limbs rubbery, his body weight was his only advantage. She snarled, twisting between forms and faces. Her mental attack shifted, heaving up all the raw doubts and fears that had shattered him during the last murder attempt.

"*Winn,*" En cried, exposed heart pounding in rapid rhythm with Caiden's. He whipped into a blur, replaced with faster and more erratic visions as Çydanza plied Caiden's feelings. Shadowy horrors flashed over his retinas. Pheromones clobbered him, demanding he believe.

Reality twisted. Caiden was armor-clad, a murderous Casthen drone. Among the flowers lay his family's corpses. Red blood, blue, and the whipkin flayed. The big nophek he'd tamed sprawled skull-smashed and oozing.

"Not me," he choked. "I didn't cause this misery."

But you belong. A little voice in his soul whispered.

The jagged parts of him that didn't fit in Laythan's crew weren't anything he could file down. They had been bred into him: violent fangs, sharp mind, a firebrand. The hate. The *proclivity* for hate.

A single sweet memory budded through savagery. Leta-vishkant proclaiming, *You are spirited and kindhearted and self-sacrificing, and that is so much more powerful.*

Visions blurred by tears, Caiden hung on with everything he had. "You've lived long enough at the cost of millions of lives. You're done."

The *Azura* crash-landed at the edge of the field like a splashing wave. The universe rind was vibrant and ready. The bay iris opened and Threi hurtled out.

Çydanza thrashed and shrieked. Caiden's nerves sawed him, muscles spasmed, but he crawled, clinging to her with his one arm while pushing them through the field with his legs, swimming through lily petals and lightflies.

The memories stopped. Flickers of emotion gnashed at him as the stimulus in his brain continued, but the visions ebbed. Çydanza's ability was exhausted. Defanged, she couldn't affect anyone else.

"*Threi!*" Caiden screamed.

The man rushed over in a blizzard of lilies.

Caiden's strength whisked away. As his grip slipped, Çydanza crawled from his arms. Threi skidded to a stop. Caiden gasped, "She's safe! She's done! Grab her! To the rind—"

They couldn't let her get away or recover her strength to attack again. Caiden couldn't withstand a second round. They were only eleven paces from the *Azura's* rind.

Threi grabbed hold of Çydanza. "My turn. My turn with you." He twitched, burying his thumbs into her skull so she couldn't run. Her screech grated Caiden's ears like a sandstorm.

Threi grappled her onto her back and straddled her waist, pinning her shoulders with both hands as she bulged between densities and appearances, rifling through his memories but exhausted of the force she'd used on Caiden. Threi's eyes suddenly widened, struck with a vision. His chest heaved and neck corded with tension.

Caiden stared as Çydanza congealed. Long brunette hair gathered to one side. Her pretty eyes dominated an otherwise ordinary face. Freckles thick as stardust in tawny skin.

The Dynast Prime. Abriss.

CHAPTER 44

MURDERER

Caiden watched in horror as Threi's long fingers curled around Çydanza-Abriss's neck. She bucked and clawed. Caiden shouted, "Get Çydanza to the rind! Destroy her!"

Eleven paces away. The *Azura*'s rind shimmered.

Between delirious breaths, Threi snarled, "I've waited. So. *Long.*"

"*Threi!*" she screamed, Abriss's voice a beautiful, glorious bell. "It wasn—"

"*Scream louder*," he hissed, laced with a Graven order. "Fight against me with everything you have. Beg for your life. Tell me again you love your dear brother, Abriss."

Çydanza-Abriss shrieked, and even though she was an illusory copy of the real woman, Caiden felt a kick of Graven response, every cell of him urged to respond. He almost missed registering the word "brother."

Abriss screamed, "*I loved you!* Please! You can't—"

For a heartbeat, Threi paused. Çydanza rolled beneath him but he caught her wrist and jerked her back. "You're the only person who could, but we didn't love each other. We *affected* each other."

Her face screwed in confusion. "You can't kill me," she choked. "I"—she garbled the words, wading through his memories for lines with meaning—"do not hate you for your greed…"

She stopped fighting and pushed into him, hugging her arms around his neck and shoulders. He stiffened, eyes glistening.

"This has to happen," Threi said, "for the multiverse to survive. I have to be able to do this." He bore down on top of Çydanza-Abriss, fingers shoveling into her neck.

Caiden gathered his strength and lurched up but stumbled as vertigo slammed into his head. He screamed through the pain roaring between his ears. "*Threi!* Get her to the rind!"

Threi's fingernails dimpled skin. Abriss's scream whittled to silence as he crimped her windpipe shut. Her beautiful, mesmerizing face contorted with horror while Threi breathlessly levered his full weight on her throat. "Your blood *is* just as blue as you believe it to be, sister."

Caiden forced himself up and shoved Threi's shoulder away as Çydanza-Abriss slumped, collared in bloody gashes. Çydanza's morphic body was wounded enough, and she exhausted enough, that her particles struggled to recalibrate. Flesh sizzled around her neck injury, healing and re-forming, which only made her choke more. She felt *real* pain. Purple lips agape for air, she attempted to crawl away but fell in convulsions.

Threi sat back and ran shaking fingers over his face, through his hair, and down his neck, panting ecstatically. "That was more satisfying than I'd imagined. I can do it. I'm ready now."

"*Nine crimes*, what is *wrong* with you?" Caiden wrestled his disgust. *Tests*. It all came together, and he reeled at the absurdity. "You...you've been orchestrating Çydanza's demise—test after bloody test, and all that weird shit in your room—for *how long* just to simulate your ability to kill someone completely different?"

Threi closed his eyes, tilting his head back with a soft, cathartic smile. "I'm just getting what I've earned. Confirmation."

That was why Çydanza had never seemed important to Threi. He didn't need her dead, he needed her to take the form of someone else.

To pretend-kill this vishkant version of a person.

The Graven research. The patience. The suffering he wrought. *Silye*. The entirety of her.

Even the damn Dynast-colored blanket on his bed.

"You intend to murder Abriss, but she's too Graven," he quested. Admission sparked in Threi's eyes, and Caiden hissed, "All this, for... Why not abuse a random vishkant somewhere else if you're just lusting after the idea of murdering someone you hate?"

"It's not lust." Threi stood, wreathed in twilight and petals. He looked down on Çydanza's spasming, misting body as the vishkant tried to recongeal. His voice quieted, breathy. "It's necessity. Most vishkant don't fear for their lives, and I needed the fear to be real. Only Çydanza—thinking herself impervious for so long—would fight with everything. Only she would scream at me to stop."

"Crimes, this is messed." Caiden grabbed Çydanza. The vishkant's body morphed into neutral vapor and spongy bones, so weakened from the damage that she couldn't take a form, couldn't draw from Caiden's memories enough to become anyone he knew. Caiden slogged through the lily field toward the ship, panting and blinking hard.

He hauled Çydanza to the *Azura*'s rind and threw her into it.

Explosive waves of force dropped him to his knees. The rind convulsed in lightning bursts and splashes of riotous color.

Çydanza's scream modulated as if a thousand voices cried out of a mutating throat. Her face engulfed in the universe edge flickered between his mother, his father, Leta, and everyone else he cared about, living or dead.

Caiden balled up the thick mess of his emotions and threw it into his fist to hold the vishkant's body in the rind. "This is for Laythan. For Taitn. For En. For Ksife. For Panca, the *Azura*, the whipkin and nophek and every being you've ever hurt or tried to break. Some of us don't break that easily."

Her screeches ceased and only a roar and hiss remained.

Threi stepped over Caiden and planted a boot on the vishkant's chest to shove the rest of her molecules into the rind. The pores in Çydanza's bones widened until no material remained. She effervesced from squiggling vapor to light to filaments of air wriggling back under the world.

Overwhelmed and wrung dry of all his past, Caiden slumped over the dying tangle of her.

The rind sputtered haze and hateful colors before settling back to a docile opaline curtain.

Threi's panting was stark and ragged in the silence.

The air smelled of their sweat and desperation, getting whisked away by perfume. Flowers whispered in the breeze.

"Congratulations," Threi said between vigorous exhales.

Caiden toppled onto his back, chilled by the reality of everything it cost: six years off his life and sanity, the *Azura*'s integrity, his family's torture.

Murderer.

He raised his palm. There wasn't even blood on his hands. Vishkant didn't really bleed. No evidence, no guilt—the Casthen way.

His breast numbed with fading adrenaline, and as tingles of elation cooled to simple exhaustion, Caiden felt filthy. He was the monster the Casthen had bred him to be all along, even though he'd done good with it. Unfathomable future pain had been relieved from the world with Çydanza's demise, but in the moment, he could only see the dirt of it, not what would grow.

I forged myself after all into the blade sharp enough, the trowel keen enough to dig under the taproot and upheave the entire thing.

"Now what...?"

Threi replied, "Some of the Casthen main command are dead, but the others I need to speak with."

Caiden hadn't meant the logistics.

What am I now?

He had been devastated by the realization that he'd been raised with only one purpose: a mechanic. But in re-creating himself, he'd become another creature with just as singular a purpose: killing Çydanza. He thought again of all the evidence in Threi's room, an obsessive theme so familiar to what Caiden was doing to himself: Threi was forging himself into a weapon sharp enough to cut the Dynast Prime. Just like Caiden, through the acceleration, the nightmares, the sparring. A single-minded design, oblivious to who or what it hurt.

Threi's cheery voice itched the wrong way against Caiden as the man maundered on. "Now the Casthen actions can be held before an ethical council. The operations can be clean—as much as that concept exists in the multiverse." Threi fussed over a small holosplay. His body steamed, and he all but vibrated with excitement. Whatever he'd chugged to enhance his

Graven effect and snare hundreds to his will had worn off. His pale, hawkish face didn't inspire love, his voice was rich but didn't build a gravity into the world, and his body wasn't burdened with an aura.

"Sister?"

Threi eyed Caiden sideways. "That's right."

Caiden tried to grapple that idea, but a headache reared in his skull. The drifting lightflies confused with sparkles foaming across his vision.

Threi was Graven enough to have more resistance against Abriss than most, but—as evidenced in her order to kneel, which he hadn't been able to disobey in Emporia—he wasn't Graven enough to exert his own will in her presence.

Caiden said, "The sensory-dulling experiments—you're trying to minimize the sensory pathways through which Graven effect is received? You engineered Silye to be extra susceptible so you could test the devices on her. And the substance that temporarily boosts your Graven rank. You're trying to match Abriss so when you plunge a knife her way she can't shout 'stop' and fix you in your tracks?"

"Vishkant can't simulate the Graven effect Abriss will have, but she felt real enough. I proved my emotional capability."

"You don't seem like someone who finds murder hard."

Threi fixed him with an icy gaze. "There is *no one* in the entire multiverse as hard to murder as Dynast Prime Abriss Cetre in Unity."

Swelling with great breaths, Threi looked across the stars, bent by lightseep fracturing the heavens. He gazed along the horizon blistered with universes.

The new Casthen Prime.

Caiden batted at lightflies and dizzy sparks. A hollowness gaped in him again, drained of the fury he'd filled it with. None of this revelation fit either. *I need family. They'll knock sense into me.*

He rolled onto his stomach and pushed up to his feet. His vision foamed black. Çydanza's attack had an unknown toll, and it wasn't good. Threi had only ever tested the memory flood on people who had died, not documented the neurological effects of survival.

"I need..." Caiden's voice ebbed in and out of a static foam in his ears.

Flickers teemed in the corners of his vision, leaving black dimples in their wake. "I need to get to my crew." *And get the* Azura *away, get myself away, everyone safe and together.*

Threi had murdered hundreds with a few words. The image of it lurked in Caiden's weary mind.

Threi dusted lily petals from his clothes. "When you're done, meet me at Çydanza's universe with the *Azura*. We need to bridge into it with the ship's universe and transfer data out from Çy's servers."

Caiden nodded and limped into the ship, closed the iris, and slipped into the pilot's seat. His brain filled with wool and slithering. Perhaps the gray matter had uncoiled and was squirming in there.

"One last flight," he muttered to himself. "Make it to the infirmary. Everyone safe."

He deactivated the universe bubble and took off. The *Azura* was serene, her engines singing. Stars peppered the view as Caiden banked to the dark side of the planet.

Slow. He took it achingly slow. Arm cramping. Vision as gray as the vapor of his old home.

Ksiñe will patch me up. I'm not alone.

At the Enforcer's pad, he descended gently.

I'm worth something to them, even when I can't identify worth in myself.

Caiden cut the engines and dithered in the seat, gathering clarity. A serrated ache roamed his head instead.

He groaned and rolled up, pushing this one last length, one more task. In the engine room, he scooped Panca up from where she was medicating against the engine block. Unable to bear her weight on his shoulder, he looped his arm under hers and murmured at her to help, to walk.

Up and out of the ship. Slow. Hallways tenebrous. A seizure slammed him. Caiden skidded on the slick floor, Panca sprawled. He scrabbled at consciousness as a migraine doubled him over.

Then hot, fanged void chewed up the last of his strength.

CHAPTER 45

SAVED AND SALVED

Consciousness seeped in. Murmured sounds, gentle touches, spicy scent. Caiden blinked one eye at a time. Gray as the vapor sky, above. A ceiling.

He tried to move and groaned, body like a bag of rocks. He lay on a plush, raised medical slab, head pillowed and body covered with a blanket of heated gossamer.

Panca tinkered on his augmented arm with a tiny awl. She looked up, and a brilliant smile creased her face.

"*Pan*..." he rasped. His own smile hurt—a lot. He winced and closed his eyes. "I'm sorry. I'll never have enough apologies for all of you."

Panca laid a soft, soft kiss on his forehead. She patted his left arm. It reactivated in a rigid flurry. He gasped and curled his arm tight. *Thank you*, he mouthed, and laughed—even more painful than the smile.

"Hey, hero." En sat on the edge of the next bed, repairing her shoulder. She still looked like shit. Pigmentation was only back on her face, and splotchy at best, but her smile was less gruesome, and her jumble of materials had been strapped back into a human figure.

Panca walked over to help with En's shoulder. En passed her the tool and beamed.

"Layth, get in here!" Taitn shouted as he approached Caiden's bedside. He walked gingerly, fitted in compression gear that oddly bulked his thin body. Hair and beard were neatly trimmed—the former even sported En's braidwork down the top.

"You look...good." Caiden meant it. Despite the gaunt paleness, something fit Taitn as it hadn't before. His softness fit better, perhaps.

Taitn shook his head. "Bone density's off. Organs failing. But I'll last to Emporia and the Cartographers' clinic. We need to get you there too."

En didn't look up, but simpered. "Lyli will help for sure."

Laythan entered. Temporary prosthetics replaced both eyeballs: eerie glass surfaces, forest green glistening over silver. He blinked at Caiden, eyelids and temples pinched by stitches right over the old scars from the last time he was blind. "You look horrible."

"So do you."

En slapped Laythan's arm. "Be nice. You're looking at a hero."

"How's..." Caiden tried to move but the signals were all jumbled up. "How's my head?"

Ksiñe slid off a bed at the far end of the infirmary and hobbled over. His countless wounds were stapled, stitched, and taped up as if the infirmary had run out of materials to patch him with. The barest amount of spotty pigment returned to his skin. Honey-colored wisps gathered across his face as he neared.

Caiden's smile was half sob. Who knew a color could be so heartening?

Ksiñe handed back the morphcoat. Its down slicked into aged leather.

Caiden nodded thanks and crushed the coat in his hands. The whipkin bounded off Ksiñe's arm and sniffed around Caiden's ear, licked his temples and eye. He reached up to scritch her head. "Love you too, little girl."

Ksiñe said, "Head will improve. Temporary brain damage. Lyli can fix."

En chuckled, then shut up when Taitn glared and Ksiñe's skin rippled irritated orange.

Caiden laughed. Sparks of pain filled his lungs. "I don't expect any of you to forgive me, but most of the stupid is wrung out of me now, if that's any consolation."

En picked up Caiden's black wrist in her jagged, glassy hand, two fingers missing. "Brave and stupid are sometimes the same thing."

Caiden sank back to the plush bed. "Thanks for coming."

"We don't leave family behind." Laythan leaned against the door frame. "And you already earned a fist for running off. Killing Çydanza...that will ripple, and make others rethink their own regime. You were brave to do something so huge. And damn stupid to waste yourself doing it."

Caiden felt both empty and overwhelmed. Exploitation was an inevitability of the multiverse, and the Casthen were in Threi's hands: a man massively accelerated, acquainted with all the Casthen's secrets, Graven enough to command hundreds to die at a whim, and singularly fixated on killing his own sister, the Prime of the ruling organization of Unity. An absurd cocktail of complications. Caiden's fourteen-year-old self hadn't realized removing one problem created space for new ones.

"I have to talk to Threi, decide what to do...Need to release a freighter of slaves to stop the re-initiation of the nophek farming."

The nophek...

"Laythan." He hesitated. "There's something I really need to do and I don't think you're going to like it."

"What have I liked that you've done so far?"

Caiden laughed. More twinges. "Let me think it through, and then... let's talk."

"Thinking things through is a good start. So is talking." Laythan nodded at the door, where Silye padded in. "You taking in strays now too?"

Caiden craned his neck to look at her, and she stopped dead-still, staring with a mix of fear and awe. He frowned. "She's just back here becau—"

"Because you've been kind to her," En cut in. "Don't forget that. Amidst it all...you were kind to her."

He shook his head. "Silye was engineered to be heavily influenced by Graven genes. Silye..." She snapped to attention and drifted over. Caiden winced. He hadn't been trying to prove a point. "You deserve opportunities and socialization free of Threi's web, so you can find out who you are, give your personality room to breathe. A chance to have your own experiences, not just watch or read them in media."

She blushed. Her long hair whisked a multitude of pastel colors as she looked away, and murmured signs, *I have a function here.*

Grief paved over Caiden's smile. "Function doesn't tie you to a place or a people. We could use your weaponry and coding skills fixing up the ship. Will you—" *Come with us.*

Caiden mashed his lips together and stared back at the ceiling.

This miserable Graven force. No off switch, no way to interact without everything being a subliminal command, no such thing as consent, no way to know if care was genuine or coerced. Threi's words kicked around his skull: *Welcome to a life of lies, Winn.*

"Oh, crimes' sake, this again, Winn?" En slid off her bed. She took Silye's shoulders and peered down earnestly. "What's your favorite media?"

Silye's eyes widened. Her reflective pink gaze saccaded, assessing En's face. She signed a reply.

"Excellent," En said. "Want to see that setting in person? Go swimming? Fly cloudforests? Ride haripeks through glittering Graven ruins overgrown with magenta sorrelvines, like in the opening scene? Let's do all the fun stuff. Come with us."

Silye blinked, then shook her head and signed, *I'm comfortable here.*

"You might be even more comfortable somewhere else, but you won't know that until you leave and stretch yourself."

He'll find me.

"The multiverse is a vast place, you're a free entity, and we'll fight for you, dear. You'll be safe."

Really?

"I insist," En said. She turned to Caiden. "See? Easy. Who cares if she wouldn't have been able to say no to you if you'd asked, she's better off coming with us."

"*I* care," Caiden replied. "Graven power turned Threi into an irreverent, reckless madman. What if I become the same without knowing it? Especially if the reactions are so subtle that they don't make my Graven effect, my privilege, as obvious as they do for Threi. I don't want to stop noticing, over time, how I'm influencing the people around me. I have to do better, be vigilant."

En rolled her eyes. "Yeah, but also not shut yourself off from any connections at all, or go gallivanting across the multiverse again, believing that you're sparing others. You're absolutely the type who would do that."

Ksiñe made a noise and crossed his arms. "You are not more noble for refusing to admit your genetics have been a gift."

That sank in. His capabilities had helped him protect Leta from bullies, had aided him surviving the desert, had let him bounce back to health and put on muscle faster after the acceleration, had healed a gruesome spinal injury, and were one reason he'd survived in the Casthen Harvest and had the stamina and fortitude to kill Çydanza.

"You're right. I just…"

"Hypocrite," Laythan butted in. "You wouldn't discriminate against Silye because her abilities weren't her choice. So stop turning that disgust on yourself. Just because someone like Threi uses power for self-gain doesn't mean the power itself is abominable."

Caiden chewed on that thought, but one acknowledgment kept intruding: the massacre on the plateau—hundreds of brutal deaths—that happened because *he* had been complicit in the whole scheme for revenge.

"You're family," Panca said.

Taitn came up next to her and nodded, adding, "In the best families, nothing about your origin or makeup or privilege matters. We love you for you."

A flush rose up Caiden's cheeks. Coerced or not, their bond was invaluable, and he would make sure he did good by it.

He struggled to push himself to a sitting position, then looked at the crew earnestly. "We're not safe yet. Threi…I need to meet with him. And I need your advice first."

He explained everything Threi had done and revealed. The crew listened. Silye sat quietly, looking pensive as Caiden laid out all of her master's deeds and promises.

When he'd finished—having thoroughly knotted up his own feelings about it—En said, "First, what are you even considering, here? Murder?"

Caiden winced at that word. "I doubt I could kill him if I tried. So I guess I'm wondering where to end things. We aren't friends, but do I need to ensure we aren't enemies? Do I need to try to take the Casthen away from him?"

Laythan rubbed his bearded chin and hummed. "Let the Cartographers deal with the Casthen. They're on their way here already. Threi may be a powerful individual, but the Cartographers are a massive organization. The two of them will have to find common ground and it's not your place to mediate."

"Laythan..." Caiden waited for the captain's full attention before he prodded an old wound. "I won't ask about whatever happened between you and Threi, but—what about Abriss Cetre? Is she really the terror Threi claims she is? Should he be loosed on her like a rabid hound?"

"Can't say. I've stayed out of Dynast business. Both Graven brats are trouble simply because of their pedigree, but it's no one's place to judge simply because they're *capable* of great harm. Capability is not culpability. Çydanza's corruption has been visible for decades. But this—Winn, this is one of those difficult decisions where there's no easy call with limited knowledge. Threi might be as much of a terror as Çydanza, or he could be a force of good, ridding the world of worse."

Something Pent the saavee had said surfaced in Caiden's mind: *Bad things can make good people. Good people can make things bad.* Çydanza had been killed through Threi's planning. Perhaps bad people could make things good.

Then the image of hundreds dead flashed in Caiden's mind again. And he recalled the countless others Threi had sacrificed over the years to test the memory flood and the rind.

Taitn scratched the back of his neck, frowning. "We know a lot about Threi, less about Abriss. Within Unity, the Dynast has eliminated most illnesses, connected planets and promoted cultural exchange, and implemented an immigration plan for inhabited planets that end up consumed by Unity's expanding rind. The organization is driven by faith in harmony, is transparent about their practices, and have only done good."

Caiden grumbled. "The opposite of Threi, who's shadowy and already piled with sin." His elevated mood crumbled. "I'm not convinced, but it's time to go speak with the bastard. Wish me luck."

CHAPTER 46

CHOICE

Caiden strode for the large data holosplays over Çydanza's white desks. Threi followed more leisurely. The *Azura*, universe active, was parked to bifurcate the rind of Çydanza's universe, forming a bridge for them to get inside so the rind didn't boil the flesh from their bones and all that.

He stopped at the central console and scrolled through reams of data. Countless planets, growth rates, mortality, harvest, product. As he absorbed the full scope, his gestures slowed until his hands hung in the air and he stared. For centuries or more across every known universe, she had manipulated, terraformed, bought and sold. She'd run species to extinction and resurrected them for profit. She'd played a long game, waiting ages for the memories of lesser species to extinguish. All for profit and expansion. All so a little number would grow larger. Every operation at some stage came at the expense of living, conscious beings, the expendable fuel of the Casthen system.

"This…" The extent of the operations and Çydanza's lack of empathy still astounded him. "I'm going to tell the Cartographers everything, if you don't."

"Naturally," Threi replied, ambling to another desk to start the offload process. "I promised to coordinate with them."

"Forgive me if I don't trust your promises."

Threi looked over with an eerie smile. "The Cartographers' aid was always my plan. They'll set this all straight." He swiped and arranged statistics, his eyes sparkling as they sifted through data. "I'll make the Casthen into an organization of passagers. But… there are things to hide first."

Caiden rolled his eyes. "There it is."

"There are things here that passagers shouldn't gain access to, for the safety of everyone, which means the Cartographers shouldn't have it to begin with. And there is one thing that the Dynast should never, ever see. By the way, your slaves," Threi deflected. "The ones you memory-wiped... I'm sending them to a refugee planet."

Guilt slid through Caiden like a hot knife. "*Refugee* planet?"

"That's not a euphemism for something horrid. Refugee planets are in universes that meet a baseline physics examination. Crime is regulated, education readily available, and biomes are cultivated for a variety of species. The Cartographers manage these planets as hospitable refuges for individuals of all origin. Aren't I nice?"

"I'll consider that a promise, and hold you to it."

Threi gave a mock bow.

Caiden fell quiet, gazing over the breadth of Casthen resources. If Threi's sole ambition was to kill his sister—to remove a threat or assume rulership of the Dynast—did that make him relatively harmless to the rest of the multiverse?

He watched Threi's face for a while as the man flitted in the Casthen servers. "You can command people. Do they become tools to you? Do you ever forge real connections?"

Threi paused, hands in the air. His smile bent. "Weren't you also using me to get what you wanted? Am I your tool because of that? Pup, everyone uses everyone else, and most of us let ourselves be used when it suits our needs."

"You didn't answer me."

"I didn't have to."

Don't forget.

That handful of seconds of pure chaos. Blades and glaves and fists and skulls. The roar of hundreds of instant suicides.

Die as fast as you can...

Threi hadn't blinked an eye afterward. He *wasn't* a mosaic cur like Caiden; he was purebred Graven, his accelerated years bleaching the freckled markers that must have been nearly as thick as his sister's.

"Abriss. Do you mean to kill her because she can do what you did, but even easier?"

Threi side-eyed him. "Now you're catching on. I'm the only person who has a whisper's chance of harming her."

"I'll believe she's capable, but not that her intentions are as bad as you say."

Threi dropped his arms and turned. The data of worlds reflected sharply over his clean-lined features and pale eyes. "Sweet soldier, you still have so much to learn. Just because you can't see treachery doesn't mean it's not there. And who better to hide it than the woman every being is genetically programmed to adore and never question?"

Caiden walked, pretending to examine more of the holosplays. "I'll need more time to see. To learn about the Dynast."

"You're sharp, you won't have to dig far. May I suggest *Graven Intention of Prima Luminiferia*, Volume One, Unabridged Edition. It's on a shelf in my room, you can borrow it. Don't dog-ear the pages."

Threi returned to his work. Caiden backed up.

What is most important, right now? Family. Getting them and the Azura *to safety.*

He surveyed Çydanza's universe. It was level sand from edge to edge, dipping into pristine pools, some of which bubbled with springs or steamed with heat. Besides the desks, there was nothing in the universe of note. He wasn't sure if vishkant ate. Most types of organic matter—including human biology—dissolved upon contact with the rind, but there were some elements allowed through, if not whole beings. Using the *Azura*'s universe as a bridge was the only way to get incompatible xenids through.

Threi stood engrossed, muttering to himself as he fussed with the data transfer.

The water looked drinkable.

Caiden ambled back to the ship. He slipped through the *Azura*'s rind and sighed. His body grew buoyant, eased. Air sweet. Decisions felt easier in her world.

He slapped the bay-door switch.

Threi turned at the sound. "*Winn!*" His shout was drowned by the liquid gasp of the door iris seal.

* * *

Droves of slaves spilled out of holding rooms, headed to the sleek vessels that would fly them to refugee worlds. Caiden and Laythan peered over the side of the catwalk to watch.

"I'm responsible for their memories being stripped from them."

Laythan patted Caiden's shoulder. "They would have been wiped no matter who pressed the button or shoved the prod. *You* eliminated Çydanza from Casthen Prime leadership in time to save these people from being shipped off to a nophek farm. And besides, most were convicts and degenerates—it's a fresh start to be rid of those memories. You're their hero, all the same. Every passager will hear the real story…about CWN82, the memory jog—all of it."

"I don't need to be a hero." Caiden had a feeling he would be staying out of the spotlight for a while.

A Cartographer fleet had arrived just in time to make things messy and preoccupy all of Threi's attention. To buy a shred more time, Caiden had sent a note: *We'll talk soon.*

Inside the prison of Çydanza's universe, Threi had access to all of Çydanza's digital fingers, the workings of the Casthen, but his Graven charm was damped by the rind and the need to use complicated broadcast systems. He wouldn't have access to whatever enhancers he'd used to amplify his power, so couldn't command the entire Casthen base as he had before. He would survive inside, while the harm he could inflict on the multiverse was lessened. Caiden was willing to become a target in order to declaw the most actively dangerous being in the multiverse.

That was the best compromise he could come up with until he knew more about the Dynast's Graven siblings.

"We need to hurry. But before we go…" Caiden motioned Laythan to follow, descended stairs through a dark rind at the end of the catwalk, and paused by a door. "Don't be mad."

He opened the door to the warehouse and waited as Laythan took in the aisle stacked with cages of nophek pups, lining the walls with frightened bundles of teeth and eyes. The space filled with the sound of struggling breaths and nightmare mews. The sight that once would have lit Caiden's temper or sent him running now wrenched his heart.

When no punch or grumble came from Laythan, Caiden asked, "Can we save them?"

A steady stream of air escaped the captain, ending in a whistle. He ran a hand through waves of white hair. "Everyone's going to want these. Who knows they're here?"

"The Cartographers don't know yet, but we won't have long to smuggle them out." Caiden walked to the first cage and crouched to make out the small, moon-eyed creature in the darkness. It was sickly like all the rest, pumped with artificial nutrients and whatever else the universe didn't have for them, staving off their inevitable demise.

Laythan folded his arms. "Another planet where they'll survive without treatments doesn't exist outside of Casthen control. That's what made RM28 so special. I know only one place they'll never be discovered... But chances are high they'll die in its environment."

The gruesome little beast whimpered, and pity swelled in Caiden where fear used to be. "I've done days of research on a live mature male," he began. Laythan raised an eyebrow high. "Don't ask." Caiden still had scars and twinges from their fight. "Between that knowledge, Ksiñe's expertise, and Panca's machining, we can design something better than the outdated meds the Casthen are using now. They'll get a chance, they'll be free for a while."

"High risk, but a chance," Laythan agreed. "Happy, for a while. Maybe even a long while. Are you sure?"

Caiden straightened. Sparkles danced in his vision—he wasn't completely recovered. Although his head swam, his resolve was clear. "A chance is better than sure death, better than exploitation. The nophek gave me a chance at fourteen years old, and however horrific it was, it's forged me into a man I'm proud to be. I can give that chance back. At the very least, Threi shouldn't have this much potential gloss."

Laythan smiled sadly. "I'm not sure what happened to you here, but you're not the same boy I picked up on RM28."

Caiden slipped a hand into his morphcoat's leather pocket and squeezed the glass chicory flower. "I'd better be different, after everything that's happened."

CHAPTER 47

STRAYS

Caiden stared at the Cartographers' white floor in Emporia, his head bent forward while a hand steadied his neck. An inscriber whined as it ground against the supercrystal shell of his upper vertebrae. He meditated to the sound and what his choice meant.

After a while, the artist—En's friend Cheza, who had built half of Caiden's arm—straightened and wiped off the nape of his neck. She handed him a square of mirror and held another behind him. The silver flashed as he angled it, stabilizing the reflection of a white symbol etched in the unpolarized supercrystal. It was his old brand, but upside down: the same Casthen circle with rays above instead of below. A dawning or setting sun. Maybe both. He imagined his augmentation back into pigment and the brand changed from white on diamond to black on skin.

His exhale fluttered with dark emotion as it left him, then he grinned.

"Looks great." En rose from where she'd waited. "Won't it remind you of once being a slave, of being designed?"

"Yes." He rose and turned to Cheza.

"Your smile's thanks enough for me, Passager," the artist said.

Caiden smiled wider, then joined En and ran his fingertips over the mark as they left the machine ward. "If the augmentation is a symbol of my reckless bravery, then the brand will remind me of my origin. Strength can rise from any wreckage. I'm free now...free to put whatever I want on this body. It's mine."

"So, you chose your slave brand, overturned." En smirked, studying him as they walked to the Cartographers' atrium.

Caiden's cheeks heated. He redirected. "How much did you get replaced?"

En was heavily repaired, with the exposed, still-gruesome parts hidden beneath her flowy clothes. "Twenty percent fresh materials. Most of it regrown. Panca still has a lot of work to do on the actuators and deeper mechanics. Until then, no fighting or f— Well, my reflexes are shit, so definitely no fighting. It's a sad time."

The Cartographers' main atrium teemed with color and pattern as its white surface reflected a diverse passenger crowd. Holographic cumulus projected in the jeweled walls of the lightseep cavern surrounding the platform. All in all, quite soothing after the dank darkness of the Casthen Harvest.

En stopped, wearing a rare pensive look. "There's a universe where selective cloning has improved due to an anomaly in their physics. Thought I might splurge for something of my old self, something I gave up too fast while finding my way." She beamed. "A heart, perhaps."

Caiden smiled. Micropigment glitched in En's cheek. Her eyes widened. She whirled around, catching Caiden in an arm to pivot him. Her hair turned pink and bounced up in curls, obscuring her face and his as she crushed him close, whispering in his ear, "Don't screw this up."

"What?" Caiden twisted to follow her sideways gaze. Through her curls, he spotted Taitn entering the atrium several paces away.

"Passenger Taitn!" Lyli spotted him too. She glided around a desk and rushed over.

Taitn's eyes rose from the floor. His shoulders stiffened, face winced.

Panic seized Lyli's white features as she stopped, ringlets spilling over her shoulders. She snatched Taitn's wrist and held it for a pulse. He froze as if a predator circled. The alarm on Lyli's face eased into clinical concern as she dropped his wrist and probed his sunken cheek with her fingertips. Her eyes twinkled with data transformations.

"You have desenescized all at once and without the appropriate therapy, Passenger." A tragic inflection strained her measured voice. "Your heart rate is shockingly high."

En sniggered at that and whispered, "Taitn doesn't know it, but Lyli had just started training here—before her accident—when Laythan brought Taitn in off Bielska, freshly accelerated. She knows who he really is."

Taitn stared down at her, mouth agape, unable to shake his paralysis.

"The Cartographers have put you and Winn in my care for treatment." Lyli caught his sleeve and pulled him over to a bench. She sat facing him, brushed his hair away from his forehead to examine him, and tilted his chin with her fingers, seemingly oblivious to his blush.

"There is serious deterioration in your retinal impl…" She trailed off and folded her hands on her lap. "I apologize. Does my touch offend you? I must examine the stressor points in your body's wave correlate, but I can do so with gloves." She dug in a pocket of her coat-dress.

Taitn gently grasped her wrist, then released it immediately. "No… please. C-continue." A lump in his throat bobbed as he swallowed and sat straighter.

Lyli gave him a luminous smile.

En was cracking. Her shoulder against Caiden's shook with suppressed laughter.

"Shh!" Caiden pulled her behind a tall chketin to hide them.

Taitn closed his eyes, half frowning, as Lyli probed his neck then leaned in, bending him toward her chest so she could palpate his upper spine. Her purple eyelashes narrowed as she concentrated, piscine eyes flickering through data.

En struggled to hold back giggles. "Oh, that poor, lucky man. The torture!" About to burst, she swept Caiden away to the lifts. "As much as I'm *dying* to see how this plays out, we need to get back to the *Second Wind*."

She adjusted a heavy bag over her shoulder. It clinked with the vials of rare, expensive chemicals Ksiñe needed to keep the nophek alive. She had bought some, swindled others, and put Caiden in fights for a few.

He pulled free of En's arm as they entered the lift. The door swashed up in front.

"Hey, En."

"Yeah?"

"The vishkant—not Çydanza, but the… What's their name?"

En fixed Caiden with a side eye. "*She* pronouns. And she likes to call herself Adwyn, but is still shy about assembling a personality of her own. Young vishkant struggle to figure out who they are, when everyone else's thoughts and memories impress on them whether they want it or not. I've tried to teach her that it's all right to change your mind, to be a work in progress."

The liquid lift door skittered open. They stepped out, and Caiden paused where the colorful navigation threads bunched in a circle and branched away.

"I want to say goodbye." Caiden backed up a couple steps along the red.

En winked. "Be back in time for food, Ksifie's cooking something special. Oh, and don't make a scene—the Cartographers are on your side but not everyone's happy about Çydanza dead or the Casthen economy upheaved."

Caiden smiled and pivoted, taking his time following the red thread, ignoring the sights and sounds. He passed the holographically painted lightseep biomes without pausing to marvel at them. Both he and the world were different now—he'd lost wonder in exchange for confidence, and confusion in favor of understanding. He wasn't the mechanic boy from the agrarian world, nor was he a Casthen Enforcer bred as a perfect Graven soldier. He was a passager: a term that incorporated so much variety, it really had no definition. And it had room enough for someone like him.

He laid his palm on the vishkant's door. Red hues cued the recognition protocols, the door opened, and there she stood, a ghost of form dressed in lavender clouds.

Fresh memories of his struggle with Çydanza kicked up nervous eddies in his stomach.

"Caiden…" Her tone mixed pleasure and surprise.

He stepped in so the door would close.

As she walked to him, her vapor tightened and resolved into tan skin, a periwinkle dress, a waterfall of sun-bleached fawn hair, and all the perfectly imperfect details of twenty-year-old Leta's face. But her placid expression messed into a frown, her eyes dulled and flicked side to side. Because of her youth, the vishkant accessed newer memories: all of the Casthen ordeal would be clear to her.

Her frown crinkled into a look of horror. Her gaze locked onto his and filled with tears as she sobbed and held his face in trembling hands.

The sight broke Caiden's dam of fortitude. "No, no, it's all right. I'm fine now." He gently wrapped her in his arms, but she continued weeping, staring at the terrors that lay inside him. Caiden had left them there to fade or fester—whichever, as long as they were gone in the end. "I didn't come here to make you cry. I'm sorry."

She held on to him and sobbed for a long while, soaking his shirt. He kissed the top of her head. "I came here to thank you."

"She…" Leta wiped at her eyes, lashes wet and stuck together. "The vishkant. How could she use her nature that way? Oh, Caiden…" She caved against his chest again. He crushed her tight.

"I'm all right, really."

Muffled, she replied, "I know you're strong, but…it's all too sad. These aren't what memories are for."

Caiden stroked her hair and breathed in Leta's sunny sweetgrass scent, then frowned, pushing her back.

"Adwyn, could you…not be *her*? I've seen her so much. She needs to fade like the rest of those moments, and remain in the past." Caiden exhaled and tried to push down all the times he'd seen Leta die. Face screaming. Child, mangled. A fountain of blood in his arms.

The vishkant's eyes widened at the use of her name, then she fell out of form into scintillating folds of vapor.

"I'm starting over," Caiden said. "En mentioned there's a form you like that's your own?"

She darkened like a storm cloud, and tilted her head down to hide her face as the particles congealed. Her hair smoked to a rich brown with bronze highlights as it curled into waves. In a new, huskier voice she said, "But what if you hate—"

Caiden lifted her chin. The last steamy wisps of formation stuck to her face, darker-skinned than before. Her features were more refined than Leta's. Less innocent.

She said, "I'm no more than what I look like, what people see."

"En's probably told you this, but what's important is that it makes *you* happy. You're more than what you look like, to me. And after everything that happened, I don't want vishkant to become another sore spot in my memory, or repeat the mistake of hating a group because of an individual. After all, I know one vishkant who's been lovely to me."

Adwyn hugged him tight. "You didn't deserve what they did to you."

"I chose it."

"Choose something better now?" She rose on her tiptoes, lingering as if to kiss him.

This form of hers was more womanly, her new clothes sheer scarlet. Her eyes dark and pretty.

Caiden smiled and shook his head. "No, thank you. And I don't have long to stay, but I wanted to thank you for forgiving me when I couldn't forgive myself."

"You're weary."

"Very. Will you just lie with me for a while? Rest?"

"Cuddle?" Adwyn gave him a radiant smile. Her dress turned opaque and downy soft as she pulled him to the bed. "You of all people deserve rest and care, Caiden."

The *Azura* perched in the shielding hollow, while the *Second Wind* hunkered in the darkness of Pent's depository, and for a moment Caiden imagined he'd never left. Hadn't joined Threi or made it to the Casthen Harvest. Hadn't spent days trapped in nightmares. Hadn't murdered...

"Who are you, again?" Pent's shriek reminded Caiden that time had indeed passed. He was older in more than looks. "Once more tell me!"

"I'm Winn, the passager with Laythan," Caiden said. "My ship's in your shielding hollow right now!"

Pent grumbled and stalked alongside him, weird eyes bright and squinty.

"Leave him be, Pent," Panca called from near the hollow. The saavee went stock-still then folded into a bow.

Caiden walked over, happy to see Panca energized again, the core in her forehead limpid and luminous. They had discussed what to do with the *Azura*'s hasty reassembly and Glasliq-pilfered new shell. The research the Casthen machinists had conducted—which Caiden wiped after copying—suggested incredible and frightening capabilities in the *Azura*'s spine.

He asked, "Do we have everything for the temp repairs?"

Panca nodded. "Glasliq material's bonded well. Twitch drive's still non-functional. Oh—En bought you pillows." Panca fluttered a laugh.

"Finally." Caiden chuckled and turned to the *Second Wind* hulking in the darkness. In front of it, En lounged on a crate while making a complicated weave in Silye's hair, almost two meters long. The creamy pleochroic locks slipped between colors as he maneuvered them, from lavender pink to dark blue and slithers of green. Silye sat on the floor, dismantling a heap of stolen Casthen weaponry.

Caiden strolled over, and En said, "I've charted a stupidly roundabout route to our destination, to clear the nophek of mandatory inspections and harmful universes. Bribed others and called on favors. We'll make it, anyway. Go see Ksiñe. He might not look it, but he's very excited. Panca's IV module design is gonna work."

Caiden lingered on the warm sight of the two of them before heading inside. The cargo bay was crammed with nophek cages, most of the little beasts sated and asleep. Each had been outfitted with one of the collar devices Panca had tinkered over during the entire trip back. It would administer the chemicals and medicaments to keep them alive in most environments, until the concoctions ran out. After that, their survival was up to the nature of the destination planet, complicated by how the gloss growth changed their physiology.

The *Wind*'s medical suite was as large as the *Azura*'s bay. Alcoves carved out the walls, and the seams of recessed compartments and drawers covered every surface. Many lay open with items strewn around in an uncharacteristically disorganized fashion indicative of Ksiñe's excitement. The whipkin leaped all over, fetching or stowing items.

On a raised slab lay a docile nophek pup out of its cage. Ksiñe probed the beast's neck and chest with a medical glove while data strung along the dimpled air above his other palm.

"You found a sedative that works on them?" Caiden asked.

"No. Designed one from your research."

Caiden swelled with pride and fascination. The little beast's pupils contracted vertically under the clinical lights, reflecting mirror silver deep inside.

"Tapetum lucidum—nocturnal?"

The Andalvian shrugged. Rose-colored sparkles bubbled happily on his face. "This generation started adapting on RM28."

"Maybe they'll have a better chance at surviving on Laythan's uncharted planet." Caiden's cheeks heated. *The one bit of this multiverse that Laythan's kept secret from everyone…and he's offering it for this. For me.*

He bent to peer at the nophek, a delightful miniature of the big male he'd tamed. Its muzzle was short and bony, face boxy, built for jaw strength, as Caiden's scars could attest. Most of its body was black-red skin and fur with rough, scaly legs and spine. He sank his hand into the thick mane around its neck and shoulders, incredibly soft for how coarse it appeared. "Down fiber…Cold climate? High altitude?"

"Probably." Ksiñe actually smiled: a frightening waver on his lips, parting just enough to reveal a fine serration of piscine teeth.

Caiden stroked the nophek, the little thing of his nightmares. The skin on its face was fleecy compared to its ridged back. Its ears were erect, cropped triangles as smooth as velvet. The beast closed drowsy eyes as he stroked it. "I was friends with your dad, briefly," he whispered to it, then chuckled, then grew very sad at the thought.

Ksiñe pushed the pup's head to show off its shaved nape. One of Panca's small devices lay freshly embedded, with tiny tubes along a skintight stretch collar. A small kinetic implant atop its nose expelled chemicals, triggered by breathing, fed by a pack of vials secured under its chest. "Expensive chems I make from scratch. Panca solved plasmic corrosion problem."

Rosy hues wafted across the Andalvian's soft cheeks. The challenge of finding a way to keep the nophek alive had absorbed him since he found out about Caiden's plan. His ill-patched wounds were worse—bruises spreading, fluid leaking through bandages—but he looked happier than Caiden had ever seen him.

Ksiñe set his tools aside and lowered the pup back into its cage. "Take to cargo."

Caiden hauled the cage out and passed Silye carrying a fresh one in. After he'd set his on the stacks, he went back to the suite hallway and stopped, smiling at the sight.

Silye wrangled the feisty nophek steady on the examination slab as Ksiñe attached a chem pack. His face boiled black with disgust or irritation. Silye tapped the nophek's head and made a gesture. Ksiñe nodded, and clucked a sound at the whipkin, who was climbing and jumping around the suite and the two of them, fetching requested items.

Caiden watched for several more arcminutes as they communicated deftly without words—Ksiñe using body language and emotions, and Silye touching or gesturing. En's braiding had gathered her floor-length hair away from her face, around her torso, and secured at her waist so the huge curls skirted over her legs.

Her fingers expertly locked the pup's clawed paws as it wriggled. Ksiñe helped her flip it on its back.

En came up to lean on the opposite side of the door frame.

Caiden asked, "How long have she and Ksiñe been getting along?"

"Ah, right away. The whipkin cuddled with her on the flight here, and you know... that was it."

Caiden chuckled, recalling how cold the Andalvian had been with him initially, and how animated he was now with Silye.

Metal creaked behind as Laythan stopped near the entrance to the bridge and beckoned them over with a gesture. "She can't stay, no matter how much Ksiñe finds her useful. You've been enough trouble. Take her on your own ship or find a home for her."

"That's not fair," Caiden argued. "You have plenty of space on the *Wind*. Let her stay until we finish dropping the nophek off. Maybe I can get her to tell me what she wants to do."

En snorted. "She'll want to stay with you, Graven boy."

Caiden winced and turned away.

"Sorry," En muttered. "Still tender, huh. *I'll* talk to her. I know somewhere she can go for a while, the same place I sent Adwyn. Mauya—even half or quarter—are coveted, and Silye is innocent enough to land in trouble fast, despite her combat skills. She needs a gentle introduction to the real world, especially since media is her only reference and Threi's snaky crew all she had for socialization."

Laythan's gaze fixed down the hall.

Taitn exited the scour room, looking so much better than before, all three of them stared. His gauntness had filled out, skin tone evened, and his eyes regained some blue. He was a trim, healthy specimen of thirty years.

"What?" Taitn flushed.

"Looks like your 'treatment' at the Cartographers' worked." En couldn't help his grin.

"An uphill battle for a while." Taitn missed or ignored En's innuendo. "Injections. Diet. More treatments. Winn, you get something similar?"

Caiden nodded. Lyli had taken him through a chain of strange procedures for the nervous-system damage the memory flood had inflicted. "She said she'd bring us extra dilu—" He cut off when he spotted Lyli approaching with Pent leching at her heels. Caiden waved.

Lyli expertly dodged the saavee's rapid-fire words. He slinked away as Taitn stalked over to meet her at the entrance. She carried a large purple canister in both arms. Snowy curls spilled around it. The hovering spotlights or the *Wind*'s ruddy glow made her appear less ghostly diaphanous than usual.

"I have brought your and Passager Winn's extra solvents and physics for your trip away," she said cheerfully. "In your case, it will not be enough for longer than your intended travel. Please promise you will return for further clinical treatment?"

En chuckled and whispered, "*Treatment.*"

Caiden walked over to take the canister from Lyli. "Thanks. For this and the earlier care."

She returned his smile and bowed. "It is a Cartographer's duty to see that all passagers are well and accounted for. I am glad you are well, and for what you have done."

Up close, her face was obviously powder-brushed white to appear more opaque. Her hands still had the ghost of bones past her milky skin. Her eyes widened when she saw that Caiden had noticed, and she dropped her gaze, for the first time losing her graceful, clinical confidence.

Caiden strolled back to En and Laythan inside the cargo bay. Taitn hesitated, then stepped closer to Lyli and brushed a palm across her cheek, coming away with a smudge of powder. "You don't need it."

Lyli blinked in surprise. Her embarrassment crumbled and she laughed—a sweet, lustrous sound. "And you do not need to be shy, Taitn Maray. If I could wipe that away, I would."

"You can." Taitn smiled, his own reservations dashed. He leaned down for a kiss.

En squeezed Caiden's arm painfully tightly. Caiden glared and tugged but couldn't pull from En's augmented strength.

"Took him damn long enough," En muttered. "Nice going, Lyli. Patience of a saint."

Lyli's heart was beating visibly faster when Taitn pulled out of their tender kiss. She covered her chest with her hands, pink flushing her powdered cheeks.

Taitn took her hands in his and curled them away. "You don't need to hide."

"Neither do you." Lyli leaned toward him.

Taitn glanced into the ship and blushed furiously. He gently herded Lyli around the corner outside.

En broke into giggles that he tried unsuccessfully to stifle.

Laythan scoffed. "Taitn may be younger and inexperienced, but you'll never stop being the immature one, eh?"

CHAPTER 48

UNCHARTED

During the long and uneventful egress-hopping trip to Laythan's secret sector of the multiverse, Caiden was able to forget everything but the present moment. The crew's routine made time irrelevant: good food and better games, banter that Caiden was old enough to contribute to, a soft bed and a beautiful ship and a family.

They took both vessels and swapped passengers at Cartographer Dens while resupplying. When they finally reached the lonely universe where Laythan's uncharted planet existed—somewhere in it, he assured them—it was Caiden's turn with En and Silye.

"Why did Laythan never sell this charting?" Caiden asked. "Habitable planets are worth a large fortune."

En reclined against a wall, surrounded by tools. She tinkered on her kneecap, which lay open like a flower, tendons draping to the floor. "The nophek we're hauling are worth an insane amount, and ten times that if their gloss ever matured. You could be set for life, yet you aren't selling them."

"The nophek need to be free to live as real animals for however long they have. Their value isn't in currency, to me."

"Exactly. Laythan is repaying your nobility by sharing something of his own. Besides, he may want the idea of a safe planet to escape to one day when he's sick of passager life, but honestly, Laythan will die before he ever settles down." She smiled. "Are you sure you're going to stay on this planet, whatever it is, with the nophek?"

"I need to rest. I spent too long looking ahead, trying to be something I wasn't ready to be, wrapping myself around feelings that no one is ever big enough for."

En arched an eyebrow. "Philosopher hero. What will you do after?"

"Depends what I learn in my research." The *Azura*. The Dynast. The Graven things Threi was hiding in the Casthen data vaults. And Caiden's own genetic sources. The *Azura*'s data storage was packed with whatever he could steal before they'd left the Harvest. "I can protect and liberate those who are too ignorant, innocent, or indentured to save themselves. Hopefully that will validate my engineered origin."

Something monstrous lingered in him, in that nightmare-carved hollow that he'd let his pain and rage inhabit in order to survive becoming Casthen. It was asleep, but he could feel the shape of it, just out of perception.

En gave him an adoring look. "Born and bred a hero! Well. If you're gonna be here a while, better hope Laythan's planet is not as ugly as RM28."

Caiden set the *Azura* on auto-course to follow the fat tail of the *Second Wind* toward unnamed constellations. He got up to stretch.

Clinks and tiny sparks emanated from En's work. "Are you gonna keep Silye?"

"She's not a pet or a slave, and can't be owned. Crimes, En, we've been over this." Caiden threw his morphcoat over the back of the pilot's seat. The ship's climate cooled in response to his heat.

There was a bout of silence while Caiden did footwork drills across the length of the bay to get his muscles moving. He glanced down the ramp. Silye had fallen asleep in one of the chambers below. "I was bred to be a manipulator, and she was bred to be manipulated. She's not staying with me. It's inhumane."

"Even if she's happy?" En asked.

"Can you drop it?"

En fixed him with a quizzical look. "Just trying to understand."

"You're good at poking at wounds, huh?" Caiden sighed. "*Even if she's happy*, coercion is inhumane, it violates rights."

En tinkered for another arcminute. "All right, but remember: Andalvian, vishkant, falvees, and others are fairly Graven-resistant; you have options."

"I'm not lonely, En."

A message prickled Caiden's neural link a moment before words formed in the cockpit holosplay: *Speeding up.*

Thankful for the distraction, he crawled back in the seat and matched the *Second Wind*'s acceleration, but it was still a long, monotonous wait until anything changed. After a while, it became clear they were headed for a large sun.

Silye wandered up from the lower level with Caiden's nophek pup on an invisible lead. A transmitter in its collar linked to a bracelet too large for Silye's wrist.

"Any change in it?" En asked, closing up her knee.

Silye shook her head. They still feared that something about the universe might kill the pups despite the chems, but no change so far was a good sign.

"The planet's biosphere will be the real test," Caiden muttered. Laythan couldn't even say if there would be enough food there. "Fish," he had said, and shrugged.

Caiden smiled as Silye brought the nophek to the cockpit and crouched to stroke it. Had they been cuddling, the two of them, when she slept? The creature was still a bit sedated, but like all animals, it was quickly taming to food. On its collar, he'd tied the glass chicory flower memento.

Caiden rubbed the nophek's plush ears, then looked to Silye. "Are you all right?"

She stared at him for a long moment before nodding. She must have used the scour: her hair shimmered in thick, weightless waves and snarls. She wore one of En's long-sleeved shirts in a pastel fiber from some far-off universe. It was a thigh-length dress on her.

Silye drifted to Caiden's shoulder and pointed out the cockpit windows. A beat later, a message appeared, signaling the *Second Wind*'s deceleration. A burning sun and a cloud-wrapped sphere dominated the view.

The *Second Wind* vanished into the deck of gray cloud. It reminded Caiden of his home planet sheathed in the ceiling of vapor, and he half expected to see green pastures beneath.

A realization unspooled a sigh from his chest. *I've been inside stations and facilities almost exclusively since RM28. The knowledge of other worlds has been rattling around in my head but I haven't smelled them, felt them, breathed them. I'm finally going somewhere* real.

The atmosphere enveloped them. As robust as the *Azura*'s glossy engines were, she still quaked. Moans of stressed material slithered through the roar of engine and flame. Silye clung to him stoic-faced, but her hands shook. The nophek pup crawled beneath Caiden's legs.

Fantastic blasts of heat and whipping vapor obscured the view before the ship broke cloud cover. Caiden leveled up and slowed in awe.

It wasn't green. A soft glow permeated the air. The sun rested on the horizon as a spectacular rose-colored sunset textured by cloud. Ocean stretched between strands of black sand, but this wasn't the choppy abyss of his homeworld's seas. The water was ice blue, shallow everywhere and without a wave. The *Azura*'s reflection streamed across it, disappearing in deep sapphire chasms.

Silye's hand slipped off Caiden's arm. Her mouth hung open and her eyes glistened.

En whistled in amazement. "Well, no wonder he wanted this untouched."

Crystalline monoliths shot up like islands. Higher, stepped hills captured water in marbled decks of obsidian and quartz. Waterfalls streamed across jet rock, fed by rivers that snaked through moss-covered highlands.

"En, is this...unusual? Or do a lot of planets look like this?"

"Laythan has a taste for the unusual, if you hadn't noticed."

More and more greenery spotted the landscape, hidden under waterfalls, in shady ravines, and hemming the beaches where sand met stony soil. On one such landmass, the *Second Wind* hovered and began a laborious descent on the beach. Caiden found a plateau just above and set the *Azura* down first.

He rocked himself out of the seat. Scalar gravity disengaged. The planet's own gravity was more silken, and he was instantly at ease. "Ready?"

He slid the nophek's leash bracelet off Silye's wrist and twisted it on his. Silye slipped her hand in his free one. He tried to decipher her blank stare and dilated pupils. "You haven't..." The words caught in his throat. It was time for the heartbreak of the Casthen's cruelty to be over. "Have you never been on a real planet, Sil?"

Never, she signed, and squeezed his hand.

Warm air blasted in as En hit the bay-door switch. Caiden grinned and headed out. Urged by the leash, the nophek pup uncurled and padded at his heels.

Expanse engulfed Caiden, rendering him small and insignificant. His worries evaporated, memories dissolved in the reality of sky and sea.

"Wow." He laughed and twisted to take in the full vista, breathing sweet, dewy air. Sunset striated the sky rose through brushstroke clouds. That alone would have been enough to entrain his attention for hours, disregarding the glow over the sea or the clouds of mist thrown up by distant waterfalls. The air felt soft and electric against his face.

A breeze lifted all of Silye's hair. En trailed a hand through the strands as she walked by. "Come on, Laythan's unloading already."

They picked their way down the rocks to the black beach. Reflective facets caught light, making the sand glitter like a night sky. The ocean had no surf but rested quiet and shallow for a good kilometer out. In the distance, a flock of ivory birds swayed in the wind.

"Laythan, this is incredible."

The captain squinted at the sunset and back at the mossy highlands. "It'll do. This landmass has shelter, water, and critters among the rocks. A good life, for a while."

"How could you leave after finding this place?"

Laythan scoffed but smiled. "You have a lot of worlds to see, boy. Some are even better than this one."

Caiden struggled to believe that. He drew another breath of clean air and a fragrant cocktail of herbs, water, and sweet florals.

Silye dropped Caiden's hand and crept to the edge of the water, letting it soak into her slippers. Her hair waved around in the breeze.

Caiden headed to the *Second Wind*. His nophek kept up, happier for the softer terrain under its paws. The *snick* of claws on sand no longer sparked his fear. The creature was playful, rooting its nose in the grains and crunching up shells. A memory flashed of the huge, intelligent nophek he'd befriended, and he felt prideful of this little echo.

"Stand clear!" Taitn shouted. A hundred cage latches unclicked at once.

Caiden sidestepped from a small stampede of black-and-red shapes. He recalled his population streaming from the open transport cube into waiting terror. Now the terror, in miniature form, rushed out of captivity into freedom. Nothing terrible waited for them.

Caiden's heart swelled. Taitn came up beside him and together they watched the beasts sniff in the sand, clamber up black scree to tuffets of moss-covered stone. Their collars jingled, vials tinkling with the chemicals that would give them a chance.

Panca watched from the bay with a smile. "Stronger chems Ksiñe made'll last them a half generation. Enough time to adjust to new habitat."

"Maybe not." Ksiñe gathered a seawater sample. "But atmospheric pressure looks good. Humidity too."

The pack headed uphill, disappearing on the plateau. Caiden's pup sat by his boot, digging in the sand.

"Hey," Taitn said quietly. "This has been a crazy ride. Bad and good… ever since you and the *Azura* saved our lives on RM28. I wouldn't be— Well, a lot of things wouldn't have happened without you. You've grown so much. Thanks for forcing me to grow too." He glanced around at the crew. "Us. Us to grow…"

Embarrassed, Caiden pushed sand with the toe of his boot, covering in the hole the nophek made. "You all started this. Could have left me in the desert."

"Come on." Laythan strode over and clapped Caiden on the back, prodding him up the slope. "I have something to show you." To the crew behind, he yelled, "Follow us but land in the water."

En startled as Taitn put his arm around her shoulders and led her inside the ship. They talked, but Caiden couldn't make out the words.

Silye ran with soggy slippers to catch up with Caiden and Laythan.

Caiden glided the *Azura* off the plateau, and Laythan directed him past more islands to a cluster of crystal monoliths lining a solitary black strand. Large curls of sand dipped in and out of the ocean. Tucked in the bosom of the largest beach lay a one-room aboveground bunker. The roof was cluttered with dishes, antennae, and transmitters overgrown with emerald and purple plants. Behind it rose a cliffside dripping with more flora.

"Set on the beach here," Laythan said. Curls of seafoam and sand whirled up around the *Azura*'s glass wings as Caiden landed. Laythan opened the bay iris when the engine roar died to whispers. "Welcome to the only place I've ever called home besides a ship. It's not much to see."

Laythan strode for the structure but Caiden froze the moment he stepped out. High-altitude winds ripped the cloudy sunset into a starry blue night, thick with stellar dust and distant worlds. Large chunks of crystal spotted the beach and refracted the view like self-contained worlds of their own.

The nophek sniffed and tossed its head, mewing in hunger, while its flashing white eyes shifted over the beach, oblivious to the sky.

Silye's head craned up, eyes wide and eyelashes wet.

"Nice to see something new, isn't it? This is no Casthen facility. No media in a holosplay. This is real."

He left her marveling and followed Laythan inside the building. It held a cot strewn with colorfully patterned, ancient-looking blankets, a storage pantry hewn into the cliffside, and an entire wall of computing clusters and ripped-out ship database drives stacked on one another. Laythan switched on a holosplay.

"Every bit of data my ship has is here too," Laythan said. "Universes, species, terminology, so forth. All my Cartographer charts. You can add whatever you brought."

"More than enough to figure out what to do with my life."

"You sure you're staying?"

Caiden returned to the beach and the view. "Yeah. I need time to recover and wrap my head around everything." *Figure out what to do about Threi.*

There was so much to see and do, but in many ways he'd lost his enthusiasm. A deep fatigue gnawed on his bones, and no treatment of Lyli's had dulled those teeth. He needed simplicity, and knowledge at his own pace.

The *Second Wind* caught up and settled in shallow water. A bank of sand joined the *Wind*'s flank with the shore. The crew disembarked.

It was time to say goodbye.

CHAPTER 49

NOW

Behave." En wrapped Caiden in a tight hug. "No gallivanting until we get back. Seventy ephemeris days will go by fast." When En pulled away, looking shy for the first time, the veneer of flesh had cleared from dramatic striped sections of his arms, chest, and neck, revealing true materials. Impressive materials. Caiden recalled Çydanza's accusation that En had been changing in all the wrong ways.

"No regretting your augmentation?" Caiden asked.

"Fluidity is what actually suits me, I realized. I like all that I am." En drew in a long breath then grinned and stole one more hug.

Ksiñe bent to examine the nophek pup's collar and implants. He stroked its back before straightening. Fair purple ripples streamed down his neck and shoulders, pooling around his many white scars. The whipkin launched over to Caiden's shoulder and arched, rubbing against his cheek while purring into his ear.

Ksiñe's face stormed. "Forgive me...for saying nothing about memory loop, before you went into biodata chamber. Could have stopped it."

Caiden shook his head. "Without it I wouldn't be here now or have become who I am. Right away in the desert, Laythan tried to tell me that with hindsight we can appreciate how horrible things have made us so much stronger. I accept what the nightmares did."

Ksiñe's complexion cleared, pink specks babbling at the corners of his eyes. He smiled, frighteningly, for the second time, then reached out to gather the whipkin.

Caiden flushed. "Where's Panca?"

Laythan nodded toward the *Azura*.

Caiden wandered into the engine room. Panca strolled along the machinery, trailing her fingers across its inner music, which only she could sense in full.

"You're always welcome on my ship, Panca, for as long as you want." His voice reverberated in the darkness. "And I'm counting on you to help me fix her up in earnest."

Panca's face was soft and loving as she circled around the other side of the engine block, her gaze moving between elements. The core in her forehead flashed now and then with a deep reflected luster.

She sought words. "Take care of her."

"I will." He followed behind as she walked up to the bay.

"Fuel prism needs rotating," she said.

"Yes."

"The stagger's flawed again."

"I know." Caiden chuckled.

"Don't use florescer till we find more Boll adapters."

"Thank you, Panca." Caiden stopped outside and caught her smile as she walked back to the *Second Wind*.

Taitn strolled over, admiring the *Azura*. Her transparent shell reflected stars. "You sure you're all right here alone?"

"You all keep asking that." Caiden gazed over the stars parading across a golden horizon. "I'm not fourteen anymore."

"I'm not forty-two anymore."

Caiden laughed. "Take care of Lyli."

Taitn wrapped him in a strong, quick embrace. "See you later, brother."

Caiden beamed and composed himself as he walked over to Laythan.

The edge of the sun set red. Monolith crags jutted up like the silhouette of teeth. A "thanks" wasn't enough to appreciate what Laythan had given him. Instead, Caiden inhaled another deep breath of real, unfiltered air.

Laythan laid a hand on his shoulder, squeezed, and left it there as they watched more stars prickle through the clouds. Finally, Laythan withdrew and started toward the *Wind*. There was no better farewell than the wordless, easy energy between them.

"Can you go get her?" En called, nodding to Silye, who stood at the water's edge.

Caiden pulled off his boots and strolled over barefoot, wiggling his toes in the volcanic grains. He stopped at Silye's side. The water was warmer than its icy blue suggested.

Her cheeks were wet.

"I've never seen anything like this either." Stars speckled the lake-calm ocean surface. Despite the encroaching night and the dimming rose, the air was still bright, as if the atmosphere bounced a glow across the planet.

"It's time to go," he said.

She slid her arms around his waist.

"Sil...it's time to go. You need experience away from Graven things. And I need to be alone, where I can think straight."

She signed, *You want me to go?*

Every statement he made was an unwitting order.

"For your own good, yes." He bent to kiss the top of Silye's head. She looked up, and the kiss landed on her forehead. Caiden cleared his throat. "And follow En's lead, but not too closely. Take care of Ksiñe and the whipkin."

She might take that as a Graven order, too, but there was in goodness in it, and that was what mattered. Silye nodded and signed, *I will.*

"En, make sure she ends up somewhere safe?"

"Oh, I'll convince our dear captain to take her in. You know he can't help himself." En chuckled and took Silye by the shoulders, leading her into the ship. She looked back the entire way.

Caiden watched the *Second Wind* lift off, stir the sea, and ascend until it was another speck among the pinprick stars.

He headed into the *Azura* to grab his morphcoat off the pilot's seat. A starburst in the idle display pulsed to indicate a message. Threi's voice filled the cockpit: "Winn, they found a food that crosses the rind of Çydanza's universe. It's sort of like a furry slug. Revolting but salty. Thought you'd be happy to hear.

"The Cartographers are setting up regulations for Casthen operations. I have no end of jobs for a passager with the best starship in the multiverse.

One of those jobs might be to let me out." The smile was even in his voice, but weakly Graven-edged. "You did say we'd talk '*soon.*' It's been so many days, I'm wondering what 'soon' means to you, darling soldier. Come let me out, let's talk, and work together again. Or I put a bounty on you for killing Çydanza, and every passenger hunts you down through the multiverse... Whichever of the two sounds more fun to you. Oh, and Winn..."

The recording stretched into silence. Caiden reached up to shut it off.

His fingertip was an inch from the message symbol when Threi continued, "I salvaged more than just nophek off RM28."

The ring of light dissolved, message ended.

Caiden's hand hovered in the air. *More than just... What?*

The ship prompted a callback option, responding to his elevated heart rate.

"No, he's baiting me to contact him. That's all. I'm not ready to talk yet."

He still had the Graven and Dynast to investigate, both in Laythan's databases, the content he'd copied from Threi's private room, and in the paper book: *Graven Intention of Prima Luminiferia*, Volume One, Unabridged Edition.

Caiden shook his head and pulled on his morphcoat. As he ambled outside into a rapidly cooling breeze, the leather's lining expanded into a thin layer of wool.

Without a surf, the planet was nearly silent. Cliff rocks dripped. Crunchy rumbles floated from distant landslides. The nophek made nasal whines as it pawed in a circle in the sand. Caiden sat beside it and rested his elbows on his knees, facing the sunset. His brain, his many thoughts, for once were quiet too.

"Caiden is dead. I said that when I became a passager." He slid the leash bracelet off his wrist, deactivated it, and shoved it in a pocket. "I transformed that person. I'm going to name you 'C,' after the first letter of everything I hated."

He watched the crystalline ocean soak up darkness and stars. He breathed sweet air and looked into the nophek pup's big, moonlike eyes.

"You really are ugly."

The beast snuggled into the sand and rolled on its back. With serrated jaws, it gently mouthed his wrist as he scratched its belly.

CHAPTER 50

BAIT OUR HOOK WITH HEART

Ten years later...

Weaved into the incorporeal, collective field of consciousness—that Graven place between the clouds of space and the ocean of time— she distinctly felt someone's attention rivet on her. At first featherlight, her spirit grazed by a wingbeat, the sensation intensified from potential to reality and struck Leta so sharply, her mind was kicked from the remote body she inhabited.

Her awareness slithered off mechanical tendons, uprooted from organs, detangled from metallic exoskeleton. Leta grappled with the last sensations of her Proxy body slumping in place, inanimate. Her consciousness drained from it and whipped involuntarily back through the luminiferity, to re-condense within her real body suspended three corridors and five rooms away.

Her eyes snapped open. The scalar gravity field holding her hovering dissolved like shackles released. Leta toppled into her handlers' arms.

Consciousness glowed back through her nerves and flesh, and her first sense was *dismay*. Her natal body was becoming a stranger the more time she spent away from it: twenty years old, a full twelve inches shorter than the Proxy she had just been entangled inside, her skin two tones drained, riddled with void-white freckles, and weak as a web-caught moth. Years of training and treatment had altered her genetic blueprint to approximate the ancient Graven, to unlock access to the chaotic, etheric collective— luminiferity—that she and the others were still learning to navigate.

Her handlers eased her bare feet to a frigid floor. Bones as sensitive as glass chimed with fresh pains while silken flesh stretched uneasily. Her breath snagged in her lungs. Deeper dismay pushed aside her worry of *who* had drawn her back to this weak vessel and why.

The hushed, low-sensory Away room was home but not homey, and the wretched memories here were slowly, thankfully dissolving with the rest of her past, like the whiteness that was now her childhood, her life before the Dynast. She'd forgotten how she arrived, or even if she had simply *emerged* fully formed. Old fears crackled off Leta's spirit, and she swallowed a rusty dread.

"Leta Nine," a handler said, gentle as the sough of a wave, but the sound still avalanched in Leta's sensitive ears. "Move slow. Come back wholly. We are holding you." The familiar, melodic phrase was like a spell. Leta eased into their hands. She attempted to stuff down the dismay.

At least the sight of family still made her smile. The spiritual presence of Leta's fellow Graves hummed in the room as they levitated above quartz plates. They saw each other's real bodies rarely now that the training trials were over, survived by less than ten of them out of more than twenty. Their minds now were away on missions within their own Proxies: those receptors handcrafted by Abriss Cetre from the geometry of stars. The Graves were as lightning arcing through dimensions, their Proxies were the lightning rods calling them down, coalescing their expansion into one stable nest of neurons. In her real body, Leta buzzed and shivered like a poorly contained bolt.

She sighed out the ache. "Why am I back?" Her atrophied voice broke, an instrument corroded and out of tune. Her purpose was to drive other, better instruments.

The handler replied, "The Dynast Prime has requested your presence in the orrery."

The Prime. Awe blushed through her before the confusion struck. "I was just...near there..."

"*In person*," the handler said. "Not in-Proxy. Just you."

A rare summons...The primarily inorganic Proxies were immune to Abriss's genetic control. Leta's real body—with soft, fallible biology—was not. Which meant this summons was to deliver an order she would not be psychosomatically able to refuse.

Another phase of trials? More soul growing pains.

Leta hesitated, splayed her hands against the floor. There was an ache still, in each freckle, the ghost of every treatment round she'd survived. One decade had faded it all to phantom pains but her skin was left a landscape of galaxies, layers of splotches and freckles and spots, palest on top, from star-white to midnight.

"Mistress?"

"Help me up." Leta stood, wobbling, on the plate of her Away station. She pressed her soles into the cold, realigned her spine, sought gravity, banished reservations. She pried herself free from helpful hands into an ungainly gait, out into the hallway to leave—so rarely in this body—the Graves' wing. She'd been all over Unity while in-Proxy, dashing on missions: infiltration, espionage, security. Another self, separate from this skin.

One of the handlers threw an ankle-length coat around her shoulders. It swished over her morphsuit and dampened a bit of the air, the flavors, the music and temperature and seizures. Unlike in-Proxy, the sensory world butchered her with dissociation. She was as raw as a nerve out here, but if the Prime summoned, it was important.

The side hallway soared a hundred meters, as tall as it was long. The Dynast hold colonized the massive skeleton of a Graven structure. Their lightseep obsidian, which vibrated and sang in frequencies only Leta and the other Graves could hear, drove deep into the planet's core. Crystalline growths formed walls, ceiling, floor, like new muscle to pad out the bones of the ancients' long-dead palace.

Leta choked on the cloying perfume of a garden. Something itched her spine: a roar echoing from far-off plateaus. They were streaked with Dynast soldiers and fleets—a drop in the ocean of the immense forces the Prime controlled. Leta squinted—no shadow today on the sun—at light blaring across salt mountains and steam clouds where hot springs gushed, and while in-Proxy she would have shrugged, bored and untouched, these surroundings were all manner of abrasive and disorienting now. Her mental map of her body rushed to *become* the flow of the springs, leaping into the sound of it, expanding as part of that distant, raging water, and as she started to lose sense of her flesh entirely, consciousness wanting to *run*, she darted to the Dynast Prime's orrery-room door and braced herself.

Under the pressure of her palm, a section of the dissolve door vibrated in phase and opened a crack.

"Enter," said the beautifully dulcet voice of Dynast Prime Abriss Cetre. Her very genetics encoded a loving demand in anything she said—to which everything obeyed.

Leta's heart swelled with response, lifting her frail bones with a tender trinity of energy, fealty, and impulse. Though her genetic conditioning had made her more like the Graven of old, she had no loving effect on others— that was inborn, not acquired, and Leta didn't know how or where she'd been born. Those years were erased by the glossy radiation of the treatments. But Abriss loved her and all the Graves, had the best ideals in mind for all of Unity, and Leta was overjoyed to obey.

She pushed through the doorway, drifted into the nonagonal orrery room, and balked at the sheer amount of input. The Prime stood on a central dais, in the heart of a perfect sphere map of Unity hovering in translucent lavender arcs nine meters tall. It outlined galaxies rife with stars and planets, conjoined by lines of relationship and necklaces of number. Zoomed sections filled the periphery. Statistics, orbits, and astrological glyphs flowed like cosmic winds around the diagram, which only Abriss could decipher. A master astrologian, she wielded unparalleled powers in Unity, able to divine information and glimpse past and future states through celestial motions.

In the middle of that web, like a slender spider, Abriss turned. "Leta. Come here." She spoke in monotone, delicately enunciated. The syllables whisked shivers across Leta's skin. Her cells aligned to Abriss's gravity and she was tugged to the dais, through nebulae salted with data. The attraction was gentle, and the closer she approached, smelling petrichor and sage, the more relaxation threaded her tendons and joints, eased her nervousness, and blossomed an awed smile on her lips.

I would die happy for her.

Abriss had poise in place of charisma, serenity more than beauty, and an austerity sharp with energy, her movements as intentional as her speech. A leader who feared nothing, ever.

"Do not be scared," the Prime said, though surely she knew fear could not exist near her.

"How do I serve?" Leta asked.

Abriss's gaze saccaded across the luminous orrery. Freckles stardusted all her tawny skin in both paler and darker spots, a mirror of the star-peppered air. "My stars have told me that a sudden message will arrive regarding family, and if the youngest of my Graves is with me, that message will ripple into something…" In one of the fields, she cupped a little sun in her palm. "Extraordinary."

Family. Abriss was the last of the Dynast family alive, as far as Leta knew. And Leta's family were the Graves, seven corridors and three rooms away.

Abriss gripped the brunette braid slung over her shoulder. Gaze fixed on orbits stationing conjunct, she muttered, "One moment. A trine forming exact. Ipsa's return on our natal—" Her eyes widened as she cut off. "*I know who will call.*"

At that moment, the call came in. A terminal pedestal flooded with symbols. Abriss stared at it for a heartbeat, beautiful in her rare startlement, pillowy lips parted and smoky eyes bright as amber. "Allow," she said.

The comm system linked.

Part of the orrery sizzled away, replaced with the projection of a man's life-size silhouette, vague behind the milky surface of a universe's rind.

On reflex, Leta's senses fuzzed and her mind sought him out across the luminiferous collective, which had no distance or time. Her expanded senses encompassed Unity, but couldn't seek past Unity's rind. Only tiny bits of knowledge made it through from beyond, sparkling in her brain. The man's universe was a prison, and he was Abriss's—

"Brother," the Prime said. "We haven't spoken in over five million arc-minutes. Since Emporia."

"Forgive me, sister, I've been…detained by matters." The man stepped closer to his prison's rind. Its iridescence billowed aside, exposing his crooked smile.

Familiarity sparked. Leta's brow creased. She *knew* this silhouette from long ago, the memory frayed at all its edges. She had been in darkness and he had reached a hand down from the light. *How did you survive, little thing?* his same voice had said.

"No doubt," he continued, "you have pawns to boss around and astronomy to read, so I won't waste our time."

"Patience was not ever your strongest trait, Threi."

Even without the literal glitter of stars all around, the air sizzled between these two like a live wire, a volatile magnetism even more primal than Leta's Graven fealty to Abriss. This was more aversion than love, which itched against Leta the wrong way, spurring her instinct to protect. She'd served in-Proxy as Abriss's guard on many missions, but her real body was no fighter, and felt even more raw and tiny in the presence of these Dynast heirs. Two truly cosmic human forces were conversing in this moment. A mere slip of insignificant shadow, Leta shrank behind the Prime to the dais end.

"A man named Winn has been forced into Unity and will be hiding somewhere in your vast, incomparable, resplendent realm, dear Prime." Haughty, sarcastic words, like syrup.

Abriss cocked her head. "Winn..." She pecked a finger at the terminal and more of the orrery sizzled into holosplays: footage of a memory jog recording, an attack in Emporia, the Casthen's blood-red emblem. "I remember. He was the... Graven Paraborn." A flavor of disgust clogged her words. "But all this occurred ten years ago. Why do you care of him?"

The holos settled on an image of the man and a block of text that was meant to chart his whereabouts over time. Instead, it tracked a ghost: wisps of velocity in the multiverse, a legend, a glass star shooting too fast to catch.

Leta's gaze locked on the picture of the man, around her current age at the time it was taken a decade ago, when he'd dismantled the Casthen's leadership. She had seen the image back then, too, and recognized him at the time... hadn't she? The memory was threadbare, fuzzed up by the abrasion of years. She'd been young, just beginning to be scrubbed blank by the Graves' treatments, the glossy starlight injections like a bleach on her spirit.

Leta grew lightheaded, her consciousness unraveling at the edges, some of it trying to travel, some burrowing into her own history as she grazed the edges of a feeling, the sharp consonants of a name, a scent..."*Caiden.*"

The sound came out a whisper, barely enough to tickle Abriss's ear and start to shift the woman's head, but Threi talked over her—

"He's evaded me for all this time. There's a bounty on his head higher than a pile of gloss, but—" Threi paused for a dramatic, conspiratorial smile. "It's proven exceedingly difficult to catch a ship that has Graven technology never seen before. Technology that can create and collapse a new universe at will."

His grin widened as Abriss gaped. She blinked at him before dashing her gaze back over the orrery, her lightning-quick mind gathering starlight and angles into knowledge that might confirm or deny her brother's wild claim. In the end, she inhaled, lifted her chin, and squared her shoulders back at his projection, but Leta could make out the quiver infesting her shoulders.

What could Abriss Cetre—the most powerful creature in Unity—do with this new technology that could make even her tremble at the thought?

Dread stitched down Leta's spine. She peered back at the image of the man with two names. Rage fired his blue eyes, short hair tousled like a pale storm, freckles dusting nose and cheekbones—was he family of theirs?

The threadbare memory re-knit some more. She'd been ten years old and he should have been fourteen but wasn't. *Why?* she'd asked. The handlers said her memory must have been damaged, or a loose resemblance, and it was no matter: time was corporeal, and her training would bring her closer to the empyreal. Her past could safely be forgotten in the wake of such a bright, bright future.

Was this recollection loosely connected, like two of Abriss's planets forming angles to each other for a brief heartbeat of orbits? Distant lights believing, for a flicker, that they were related?

Threi Cetre drawled on, "I've piqued your illustrious interest, sister. May I suggest we make a deal?"

"Fair deals are, again, not one of your strongest traits." Serenity paved over Abriss's surprise. She glanced at Leta behind her.

Happy shivers almost melted Leta's knees. Abriss's attention cut bladely, spilling awe like lifeblood.

"Why did you not contact me sooner, if this is real and so critical to you?" Abriss asked.

"You wouldn't have believed me about the ship's Graven tech until you could confirm it with your darling stars. And you wouldn't help unless he was in Unity. It's taken me a decade to force the boy there, but finally catching him will be easy now that he's in your universe, within the spider Abriss's great web." Threi's pauses were filled with smiles. "Give my fleet unrestricted access to Unity. Assist in Winn's capture, with all your Dynast immanence and astrologian precognizance determining his location and intention. I'll use the Graven ship to release myself from this universe I'm stranded in, and you can pry apart the ship's shell and suck the crystal innards or whatever you wish for your Graven research."

Silence leadened the room as Abriss considered. The astral terrain shifted around them. She observed it, but her brow twitched—there was something she couldn't read about this situation. In the end, she donned a combative smile and said, "If this Graven ship is in Unity, I am free to acquire it myself. Why should I buy your assistance?"

"Because he won't be there long, and your beloved Unity is too vast, and you know too little about him. The reason it took me a decade to force him there is because he's sharp and he knows you can find him. But if I share everything I know about Winn's natal details, your astrology will be just as razor-sharp. I can give you the exact Paraborn brood, the astrocartography, the universe where he grew and his little egg hatched. All of it."

Abriss considered again, amber eyes sparkling with reflections. Patient, she tended to silence as strongly as her sibling loved to speak. When the wordless space grew unbearable, he filled it: "Besides," he said, with a slight quaver. "You miss me. I can tell."

"You think very highly of yourself."

"How *long* has it been since you were in the presence of someone who didn't automatically adore you?"

Abriss scowled. "I might ask the same of you. Power always did go straight to your head. You still have no—" She twisted fiercely, fixating on one planet. New lines sprang up and converged, reflecting periwinkle in Abriss's glassy stare.

Whatever cosmic shift she was entranced by was palpable to Leta's enhanced spiritual senses as well: a roar in the luminiferity, gaining force. The periwinkle planet glided closer to a line that aspected at a harsh angle. The Prime's lips parted and her gaze darted to a star on the opposite end of Unity's sphere. A ring of numbers filled with nines.

Abriss cocked her head, smiled a little, and whispered, "I agree to your deal."

For the first time, her brother looked troubled. "You do miss me."

The rising, vibrating curl of empyreal power that Leta felt finally broke over her in a wave. Her awareness mushed between the vast dark of time and the orrery and snatches of the present like glitters on a brackish pool. Her sensory world roiled. Whispers of a childhood scent, a field. Leta clutched her skull as the intensity blotted her brain. Then Threi's voice—"Well. Splendid. This is all of him, for your predictions..."

Promised data beamed in and inhabited the air: Caiden's birth details, brood and shipment, destination planet... pictures, a landscape Leta recognized as... home?

Footage.

Pastures as vast as a sea. Holes of fire punched in a faraway sky. Black cubes. Stench. Death. Teeth and teeth and teeth.

Then not footage but *memories*—blushes of color and fragrance and touch—filling up the white spaces in her soul that her training had scrubbed clean.

Rough, grandfatherly oak trees, spicing the hot air, shading her face as the tall grass swayed with a *shush*. Blue chicory bobbed among greens. Caiden lay beside her and time had stopped. Marred in grease from the work, sweat from their run, fatigue from helping her climb to the highest limbs, he was falling asleep. Breathing soft. Blond locks falling over his eyes.

Leta blinked hard back to the orrery. Her lips shaped his name. She smelled green earthiness, rich chicory, alfalfa, musk, and metal. Things were still happening in the room, gauzy and time-lagged.

She fought the urge to let her consciousness dissimulate and wriggle out of her body into the luminiferity, to seek out Caiden's soul in empyrean dimensions where no multiversal distance could separate them. He was alive. *Caiden.* Her pulse unwound to a stop, she tried to breathe—and was slammed back to her body and the present moment by Threi hissing, "*I recognize her.*"

Abriss swiveled around to face Leta.

"And you, sister, arrange nothing without a reason, so she's here for a reason and I know what it is."

"Tell me." Abriss motioned a freckled hand to Leta. "Come closer."

Leta obeyed immediately, her feet tripping, body vibrating with energized confusion. Joyously, she obeyed.

Threi said, "Your Graves project has transformed her, but I recognize the girl at this age. I've seen her in Winn's memories. She's important to him, a keystone in his heart and mind."

Important to him. Her own heart lurched at that. Crisp memories with sharp edges jammed up through her love of Abriss.

"Darling sister"—this, a snarl—"I think you have both hook and bait for our dear Graven boy."

A dark chord in Leta strummed viciously. Neither of these powerful individuals had good intentions for Caiden.

Her family. Her childhood hero.

Then Abriss turned to her.

With Graven charm.

"Leta Nine…"

The edges of her resistance melted in the warmth of Abriss's magnetism. Among all the orrery's luminous forms, the stars, the concatenations and planets and swirls, Unity still moved with Abriss, its heart.

"Reseat in your Proxy and prepare a solo ship."

The storm in Leta's body polarized into obeisance, relaxed into a unified chord, the deep genetic love of this Dynast Prime. Adoration lifted her from a sinking sense of something *wrong*: a flicker of feeling spread thin by the blunt, heavy blade of time.

Leta replied, "At once, Prime."

Look out for

AZURA GHOST

by

Essa Hansen

Caiden "Winn" has been on the run for a decade, deserting family to keep the Azura out of enemy hands. His pursuers finally craft the perfect trap: a new bounty hunter possesses the memories of Caiden's dead childhood friend Leta, whom he'd abandoned to slaughter after promising he'd return. This hunter claims to be that same girl, her real body captive on the Dynast faction's homeworld.

Even if she's an impostor infused with memories to lure him, Caiden can't forget his shattered promise. If there's any chance it's really Leta, he must atone. If it's not, he'll deliver retribution on whoever would violate her memory. But in order to have a fighting chance against the Dynast's Graven descendants—the most powerful pair in the multiverse—he'll need to confront his own genetic origin and uncover the Azura's true form.

www.orbitbooks.net

GLOSSARY

Abriss Cetre—The Prime of the Dynast faction of Unity. She is a direct descendant on the Dynast family line, able to claim the highest rank of Graven genetics in any current living being. By her genetic nature, her presence inspires love and loyalty in all individuals and gives her immense control over her subjects in Unity. She is a master astrologian, able to read the motion of celestial bodies and divine information about events, individuals, and the past and future. Abriss maintains peace in Unity and pursues research into the Graven civilization. She believes that the Graven aimed to correct the erroneous multiplicity of the multiverse, uniting it back into central Unity to make space and time one continuum.

acceleration—Expensive and energy-intensive technology that can enhance an individual's age by a specified time duration while also programming the brain and body with skills and knowledge. The process takes mere moments regardless of the amount of time the individual is accelerating. Acceleration can be paired with desenescence—reverse-aging—to invest an individual with abilities without affecting physical life span. Not all species are able to undergo acceleration.

Andalvian—A humanoid species whose chromatophoric skin cells act like colored pixels, reflecting their brain activity in changing patterns and colors. Andalvian emotions are expressed involuntarily on their skin, but their culture is stoic and dispassionate, valuing composure. They are sharply intelligent, straightforward, and honest, most often involved in the sciences. Their native language is rich with multiple meanings and contextual nuance, able to condense multiple phrases into one.

atmoseal—A thin membrane of energy and particulates that acts in the place of an airlock, sealing in pressure and gases without the need for physical doors. The atmoseal stretches over the opening of a passageway or ship aperture.

Cartographer—The Cartographers are a long-standing and diversely membered organization dedicated to mapping the expanding multiverse, understanding its content through study, and making it safe for travelers. They facilitate first contact with newfound cultures and organize ambassadorial trips to invite isolated worlds into the wider multiversal culture. They maintain a free, public database of information, and charge for specific chartings, while paying passagers for data on newly charted territory. Their resource and service hubs—Cartographer Dens—are scattered throughout the multiverse. Cartographers believe there is a holistic purpose behind the multiverse, and that basic knowledge must remain free and new worlds integrated into a sum whole of understanding. The Cartographers' efforts in cultural exchange, education, and mediation has prevented or alleviated galactic wars throughout centuries.

Cartographer Den—Resource hubs on space stations or planets, scattered throughout the multiverse. There is at least one Den per universe of habitable size, located near a stellar egress when possible. They provide Cartographer services, including sales and purchases, medical, and mechanics. Neutral ground is strictly enforced in the "bar" section of every Den. Within Unity, the only Cartographer Den is located in Emporia.

Casthen—A private organization that has been monopolizing economy, trade, and mercenary services for centuries. They are governed by a Prime. Their ranks are populated primarily by hybrids from interbreeding and genetic engineering projects, focused on generating adherents adept at their roles or resistant to multiversal variances. It is rumored that the Dynast—who does not interact with the multiverse outside of

Unity—contracts the Casthen to procure goods. The location of their headquarters, the Casthen Harvest, is a closely guarded secret.

chketin—A humanoid species common in the multiverse. Though muscular, powerful, and never shorter than two meters tall, they are a shrewd and intelligent species integrated deeply into Cartographer function. Chketin are slow to deliberate but stubborn in their final stance, leading others to nickname them "walls."

clarient—Ethereal beings that parasitize physical systems. They are sometimes captured in machines and enslaved for computing. One theory suggests that they parasitize the brains of young nophek and are responsible for the gradual crystallization of gloss.

cloudsuit—A body harness netting that emits a membrane across the user's body, like a second skin. The membrane's material puffs apart into a vaporous field of protective particles that regulate personal atmosphere and protect from external factors. It allows for complete freedom of movement and condenses back against the body under extreme pressure but does not provide armoring. There are variations of this style of suit for use underwater.

crossover—The process of crossing through a rind from one universe to another. As physical and etheric parameters may shift between universes, crossover involves the individual's adjustment to existential changes on the other side. Depending on the unique nature of the rind, crossover may harm or destroy certain species or transform others.

CWN82—A medium-size universe that was falsely reported to be unstable for crossover. These reports propagated by the Casthen faction allowed them to keep the universe exclusive to their use and away from scrutiny. Upon planets within this universe, Casthen organized the cultivation of nophek and feed production.

Çydanza—The Casthen Prime, who has been in office for the recorded centuries that the Casthen have existed. It is unclear whether Çydanza founded the Casthen or merely assumed control. Despite general opposition against the Casthen's morally questionable scope of operations, Çydanza has never been accessed or assassinated, nor has she perished, leading to various rumors about her physical nature, or whether

"Çydanza" is more of a title than an individual. Though she makes broadcasts verbally, her appearance has never been recorded.

Dynast—The governing endarchy of Unity. The Dynast are dedicated to the harmonious functioning of all planetary systems within Unity, and the search for knowledge about the ancient Graven species. The Dynast's centralized government is led by an assembly under control of an appointed Prime descended from the Dynast family. The Dynast believes that the fall of the Graven civilization happened at the same time that Unity was divided into the new, expanding worlds of the multiverse, and that these outer worlds are corrupt and unsuitable to touch.

Emporia—A large space station of colonized lightseep obsidian that is a hub for various factions in Unity. It is said that anything can be bought, sold, or sourced in Emporia. The station is located close to the border of Unity.

Glasliq—A rare type of starship, one of which belongs to Threi, a Casthen Enforcer. Its hull is constructed of a morphic liquid glass material adhered to an adjustable metallic frame, making it supremely agile and resilient against universal conditions. The outer material can change phase between a solid, liquid, or gaseous state depending on conditions.

glave—General term for a personally equipped defensive or offensive weapon. Glave technology varies in type and effect, and is sourced from a variety of cultures.

gloss—The most valuable substance in the multiverse, gloss is an extremely rare energetic material, developed inside the maturing brains of nophek creatures. It can take both solid and liquid form, and is utilized to power Graven technology and generate starship fuel. Some believe that gloss is produced when clarient parasitize the brains of nophek and crystallize the pineal gland and surrounding tissues.

Graven—An ancient civilization about which much is still unknown. In the distant past, an extinction event wiped out most traces of the Graven, leaving behind ruins and technology all over the multiverse. There are various theories as to whether the Graven participated in or even created the multiverse, or if they were wiped out in the same event that divided Unity into expanding daughter universes. Pure Graven genetics remain in the human descendants of the Dynast family, but their true biological form is undocumented. Graven genetics create a biological resonance that coerces loyalty from other beings. The effect intensifies by proximity and sensory exposure, and affects some species more fully than others.

Graves—A project in the Dynast's Graven research that seeks to approximate the Graven species's consciousness and sensory extension by conditioning a group of individuals through a complex biological process of radiation and gene transfection. The goal for the surviving individuals—the Graves—is to consciously access the luminiferity, a spiritual domain of collective consciousness freed from space and time, where information and shared consciousness is available non-locally. The Dynast hopes that this new information domain will give them fresh insight into who and what the Graven were.

holosplay—A detailed holographic display. Light organizes along a three-dimensional gridded field of tensor points in the air.

lightseep obsidian—The physical condensation of energy structures previously existing in spiritual, immaterial dimensions un-phased with physical reality. After the fall of the Graven civilization, the vibration of their lightseep slowed and materialized into visible matter, appearing crystalline and transparent. Lightseep is impossible to move, break, or tool, but many of the lightseep ruins throughout the multiverse have been colonized and repurposed using other materials inside.

luminiferity—The etheric, collective field of consciousness that exists outside linear spacetime. It is believed that individual consciousnesses are condensations of this field, and after death the consciousness re-expands into the luminiferity. The Dynast has been studying how to access the accumulated knowledge and experience inhabiting the luminiferity.

mauya—A delicate, semi-humanoid species accustomed to low gravity. Mauya are highly intuitive, and physically remarkable for their fleshy wings and long, crystalline hair.

memory jog—A process that stimulates the subject's memory and records brain activity, which is then reconstituted into a visual recording of events. The process does not work for all species, and some experience debilitating side effects.

morphcoat—A jacket made of a morphic material that changes qualities in response to mental state or mood. Useful when traversing frequently between environments and temperatures.

multiverse—The whole conglomerate of variously sized bubble-shaped universes embedded within one another or stuck together like a foam. Their surfaces are "rinds" of energy that separate the differences in physics and other features between universe interiors. At an unknown point in history, smaller universes began to bubble off the outer border of Unity, the original singular universe and now the center of the inflating multiverse. On the fringes of the multiverse, new universes are constantly developing and expanding.

nophek—A rare quadruped mammal species from an unknown native planet. Their biology can only exist in specific universal parameters without medical intervention. Nophek are vicious and intelligent carnivorous pack animals. Reddish black in color, their muscular bodies range from one to two meters tall at the withers. They are covered in a mix of fur, mane, and rough skin. As a nophek matures, highly valuable gloss crystallizes within a gland in its brain.

passager—A free individual registered with the Cartographers as a multiversal explorer, bound to a code of rights and allowed access to Cartographer services.

Prime—The singular leader of a sufficiently large organization. Within the Dynast, Prime status is hereditary.

Proxy—One of the hybrid organic-inorganic mechanical bodies designed by Abriss Cetre specifically for each of the Graves. The Proxies remotely contain and are driven by the Graves' consciousnesses, allowing their real bodies to remain safe within the Dynast hold.

rind—An interstitial space between universes, like an energy membrane, dividing universes from one another. Rinds can be passed through without resistance, but not all physiologies or technology can cross over without damage. The alterations in physics that rinds impress on objects passing through are individual to each rind.

RM28—A mostly desert planet with the right environmental conditions to sustain nophek. The Casthen established nophek packs here, and sustained them with periodic feed shipments.

saavee—Roughly humanoid in shape, but with unusual skull structure and facial features. Saavee are common across the multiverse and take up a variety of jobs, especially prevalent in mechanical technology disciplines. From a curious and gregarious culture, they are generally considered friendly and helpful to all species.

saisn—Tall, lean humanoid xenids known for their fine muscular control and sensitive nervous systems. All saisn develop a specialized sensory organ in the brain that is visible as a transparent, faceted core in their forehead. They are immersed in a "sense-sea"—a broad frequency range of sensory detail. Saisn culture is philosophical and refined, politically complex, and quite secretive to outsiders. Within the Cartographers, saisn often serve on the culture council and as ambassadors to newly discovered worlds and first-contact missions.

scalar gravity—Artificial gravity generated in a patterned matrix of nodes and antinodes within a short range. These scalar gravity fields pattern force in space to levitate objects or to anchor them against a surface such as a floor. This gravity system is used for starships and stations, and on a small scale for maneuvering objects or creating force fields.

scour—A tubular chamber of adjustable size that can cleanse and restore xenids of all biological type. It cleans skin and clothing, heals minor wounds, kills parasites, and eliminates internal waste. Scour technology is common throughout the multiverse.

stellar egress—Instantaneous spacetime shortcuts from one specific location in the multiverse to another specific location. All egresses are both entrance and exit points. They not only cut down on travel time but allow entrance into universes while bypassing the need to cross through their rind. This can open up exploration in universes otherwise too dangerous to cross over into. Egresses are remnant Graven technology.

tal—With vaguely humanoid skeletal structure, these xenids have morphic flesh, a ruffled, smokelike solid matter that flows between shapes: solid and limblike, or fanned out like broad cloth. Tal are fairly uncommon in the multiverse.

twitch drive—A ship flight-control system that uses the pilot's muscular control, rather than conventional neural control. It is considered more reliable and comprehensive. Twitch drives usually consist of two or more pliable panels to encase fingers or comparable appendages, but may also involve—via the seat—the full musculoskeletal system of the body. The theory behind this flight method emerged from the technical riding of creatures, where the flow of energy and pressure links the two neural and musculoskeletal systems together in a feedback circuit.

Unity—Once the sole universe, Unity is the largest and central world of the multiverse. It is slowly inflating and absorbing planets and other celestial bodies at its expanding border. The Dynast faction governs Unity, and has immigration programs for affected border planets. The physical and metaphysical laws within Unity are so well understood, nearly all disease and ailment is preventable, life spans can be lengthened, education is free, one language is standard, technology has perfected resource generation and waste management, and citizens understand how to align with reality to manifest their desires and needs. For many, Unity is considered the paragon of safety and comfort.

vishkant—Rare, mostly incorporeal xenids with vaporous bodies that congeal into solid form in response to an observer's consciousness—thoughts or memories—and assume the form of a familiar person. The vishkant's appearance and solidity is partially real and partially observer hallucination elicited by pheromone. When the impression of external consciousness is removed, the vishkant's molecules return to a neutral, vaporous state. Older vishkant can maintain a form of their choosing and resist exterior influence. Due to their shapeshifting ability, vishkant are often employed in espionage as manipulators, or in pleasure trades as manipulated.

whipkin—A short-furred, egg-laying mammal around one-half meter long from nose to tail. They are omnivores adapted to a saline woodland environment, with long-fingered paws for climbing, and patagia between forelimbs and hind limbs for gliding and swimming. They are extremely intelligent, but shy and reclusive in the wild.

xenid—Generic term for an individual of an alien species, usually applied to nonhumans.

ACKNOWLEDGMENTS

Huge gratitude to my agent, Naomi Davis, who grasped the heart of this book immediately and helped me run with it. Thank you for your keen editorial eye, unwavering support, and showers of digital glitter. Much love to the BookEnds Literary Agency for all their encouragement.

My deepest thanks to Brit Hvide for being this story's steadfast champion and for her powerful edits; the book has transformed in ways I couldn't imagine, and I leveled up immensely in the process.

Thank you Bryn A. McDonald for ushering this book so smoothly, along with production coordinator Xian Lee, and my copy editor, Rachelle Mandik, for such detailed polish and for getting my eye on even more ways I can improve. Angeline Rodriguez, for being so thorough and patient with my newbie author questions. Thanks to my proofreaders, Amy Schneider and Janine Barlow for their eagle eyes. The amazing and dedicated team at Orbit has made me feel so warmly welcomed—Francesca Begos, Paola Crespo, Laura Fitzgerald, Angela Man, and the many people behind the scenes who I have yet to meet! And immense thanks to Anna Jackson for acquiring this book for the UK!

It is incredible to see the *Azura* rendered so beautifully by Mike Heath on this sleek dark cover by Lauren Panepinto—I can't thank you both and the Orbit cover coven enough.

The interior design and typesetting team Six Red Marbles & Jouve India have done magic—when I saw my words laid out, the reality finally struck me that this was going to be a real book I could hold in my hands one day.

I am indebted to all my very first readers who trudged through the early drafts, for their sensitivity, fresh eyes, and craft expertise—and special thanks to my Alliance crew for the laughter, commiseration, and brainstorming that kept me afloat these past couple of years. My growth is all due to your encouragement: Alia Hess, Cassie Greutman, Darby Harn, Jennifer Lane, Nick Lilic, Shelly Campbell, and Sunyi Dean, who hauled me to dry land in those early days and helped me weather a lot of "soon."

Finally, a warm thank-you to Philip Athans for giving me the first big push out the door on this publishing journey. I think I'd be somewhere else without it.

extras

www.orbitbooks.net

about the author

Essa Hansen is an author, swordswoman, and falconer. She is a sound designer for science fiction and fantasy films at Skywalker Sound, with credits in movies such as *Doctor Strange* and *Avengers: Endgame*.

Find out more about Essa Hansen and other Orbit authors by registering for the free monthly newsletter at www.orbitbooks.net.

if you enjoyed
NOPHEK GLOSS

look out for

CHILLING EFFECT

by

Valerie Valdes

Captain Eva Innocente and the crew of La Sirena Negra *cruise the galaxy delivering small cargo for even smaller profits. When her sister is kidnapped, Eva must undergo a series of dangerous missions to pay the ransom. But Eva may lose her mind before she can raise the money. The ship's hold is full of psychic cats, an amorous fish-faced emperor wants her dead, and her engineer is giving her a pesky case of feelings. The worse things get, the more she lies, raising suspicions and testing her loyalty to her found family.*

To free her sister, Eva will risk everything: her crew, her ship, and the life she's built on the ashes of her past misdeeds. But when the dominoes start to fall and she finds the real threat is greater than she imagined, she must decide whether to play it cool or burn it all down.

Chapter 1

SAVE THE CATS

Captain Eva Innocente crept down the central corridor of *La Sirena Negra,* straining to hear the soft rumble of her quarry over the whine of the FTL drive and the creak of space-cold metal.

((Getting warmer,)) Min pinged over her commlink.

Min would know, since the ship was essentially her second body when she was connected to the piloting interface. But the critter Eva was tracking wouldn't stop moving. It had gone from the cargo bay down below, up through the mess, and was now somewhere between the crew quarters and the head. If it got to the bridge—

((Warmer.))

A hiss of steam sprayed Eva's hair. Startled, she nearly dropped the vented box she carried onto her foot, juggling it awkwardly before settling it against her hip. She resumed her barefoot tiptoeing with a scowl. Vakar would have to fix that leak later, once the more immediate problem was taken care of.

((Red hot!))

Eva crouched, held her breath, and listened. At last, in a gap between two panels, she heard it.

A lone kitten, purring.

Eva reached in, grabbed it by the scruff of its neck, and dropped it into the box.

((Got it,)) she pinged back at Min. Eighteen down, two to go. Her arms were covered in scratches and her black hair was a mass of tangles from being woken up in a hurry, but on the plus side, she'd gotten pretty good at catching the little mojones.

On the minus side, they were only a few hours from their drop point on Letis, and she wouldn't get paid unless she delivered the full cargo.

The kitten mewled, and Eva lifted the box to glare at it. "Don't start with me," she said. "This is the third time you've escaped and I'm ready to throw you all out the airlock."

Green eyes stared her down, the slitted pupils dilating to black discs.

"And stop trying to hypnotize me," Eva muttered. "It's rude." Fucking psychic cats.

The cat yowled in reply.

Eva carried the box down to the cargo hold. The tall ceiling allowed for multiple stacked containers, with catwalks near the top that had earned their name repeatedly over the past cycle. Metal plates were bolted onto the ship's frame, some hinged to allow access to the guts underneath, with no exposed pipes or wires to break the monotony. A blocky passenger cabin sat in the corner, for the occasions when someone hired them for transportation instead of delivery. Mostly it transported broken parts Eva hadn't bothered to sell or scrap.

Leroy stood in the middle of the room, sweat beading on his upper lip, his curly red hair sticking up at odd angles like it had been licked into place. Since she'd found him on the floor covered in cats earlier, that was to be expected.

Eva was almost a half meter shorter than him, and each of his pale, tattooed arms was thick as a steel beam, but he stiffened into the straight-backed pose of a soldier about to get chewed out as she came closer.

"I'm sorry," he said.

"I heard you the last ten times. Relax."

His shoulders hunched. "I thought maybe, just one, for a minute—"

"I know, Leroy. They're hypnotic." And you're prone to suggestion, she added silently. One of many unfortunate side effects of his years as a meat-puppet soldier, being thrown into whatever corporate war needed warm bodies instead of tactical nukes, controlled remotely by people with an eye in the sky and no skin in the game. Other side effects being anxiety, nightmares, and the kind of sudden, extremely violent outbursts that turned an asset into a liability.

Eva knew how those nightmares felt. She was also good at turning liabilities into assets, and Leroy was no exception. He'd been responsible for managing supply chains and tracking inventory when he was deployed, so handling smaller, less-frequent cargo logistics came easily to him.

She dropped the cat into the spacious, climate-controlled shipping container from whence it had escaped. It had food, water, self-cleaning litter boxes, toys, tiny hammocks, raised platforms on which to run or recline—anything a cat could want, or so the person who designed it had thought.

Apparently, what a cat really wanted was freedom.

Eighteen balls of fur sat, or splayed out, or licked their butts, most of them studiously ignoring Eva and Leroy. A few glanced up and blinked languidly, as if they had not been slinking around the ship getting into trouble only minutes earlier.

This was what she got for taking on live cargo. If she weren't doing this for her former captain Tito, and if he weren't paying better than their last four jobs combined . . . That smiling comemierda hadn't told her the critters were genetically engineered mind-controlling geniuses. It was exactly the kind of casual not-quite-lie that had made her quit his crew seven years earlier, over her father's objections. Given that her father preferred whole-ass lies, and given that he was Tito's boss back then, his opinion had mattered as much as a fart in a hurricane.

Fuck 'em both, she thought, not for the first time.

"Found another one trying to get into a supply cabinet in my med bay." Pink sauntered in holding a kitten to her chest, rubbing its face absently with one dark finger. Her dreads were tucked under a sleep cap, and her eye patch was flipped down to cover her cybernetic eye, while her organic one took in Eva's scruffy condition with a raised brow. "You're looking splendid," she said.

Eva examined her welt-striped arms. "I look like I wrestled a needle-bear."

"Are those real?" Leroy asked.

"No," Pink said.

"Says the lady who hasn't wrestled one," Eva retorted.

Pink rolled her eyes. "I'll clean you up and synthesize you some allergy medicine when I'm done making my hormones. How many cats left?"

"Just one." Leroy paused for dramatic effect. "The leader."

"Cats don't have leaders, honey," Pink said.

"Tell that to . . . the leader."

Pink may have been right, but Eva knew who Leroy meant.

The one who kept busting everyone out was the smallest cat, a calico with mottled brown and black fur with patches of orange, and hazel eyes that looked like they had seen some shit. They probably had. She didn't know what it took to make the kittens more intelligent, but she doubted it was nice.

"Viva la revolución," Eva said. "But not on my ship. Min, can you pinpoint its location?"

No response.

"Min? Can you hear me?" The silence grabbed her stomach and slid it up to her throat.

((Bridge, help,)) her commlink pinged, the limitations of the mind-to-mind communication feature more frustrating than usual at the moment. It was Vakar, who for some reason made the cats nervous. Maybe it was the quennian's pangolin-like skin, or his twitchy face-palp things, or the fact that his smell changed to match his mood. These particular psychic cats probably weren't designed to work with nonhuman people.

"Me cago en la hora que yo nací," she muttered. If the cat had gotten into the bridge, there might be more trouble than lost wages. "Leroy, stay here. Pink, with me."

Pink shook her head. "I'm not leaving Leroy alone with these babies when we're so close to docking." She punctuated this by placing her kitten in the container and closing the lid firmly, then standing next to Leroy, hand on hip.

"Fine. I'm sure Vakar and I can handle one damn cat." Eva stalked out of the cargo bay, back up past the mess and crew quarters and head, past her cabin and the med bay, all the way up to the short hallway that led to the bridge. Min's neural implants—originally meant for controlling repair mechs on her family's solar farm, later used for the bot fights that had earned Min her reputation—let her control and monitor *La Sirena Negra* from anywhere on the ship, but the pilot still preferred to be near the physical controls. Eva had told Min to ping her if a cat made it inside, and she had assumed the comm silence meant good news.

She should have known better.

Vakar waited outside the door, smelling like tar. Nervous, Eva's scent translators supplied. He had taken off the gloves he normally wore and was trying to dig his four-fingered claws underneath the handle of the emergency door release.

"You know your hands are too big," Eva whispered. "What's the situation?"

"I tried to reason with the cat," he whispered back. "It ran in and the door locked. I managed to bypass the security protocol, but the manual override engaged. I must say, for creatures without prehensile extremities, these cats are remarkably—"

"Later." She gripped the handle and tugged it out, then twisted it clockwise to disengage the dead bolts. Each unlocking pin made a loud grinding sound as it moved.

"When was the last time you lubricated this?" Eva snapped.

"I would have to check my maintenance logs, but I have been rationing lubricant and this was lower priority than other items."

Eva suppressed a joke. Vakar was always so sensible, and it wasn't his fault she'd been denying his requisitions.

"On three, you open the door and I bust in," she whispered. "Ready?"

He shrugged assent.

She moved aside and drew her pistol, loaded with tranq rounds for the occasion. Hopefully she wouldn't need them. Hopefully they weren't strong enough to kill a cat. Hopefully she wouldn't miss and hit something that would blow up the ship.

Hope in one hand and shit in the other, and see which gets full first, she thought. She leaned against the bulkhead next to the door and pinged the countdown silently at Vakar.

On three, he slid the door open and she leaped in, scanning the room with her pistol leading.

Min lay in the pilot's chair, black eyes open, short dyed-blue hair in disarray. Because she was connected to the ship's systems wirelessly, she didn't have to look at the instrument panel in front of her, so her chair was reclined as far back as the small bridge allowed. Where some ships had holographic controls, *La Sirena Negra* was all old-fashioned buttons and switches and blinking lights—less fancy, but cheaper to maintain and not as prone to sudden catastrophic failure. Above that, the display connected to the fore hull cameras was turned on, projecting an image of the dizzying streak of stars passing them as they flew through the red-tinged blackness of space.

Sitting on the instrument panel, pawing at the manual control override, was the calico cat.

It hissed at Eva, hazel eyes flashing. She felt a sudden vertigo, as if the artificial gravity had shifted. Shaking her head to clear it, she leveled her gun at the critter.

"Get down from there, you cabrón revolutionary," she said, "before you break something."

"The little cuddly-poof accidentally blocked my commlink access, Cap." Min spoke through the speakers in the bridge instead of her human mouth, as usual.

Eva snorted. "Accident, sure. You okay?"

"Yeah, comm's almost back up."

"But are you okay?"

"A few bites and scratches in random spots. Nothing Vakar can't fix."

"I meant your— Never mind." Eva was going to say "real body," but after four years the ship was as much Min's body as the one she'd been born with.

The cat crouched, its butt shaking in the air. Then, in a fluid motion, it jumped onto another part of the panel.

"Idiot," Eva hissed. "Get away from there. You'll jettison everything in the cargo hold."

It raised a paw threateningly.

"You're seriously going to kill all your little cat buddies? Flush them right out into space?"

It hesitated and cocked its head at her.

"Cap," Min said, "you're talking to a cat."

"I believe it can understand us quite well, Min," Vakar said, peering around the edge of the door.

"Right, okay." Eva hunkered down and stared at the cat, face-to-face. "Listen, kitty. I'm taking you to a nice new home somewhere. A café where millions of tourists will come every year to pet you and feed you canned meat. I don't even get to eat canned meat."

The cat's tail lashed back and forth.

"Yeah, I don't know, maybe that's not your idea of a good time." Eva ran a hand through her tangled black hair. "What do you want me to do? Someone is paying me to take you to another planet, and if I don't deliver, I don't get paid. And if I don't get paid, I lose my ship, so pretty please with sugar on top, get in your cabrón crate already, coño!"

The bridge was silent for a moment.

"That did not sound like a compelling argument," Vakar said.

Eva made a disgusted noise and threw her hands in the air. As if in response, the cat leaped onto Min's human lap, where it settled down and began to lick its paw.

"Okay, what the hell," Eva said.

"Ooh, I think it likes me," Min said. She scratched the cat's ears with a pale hand.

"Too bad. Twenty kittens, cash on delivery. We don't get paid for nineteen."

The cat yawned, showing tiny sharp teeth and a throat pink as a guayaba.

"It is arguably cute," Vakar said.

"It broke out of its cage, locked itself in the bridge, and tried to take over the nav systems!"

"Cap, come on. How would it know how to use the nav systems?" Min scratched the cat's chin and made soft cooing noises at it with her human mouth.

"Psychically," Eva said. "Mira, cute or not, I want these sinvergüenzas off my ship as soon as we dock. If that cat isn't in its box in the next—" She glanced at Min. "How far out are we from Letis?"

"We'll hit the nearest Gate in about an hour, then two hours to orbit, plus docking time and customs."

"Madre de dios. I was supposed to call Tito to find out who we're meeting and where." Eva cast one last snarling look at the kitten, which had the gall to wink at her. "I'll be back for you, cat, so don't get comfortable. Vakar, keep an eye on them."

She stalked past Vakar, back straight, fighting the urge to scratch her welted arms until they bled. Could one thing go right for her this cycle?

"You're shitting me."

Eva sat in the mess room, clenched fists resting on the big oval table in the center. The smirking face of Tito Santiago, patron saint of smug assholes, floated in front of her. His dark, wavy hair was precisely tousled and his brown eyes twinkled with barely suppressed amusement.

"Shit happens, Beni," he said, his holo image crackling slightly. "It's not my fault the buyer went bankrupt."

"Cómetelo. Now I know why you convinced me not to take the usual half up front."

"I'll owe you a favor."

"My ship runs on fuel, not favors."

His smile didn't change, but his eyes narrowed. He was getting annoyed. Back when he was her boss, it had worried her; now it just pissed her off more.

"No es pa tanto," he said. "You can sell the cargo on the black market for triple what the buyer was going to pay."

She ran her finger along a scratch in the table's metal surface. "You know that's not my game anymore. Not to mention the damn things are a righteous pain in the ass."

"You wouldn't know anything about that, I'm sure." He ran a hand through his hair. "Decídete, mi cielo, I haven't got all cycle."

Mierda. It wasn't like she could return the cats as defective, either; the sellers would credit the original buyer. And probably reprogram them, whatever that entailed. Animal protection laws got flexible in certain sectors.

Eva thought of that stupid little ball of fluff curled up on Min's lap and sighed.

"A big favor," she said finally. "An expensive favor."

"Claro que sí, mi vida. You know I'll take care of you."

"You take care of your boyfriend. Me, you just fuck."

He glanced at someone over his shoulder. "Bueno, speaking of boyfriends, te dejo. I'll let you know if any more jobs come in that will fit your . . . particular preferences. Adiós." The holovid flickered off.

"Particular preferences." Only Tito could make her desire to avoid illegal or unethical work sound perverted. Hell, he'd probably given them the job in the first place because legality shit all over his bottom line.

Why was it so hard to make a living without killing strangers or screwing people over? Seven years of cargo delivery and passenger transport, of building up a reputation from nothing, and what did she have to show for it? A few regular clients, a handful of shell companies under various aliases, and a message box full of unpaid bills.

Eva forced herself to unclench her hands, placing her palms on the table. ((Mess room,)) she pinged to the whole crew. Time to deliver the bad news. Not to mention—

"The fuck am I going to do with twenty cats?" she muttered.

Everyone sat around the big table in the mess—even Min, who was flying the ship remotely while curled up in a chair, drinking a misugaru shake. Pink munched on a protein bar, her dreadlocks tied back from her face. Leroy leaned forward, hands clasped together under the table in his lap, his hair still a frizz of red and his tattoos programmed to look like barbed wire. Vakar sat on a stool, his double-jointed legs straddling the metal seat, smelling like incense but with a faint undercurrent of something else. Vanilla? Eva couldn't place it, but her translator told her it was anticipation.

Eva stood, bent forward so her palms rested on the table. "Do you want the good news or the bad news?"

A chorus of "Bad news" answered her.

"The bad news is, Tito shafted us, so we're not getting paid."

Pink chewed slowly, pinning Eva with a glare from her visible eye. Leroy groaned and dropped his forehead to the table.

Vakar's smell transitioned to cigarette smoke with a hint of fart.

"What's the good news?" Min asked.

"We can do whatever we want with the cargo, and Tito owes us a huge favor."

"Favors are delicious," Pink said. "I ask myself, 'Dr. Jones, what do you want to eat for lunch?' and favors are the first thing—"

"I told him that, but there's nothing we can do to him, and he knows it." She squinted at Pink. "Unless your fancy lawyer brother might be able to help?"

Pink scowled. "He's still up to his nose hairs in our habitat's lawsuit."

"Assholes." The only thing worse than scummy freelancers like Tito was corporations. In Pink's case, a Martian megacorp had encouraged a bunch of idealistic people to take out big loans to set up a habitat on an unclaimed world and do all the hard work of making it self-sustaining, then started shipping tainted seed and faulty tech to sabotage them. Inevitably, the settlers sold off their assets dirt cheap or had them seized to cover their debts, then the corporations rolled in, slapped on a coat of fancy, and resold everything at a huge profit.

Where most people gave up on fighting an impossible enemy, the Jones family got mad. And when they got mad, they got busy.

"What will we do now, Captain?" Vakar asked, interrupting her dour thoughts.

Eva straightened, her hand creeping to the back of her neck to pick at a scab. "Since we're already about to Gate to Letis, I say we dock and see if we can find a cat buyer or pick up a new client. Or both."

"I'll post an ad on the q-net," Min chimed in. That meant she would also steal some time to play a VR game with her friends, but Eva didn't mind. Pretending to shoot and stab imaginary bad guys was much safer than dealing with real ones.

"Use the Gato Tuerto Enterprises q-mail address," Eva said. "And keep an eye on the box in case someone responds while we're there."

"Any chance of shore leave?" Leroy asked, perking up.

"Sure, but take Vakar." She pointed at the quennian with her free hand, still scratching her neck with the other. "Vakar, start making a list of the damage the cats caused so I can send Tito a bill he can wipe his ass with, and pick up anything you need while we're there." She winced as her neck scab gave way to blood. "Anything we can afford, that is. Pink, same for you."

"Aw, that's work, not shore leave," Leroy whined.

"Make it a game. Whoever finds the cheapest rations that don't taste like shit gets to eat them." Her crew wore expressions ranging from dismay to anger. "Any questions?"

"Yeah," Pink said. "Next time I see Tito, how many times can I punch his sweet little face?"

"Once for every cat we still have in our hold." She pursed her lips and squinted. "In fact, if you need me in the next twenty, I'll be beating the shit out of a heavy bag with his picture on it. Dismissed."

The others stood and left, but Vakar lingered. "Would you like company?" he asked.

Eva opened her mouth to accept, then shook her head. "You need to get that parts list together. Next time, though."

"Of course." He stood, his disappointed smell making her feel inexplicably guilty.

"I'll help you with the list," she said. "It will get done faster, and then we can—"

"No, that is all right. I still have the scar from the last time we sparred when you were angry."

She grimaced. "I'm still sorry."

"That was not an admonishment. It was my fault for being careless."

He smelled less distressed, but she flapped a hand at him anyway. "You take aft, I'll take fore. If we finish early, we can hit each other until I feel better. Deal?"

"Terms accepted." He left, humming softly. Another smell snuck in under the others, dark and vaguely fruity. It had started a few months back and it was driving her up the wall. She'd even had the scent translators installed to supplement the rest of her translation suite, but the damn things were still learning.

Well, she'd figure it out eventually. Eva grinned, feeling cheerful despite herself, and got to work.

The inspection took longer than expected, so they were almost to the Gate before Eva finally crawled out of the last access tunnel and went back to her cabin to change her clothes.

It had been a long time since her every waking moment was spent in a spacesuit. Its impermeable quick-rigid material doubled as armor in a pinch, and the isohelmet that popped into existence with a thought could deflect projectiles and scrub bad air. And, of course, there were the gravboots, perfect for kicking asses when she didn't care what anyone's name was.

She'd just finished pulling on her boots and activating the pressure seals when Min poked her voice in.

"Hey, Cap, you have a call on the emergency frequency."

Eva froze. The only people who knew that frequency were her crew, who were all on the ship, and her family, who had barely spoken to her for years. A tickle of unease slid up her back like phantom fingers.

"Send it in here, and give me privacy," she said, sitting on the lone chair near the closet.

The lights in the room dimmed to allow a better view of the holo image that projected from her closet door. At first, nothing happened, and Eva leaned forward as if she could reach into the transmitter and pull the person through.

Then, a crackle of static appeared, formless and vague. Eva's eyes strained to turn the visual gibberish into a face or a body.

"Captain Eva-Benita Caridad Larsen Alvarez y Coipel de Innocente," a voice said. It sounded gravelly, like it was being modulated.

"Who is this?" Eva demanded. Not many people knew her whole name, and she'd dropped Larsen permanently after her father—

"I am an agent of The Fridge," the voice said. "We have apprehended your sister, Marisleysis Honoria Larsen Alvarez y Coipel de Innocente, and will hold her until her ransom is paid."

The Fridge? The intergalactic crime syndicate? Yeah, right. And she was a secret Martian princess with millions in frozen assets.

"Fuck you," she said. "Prove it." This couldn't be real. It had to be some twisted joke. But they knew her name, the emergency frequency—

The quality of the sound changed, and a blurry image of her sister took the place of the static. "Eva, it's Mari. Please, you have to help me."

She sounded scared, and Mari had never been scared of anything except her wild little sister getting lost or hurt. Eva's stomach shriveled like a freeze-dried fruit.

"They said to tell you something no one else knows but us. Remember when you were eight, and I was eleven, and you climbed into Abuelo's closet and found his gun safe?"

The memory rose in Eva's mind. She'd thought she would be able to crack the code, because she'd seen a holovid where someone did it and it looked so easy.

"You couldn't get it open, and you accidentally pulled the shelf down and everything fell, and you didn't want to get in trouble. I never told anyone, Eva. Never."

Mari had told their mom that Eva was with her the whole time, reading about alien cultures. Abuelo had said something about shoddy construction, fixed the shelf, and forgotten all about it.

Mari always did have her back, even when Eva didn't deserve it.

"I'm not buying this," Eva said, but she was already half-convinced. Only a handful of people knew the frequency they were using. Spoofing someone's identity wasn't impossible, but only her family used their full name—it was shortened on legal documents, and Eva operated under enough aliases to form her own fútbol team. She also doubted Mari would have a reason to randomly drop that story on someone, then for them to concoct a wild plan to use it like this.

Mari's face faded to static and the modulated voice returned. "You may ask one question for proof."

One question. She had to make it good. What was something only Mari would know, something that couldn't be found on the q-net quickly?

"How did you almost die while you were doing your dissertation?" Eva asked.

Mari's face returned, her voice trembling. "The Proarkhe ruins on Jarr. I still have the scar. A cabrón giant spider took a bite out of my leg while I was trying to dig up an impossibly well-preserved metallic container. Mom was so mad, she almost didn't come to my graduation ceremony."

Mierda, mojón y porquería. That was Mari, no doubt.

"Are you all right?" Eva asked, feigning a bravado she hardly felt, but Mari disappeared and the sound changed again.

"Your pilot will be provided with coordinates at which you will meet your assigned handler," the modulated voice said. "You will receive more information when you arrive. If you ever want to see your sister again, you will do exactly as you are instructed. Tell no one, or she will be terminated."

The transmission flickered off. Eva stared at the space behind the projector in disbelief.

Equal parts rage, fear, and determination fought for supremacy inside her. How dare these assholes fuck with her family, her flesh and blood? Especially Mari, sweet Mari, who used to save snails from hot sidewalks because she couldn't stand the thought of someone stepping on them. What if Eva couldn't do what they asked, and they killed her sister? How would she ever face her mother again?

No, she wouldn't let that happen. She'd play their game, bide her time, and figure out some way to free Mari in case honor among thieves turned out to be less applicable to kidnappers.

Min spoke through the speakers. "Cap, someone sent me coordinates for—"

"Set a course."

"But Cap, what about Letis?"

"Forget Letis," she snapped. Then, more calmly than she felt, she added, "Don't worry, it'll be fine. Send those coordinates to my commlink, please?"

Tell no one, the message had instructed. How would they even know? Was that a chance she was willing to take? Not especially. Acid climbed her throat at the thought of lying to her crew. Maybe this was all a setup, and she could blow in, bust heads, and get back to her real problems.

The Fridge was like the chupacabra: everyone knew of someone's cousin's friend's acquaintance whose goat had been sucked dry, but no one really believed it. Secret organizations didn't actually go around kidnapping people and throwing them into cryo, or running illegal labs and asteroid mining operations, or stealing artifacts from ancient civilizations for mysterious evil purposes. Only conspiracy theorists like Leroy believed in that nonsense.

And yet. Her father had warned her about The Fridge years ago, after one of his best clients suddenly sold every spaceship they owned and ran off to casa carajo. They wouldn't tell him why—got extremely nervous when he asked—but he'd looked into it. He'd found people going on mystery vacations or suddenly quitting their jobs, their loved ones liquidating assets or, if they were big shots, throwing their weight behind causes or projects they hadn't previously supported. Some of those people came back from wherever they had disappeared to, only to move away for good after a few cycles. Some stayed gone, and some, well . . . Not every culture published obituaries. Still, he told Eva, it was more void than substance. It might all be coincidence.

Also, he had told her not to fuck with The Fridge.

She stared at the fish tank on the panel above her bed, her only real luxury, and a reminder of the family she had left behind when she went into the black for good. One fish for every family member: a brilliant green one for her mother, dark red for her father, striped ones for her grandparents on each side, yellow and blue respectively.

And one for her sister, of course. Indigo and black, it tended to hide among the rocks and corals, avoiding the light. Mari, who finished schooling two years early. Mari, the brilliant historian and scientist with the cushy government job studying ancient ruins. Mari, the quiet one, whereas Eva was like their mother, loud and outspoken, quick to laugh but also quick to shout.

But Eva remembered their last big fight: her at twenty-three, thinking she knew everything there was to know about everything since she'd already been in space for five years. Mari telling her to stop being so selfish, to stop letting their father drag her into his line of work, the work that had pushed their mother into leaving the man after a decade of marriage even though it meant raising two young kids on her own. "Think of Mom," Mari had said. "You're breaking her heart." Eva had stood there and let her scream, let her vent, like she was a barnacle and her sister was a wave. She'd even let Mari hit her, once, and then she'd left.

Mari had been right, of course. And here Eva was, trying to do what she'd been told so many years ago, only to have this happen. Mari would see the irony, perhaps, but she wouldn't like it. She'd always thought Eva had it in her to do better, to *be* better, and Eva had resented the endless pushing.

Still, maybe she could unload the cats, get paid, keep to the straight and narrow path.

And maybe she'd find a café that sold some actual pastelitos de queso. Or a chupacabra.

The Fridge was bad news. She couldn't drag her crew into this, but until her handler gave her instructions, she could only guess at what to expect. What a genteel word for it: "handler." As if she were some famous person who needed a combination supervisor and assistant. Nicer than "master," or "controller," or "overseer." And yet it made her feel like an animal instead of a celebrity.

Maybe those cats had the right idea after all, wanting to escape their cage.

There was a polite knock at the door, and Eva realized she

had stood up at some point and taken a fighting stance, hands curled into fists. She forced herself to relax and sent a mental command at the door to open it.

Vakar stood outside, his gloves back on. "I was thinking, are you sure you want me to go with Leroy? I can find anything we need myself, and he can—"

"Never mind," Eva said. "Something came up. We're diverting to . . ." She checked her commlink. "Station U039F." Even as she finished saying it, she stifled a groan of realization.

"Omicron?" Vakar asked incredulously.

"You've been to worse places. Can you stock up there?"

"Probably. Are you well?" He smelled of incense. Concern.

She met his gray-blue eyes long enough to feel like she'd licked a battery, then looked away.

"I'm fine," she said.

"Are you sure?"

"As the night is long." She didn't feel like sparring anymore, but she plastered on a smile. "Come on, your ass needs kicking and I've got my boots on."

The incense smell strengthened even as he stepped aside to let her take the lead. She thought of her one time in a church, with her abuela, that heady, dizzy sense of something watching her, invisible and dangerous.

Just as she had then, she stared at her feet and prayed.

Enter the monthly
Orbit sweepstakes at
www.orbitloot.com

With a different prize every month,
from advance copies of books by
your favourite authors to exclusive
merchandise packs,
**we think you'll find something
you love.**